BLOC

CW01044111

BLOOD TORN

BOOK THREE

LINDSAY J. PRYOR

bookouture

Published by Bookouture

An imprint of StoryFire Ltd.
Carmelite House
50 Victoria Embankment
London EC4Y 0DZ

www.bookouture.com

ISBN: 978-1-909490-19-2

For Moth

With *very* special thanks to:

Aimee, Anita, Fiona, Incy, Jane, Kelly, Linzi, Tima and Tracey
for your openly-unremitting support for Blackthorn.
You ladies are incredible.

Every reader who has got in touch to share your enjoyment of the
books so far – you make more of a difference than you know.

And Bookouture
for your continuing dedication both to this series and to me as a
writer. I'm *so* proud and fortunate to be a part of
such an awesome publisher.

Chapter One

This was not good. This was not good at all.

Just when she thought the night couldn't have got any worse, Jask Tao walked into the equation.

Sophia glowered into the lycan leader's exquisite azure-blue eyes, his dark lashes a sharp contrast to the untamed fair hair that fell around his defined, stubbled jaw.

'You need to let me go,' she said, as he remained crouched in front of her at eye level, his firm grip on her jaw as unrelenting as his gaze.

'And why would I want to do that?'

It undoubtedly sounded like a ludicrous suggestion, surrounded as she was by four lycans, her outstretched wrists roped to the rusted rings embedded in the dank, subterranean walls. But she said it anyway. 'I'm warning you – you're making a mistake.'

He examined her pensively – those uncompromising eyes betraying his angelic, albeit rugged, appearance. He let go of her jaw and stood up, his candlelit shadow looming on the moss-encased walls of the ruins.

It had been three days since Marid had abducted her – ambushed her. The sleazy vampire knew about The Alliance. And if word was out there about the covert operation, the others were at risk too. She'd already wasted the time Marid had held her hostage, let alone the past three hours she'd been trapped down there since he'd sold her on. She needed to get back to the rest of the group. She needed to warn them.

But more than that, more than anything, she needed to find out what the hell was going on with her two sisters.

She glanced at the two dead vampires lying on the stone-slabbed floor ahead – the vampires that had bartered with Marid over her like she was nothing. Her skin crawled as she thought back to the way they'd grinned conspiratorially at each other as they'd tied her to the wall. And she'd known from the malicious look in their eyes, let alone the conversation they'd had whilst drinking and laughing at the table, they'd planned far more than just a feed.

But the events that had followed had been a surprise to everyone.

She'd realised what had happened the minute the shock had subsided. There was only one explanation – only one type of blood that killed a vampire that quickly and that painfully: serryn blood.

She sure hadn't been a serryn before she'd entered that chamber – the leech, Marid, had proven that point. But the evidence spoke for itself – the vampires' bodies now twisted and contorted from biting into her, her blood having imploded every one of their veins. It had taken only seconds for her toxic blood to penetrate their systems.

She knew only too well from her research that only serryns caused that reaction – a rare bloodline of witch long thought extinct. Just as she knew there was only one way anyone not born a serryn would become one – the so-called curse jumping from an older sibling to a younger one if the former committed either of the two serryn taboos: suicide by their own hand, or falling in love with and consummating that love with a vampire. Right then, both ideas seemed as implausible as her big sister Leila being a serryn in the first place.

If the indisputable proof hadn't been plain in front of her, she would have laughed off the possibility. Now she needed to know *exactly* what was going on. Forget The Alliance's rules about no outside contact – this was family. Not only was her little sister, Alisha, in trouble, but now seemingly so was Leila.

Which meant, even more so, that she had no time to waste on lycans.

She glowered back up at Jask.

Feet braced apart, hands low on his lithe hips, she had no doubt his stature was imposing enough when stood eye-to-eye with him. The last thing she needed was her forced submissive position on the floor exacerbating it.

It wasn't helped by the fact she knew more about the uncomfortably good-looking lycan than just his zero-tolerance leadership – he was bad-tempered, temperamental, and fiercely protective of his pack. And – though it was irrelevant it slipped into her mind anyway – rumoured to be proficient in bed. He was certainly well-equipped enough to live up to his reputation – his jeans temptingly fitting those solid thighs, his biceps distractingly taut through his shirt, those rolled-up sleeves exposing well-toned forearms. She lingered over the brown leather straps wrapped around his wrists, matching the ones around his neck, a small platinum pendant nestled in the hollow of his throat.

She glanced at the other lycan beside him: Corbin Saylen – Jask's second in command, with a reputation as equally uncompromising. He had a presence all of his own, stood there, arms folded, his grey eyes locked on hers.

But then, when you were one of the minority third species in Blackthorn, you had to have a reputation to survive.

'Get in here and tell me what happened,' Jask demanded, summoning the two lycans from beyond the doorway.

The one she knew to be Rone entered first. On appearance they had to be twenty years younger than Jask – but it was as impossible to tell with lycans as it was with vampires. Rone and his comrade, Samson, had deliberated over what to do with her for the best part of an hour after gatecrashing the vampire feast gone wrong. They'd paced the room, arguing over whether to just leave her there. Despite having tried to barter with them, she'd seen their faces and that was finally enough for them to relent into calling for backup.

Backup being Corbin and, from what she had picked up from overhearing their panicked phone call, and despite their protests, Corbin deciding to inform Jask.

'We were across at the warehouse,' Rone stated. 'We heard the noise she was creating so came out to look. She was putting up a hell of a fight.'

'And then?' Jask asked.

'We saw them bring her down here.'

'And knowing you never interfere in vampire business, you walked away,' Jask added, the disapproval emanating in his eyes.

'We were going to,' Samson said.

'But it was two on one,' Rone interjected. 'They were getting violent with her.'

Jask looked back at Sophia, but she knew he wasn't looking at her – he was examining the evidence of the cuts and grazes on her face. 'The vampires do their thing, we do ours,' he said, looking back at Rone and Samson.

Sophia raised her eyebrows at the indifference in his words. Seemingly his reputation as a heartless bastard was equally justified.

'That's the only way the segregation works and you know it,' he added. 'We have enough to do in protecting our own, without trying to save every helpless victim in this district.'

She nearly protested at the victim remark, but resolved to keep her mouth shut. All that mattered was getting loose.

'We thought she was just a girl,' Rone explained. 'What did she do to them? I've never seen vampires go down that fast. It was all over within minutes.'

'Just be grateful your discovery is sufficient enough to save me ripping into you right now. What were you doing on this side of the district?'

The two youths glanced nervously at each other.

'We had a deal going,' Rone declared, instantly dropping his gaze to the floor in response to Jask's thunderous glare.

'A deal? With vampires?' he asked, distaste exuding from his tone.

After a moment's hesitation, Rone gave a single nod.

Jask exhaled with exasperation. 'So there's someone who knew you were here?'

'What if they think this was something to do with us?' Samson asked, echoing the line of thought that had no doubt provoked Jask's further irritation with them.

He took two steps towards them. '*This* is why you don't come here. *This* is why you stay in Northern territory. *This* is why we're going to clear up this mess and get you back to the compound so I can deal with you properly.'

He removed something from his back pocket, flicked open a switchblade that glinted in the candlelight as he turned to face her.

Sophia braced herself as he expertly sliced through the ropes that bound her arms to the wall. She barely had time to rub her throbbing wrists or rotate her aching shoulders before he'd grabbed her by the upper arm and tugged her to her feet as if she was weightless.

'Corbin, get her up to the bikes,' he said, shoving her towards him. 'We've spent too long here already.'

She was a little unsteady for a moment, but quickly regained her balance as Corbin wrapped a firm hand around her upper arm.

She refrained from struggling, knowing she stood a hell of a better chance one-on-one against Corbin if Jask and the other two remained distracted for long enough.

As Corbin led her towards the door, Jask stepped over to the table to pick up what was left of a bottle of whisky and the remains of one of the burning candles. It took no imagination to work out *how* he planned to get rid of the bodies, especially all traces of serryn blood.

Corbin tugged her out into the corridor before she could see any more.

His eyes were fixed ahead, his grip on her arm unrelenting as she tried to match her strides to his. His shoulder-length hair blew in the mild breeze as they turned the corner. Tall, broad and with the lithe strength of all lycans, they may have been no match on appearance, but she'd taken down bigger than him.

Just as she'd take Marid down when she caught up with him again. Because she would. And the sharper the object she used to say what she had to say, the better.

The stone corridor seemed endless. She hadn't seen much of it on the way there – she'd spent too long slamming her heels or fists into every available inch of soft flesh on the two vampires who had dared to drag her down there.

The stairwell, when they eventually reached it, was as narrow as she remembered, her knees having scraped against stone as one had held her legs, the other restraining her arms around her as they'd carried her bucking and protesting down there.

Now Corbin pushed her up ahead of him, his size forcing him to be more behind her than next to her, but he didn't let go of her arm.

As soon as she saw moonlight on the steps, she tried to yank her arm free. 'You're hurting me.'

'Then keep moving.'

'Seriously,' she said, stopping abruptly. 'Just give me a second, okay?' She wrenched her arm from his as she feigned weakness. 'I don't feel too good.' She slid down the wall to collapse onto the steps.

He let go of her just for a second.

It was what she needed.

She snapped her head towards the top of the stairwell and faked a look of shock. As she'd hoped, it was enough to evoke his curiosity – a luxury of a split second when his eyes were averted from her.

With both hands she grabbed his lower leg and yanked with every ounce of strength she had left.

Corbin's startled gaze met hers as he slammed his hands onto either side of the wall to brace himself.

It granted her another split second to slide along to the middle of the step, to pull back her leg before slamming her foot hard into his groin.

He instinctively bent over double and lost balance. He tumbled backwards, but she didn't stop to watch.

She turned and clambered up the remaining steps, her thighs heavy as she struggled to her feet to take the last few steps two at a time.

She heard Corbin's voice echo up the steps behind her – one single call: 'Jask!'

She fell up the last step, her palms scuffing concrete. The dark and barren wasteland loomed ahead – nowhere to hide for at least seventy feet to where the outline of some old factory buildings lay in the distance against the overcast night sky. She had to get to them. Hiding was no use with the lycans' proficient sense of smell, but something would be there that she could use to defend herself. Damn it, the outskirts of the east side of Blackthorn were renowned for their reclusiveness.

Like a runner at the start of a race, she lunged forward, taking off with as much speed as her aching body would allow. She kept her attention firmly on the closest building, her eyes blurring against the cold night air, the terrain rough and uneven beneath her boots.

She told herself not to look over her shoulder, not to dare lose her pace for one moment, but instinct overwhelmed her.

She turned to see an outline closing in on her from maybe only forty feet behind.

Her heart lunged and she ran faster, her throat parched and constricted. She ignored the shooting pains in her chest, the laceration of agony in her side that under any other circumstances would have forced her to stop.

But common sense screamed in her head – she couldn't outrun a lycan even on the best of days. She had to conserve what little energy she had left if she ever wanted to escape.

She forced herself to stop despite her instincts urging her to keep running.

She struggled to catch her breath in the few seconds she had as she turned to face Jask coming to a standstill a few feet away.

He clearly hadn't expected her to stop. The dance of amusement in his eyes almost masked the irritation, had the latter not exuded from him so intensely. 'Don't you think you've had enough fights for one night?'

'I'm not going with you,' she said through annoyingly ragged breaths.

He raked her swiftly with his gaze. 'So you seem to think.'

'Walk away, Jask, and save yourself the trouble.'

She could have sworn she saw another glint of amusement in his eyes.

'Walk to the shed over there with dignity,' he said, cocking his head over his shoulder. 'And we can forget you tried to run on me.'

'I have a better idea. Go join your puppies and bike it back to your Northern pound. You've got no business being here. And you've got *no* business with me.'

He took a few steps closer. 'I'll let that first comment go, on account of it being a stressful night for you. But as I'm *making* what's in those veins my business, you either be a good girl and do as you're told or I'll be a bad lycan. Your choice.'

The sincerity in his tone, the slight darkening in his eyes, made her stomach jolt and, to her distaste, not just with apprehension. She rolled back her shoulders, preparing herself for battle. 'You've got to get to it first.'

He raised his eyebrows slightly, only this time a smile escaped – a stunning, fleeting smile that ignited those azure eyes and annoyingly only enhanced his handsome face further. He rested his hands back on his hips. 'Seriously?'

It was one mocking look too much.

She closed the gap just enough to lift her leg with lightning speed, less than an inch from making impact with his chest before he moved his foot just as swiftly, swiping her other leg from under her, causing her to hit the floor.

Leaning back on braced arms, she stared up at him; not so much as a hint of a glitch in his composure.

It was a move she'd developed to perfection, and he'd kicked it from her as if it was nothing. His self-assurance riled her as she looked squarely into his unperturbed eyes.

Feeling an alien flush in her cheeks, she moved back slightly to forge some distance between them before getting to her feet.

She was going to wipe the smug look off his face.

But as she lifted her leg again, he knocked it aside, as he did her right fist and then her left as she tried twice to strike him.

Since she'd joined The Alliance, Zach had taught her everything she needed to know about one-on-one combat – if not to take an opponent down completely, then at least long enough to get away.

She paused for only a split second before increasing the on-slaught, hitting out at him with clean and precise moves, only to have him fend them off swiftly and accurately before knocking her leg from under her again.

She fell back down, brushed her hair from her eyes in irritation before glowering up at him.

'You've spent too long fighting vampires, honey,' he said.

The playful challenge in his eyes incensed her. The mocking in his tone, the derision in his eyes, triggered her indignation more.

She knew better than to fight unless she was in complete control of her temper but this was now just as much about pride as escaping. Instead of taking the moment she needed to escape, she got back to her feet.

She picked up pace, using every move she had been taught in quick succession, catching him several times but never with enough force or at the right angle to make any impact.

'Are you scared to fight me?' she demanded, frustrated by his purely defensive moves.

'You want to exhaust yourself, you go ahead.'

She sped up, increasing the speed of her moves, adrenaline pumping as she went at him harder. He missed a couple of her shots, allowing her to make impact with his chest and knee, but it was nowhere near enough to take him down. She knew she was being less precise, fuelled by her anger rather than tactics.

And this time, when he kicked her legs from under her, he purposefully went down on top of her.

She lifted her knees nimbly against her chest, ready to use the remaining strength in her thighs as leverage to force him off her, but he instantly closed the gap. He forced her thighs to part either side of his hips, spreading her legs further with the power of his, locking her ankles down to the ground with his own at the same time as pinning her arms to the ground either side of her head.

Despite the futility, she tried to writhe and buck beneath him, but not one inch of his hard, tensed body was moveable.

Gasping, she let the back of her head hit the ground, panting as she looked up into his eyes, every inch of her resounding in umbrage at her helplessness.

'Done?' he asked, the calm in his eyes infuriating her as much as the effortlessness with which he held her to the floor.

She tightened her hands into fists. 'Get off me,' she all but growled.

'Are you *done*?' he repeated, his tone taking on an impatient edge that escalated her agitation.

She defiantly held his gaze, feeling every inch of the power behind his body, the heat emanating between them. As he watched her a little too intently for comfort, mesmerising her with his quiet confidence, she felt another unfamiliar stirring. 'If it means you'll get those feral hands off me, yes, I'm done.'

She grudgingly stilled as she awaited his response; gazed at the masculine lips that hovered inches from hers before looking back into his eyes.

He lowered himself a few inches, his biceps straining distractedly against his shirt. 'Vampires might bite, honey, but lycans tear. You might want to bear that in mind next time you try and take me on.'

With only another moment's linger on her gaze, he released her wrists, eased off her, grabbing her arm to pull her to her feet along with him.

'You don't know what you've got yourself into,' she declared, unable to suppress her indignation.

'You can tell me all about it back at the compound,' he said, only to hoist her up over his shoulder.

Her cheeks flushed from the blood rushing to her head, let alone the humiliation. 'Put me down!' she demanded, slamming a fist into his back as she tried to kick at his groin.

Her retaliation only evoked him to hold her tighter though, her clenched fist barely having any impact on his solid back.

She glowered down at the ground that swayed beneath her, forced her elbows into his back to regain some kind of control, but they reached the shed in no time.

He slid her down onto her feet, catching her forearm as she stumbled with the motion.

Rone and Samson were already helmeted up and astride their motorbikes in the far corner.

Corbin stood nearer by, his arms folded as he smirked in amusement at Jask. 'She's going to be a lot of trouble. Are you sure she's worth the effort?'

'You know me – I love a challenge. Taming could become my new favourite pastime,' Jask said, tugging her over to the nearest motorbike. He unhooked something from the seat, and turned to clasp one cuff of the handcuffs over her right wrist.

He lifted the helmet off the seat and shoved it on her head, before guiding her astride his motorbike. Sitting in front of her, he pulled her other wrist around his taut waist, cuffing her hands together at his lap, the position forcing her intimately against his back.

She clenched her hands and fought against leaning against him. But she was given no other option as Jask revved the engine.

Sophia quickly found somewhere to rest her feet and braced herself just as they sped off, kicking up dust behind them.

Chapter Two

Sophia held on tight as Jask's bike ripped through the barren outskirts of the east side of Blackthorn, the wasteland and abandoned warehouses soon replaced with the high-rise, compacted buildings that enclosed the district's hub.

Blackthorn: just one rotten core of thousands more. Cores set up and partitioned off to contain the third species since their outing eighty years before.

The Global Council, a panel of humans elected as advocates for their own race, had done so as their promise for safety for *all* humans. What were once cities, towns and villages had been disbanded under the regulations into socially segregated areas now called locales – the third species contained in the nucleus of a further three encircling districts. Contained until they'd proved themselves safe, as they so claimed.

And each locale was managed by its own law enforcement division ensuring that happened. Established as part of the Global Council's regulations, the Third Species Control Division was responsible for maintaining order amongst the vampires, the lycans, and whatever other third species crawled the dark streets in their patch.

But the system was failing.

Not least because there *was* no segregation anymore. Not unless you were part of the elite – humans who had earned their place in the far reaches of the locale, across the most highly guarded of all the borders in the exclusive third-species-free Summerton. Or even Midtown – the next notch down. The rest of the humans were forced to live in the under-privileged Lowtown, mingling with the third species allowed to reside there, right next to the now weak borders of the infested Blackthorn.

Back when the regulations were put in place, residents of Lowtown had been promised that, despite being given the dregs in terms of provisions, opportunities and medical care, they would at least get protection. But along with many other changes in the authorities' priorities, the resources to fulfil that promise soon dwindled. And vinegar was only smeared onto the wound of their neglect by the fact that some third species, such as the Higher Order – vampire royalty – were deemed *more* worthy than humans, their privileged residence in Midtown a painful contention.

For too long now, humans outside of Summerton and Midtown had been nothing more than by-products of a deteriorating system. The authorities had long lost sight of what was really going on – both Lowtown and Blackthorn now rife with corruption under the rule of a few pivotal third-species leaders. Worse, those same authorities no longer gave a damn about the humans caught in the crossfire.

And very few had opportunities to improve their situation, especially financially. Those that did were ousted with threats against themselves or their families if someone bigger or better connected wanted to take their place. Because with opportunities so few anyway, only the very toughest survived or those who were in with the right cliques.

Subsequently, a selfish human society had formed. Humans learned survival of the fittest by down-treading, down-beating, threatening, bullying and controlling even their own.

As a result, increasing numbers of humans opted to live in Blackthorn instead – to become permanent residents in the protective cocoons created by their vampire owners or, as they liked to call themselves, sires. It was a derogatory and controlling term that Sophia loathed. But that's how the feeder-vampire relationship was, no matter how they painted it. The sires fed and housed their human feeders and, above all else, gave them protection in a place where the latter was top of the hierarchy of need. Without protection, you didn't survive long enough to need food and shelter. In the wrong hands, you'd rather starve.

It was a part of the Blackthorn culture that sickened Sophia and one that she'd long believed the TSCD should do more to control. But feeders never grassed on their sires. Treachery was dealt with brutally. And with no way of ever getting out of Blackthorn or Lowtown, they knew only too well that the authorities were the last ones able to help them. Once you fell, you just kept falling.

Which is why The Alliance, a cohort of human vigilantes, had taken it upon themselves to succeed where the authorities failed. Which is why Sophia worked Blackthorn every night, weaving her way into the third-species underworld. For the past ten months, she had mingled in the very abyss of it, seeing for herself that, like mould, its rankness was seeping into every aspect of the district and that it had to be stopped.

The Alliance would bring back equality for *all* humans. And it would start with ending third-species control in Blackthorn – the bullying, the blackmail, the protection rackets. The Alliance would bring down the key underworld players one by one. Control would be regained. The humans forced to live in Lowtown or Blackthorn would finally be safe, just as had been promised by the very authorities who had since abandoned them.

If she could get back to The Alliance to warn her colleagues their furtive operation had been exposed.

When she escaped the uncompromising lycan leader she was cuffed to.

Through the darkened shield of Sophia's rain-spattered visor, the streets were nothing more than blurred, opaque shades of grey against the backdrop of the pending dawn. The throbbing growl of the bike drowned out the noise that consistently permeated the dense core of the district – not least the low, rhythmic thrum of bass music that could be heard even at the periphery of Blackthorn where they were heading.

Despite her suppressed senses creating a sense of detachment, let alone the surrealism of *who* she was cuffed to, she couldn't escape reality entirely. Her head may have been cocooned in the visor, but her body certainly wasn't – her arms locked around the lycan leader's toned waist, her chest pressed up against the heat of his solid back. Jask must have been laughing to himself at her attempt to take him on out on the wasteland. *If* he was capable of laughing, that was. From what she'd heard, a sense of humour was one department he was severely lacking in.

Not that it mattered. She wouldn't be around long enough for any of it to matter. This was just a temporary setback. And that's what she had to keep telling herself to stop the tightness in her chest developing into panic.

Not that her panic couldn't be justified considering where she was being taken. But, for now, it was panic suppressed by curiosity. Insight into the compound was something a rare few outside of the lycan community ever had access to – unless Jask planned on you never getting out again. She had no doubt he intended the same for her. But he'd learn soon enough.

Avoiding the complication of navigating the motorbikes through the compacted and overpopulated hub, the lycans wove through the backstreets and alleys. And despite her indignation at being manacled to her captor, even she had to admire the smooth proficiency with which he controlled the powerful machine. The lycans' reputation for swift responses and superior spatial awareness was unarguably confirmed as Jask and his pack skimmed through narrow gaps and skirted obstacles before Sophia even had time to process what they'd passed.

But then the whole of the past three days had been difficult to process – ever since she'd woken up flat on her back on a stinking mattress. She'd woken groggily and with a heavy dose of disorientation from the blow to her head. Woken to a vampire feeding on her, her inner thigh wet from her blood and his saliva.

Marid.

The restraints that held her to the rusty metal bed-frame had left her helpless. And if there was one thing that sent her temper soaring, it was being helpless. Despite her weakened state, she'd bucked and cursed and threatened.

Marid had responded with a sharp slap to her face, adding to her humiliation. And she'd glared back at him with gritted teeth despite the tears welling.

She'd been convinced it was all over for her. Not least in the hours that had passed. And, at times, she'd wanted it to end. Contemplated if death was better than the pain. The pain that she had lived with for years which was nothing to do with Marid.

Then when Marid had finally told her she wasn't just another in his long line of human victims – those kidnapped and sold on for profit to the underworld – that he knew of The Alliance, and that he was next on her hit list, she'd turned her anger inwards. She'd been overheard mentioning his name, no doubt when she'd had a drink too many. Somewhere along the line she'd been stupid, careless, reckless – all well-established traits that she'd always known would eventually be her downfall.

And she had no doubt they would have been if two other vampires hadn't turned up to collect her. Two vampires that had apparently heard whispers that Marid had got his hands on an Alliance member. And luckily, if there was one thing Marid valued more than vengeance and a free feed, it was money.

She only wished she possessed as much insight into the mystery that was Jask Tao.

They swept past the carcass of the museum that marked the entry into the northern side of Blackthorn – lycan territory.

Jask's territory.

Kane Malloy ruled the east of Blackthorn and Caleb Dehain the west, with both vampires rumoured to have vested interests in the south. Both had become far too powerful. Both were top of The Alliance's hit list.

As for Jask, he may have been leader of a minor third species in comparison, he may head up a pack that kept themselves to themselves, but he wasn't to be underestimated. This was reinforced by the fact he'd recently courageously spoken out against the Third Species Control Division and played a significant part in exposing their corruption.

Worrying enough had been Jask's unprecedented appearance in court two weeks before to do so. An appearance that had corroborated the claims of the Vampire Control Unit's golden agent, Caitlin Parish, that the elite subdivision of the TSCD had used two of his lycan pack as pawns in an attempt to bring down their most wanted, Kane Malloy.

Even more troubling was proof that, with the authorities having been brash enough to take on the notorious master vampire, not least because of the potential aftermath for the human residents of Blackthorn and the surrounding Lowtown, *no one* was safe from their insane judgement.

Not only had even more mistrust of the authorities descended on Lowtown and Blackthorn; many had been left uneasy that the whole situation was anything but concluded despite the prosecution and incarceration of those responsible.

More so, Jask's alleged association with Kane Malloy in bringing the TSCD to so-called justice had left many nervous of what a collaboration like that meant for the future of Blackthorn. Any vampire and lycan associations or conflict made the authorities nervous – and those suspected of such were ousted and incarcerated.

And now there was Jask claiming he'd found her at the perfect time. Nothing good could come from lycans having a serryn – not where keeping the peace with the vampiric community was concerned. On top of everything else, the last thing the humans in Blackthorn needed was to be trapped in a civil war between the third species.

Which was why being up close and personal with the usually inaccessible Jask Tao didn't have to be a disaster. Instead, she needed to turn it around to the perfect opportunity to find out not just what went on inside the lycan compound, but what was currently going on inside Jask's head.

As they weaved closer and closer to the lycan compound, even the comparatively quieter streets had their fair share of revellers spilling out from the closing bars. A few inebriated residents stepped in front of the bikes, and Sophia tightened her grip on Jask as he and the others swerved effectively around them.

Jask took a sharp right down a back alley, skimming through a gap in a chain-link fence before slowing his pace as they arrived at the far side of a courtyard.

Coming to a standstill outside corrugated metal doors, he switched off the ignition as the others drew up behind him.

Sophia took a moment to collect herself – her body still buzzing from the reverberations of the engine, adrenaline still pumping from the ride, her heart pounding. She had to stay calm – not let him see or hear her fear.

Jask promptly unfastened Sophia's cuffs at his waist as the corrugated door was pushed open from the inside. Easing off the bike, he gave the lycan now looming in a doorway an acknowledging nod before turning his attention back to Sophia.

Despite her conviction during the ride that this was all under her control, self-doubt took the lead again.

'You want to walk this time?' he asked as she freed herself from the enclosure of the helmet.

Regardless of the unnerving heaviness of her legs as she dismounted the bike, the amusement in the cocky bastard's eyes grated too much. 'Whatever makes you feel more masculine,' she said, refusing to disguise her sneer. 'You're the one with something to prove it seems – not me.'

But she had no doubt that the glower in her eyes had gone no way to match the one in his.

'Keep your head down and your mouth shut,' he warned as he led her over to awaiting door.

'Recent graduate, were you?'

His eyes narrowed questioningly as he looked across his broad shoulder at her.

'From charm school,' she quipped, sensibly breaking eye contact again before sidestepping him and slipping through the doorway first.

The desolate, wide corridor loomed ahead.

As the door scraped to a close behind her, Sophia kept her head up, her shoulders back and her strides purposeful, Jask alongside her.

'I like what you've done with the place,' she remarked, the fluorescent tubes above buzzing in the silence. 'Very institutional.'

She looked across at him and sent him a glib smile in retort to another of his frowns, before she glanced over her shoulder to attempt to make eye contact with the younger lycans.

They hadn't just stumbled on her like they'd made out to Jask and Corbin. The two vampires who'd held her had been *awaiting* the arrival of two others – two lycans, from what she'd overheard.

But not once had Rone or Samson mentioned The Alliance or her role in it. Yet neither had any other lycans turned up.

She could have used her suspicions as a bargaining tool back in the ruins but had quickly resolved that if they truly didn't know, disclosing her links to The Alliance was potentially more suicidal than keeping her mouth shut.

Now what she needed to know was, if they *had* lied to their lycan leader, why? More importantly, how she could turn it to her advantage to get out of there.

But there was no way she could catch their eye without making it obvious with Corbin between them. She'd have to practise a little bit of uncharacteristic patience.

Jask pulled open another corrugated door and led them into what resembled a warehouse.

Two groups of males looked up from tables on opposing sides of the room. One cluster abruptly ceased their conversation. The other momentarily suspended their game of cards. All gave Sophia the once over.

As Jask marched her across the room, she struggled to keep her arms lax by her sides – the temptation to wrap them protectively around herself overwhelming under the oppression of their stares. Instead she looked a couple of lycans direct in the eye as she passed, swiftly giving them an equal once-over by way of retaliation.

As they reached another door on the far side, Jask keyed a code into the security panel before pushing the door open.

They stepped into a courtyard encompassed by chain-link fences – their twenty-foot height overshadowed only by further chain-link fences some fifteen feet beyond. The latter were at least fifty feet in height and topped off with coiled barbed wire – a sight made increasingly ominous by the eerie glow of dawn pending from behind the dense clouds.

Dawn meant another night gone. Another night wasted when she needed to get back to The Alliance. More importantly, to make contact with her sisters.

'If a subtle sense of paranoia was the theme you were aiming for, it worked,' she added, as much to ease her own tension in the dominating silence as maintain a mask of nonchalance.

But this time Jask didn't acknowledge her as he led her directly to the door opposite, keying in another code. The door made a sharp buzz before opening automatically. He stood back and indicated for Sophia to step through first.

She entered a low-arched, red-brick tunnel, her eardrums struggling to adjust to the oppressive enclosure. As the door clunked shut, a terrifying sense of disquiet encompassed her. Instinctively she picked up pace towards the open exit some twenty feet away, not least because of the unsettling echo of lycan footsteps close behind her.

The last thing she expected to enter was a large, open space, let alone be faced with greenery.

Apart from a scattering of hardy trees on the outskirts of Black-thorn – trees surviving despite the odds against the unrelenting polluted atmosphere – greenery was non-existent in Blackthorn. Occasional glimpses were only fractionally more apparent in Lowtown. Greenery was a privilege reserved for Midtown and, not least, Summerton, her true home – the latter having an abundance of parks, fields and woodlands.

But here in the lycan compound, in what was once an affluent city hotel, was not only a green lawn, but a scattering of small fruit trees.

She stood in the corner of the quadrant and scanned the three-storey building ahead, as well as the adjoining two-storey building to her left, both dark and geometric against the swirling mass of clouds. The sky appeared even heavier there, closeting the compound and encapsulating the cold bite that crept with the subtle breeze. A breeze that stirred a damp and earthy aroma evoked by the recent rainfall.

The place was scattered with lycans. Some relaxed on low walls and steps, others gathered at picnic tables, chatting in clusters. But it wasn't long before she caught their attention, her hands involuntarily clenching at her conspicuousness.

'Take them to the holding room,' Jask said to Corbin, referring to Rone and Samson. 'I won't be long.'

Corbin nodded, shooting Sophia a glance, before cocking his head towards Rone and Samson as an indication for them to follow.

Her pulse rate increased a notch. Jask wanted her alone. That could be a good thing or a bad thing.

She followed Jask around the paved periphery to the left whilst Rone and Samson were led to another tunnel on the far right of the quadrant. And from their perturbed faces, their leader was certainly living up to his reputation.

As Jask cut across the corner before continuing along the path to the three-storey building, she mindlessly rubbed her wrists – the wrists he had pinned so easily. Humiliation consumed her again at the recollection, as did the knot of nerves in her stomach as he led her up the broad stone steps to the impressive stone-arched entrance and through the open front doors.

Passing through a tile-floored entrance hall, they entered the lobby. Sophia stared ahead at the sweeping central staircase – one which she had no doubt would have been breathtaking in its day. At its pinnacle, the galleried landing split into two either side of a distant, dominating arched window.

Just like outside, lycans mingled in clusters – some reclining in worn armchairs, others strolling leisurely through the open doorway to the left or heading out of sight down the corridor to the right of the foot of the stairs.

She followed Jask across the mosaic floor, past an ornate stone fireplace to her right, and what would have been the reception desk to her left. Ascending the stairs alongside him, her attention was drawn to the opaque glass dome that crowned the ceiling, until the scorch of stares was too much to bear.

She glanced over her shoulder to see every pair of piercing eyes watching her. Even the lycans descending on the opposite side of the staircase frowned in curiosity as they passed.

She tugged at her knotted bobbed hair behind her ear, rubbed her thumb beneath what she assumed were now clown eyes, before glowering back at them. 'What the hell do they think they're staring at? Anyone would think they'd never seen a woman before.'

'Number one, you're with me, number two, you look a mess, and number three, you reek of vampires,' Jask declared. 'Everyone in this building can smell you coming from a hundred feet away.'

Despite his insults coming without so much as a glance in her direction, she still flushed with embarrassment. But she promptly reminded herself it didn't matter what anyone thought of her – least of all what Jask or any other lycan thought of her.

As they reached the top, she was tempted to turn and perform a theatrical curtsey for her captive audience, but Jask didn't give her time as he took a sharp left across the galleried landing.

He opened the only door on that side and she stepped in behind him, her heartbeat audible in her ears as he sealed the door behind them.

She took a steadying breath, taking her eyes off him only to scan the enclosure.

Aside from a cluster of three armchairs in front of the dominating window to her right, the fifty-by-thirty-foot room was void of furniture. Even the window was bare, doing nothing to hold back the muted early dawn glow across the exposed floorboards.

Jask kicked off his boots, his bare feet now silent as he led the way towards the jacquard bottle-green curtain ahead.

He brushed it aside to reveal a room about half the size of the last one, only this one had a much more homely feel.

A large, deep-pile rug lay against the wall to her right, conquered by a mass of floor cushions, pillows and a duvet. Clearly the rumour that lycans didn't sleep in beds, preferring to nest down on the floor, was true.

Another window dominated the wall ahead – this one a bay and housing an impressively deep window seat. But again, it was void of curtains. It seemed privacy wasn't an issue for lycans – not within the pack at least.

They passed scuffed, white-glossed inbuilt wardrobes as Jask led her to another curtain in the middle of the wall to her left. He tucked the fabric up on a hook and indicated for her to step inside.

She crossed the threshold into a bathroom. A shower cubicle big enough for four sat ahead, the white plastic curtains pulled back but still covering the sides left and right. A toilet was tucked in the top left-hand corner of the room. In the top right-hand corner, were two adjacent sash windows. A lengthy vanity unit containing a sunken sink spanned the rest of the wall to her right.

She caught a glimpse of herself in the broad mirror that sat above it – a small figure in loose, unflattering black clothes with skin too pale for her mussed, dyed-black hair.

'Strip to your underwear and shower,' Jask said.

Her heart skipped a beat. She turned to face him as he leaned against the door frame. 'You've got to be kidding me.'

He folded his arms, the taut bulge the position evoked reminding her of his strength. 'I want the war paint off your face so I can see what I'm really dealing with, and the repulsive vampire scent off your skin.' He cocked his head towards the cubicle. 'Now.'

She exhaled tersely. 'Screw yourself, Jask. Go find some other way to sate your guilty little pleasures – I don't strip for anyone.'

He held her gaze in the silence.

She held her breath.

A split second later, his chest was a solid wall against her back as he pulled her to the floor between his legs. He looped his ankles over hers, spreading them with his. Locking her arms to her chest, he unlaced one of her mid-calf army boots.

'I ask nicely once but never twice,' he said, as he tore her boot and sock from one foot before swapping hands and unlacing the other. 'If you want to continue being a belligerent little madam, fine. But you need to know I've no qualms treating you like one.'

He discarded her other boot and sock before lifting her to her feet with ease.

Arm locked around her waist, he carried her into the cubicle and switched on the shower. He let go of her only to yank her sweater and T-shirt up over her head, casting them aside. Re-pinning her arms pinned around her waist, he retained a faultless hold despite her furious kicking as he reached low down her abdomen to unfasten her combats.

'You can't do this!' she said through gritted teeth as she tried to buck futilely against him.

But as she lifted her feet to the wall to give herself leverage, she only gave him easier access to tug the clinging, soaked fabric down to her knees.

'No?' he asked. 'Then you clearly didn't learn from your lesson the first time.'

He pushed his foot down between her knees, taking her trousers the rest of the way to the floor. Lifting her out of them, he kicked them aside.

He reached for the shampoo bottle on the nearby shelf as she tried to elbow him away. Squeezing some onto her hair, he rubbed it in, using some of it to wash her face.

Sophia spat out bubbles, the shampoo stinging her eyes as she was forced to close them, let alone keep her mouth shut to avoid the foul taste.

She winced as it stung the wounds, scuffs and grazes from both her encounter with the vampires and the rough treatment of Marid who had made it quite clear he preferred his goods silent – something she'd had a lifelong difficulty with.

'I trust you can finish yourself off?' he said, finally letting her go.

She spat the last traces of shampoo from her mouth and hurriedly rinsed her stinging eyes with water before turning to see he had exited the shower. Through the thin fabric of the curtain, she could see his dark shadow in the corner of the room as he stood staring out of the window.

She ran her trembling hands back through her hair and rubbed her eyes until there were no more smudges of the heavy grey eye make-up she always wore.

Once she'd soothed the sting in her eyes, she sulkily grabbed the shower gel and gave herself a wash down. Although she wouldn't admit it to Jask, she was equally as keen to freshen up after being locked in a filthy room on that putrid bed for the past three days.

She glanced back at the shadow beyond the curtain and felt another flush of embarrassment at the state she'd been in, but immediately quashed the needless emotion.

She rinsed and turned the shower off, but as soon as she turned to look for something to wrap around herself, Jask was back at the opening.

She'd never been particularly shy about her body, and even less so serving with The Alliance – stripping off and tending wounds was a regular occurrence. But something about Jask's unashamed appraisal whilst she stood in her sodden, thin black underwear gave her a sense of unfamiliar inferiority that didn't rest easy.

'Do you own a towel or do you just shake dry?' she asked as she thrust up her chin, her gaze locked defiantly on his. She placed her hands on her hips. 'Or would you like to admire me for a little longer?'

He persisted, taking in every inch of her to the point she nearly lost her temper. Until she realised what he was doing. He was checking her inner arms, wrists, neck, thighs, stomach, ankles. He wasn't examining her for his own satiation – he was looking for bite wounds.

Of course – he assumed she was an experienced serryn and was assessing how many vampiric encounters she'd had recently.

She had almost forgotten what she was now. What she had become. After the night's events, let alone the previous three days, it had barely registered.

She should have been ecstatic and overwhelmed by the power that now, for a reason she had yet to uncover, flowed through her veins. For years she had dreamt of one day finding a serryn still alive – their blood the ultimate weapon against vampires and subsequently a platinum resource for The Alliance. And the whole time Leila – her sensible, shy, reserved big sister – had been harbouring a secret she would never have seen coming.

A secret she may never have discovered if something hadn't clearly happened that very night to cause the serryn line to jump to her.

A pang of sickness lingered at the back of her throat. Leila had to still be alive. She *had* to be.

'Turn around,' Jask said. 'Put your hands on the wall, bend forward and open your legs.'

She inhaled deeply, nearly gave him a mouthful of expletive-filled abuse but, despite what he thought, she *had* learned her lesson. Temporarily, at least.

She turned, placed her hands flat against the white tiles, spread her legs slightly and leaned forward just enough that he could see both the backs and inners of her thighs.

'Let me know when the thrill is over,' she said.

But when she looked over her shoulder, he'd already draped a towel over the rail above and was removing a shirt from the hook by the doorway.

He threw it at her.

'Get rid of the underwear and put that on.' He turned away. 'You've got two minutes.'

Stepping outside, he let the door curtain drop back into place.

Chapter Three

Jask stood in front of the window seat, arms folded as he looked out beyond the fences and barbed wire. Dawn had defeated the darkness on Blackthorn's horizon, early sunlight diminishing the shadowed recesses of the compound.

From the pivotal viewing point of his quarters, he looked left, down at the archway that led to the outbuildings where Rone and Samson had been taken. He didn't have time to wait around. He needed to get down there and find out as much as he could of exactly what they had been doing on that side of Blackthorn, let alone what mess there could still be to clear up.

But clearly his idea of two minutes and the serryn's idea of two minutes were two entirely different things. The bathroom was silent and it sure as hell didn't take a woman more than two minutes to put a shirt on.

He pulled away from the window and drew back the curtain to the bathroom.

She was sat cross-legged on the vanity unit, her small frame swamped in the towel, arms lax in her lap, her head resting back against the wall. She stared back at him – her brown eyes still brimming with anger and resentment, despite the lack of harsh makeup to emphasise such. Make-up without which, as he'd suspected, she was even prettier.

Her sodden combats, sweater and T-shirt were draped over the rail to dry. Her exposed slender shoulders still revealed the straps of her bra. *His* shirt had been thrown to the floor.

As aggravating as her non-compliance was, he'd give her spirit its due. He rested his forearm above his head against the architrave. 'What's your name?'

'Does it matter?'

'I asked you a question.'

Her gaze remained unflinching. 'Give me multiple-choice answers and I'll pick one.'

A pang of irritation sliced his chest at her insolence. But it was fascinating insolence all the same – especially from something two-thirds of his size, let alone in her situation.

He folded his arms and rested his shoulder against the door-frame. 'I'll just call you serryn then, shall I?'

'It's the closest you'll get to the truth.' She broke eye contact only to assess him slowly from feet to chest.

He'd changed into a dry shirt and jeans in the time it had taken her to do the exact opposite. But that wasn't the reason for the ser-ryn's appraisal. She was checking him out – and unashamedly so. He would have laughed had the blatancy of the act not been so intentionally defiant.

'You're even better-looking in the flesh than they say you are,' she said, those eyes locking on his again.

Coming onto him in his private quarters, or mocking him – both were intrepid acts. But then he had to remind himself this *was* a serryn he was dealing with, despite how small and helpless she looked. In Blackthorn, neither of the latter meant a thing.

'How long have you been working the streets of Blackthorn?' he asked. 'Only I haven't heard whispers of a serryn on the loose.'

'That's because I'm good.'

'So good that you got caught?'

She frowned. 'That's not how it was.'

'Then how was it exactly? Only going from the lack of recent bites I saw on you, you're not very successful.'

'I'm picky.'

'Is that even possible for a serryn? I understood you'd go with anything.'

Her eyes flared, but almost undetectably had he not been looking so closely. 'What exactly does any of it have to do with you? The vampires are none of your business, right? That's how it works around here – you stay in your little pound and they run Blackthorn. Which raises the question as to what I'm doing here.'

'You'll know when I want you to know. Until then, you'll do as you're told – starting with getting dressed.'

She used the leverage of one arm to lower herself nimbly from the vanity unit, the other hand keeping the knot of the towel at her chest. She stopped in front of him.

'Because *you're* going to tame me, right?' She dared to smirk as she echoed his words from in the ruins.

It was a smirk he'd seen once too often for one day.

As she sidestepped to slip past him, Jask braced his arm across the doorway.

'Did I say I'd finished with you?' he asked.

She took a step back, but not out of intimidation it seemed – instead to look him direct in the eyes. She folded her arms, emphasising the enticing upward curve of her small breasts now brimming the top of the towel. 'Why, Jask? What have you got planned next? Strip me all the way this time? And then what? You lycans like to come across all civilised, but we both know what you are underneath. You scratch behind your ear and howl at the moon with the best of them, I bet.'

Her ignorance, intentional or otherwise, was about as appealing as the way she looked at him as though she'd fallen face first into sewage.

'You've got a lot to say for yourself for someone in your predicament, serryn.'

'I've got a lot to say for myself whatever the predicament.'

His heart rate hitched up a notch. The first signs of tension formed in his chest. He kept his fists clenched to remind himself not to allow his talons to slide out from beneath the protective covering of his nails.

Corbin had been right – she was going to be hard work. And despite his light-hearted remark back on the wasteland for Rone and Samson's benefit, both he and Corbin knew the gravity of the situation. The fact was that he *did* need to tame her – and tame her he would. And that's what he had to keep his focus on – not on the blood pounding from his heart at the arrogant witch staring him down. Not on the thought of other circumstances, another time, when she'd have spent the next few minutes on her knees begging for his mercy – and doing whatever he asked of her to secure it.

He'd let his pack down before by letting his instincts take over – and he wasn't going to do it again. Which was why, first and foremost, he needed to work out exactly what he was dealing with.

Jask took a couple of steps towards her but she didn't flinch.

She didn't just have spirit; she appeared to believe she was titanium-coated – her inherent gift deluding her with a sense of impenetrability that, if the rumours were true, was characteristic of all serryns. Seemingly their spat in the shower hadn't quelled that confidence, nor had losing to him out on the wasteland.

But even he had to admit she'd put up a decent fight out there. If her moves hadn't been so learned, so predictable, she may have got one or two more to make impact. She'd soon discover though that her toned, nimble body wasn't anywhere near as invincible as she liked to believe – not if she continued to look at him with such contempt.

'You smell better already,' he said. And it wasn't a lie. Not only did she smell good now that her own scent took over but the closer he got, the better she looked. Her eyelashes, now free of thick black mascara, were fine but generous and with a feminine upward kink. Her earth-brown eyes were glossy despite being bloodshot – the latter either from the recent onslaught of soap or too many sleepless nights. Haughty eyes that were perfectly complemented by her delicate, slightly upturned nose. But it was those full, shapely lips that spoke too quickly and too cuttingly that would cause her the most trouble if she wasn't careful.

She frowned. 'I bet you really enjoyed that, didn't you? Stripping me like that.'

'I was fighting to contain myself.'

Her eyes narrowed in defensiveness. It seemed she took sarcastic insults less well than losing in combat. 'I bet you say that to all the girls. You *are* into girls, aren't you, Jask? Or is there something between you and Corbin you'd rather not share?'

It was an impulsive retort. A revealingly childish retort.

It was his turn to smirk. 'You're nothing but a kid, are you?'

Her eyes flared again. 'I'm twenty-nine, you patronising git.'

'Like I said – nothing but a kid.'

Her folded arms tensed, revealing any slight against her status was another button-pusher. 'The reputation that precedes you is quite phenomenal, Jask. I must admit I was a little worried when I knew you'd been called. But you're nothing but a pretty boy hiding behind the rumours, aren't you?'

He'd already had enough questions forming during the return journey about how she'd allowed herself to be manacled to a wall by two vampires. But now it seemed she was as poor at handling herself as she was them.

She certainly wasn't what he'd ever imagined – the mature, smooth, seductive females he'd always understood serryns to be. She got frustrated too quickly. Was impatient for control. She was too erratic, too impetuous – particularly in response to any of her weaknesses being exposed. Let alone too temperamental and emotionally vulnerable, from the way those eyes brimmed with self-preservation.

Her serrynity was undeniable – the macabre evidence on the floor back in the ruins proved that – but her adeptness at using it was questionable. And that was the last thing he needed.

'I don't think I've ever been called pretty,' he said, resting his hands low on his hips, skilfully diverting her attention there. 'And it's been a *long* time since I've been called a boy.'

It could have been a hint of a blush he'd seen – or a symptom of her anger.

Her gaze shot back to his. 'Like you said, I'm too used to fighting vampires.'

From what he'd seen in the shower, she certainly had a few minor scars to confirm it. But aside from the fresh wounds to her neck and arm from the vampires in the ruins, there was only one other slightly older set on her inner thigh.

'Don't make this any harder on yourself than it needs to be, serryn.'

As unpredictable as she was, he didn't expect her to flash a playful smile in response. And he didn't need to feel tension now tighten in his groin as well. Thoughts switching to the sexual potential her kind was notorious for was most definitely one distraction he could do without.

'That sounds like an enticing promise,' she dared to say, that unsettlingly sexy smile lingering. She closed the gap between them. 'Why, what bad things are you planning to do to me, Jask? Are all the rumours about you true? Are you really as insatiable as they say? Only you may have a few thousand years of evolution under your belt but I'm right, aren't I, about the animal still lurking inside? And unleashed during the sex act more than any other time, right? I hear you got so carried away once that you tore your partner's throat out. Is that true? Only I *love* a bit of risk between the sheets.'

As every part of him stiffened, he resolved to add painfully naïve to her profile. 'Been with a lycan before, have you?'

Her tongue played over her top teeth, drawing his attention to her lips. 'No. I never thought it worth my while. But being around you is changing my mind.' She *dared* to look him direct in the eyes as she said it. 'For you I could *definitely* make an exception to the rule.'

He promptly added suicidal tendencies to the list. 'Is that right?'

'You're very restrained, Jask. Just like you were back on the wasteland. That kind of self-control is an extremely attractive quality. But tell me, what does it take to break it?'

Confident words. Confident stance. But he'd seen the way she'd looked at him as he'd pinned her on the ground. For that moment, she'd panicked. Being out of control had scared her. And now he'd seen enough to know that smart retorts and gaining the upper hand sexually were her most trusty defence mechanisms.

Only she'd learn that self-control and restraint, fortunately for her, *were* now his most trusty defence mechanisms. And no smart-mouthed, attitude-laden little witch was going to make him lose what he had spent decades refining.

Not now. Not when he needed it most. Not when his pack needed it most.

'Take the rest of your clothes off,' he said. 'Or I *will* strip you. And I will drag you naked down the stairs, through the lobby and out onto the green, where I will rope you down and spread you on the lawn for all my pack to see. If you think I'm joking, you keep glowering at me like that.' He stepped around the back of her, picked up the shirt she had discarded and slammed it against her chest as he drew level again. 'Or you can do as you're told.'

Her scowl deepened as she bunched the shirt up in her hand, but it only took a few more seconds for her to choose the smart option.

She abruptly turned away from him, away from the windows. Lowering the towel to her slender waist, she unfastened and slipped off her bra with curt movements before tugging on his shirt and letting the towel drop to the floor. She fastened the buttons before turning to face him again. Eyes fixed on his in the only act of defiance she had left, she bent over to yank off her knickers before dropping them to the floor. But the whole sullen act was ruined as she folded her arms, the too-long shirt sleeves flapping over each other adding an unintentionally comical touch.

But he wouldn't let himself smile. This *was* about taming, not playing.

He gathered her wet clothing from the rail before scooping up her underwear from the floor.

'What are you doing with those?' she asked.

He turned away from her and pushed back through the curtain. 'Hey!' she called after him.

But he was already through the next curtain and approaching the door, collecting his boots along the way.

'You can't just walk off with my stuff!' she protested as she swept through the curtain behind him.

Less than an hour and already every one of his nerves were sparking.

He slammed the door behind him and locked it before heading back towards the stairs.

He glanced over his shoulder as he heard something make contact with the door from the other side. And this time his smile reluctantly broke through. Grating though she was, she was undeniably entertaining.

Another time, another place, another him, and he could have spent the next few hours reminding the serryn that, though lethal to vampires, she was in a lycan den now.

To some extent, he still could.

He descended the broad steps, handing the bundle of wet clothes to one of the lycans he passed at the foot of the staircase. 'Incinerate those, will you?' he directed, before making his way back outside.

❄ ❄ ❄

Sophia pursued Jask across the outer room, but not in time to stop him slamming and locking the door behind himself.

She turned the handle regardless, but it didn't budge. She slapped her palm against the doorplate in frustration before turning and slamming her bare heel against the base of the door.

'Bastard,' she hissed under her breath as she marched back into the bedroom.

She stood at the window and looked to the exit beyond. From what she had seen while heading in and from what she could see now, the rumours about impenetrable security were true. And with security like that, let alone with lycans dotted around everywhere, there was no way she was getting out of there unnoticed.

Even if she had been a witch long enough to know any spells off by heart, let alone had access to what she needed to perform them, Jask was guaranteed to have the place surrounded by wards to prevent any semblance of casting. He would never have left her unbound if not.

If Rone and Samson couldn't get her out, she was screwed.

They were who she needed – *after* she'd worked out why Jask wanted her. Because one way or another, more was at stake here and she needed to find out what.

Her heart skipped a beat as Jask headed out from the lobby and down the steps, his fair hair blowing in the breeze. She rolled up her dangling sleeves before folding her arms, irritated at how she trembled. But after her close encounter with him, she wasn't entirely sure it was just out of anxiety or fury.

She'd been speaking the truth when she'd said he was even better-looking than the rumours – even if she had said it to wind him up, a refusal to be intimidated. But he was most *definitely* more than just a pretty boy. Jask Tao was in a league of his own. And his calm resolve in the bathroom, despite her prodding, was one trait that left her far too unsettled for comfort.

Composed, methodical and controlled – Jask was aggravatingly everything she wasn't. Worse, she was already sensing the one-upmanship that only fuelled her irritation further.

He sat on the steps for a moment to lace up his boots, leaving his jeans bunched up against them as he descended the rest. As he crossed the quadrant towards the arch to the left, she admired his broad shoulders, the perfect triangle to his taut waist now a visible shadow as the early sunlight shone through his shirt – a shirt that skimmed his pert behind. And those arms that had held her down so easily, despite now being lax by his sides, still oozed power.

Lycan or not, that was one bedroom encounter she could do with experiencing – but the fact he *was* in that other league only exacerbated her barely contained frustration. Especially when he looked at her as though she was nothing more than a convenient commodity.

She watched him disappear through the arch where Rone and Samson had been taken and rested her hands on her hips as she turned around to scan the room.

First plan was to get to a phone. She'd try and call Leila or Alisha – find out what the hell had been going on. And then she'd call The Alliance and warn them.

She knew it was probably a long shot, but she'd try anyway. She rooted through his bed before searching the sole piece of furniture in the room – the chest of drawers nestled in the corner by the window. As possessions clearly weren't a preoccupation for Jask, it was less than a minute before she turned her attention to his wardrobe.

She stood on tiptoe as she fumbled through the top shelf, finding little amidst a few sweaters and miscellaneous items. She prized apart the clothes on the rail, checking pockets, until she came to a few dresses tucked away in the far left-hand side. It seemed Jask didn't sleep alone despite the rumours he didn't have a mate. She quashed the stirring sense of disappointment. No wonder he was so contemptuous of her advances – it appeared the third-species leader had something of a rare honourable streak.

She turned her attention to the bathroom. She pulled out the drawers of the vanity unit, finding most of them empty aside from some scent bottles along with some hair accessories and a few brushes – clearly belonging to the same female who owned the clothes. She picked up the nearest brush and examined the fair hairs it had trapped. She glanced back at her muss of dark hair in the mirror, before throwing the brush back in the drawer and slamming it shut.

She picked up her boots and marched back through to the lounge, but there was nothing there *to* search. She needed to look further afield.

Kneeling in front of the door, she upturned her left boot and slid the heel aside. Removing the pins hidden inside the hollow of the heel, she cast the boot aside again.

It was a basic lock and ridiculously easy pickings. Unlocking it within seconds, she turned the handle and opened the door ajar slightly to peer outside.

All was quiet.

She tucked her head through the gap and peered out fully onto the landing.

Countless bedrooms lay in the hallway beyond. And she knew from the fact they were only on the second floor that there were even more bedrooms above. Someone had to have left a phone around somewhere.

She got to her feet and opened the door.

But stopped herself crossing the threshold.

Giving away her escapology skills at that stage was not going to be helpful – not until she could guarantee contact with Rone or Samson. Not until she found out what they knew and, more importantly, what their motivations were for hiding it from Jask.

Strategy was more important than ever.

She closed the door again and relocked it. She tucked the pins back into place and sat on the floor to pull both boots on. She laced them up before resting back against the wall, stretching her legs out and crossing one over the other.

He may be stronger, but she was smarter.

She *would* turn this to her advantage. To the advantage of The Alliance. To the advantage of their cause.

She may have failed to take down powerhouse vampire, Caleb Dehain. The notoriously most wanted Kane Malloy may have re-mained as consistently elusive from the authorities as always, let alone from The Alliance. But she was right in the heart of lycan territory now with third-species ringleader number three.

An assassination from the inside was the last thing anyone would expect. And if that wouldn't send a message to the untouchable un-derworld, the likes of Caleb Dehain and Kane Malloy, nothing would.

❊ ❊ ❊

Jask headed to the arch on the far side of the green and strode through the short tunnel. He passed the gate to the greenhouse on his left and then the oak on his right, the centuries-old tree marking the middle of the courtyard partially concealing the outhouse beyond.

Turning the handle, he pushed open the weighty door and crossed the bare foyer to the holding room opposite.

Rone and Samson sat at the table with their backs to the door. Corbin sat in a chair opposite them, leaning back against the wall. The atmosphere was dense with sullenness.

Samson immediately looked across his shoulder as Jask closed the door behind himself. But Rone remained facing forward.

Usually he'd take the head of the table, but this time Jask took the seat beside Corbin instead so he could look Rone and Samson direct in the eye.

But both youths kept their eyes lowered.

Jask knew he shouldn't be allowing himself to be so personally affronted by the fact Rone was involved yet again. But the youth's habit of walking into danger, especially so innocently, irritated too much. This time, even Corbin – usually the youth's advocate – was going to struggle to justify his behaviour.

'What was the deal?' Jask asked.

Samson glanced at Rone, the latter finally meeting Jask's glare.

'A few herbs,' Rone declared.

The revelation was worse than a stab to the lungs, the breathlessness making Jask's chest clench. It was an act worthy of banishment. There was a time when he would have embraced getting Rone out of his sight, but now he was actually facing the prospect, it only made him feel sick. 'You were *supplying*?'

Both youths glanced nervously at Corbin whose upright posture now echoed Jask's disapproval. Corbin who equally knew of the punishment for the unthinkable crime against their pack.

Wide-eyed, Rone switched his attention back to Jask and nodded.

'You were supplying *this* community's herbs? The herbs we fight to keep alive. That ensure *we* stay alive. The herbs that allow the only semblance of freedom we have left. You were selling them off to vampires? And in Kane's territory of *all* places?'

'It was a one-off,' Rone said, struggling to maintain eye contact under the weight of his leader's glare. 'I swear. A vampire approached us. She said she only needed a few. She needed to sell something on to some witch in order to get something to help her kid out. I felt sorry for her.'

'So you struck a deal?'

Rone looked back down at the table.

Something wasn't right. Something in his story didn't ring true. Not just that, but he could read far too much in the youth's eyes. It was a story they'd concocted whilst awaiting his and Corbin's arrival, no doubt. As if Rone couldn't disfavour himself to Jask any more, the youth was daring to lie to him.

'And that's who you went to meet?' Jask asked. 'Some lone female vampire in an isolated part of Blackthorn?'

Rone looked back at him, but dropped his gaze just as quickly as he seemingly realised how flawed the possibility was. 'We didn't want to be seen. And she was desperate.'

No vampire female would have been that desperate and they all knew it. They'd been up to something else. But they weren't ready to talk yet, for whatever reason.

But they would.

Because that reason for holding back worried him more – and not just for the pack. Something told him Rone had got in over his head this time, and his resulting protective instincts were irritatingly kicking in against his will.

'What's her name?' Jask asked, his glare burning into Rone's lowered head, his mop of fair hair covering his eyes. Harsh impatience edged his tone as he turned to the other youth instead. 'Samson?'

'I don't remember,' Samson said, glancing up from under his eyelashes.

Whatever was going on, it was bad enough for them *both* to risk being avoidant.

'So I've got no way of tracing this mystery vampire?'

'We thought the less we knew about each other, the better,' Rone said, his continuation to lie escalating both Jask's fury *and* concern.

Jask rested his forearms on the table and leaned forward.

Sensing his leader's irritation, Corbin leaned forward to mirror him – the cautionary measure one he rarely took anymore.

It was sign enough to the youths that they had overstepped the mark. How little chance they'd stand if Jask took the decision that he wanted the truth instantly. Under those circumstances, Corbin would be his reasoning head. Or from the way the youths glanced at Corbin, they certainly seemed to hope so.

'You know the implications if it leaks out we're willing to sell our substances,' Jask said. 'You know what threat that puts us under from the authorities. That's why the answer is no. The answer is *always* no. No negotiation. You showed weakness. Your stupidity tonight could have massive implications – a ripple we cannot control. If the Lycan Control Unit hear of this they will come in and rip every herb from this place, then what do we do? Morph and be shot down on the streets? Or go on the Global Council's meds and be filled with whatever shit they secretly put in those things? Our herbs are our lifeline and you know it.'

Neither youth dared look up.

'What do you know about the serryn?' Jask asked. 'The one you so happened to stumble on.' Though, more worryingly, he now believed that a coincidence even less than the existence of the mysterious female vampire.

'Everything we saw, we told you,' Rone said, still unable to make full eye contact despite the change of focus.

'You were down there at least an hour. You're telling me she said nothing to you?'

Rone shook his head. 'Other than to try and persuade us to let her go.'

Jask looked from Rone to Samson and back to Rone again. 'I'm casketing you both for twelve hours.'

Their gazes snapped to Jask's in an accumulation of abject panic and horror.

'No,' Rone gasped instinctively.

'You chose outsiders over your pack. That is unforgiveable. Worsened by the fact you may have jeopardised our freedom. You know the rules. You protest and it becomes twenty-four.' Jask stood. 'Immediate effect.'

He could feel Corbin's disapproval burning into him, but his second in command didn't say a word. Instead, he followed suit and stood.

Samson reluctantly did the same, the whites of his eyes upsettingly exposed.

Rone pushed back his chair and stood more slowly. This time he did dare to meet Jask's glare long enough to make his umbrage obvious. But he at least had the sense to remain tight-lipped as he followed Jask out of the room, Corbin bringing up the rear.

Jask took a sharp left down the few broad steps to the stone corridor, dawn light paving the way from the high, rectangular windows nestled deep in the stone above. Their footsteps were the only things to break the ominous silence as they passed the first and then second door on the left.

Opening the third, Jask stepped inside the forty-foot-square cellar. The walls left, right and ahead were lined with upright caskets – five in total.

Striding past the stone table that lay central to the room, Jask chose the casket to the right.

No lycan could handle being contained. And the smaller the space, the greater the torture. It was a punishment he rarely had to use. A punishment that sickened him.

But the youths had to learn responsibility for their actions. Rone, in particular, needed to accept that his past wouldn't save him from being treated like every other pack member.

Corbin stepped up to the wall directly ahead of the door, selecting the middle of the three caskets. He summoned Samson, whilst Jask summoned Rone.

Knowing any protest was futile, the two youths did as they were told, backing up inside the encasements.

Jask and Corbin proceeded to regimentally strap in their ankles, calves, thighs, hips, waist, chest, arms and shoulders, before finally strapping their necks.

Rone looked Jask in the eyes, his sense of being betrayed over-shadowing his fear, but still said nothing as his leader closed the casket door.

Discomfort lodged in his chest and throat, Jask crossed the room and stepped back out into the corridor. He stared up at the windows, at the shadows of the dead climbers behind the misted glass.

He had to ignore the guilt. He'd do what he had to. This would make the point that the line was never, ever to be crossed. Something more important than ever with recent events.

Corbin stepped out behind him, locking and sealing the door before hanging the key back on the hook. 'You okay?'

Jask turned to face him. 'Something else is going on, Corbin.'

Corbin slammed the viewing window shut. 'I know. Are you thinking the same thing, I am?'

'That this is a set-up?

'Like I said on the way there, it's a big coincidence, Jask. Five days ago a witch tells us the only way to save our pack is to find a serryn, and then one just turns up? What were the chances? Let alone one who managed to get herself manacled to a wall despite being alive and kicking. Maybe fate finally decided to cut us some slack, but I'm not convinced this is as easy as it looks. I hate to be the one to say this, but what if the witch who told us a serryn was the solution had lied? What if the witches *wanted* her in here?'

'The witches in this district have nothing to gain by going up against lycans.'

'But *we* went up against the TSCD, Jask. We both know they're only biding their time before they get back at us. You saw the look on Xavier Cross's face when you gave evidence against him. His division would have had Kane Malloy in the bag if you hadn't scuppered their plans. So what if history is repeating itself? The TSCD used us to get to Kane, so what's to say they're not using the witches to get back at us? They know as well as we do that if word slips out that we've got a serryn hidden away here, we can kiss goodbye to our peaceful pact with the vampires. What if somehow they tricked Rone and Samson into being a part of that, and those two have only now realised it?'

Corbin stepped closer to Jask, his tone lowered.

'It makes sense why they'd opt for casketing instead of coming out with the truth, Jask. Especially Rone. You know how much he wants your approval, reluctant though he is to admit it.'

'Which is why he thinks it's okay to insult me by lying to my face.'

'Which is why he's scared every time he messes up.'

'Which is why he should have learned by now to stop messing up.'

'I hate to do this to you, Jask, but doesn't he remind you of someone?'

'I learned from my lessons.'

'And from what I hear, you ran wild for years when you were his age on the way to learning those lessons. He doesn't have that liberty.'

Jask looked across at his friend. 'Which I don't need reminding of. And which is why he needs to learn to fall in line before he ends up dead or this pack ends up in trouble.'

'So instead of this,' Corbin said, cocking his head back to the chamber behind, 'scare the shit out of them. It might be unpleasant but less unpleasant than this – and we'll get to the truth a hell of a lot quicker. We don't have time to waste here, let alone if we *have* been set up.'

'I'm giving them time to think. I want them to come out with the truth themselves, Corbin. I want them to accept it's their responsibility to do that. If Rone's got any pretentions about one day leading a pack of his own, he needs to learn to put that pack first. So I'm not going to wrench it out of them. Not yet.'

'Do you think they know we need a serryn? Do you think that's why they were there?'

'You saw as well as I did their shock at seeing what she is. Whatever reason they had for being there, I don't think it was to collect a serryn.'

'What about her? Has she said anything?'

'I've held off until speaking to them.' Jask headed back along the corridor and up the steps. 'Now it seems I have no choice.'

'And if you've torn off more than you can chew with her? There's a reason no one fucks with serryns, Jask. And we don't have time for maybes. Perhaps we need to focus on finding another way.'

'In the next six days? Like we have been for the past five?'

'As opposed to you getting her full co-operation in less time?'

'If I can't persuade her, I'll find leverage and *make* her do what I want.'

'They don't care about anyone or anything. You know that.'

'There *is* no other way, Corbin. The *only* way is through that serryn.' Jask held out his hand. 'Forty-eight hours and she'll be doing whatever I want.'

Corbin forced a smile at the familiar playful challenge as he took his friend's hand, despite them both knowing the severity of the situation.

They'd survived worse. And they'd keep surviving – one way or another.

'Forty-eight hours and I reckon you would have killed her out of frustration,' Corbin declared, sealing the deal, the concern emanating from his eyes despite his acceptance.

'Such little faith.'

'Not at all, Jask – I just know you. Better than anyone, remember? One way or another, that serryn will be out to break you. Just you make sure you get what we need before *you* break her.'

Chapter Four

Sophia sat on the window seat, her legs stretched out in front of her along its length. A light frost glistened on the window rims, the thin pane doing more than she would have anticipated in limiting the penetrating breeze whistling against the glass. Laughter emanated below, breaking the silence as lycans made their way up the steps and into the lobby.

She gazed out at the tightly knit buildings beyond the compound – at the myriad of rooftops, the weak early morning sun catching their crescents, not least the spire of an old church she knew lay as derelict as many other buildings in Blackthorn.

She knelt up and slipped her fingers under the sash window's handles. It took a surprising effort to lift. She locked it into position to make sure it didn't slam back down on her before bracing her arms on the window frame to peer out. The drop was at least twenty-five feet below and not so much of a hint of a climbing plant or trellis for her to cling on to. She twisted her neck to look up at the overhanging roof. Maybe if she was desperate…

'You'd clear it if you were a lycan.'

She flinched, whacked the back of her head on the window before glowering over her shoulder to see Jask stood behind her.

'But I wouldn't risk it,' he declared, as she ducked back inside. He leaned past her and slammed the window shut, his arm almost brushing her legs had she not drawn them back so abruptly. 'Even if you did get out of here, you're not getting out of the compound. And you know it.'

She rubbed the back of her throbbing head as she eased back against the wall. 'We'll see, shall we?'

He sat at the opposite end of the window seat, facing her. He stretched the leg nearest to her along the length of the seat, trapping her between him and the glass. Bending his other leg to his chest, he rested his forearm loosely on his knee, creating an irritatingly casual pose.

But it was a pose she equally hoped was reassuring. Because if Rone or Samson did know anything about The Alliance and had finally disclosed it to Jask, she was sure there was no way he would have retained his current composure.

'Clearly personal space doesn't mean anything to your sort,' she said

'Not when it's my space to begin with – no.'

She dropped her hand from the back of her skull, despite it still hurting. 'How characteristically territorial.'

He rested his head back against the wall, assessing her from under those dark lashes. There, in the tepid morning sunlight, the depths of his azure eyes glimmered in all their beauty – his pupils remaining characteristically dilated despite the light. It was a shame sharks circled beneath their enticing surface. Because, despite her stomach knotting, she'd heard too much of what lay behind the handsome exterior to be contemplating what those lips tasted like.

Despite it being justifiable, killing him was still going to be a terrible waste.

'Have you got a problem with lycans, serryn?'

'Like I said before, I've never really given your kind much thought,' she said, dismissively looking back out of the window, annoyed to feel a glimmer of intimidation at his silent contemplation.

'Those vampires didn't know what you are. Or they wouldn't have been stupid enough to take you down into those ruins,' he remarked, clearly wanting to get straight to the very point she needed to avoid.

The point that the serryn line had jumped to her *whilst* she had been chained up.

'So?'

'Why did you leave it that long before making them bite? If you were unconscious, fair enough. But from what Rone and Samson tell me, you were very much kicking. Why wait until you were chained up, minimising your chance of escaping?'

She needed to make her brain fire quicker than it was, made eye contact again to grant herself an extra couple of seconds. 'I made them bite as soon as I could.'

Jask's eyes brimmed with scepticism, but he still retained that patient resolve.

There was no way she could let him discover that she had been a serryn just a matter of hours – firstly because she suspected he needed an adept serryn for whatever she'd been kept alive for and, more significantly, not when it would evoke the inevitable questions of *how* it had happened. Until she knew her little sister, Alisha, was out of Blackthorn, let alone that Leila was okay, she was saying nothing.

'I got myself in a mess,' she added. 'It happens. And I got out of it.'

'My pack got you out of it, you mean. Or you would have stayed chained up until the next batch of vampires found you, with the evidence of what you are spread all over the floor. I hear vampires can do some nasty stuff to serryns.'

'So can those who want to use serryns against vampires, right, Jask? Is that why I'm here? Doesn't that break that pact of peace you have going on?' In that instant, her purpose to him became all too probable. She'd already said to The Alliance that she had the feeling it wasn't over. 'Unless that's what you want. Is this something to do with Kane Malloy?'

His eyes flared just at the mention of his name, seemingly confirming her fear. 'Why would this be anything to do with Kane Malloy?'

'Do you seriously think I don't know about that? It's been on every channel and station this past two weeks. *Everyone* knows about it: you and the master vampire collaborating to expose the corruption in the Third Species Control Division. I read the reports of you giving evidence of how those three agents used two of your pack to kill Kane's sister – all in their attempt to finally incarcerate their most wanted vampire by sending him on a rampage against you.'

Jask's eyes narrowed slightly, clearly not liking her insight. For those moments, it gave her *her* turn at the one-upmanship she craved.

'Only rumours are that you weren't happy you had to give evidence,' she added. 'That you only did because Kane Malloy backed out of whatever deal you two had. Of course, no one knows what that deal was. But knowing what I do about your species, it's all an eye for an eye with your kind, isn't it? I'm guessing you wanted those responsible dead, not least the mastermind behind the plan, the now *ex*-head of the TSCD, Xavier Carter. But more than that, you also wanted the only link between all four dead: the golden agent of the Vampire Control Unit, Caitlin Parish. After all, there's no better way to stick it to the ones responsible than to do the same to the one they all cared about. A pawn for a pawn, right? Only rumour has it things got hot between her and Kane, leaving you out in the cold with his change of plans in *her* favour. I'm guessing I'm here because you want to turn that back around. Why else would you need a serryn, Jask?'

'That's a lot of speculation.'

'But you're not denying it.'

'You think you're capable of taking on Kane Malloy?'

Not a chance. An hours-old serryn against one of the most notorious vampires in Blackthorn – he'd rip her apart as soon as look at her. But she didn't need Jask to see any indication of that. If that *was* his plan for her, she was useful to him. And as long as she was useful to him, she stayed alive. And the longer she stayed alive, the better chance she stood of finding out everything she needed to before taking him down – let alone staying alive long enough to find out what was going on with her sisters.

And if he *was* planning a retaliation against Kane, something that would be seen as a retaliation against all vampires, Blackthorn was about to implode. The consequences for the humans caught in the middle didn't bear thinking about. And now she had been granted the perfect opportunity to do something about it.

She just had to make sure she came across as everything he was expecting. One slip of vulnerability and she was defunct. And that meant dead.

'You clearly think I am or I'd be dead already,' she said. 'Come on, Jask – admit I'm right. Maybe we can come to an arrangement quicker that way and save us both some time. Why else would you need to tame me if not to make me co-operate? And you'd *need* me to co-operate for this one, wouldn't you?'

She was sure she saw a glimmer of amusement in his eyes. 'You still haven't told me your name.'

'Tell me why you want me.'

'How long have you been in Blackthorn?'

She couldn't let her frustration at his deflection get the better of her. The notorious closed book that was Jask Tao would have to break at some point to get what he wanted. 'Long enough.'

'How many vampires have you killed?'

'I'm working towards all of them so, as you can see, still a long way to go.'

'Where are you from? Originally.'

Disclosing where she was from wasn't going to have any impact. And she could hope it would go some way to placating his curiosity enough to stay clear of the more revealing questions. 'Summerton.'

He raised his eyebrows slightly. 'Really?'

'Don't sound so surprised.'

'And what did you do to earn that privilege?'

'I had a special talent for keeping my head above water. Still do.'

She was sure she saw another hint of a smile, clearly from the irony of the statement in light of her predicament.

'Summerton to Blackthorn,' he said. 'That's quite a lifestyle switch.'

Sophia lingered over his lips as he spoke, catching glimpses of those well-formed, powerful canines. Just like their wolf heritage dictated, they were said to still use them to kill when they needed to. It may have been a rare occurrence, but the potential was there. And from the way he had brought her down on the wasteland, let alone manoeuvred her in the shower, they were also as physically adept as their reputation dictated.

She glanced down at his hands held lose on his knees. Strong, masculine hands. His underlying talons, hidden beneath his nails, were as retracted as his canines, but they'd extend soon enough if he wanted them too. Just as he could have snapped her neck in seconds if he'd chosen too, let alone been more than capable of ripping her heart out – a rumoured personal favourite of lycans wanting to add a personal touch.

'Not unlike you wolf-boys – once running wild, now locked in here,' she said, meeting his pensive gaze again.

His eyes narrowed slightly. 'I'm a lycan – not a wolf.'

'Are you embarrassed of your heritage?'

'Dual heritage.'

'Managed by your special herbs, right? Those of you who don't opt to take the meds issued by the Global Council, that is. But take all of that away, and you have nothing left but the animal inside.'

'And the human too.'

'Still soulless though,' she reminded him. 'Having nothing but a shadow where your soul *should* be, just like with the rest of you third species.'

His eyes narrowed a little again. The silence became thick between them. But to her relief he broke away a few seconds later, easing off the windowsill.

'I'm going down for breakfast,' he said, stepping away. 'If you're not into being force-fed, I suggest you join me.'

Under any other circumstances, she would have told him exactly where to anatomically shove his breakfast. But following him meant getting out of the room, seeing more of the compound and hopefully Rone or Samson. Besides, she was starving – and her stomach frequently won over her pride.

She crossed the room behind him. 'How very civilised. Usually I have to sleep with someone before I get a free breakfast. Or maybe you lycan boys need sustenance to build up the energy? I can work with that.'

He opened the door, stepping back to allow her to exit first, his frown his only response before he followed her out.

'You know, you're really going to have to develop a sense of humour if we're becoming roomies,' she said. 'Actually, are your kind even capable of laughing or does it just come out as a growl?'

His fingers encircled her upper arm. She lost her breath as he slammed her back against the door, his grip not easing as he equally pinned her there with his glare. But she knew it was anything but fear she felt as heat rushed to the pit of her abdomen.

'Quit,' he said, 'with the irritating remarks. I'm trying to be nice. You're not making that easy.'

'I'm not an easy kind of girl,' she said, her throat too dry for comfort. But she wouldn't look away. She wouldn't break from those entrancing eyes, those rapidly dilating pupils – now almost encompassing their azure bed – a sure sign of his annoyance.

'Then I suggest you learn. Quickly,' he said, the tips of his extending razor-thin talons purposefully on the cusp of embedding themselves in the flesh of her upper arm.

'Sir, yes, Sir,' she quipped, but refrained from saluting despite the temptation.

He frowned again as he pulled away.

A part of her felt a scratch of disappointment.

She regained her breath, checked the imprints on her upper arm, impressed he'd managed not to draw blood, before following him across the landing and down the stairs.

There were less lycans around now and those that were, were heading through the open doors to her left. The sound of chatter echoed through from the room beyond, along with the clink of cutlery and the distant aroma of freshly cooked toast. Her stomach grumbled. Marid had barely fed her and the crap he'd served up had been hard to swallow.

She followed Jask towards the open doors into the wood-panelled dining hall, seated lycans filling the multitude of tables that spanned the room.

She stopped abruptly at the threshold as more slipped past her. Amidst the buzz of chatter were an increasing number of glances in her direction, a few suspended conversations as others stopped to scrutinise the stranger in their midst.

She scanned for any sign of Rone or Samson. But there was none.

And as more and more eyes turned to her, she started to feel like the only one in fancy dress at a party. Stood there swamped in Jask's shirt, naked beneath, her skinny legs thrust into her tough army boots, heat rushed to her cheeks. She instinctively smoothed down the back of her hair, but it took only a second more to resolve to retreat.

But Jask was quick, grabbing her wrist.

'I'm going to get some fresh air,' she declared, with a single attempt to yank her wrist free.

'You'll stay where I can see you.'

'Let me go,' she warned.

But his hold only tightened as he turned to face her head on, his back to the room. 'If you wanted everyone's attention, you're getting it. You seriously think I'm going to let you walk away now that everyone has seen this little battle of wills?' He leaned close to her ear and whispered, 'You are one more defiant glare away from me publicly putting you over my knee. How much humiliation do you want in one day?'

'Bastard,' she hissed.

'You'd better believe it,' he said, lingering on her gaze a second longer than was needed. An unsettling intimacy that was reinforced as he slid his hand down from her wrist to encompass her hand as he turned away – a hand that was surprisingly gentle despite the harshness of his words.

He led her around the periphery of the room, letting her go only to place his selection from the buffet table onto the compartmental tray he held.

Resentment coiled in her stomach to the point she finally lost any semblance of appetite, despite how enticing the smell of the herb-infused toasted bread and sautéed potatoes were. Instead, she opted for a glass of freshly squeezed orange juice along with a bread roll, before following behind Jask.

But whereas he headed over to the table at the back of the room, Sophia held back. Seeing an empty table for four against a wall, she opted for that.

She placed her juice on the table, yanked out a chair and plonked herself down, glowering over to where Jask was pulling out a seat beside a blonde female. Corbin, his back to Sophia, was sat opposite them both.

The blonde eyed her with curiosity as Jask leaned forward to say something to Corbin, Corbin glancing across his shoulder in Sophia's direction.

They were clearly talking about her. Worse, they were smiling.

She looked down at her bread roll before glancing back up to meet the blonde's gaze. The beautiful female swiftly responded with a hint of a friendly, if not slightly wary smile. With her baby face, full lips, sun-kissed complexion, and enviably waist-length braided hair that trailed over her full chest, she was everything Sophia wasn't.

No wonder Jask had found it so easy to turn down her advances, to be so dismissive of her flirtatious remarks. It must have been *her* clothes and fragrances in his room.

A knot of embarrassment, of envy, formed in her chest as Jask draped his arm around the back of the blonde's chair whilst he continued to talk to Corbin. She instantly wanted to hate her, but the female who glanced back at her again was only trying to make her feel a little more comfortable – one female reassuring another, despite the species divide, that she understood her awkwardness.

So Sophia forced a hint of a smile back. She had to at least let her know she appreciated her effort if nothing else – even if she clearly was Jask Tao's mate.

But as Jask recaptured her gaze, one laced with the triumph of having got her in there, even if not to sit with them, Sophia tore off a piece of bread. And plotted how to even the score.

❋ ❋ ❋

'Is she not willing to mix with our kind?' Corbin asked.

Jask placed his breakfast tray on the table as he pulled out the seat beside Solstice.

Sitting down, he looked across at the serryn.

She looked so small sat alone at the table for four – shirt held down between her thighs with one clenched fist, her long, shapely legs slightly parted, her heavy mid-calve boots unflattering to their slenderness. Her scowl darkened her eyes, her body tense with resentment. He would have found it amusing had it not been so childishly annoying.

'I think that might have been asking too much,' Jask remarked, tearing his gaze away to focus his attention on eating.

'Why's she in your shirt?' Solstice asked.

'A small lesson,' Jask replied.

'And from the death stare she's giving you, I'd say this is round three to you,' Corbin declared with a smirk.

Jask smiled back.

'Round three?' Solstice asked, her gaze switching between her companions.

Jask swallowed a mouthful of food. 'Will you get some clothes for her, Solstice? And leave them up in my room. Anything else you think she might need as well.'

'So she's staying a while?'

'Long enough for her to need to get dressed.'

'Is this what the call was about earlier? Is this why Rone and Samson are in the chamber?'

'They crossed the line,' Jask declared.

'Did they do something to her?'

'No, but they found her where they shouldn't have been.'

'Vampire territory?' Solstice glanced across at the serryn again, eyes wide with concern. 'Was she attacked?'

'Bitten, yes.'

'Did Rone and Samson intervene?'

'Not exactly. Not that Rone and Samson should have been there to see it in the first place.'

'Which is why you're angry with them.'

'They know the rules, Solstice.'

'So do you, Jask. You made them. So what's an outsider doing in the compound?'

'She has something we need.'

'Like what?'

Jask took a mouthful of bread, chewed and swallowed as he glanced at Corbin before returning his attention to his food. 'Like very precious blood.'

Solstice frowned. She stared at Jask before glancing at Corbin, looking for his confirmation too. Her eyes flared, her fair eyebrows knocked up an inch. 'No.'

'In the flesh,' Corbin confirmed.

'But I thought they were extinct?'

'Rumour is they are,' Jask said. 'Yet clearly not.'

Solstice lowered her voice as she leaned closer. 'And you brought her back *here*? She came voluntarily?'

'Not exactly,' Jask said.

Solstice snapped back a breath, her gaze switching between them both again. 'Are you both crazy?'

Jask took a mouthful of food. 'She can't do anything.'

Solstice lowered her voice to a whisper. 'She's a serryn, for goodness sake. Is there anything more lethal? Need I remind you we have young ones here, Jask? You know what her kind are capable of doing to them. And what if she takes one of them hostage or something to get out of here?' She flashed an accusatory glare at Corbin before staring back at Jask. 'Have you thought of that?'

Jask looked across at the serryn again. Her knees were now locked together, her feet slightly parted and in-turned. She was half-way through her bread roll, tearing off pieces, chewing them with her head lowered, her bobbed hair partially covering her face. The prospect of her being the most dangerous, not least vicious witch there was seemed improbable. But he couldn't be fooled. 'She's not that stupid.'

'Trapped in here with no other option? You don't know *what* she's capable of. And if the vampires get word we have a serryn here… Kane or Caleb…'

'We have no choice.' Jask glanced at Solstice then lingered on Corbin before turning his attention back to his food.

'What does that mean?' Solstice asked. Her attention switched to Corbin. 'What's he talking about, Corbin?'

Corbin glanced at Jask to acquire his approval. 'We need a serryn,' Corbin told her. 'That afternoon, after what happened to Nero, when we both headed out, we saw a witch. He told us there's a supply of turmeric here in Blackthorn. Enough of a supply for what we need.'

Solstice's lips parted slightly, her grip on her spoon tightened. 'But I thought there was no more turmeric here. That we had the last of it. Is it not still banned?'

'Oh, it's still banned,' Jask said. '*And* still illegal to trade.'

'And now we know why,' Corbin added.

Jask took a mouthful of water. 'Which is why we have to play this carefully. They get one hint that we don't have enough this time around, and this is over.'

Solstice frowned. 'No way. I know those bastards at the Global Council are willing to stoop low, but seriously? You think they knew we'd need it at some point? How?'

'This is proof that they know far more than they're letting on,' Jask said.

'All this so-called respecting our heritage and they've just been biding their time, haven't they?' Solstice said. 'They've been waiting for our supplies to run out.'

'And they can keep waiting. Because *if* the witch we met with is telling the truth, I also know where it is,' Jask explained.

'Then why don't we have it already?'

'That's where the serryn comes into it,' Corbin said.

'The supply is with another witch,' Jask announced. 'And, as we all know, they're a tricky bunch when it comes to dealing with the third species – especially with a lengthy penitentiary sentence looming over them for even looking in our direction. So if I storm in there and create attention, we're going to have every witch in this district baying for our blood, plus risk word getting back to the authorities that we're in trouble.'

'And they'll force us to go on the meds,' she said. 'Or incarcerate us.'

'Exactly,' Jask said. 'But a serryn going in to collect it is a whole other story. The witch will have no choice but to hand it over without question. Defying the most superior of witches is justifiably punishable by death apparently.'

'*If* Jask can tame her enough to co-operate, that is,' Corbin added. 'Because if she leaks word of any of this whilst she's in there, it's over for us.'

Despite the high odds, Jask could feel the weight being lifted off Solstice's shoulders. But it only added to the weight on his own. 'That's why there's no guarantee yet.'

'But if there's hope, the pack have a right to know,' she said.

'And when I'm convinced that the solution is obtainable, I will tell them. False hope is crueller.'

'Even false hope is better than no hope.'

'This is my decision, Solstice.'

Her flawless brow crumpled as she glanced with concern over at the serryn again. 'And in the meantime you're going to give her open access to the compound?'

'Locking her in a room won't help me get her on side.'

'But this will?'

'Jask knows what he's doing,' Corbin assured her. 'You know that.' He looked over his shoulder as the serryn pushed back her chair and stood, attracting all their attention. 'Which might be a good thing as it looks like breakfast is over.'

Jask watched the serryn skirt the periphery of the room back towards the buffet table.

'Jask, I'm sorry but you *can't* just let her walk around,' Solstice declared. 'You might be able to handle her, but think of the others.'

The serryn stepped up to the cutlery trays and, in plain sight, removed a knife.

Jask's heart skipped a beat. 'Minx,' he hissed under his breath.

Corbin looked across his shoulder again then back at Jask. Even his eyes turned grave for a moment. 'You can't guarantee she's not going to use it, Jask.'

'She's looking for a reaction, that's all.'

Instead of returning to her table to finish her drink, she slipped out of the doors.

'She's also got an impulsive streak,' Corbin reminded him. 'I landed on my arse in those ruins because of it, remember? If you'd told me a little thing like that would shove me down a staircase, I would have laughed in your face. We still know nothing about her.'

Jask caught a glimpse of her out the window, heading down the steps and out onto the green. 'She knows I can easily get the knife off her.'

'And what if she hides it somewhere for later?' Solstice asked, her fair eyebrows raised again, her eyes echoing rebuke.

'Shit,' Jask hissed. He shoved his half-empty tray away, hating the fact he was going to have to respond. And that by doing so he was doing exactly what she wanted – showing he was worried, that he was acknowledging her potential.

It was a game of kiss-chase, and he was chasing.

He pushed back his chair and stood.

'Like I said, Jask – hard work,' Corbin declared with a wink, before plunging a chunk of bread into his mouth as Jask reluctantly left the table.

❊ ❊ ❊

As soon as she'd done it, she'd wished she hadn't. Reaching for the knife was one of her frequent do-now-and-think-later moments. She'd gain nothing from it other than get Jask's back up, but even that seemed a better option than letting him continue to sit there so smugly – let alone with the blonde by his side.

Sophia stepped out into the fresh morning air. The invigorating breeze swept across the quadrant, something intolerably biting still accompanying it now that the overcast sky masked any hint of sunshine that had broken through earlier.

She took the steps down onto the path, holding down her shirt hem as the breeze caressed her thighs. She looked left towards the archway where Rone and Samson had disappeared earlier and it took only a split-second longer to decide that was exactly where she wanted to go.

She had no doubt that Jask was watching as she made her way along the path past the dining-room bay window.

He had to have seen her take the knife. She'd hardly been subtle about it. She also had no doubt of how ineffective it would be if Jask took her on, despite how adept she was with her primary choice of weapon on the streets. The blade, unlike the six-inch serrated edges she usually dealt with, didn't stand a chance of making enough of a wound before he got it from her.

But that hadn't been her intention. Walking past the cutlery had simply been too much temptation. She'd had to make his heart skip a beat at the very least – a small yet satisfying triumph on her part.

Now, in the metaphorical as well as literal cold light of day, it seemed painfully immature. A move that was hardly going to encourage him to let her roam freely around the compound like she needed to.

There were times when she hated her impetuousness. But there was something about him, something that triggered her need to prove herself to be anything but weak or vulnerable.

Stepping through the arch, she glanced left beyond the gate at what looked like a run-down outhouse. But it was what lay ahead of her that snagged her attention. Beyond the wide-girthed oak was a single-storey stone outbuilding.

She crossed the stone slabs, the paving cracked and buckled from the tree roots forcing their way through the earth like contorted spines. Surrounded by the array of plants, albeit many now nothing more than bark shells, was like entering a whole other world a hundred miles from urban Blackthorn.

She turned the handle on the single deep-set door. When it didn't budge on her second or third attempt, she stepped back to examine the two barred windows either side. Either the intention was not to let anyone in, or not to let anything out. She peered inside to see an empty foyer. Ahead to the left was an ajar door. Parallel to the right of it was a passageway leading off into the dark distance.

Strolling around to the far left of the building, she lifted herself onto tiptoes to peer through another barred window. An oak table sat near the far wall, six chairs splayed around it.

Running her hand over the dead climbing plant that encased the stone wall, Sophia continued around to the back. Behind the building was another outhouse beyond, this one derelict. Another barbed-wire-topped chain-link fence stood behind that – the only division between the compound and the demolition site beyond.

And beyond that was the border into Lowtown – the way back to what her life once was. Not that she'd ever get that back. Not that she'd ever–

She slammed to the ground, losing the knife as she broke her fall with her splayed hands.

'Fuck,' she hissed beneath her breath, debris grazing her bare knees and palms. She scowled back at the distended root that had been responsible for tripping her.

'Enjoying your tour?' a familiar, painfully masculine voice asked.

Chapter Five

Jask had pursued, so that was most definitely one point to her – even if disapproval emanated from his stance as he stood a few feet away, arms tightly folded.

She reached for the knife, the glint amidst the turf unmistakable. If he hadn't seen her take it before, he sure knew now.

She pushed herself to her feet and dusted down her grazed knees, flinching as she made contact with the minor wounds. 'It's better than sitting in a room full of lycans and experiencing Pavlov's experiment first-hand. It was putting me off my food.'

She hadn't meant it to come out so cuttingly. Part of her hadn't meant for it to come out at all. She glanced at him warily, wondering if maybe she'd overstepped the mark this time.

Jask didn't just frown, he scowled. 'I didn't give you permission to leave the room,' he stated, unfortunately too matter-of-factly not to pique her irritation.

She placed her hands, the knife, behind her back. She scraped an arc through the dirt with her boot as she tauntingly looked up at him from under purposefully downturned lashes. 'Does this mean you're going to threaten me with another spanking?'

The last thing she expected was to see a hint of amusement at the mocked submissive pose.

'I'm getting the feeling more and more that a hard spanking is exactly what you need. What is it they call that – negative reinforcement?'

Either he meant it, or he was actually *playing* with her. She wasn't entirely sure she could handle the latter. But whichever, he was definitely making fun of her. And *no one* made fun of her.

She folded her arms to mirror him. 'But that would show weakness, right, Jask? Relying on your brute strength because you can't manage me any other way.' She sauntered past him. 'What a real let down *that* would be.'

'If you wanted my undivided attention, you only had to ask,' he remarked, as her shoulder skimmed his upper arm.

His arrogance, let alone a need to disprove the uncomfortable truth of his words, evoked her to turn and face him as she reached the corner. 'Most would interpret me leaving the room as wanting anything but.'

'If you hadn't decided to take a knife with you, maybe.'

'This little thing?' She twirled it tauntingly in her fingers for him to see. 'I'm hardly going to be doing much damage with this. Not worried are you, Jask?'

He frowned again. 'Why do you do that?'

'Do what?'

'Defy me when you know I can do something about it.'

'Physically maybe.' She shrugged. 'But like I said, what's impressive about that? You said you could tame me, but what you clearly meant was suppress and oppress me. And you need to learn I don't respond well to that. Let this be *your* first lesson,' she said, heading back towards the courtyard.

And also a lesson to her to keep herself focused – not sate her urge to provoke the lycan leader purely to get the upper hand for a few moments.

She had to remind herself of his potential intentions towards Kane Malloy and the implications for Blackthorn. She had to stay on task and not make it personal.

'You're going to be here a few days, serryn. So you *will* learn how to behave in my presence.'

A familiar and unavoidable surge of adrenaline flooded her system.

Keep walking, Phia.

But on irritation-induced automatic pilot, she slowly pivoted on her heels.

Jask was leaning against the corner of the building, the resoluteness in his eyes unflinching.

'How to *behave*? Sorry, Jask – am I not as submissive as your lycan females? Would you rather I bend over now and wait for you to take me at your leisure?'

He raised his eyebrows slightly. Worse, he dared to give her the once-over. 'You're a hell of a lot more irritating than lycan females, that's for sure.'

'Why, because I stand up to you? Because I'm not afraid to say what I think?'

'You say that with pride. Honey, five-year-olds say what they think. Knowing what to say and when is called being an adult.'

Something inside her sparked. '*Don't* patronise me.'

'Then stop scowling at me like some sulky teenager. You look ridiculous.'

Her thoughts flashed back to the female sat beside him in the dining hall. As insecurity flooded her, the spark ignited.

She *had* wanted his attention. And part of her hated herself for that immaturity, let alone the fact he seemed to be picking up on it.

And he had called her ridiculous because of it.

Ridiculous.

She exhaled tersely and turned away to stop herself closing the gap and kicking him hard between the legs. 'Fuck you, Jask.'

'My point exactly. One bit of criticism and you retaliate.'

She spun to face him again. 'Who the *fuck* do you think you are, huh? You may have all of them cowering in fear of you,' she said, thrusting a pointed finger back towards the main building, 'but not me,' she added, slamming her hand to her chest. 'Arrogant tosser,' she muttered under her breath as she turned away again.

'You *really* need to learn some manners, serryn.'

She closed her eyes. Pressed her lips together for a moment. 'Oh, my apologies,' she said as she turned to face him just briefly enough to curtsey. 'Fuck you, Jask, *please*.'

'I'm willing to let the knife incident go, but walk away from me and there *will* be consequences.'

She stopped again. She didn't want to. But she did. She turned to face him once more. 'Is that right?'

He pulled himself away from the wall. 'I won't have you talking to me like that.'

'No?' She opted to be the one to close the gap between them. 'Then what are you going to do? Only the way I see it, I'm still alive because you *need* me alive. So is this how it's going to be? I don't toe the line so you threaten to punish me? There's one problem with that,' she said. 'I'm likely to enjoy it.'

But, this time, far from looking affronted, even irritated, his eyes glimmered with something else. Something she hadn't expected to see. Something that told her he was only too willing to test the theory.

She instinctively stood up straight to let her five-foot-seven-inch frame match his stature as best she could as he consumed the personal space left between them.

'Like you enjoyed me holding you down on the wasteland?' he asked. 'Like you enjoyed what I did to you in the shower?'

'Made you feel good did it – controlling someone half your size?'

'I didn't have to restrain you to control you just now though, did I? Yet not only did you stop walking away, you came back.' His eyes glinted with triumph. 'I'd call that progress, wouldn't you?'

Her heart pounded at the intimacy of his proximity.

'I've made my point twice about who's in charge here, serryn. If you push me, I'll prove it once and for all.'

Her stomach flipped, the prospect as unforgivably enticing as the lycan who dared utter the threat. 'You know,' she said, holding his gaze, tilting her mouth up towards his to regain some semblance of control. 'This whole alpha leader-of-the-pack thing is sexy enough, but when you get all masterful it's just too much.'

He almost broke a smile. Almost. 'You're not as hard as you like to think you are, little girl. You might play at being tough, but that's all it is. I saw you crumble when I pinned you down. You can't handle me any more than you can handle yourself.'

She gazed into his eyes as they searched deep into hers. He smelt dangerously earthy – something between freshly cut grass and humid rain. She hadn't noticed it before, but now it felt all-consuming. 'Pin me down again and see.'

'You're out of your depth, darling.'

The term of endearment, despite its intention to belittle, still struck her deeper than it should have. 'And you don't want me to prove you wrong. I'm so much easier to handle if I'm scared of you, am I not?'

He leaned closer so his lips almost touched hers. 'You know when I said I tear? I wasn't kidding.'

'Tease.' She lifted her mouth to his, as close as she would dare without physically touching him. 'I don't mind not playing gentle. Let's see if the pack leader is as badly behaved as his reputation dictates. Right here. Right now.'

As their breaths mingled, her stomach clenched, every nerve ending tingled.

But that cold, calm gaze made it all too obvious that he had no attraction towards her. His restraint was insulting. Worse, it was humiliating.

He pulled back with a smile and brushed past her, daring to turn *his* back on *her*. She wanted to ram the knife into his behind just for the arrogance of it.

Just for the pain of his rejection.

For the defeat.

Damn it – round four to her only to have him claim it back again.

She clenched the knife handle tighter as she watched him leave. 'I actually pity you, locked away here in your cage, spouting your propaganda to your masses!' she called out. 'The evidence speaks for itself. The barbed wire. The guards. You're scared of what's out there. You're hiding. Everyone knows it. You may be the big pack leader in your cage, but you're the vampires' bitch and bitch to the TSCD, and you know it.'

Jask turned to face her again – a six-foot solid frame of lycan proficiency. That, let alone the look in his eyes, was enough to make her temporarily stop breathing.

But she squared up ready to face his retaliation – the humiliation of his rejection still scorching too deep for her not to.

'What did you say?' he asked, his narrowed eyes fixed on hers.

Shut up, Phia. For fuck's sake, shut up.

But she'd ignored the voice of reason too many times for it to win through on this occasion.

'You heard me,' she said. 'Impenetrable, huh? The powers that be still managed to get to two of your own though, didn't they? And reveal just what you lycans *really* are beneath the surface. We all know how they butchered Arana Malloy – excuse of no meds or not. And what happened after still proves you're nothing but a pawn in the big boys' game and everyone knows it. Putting those responsible away in the safety of the penitentiary when you know you should have dealt with them yourself is evidence enough. That incident didn't just show the VCU for what they are, it showed what *you* are – doing Kane Malloy's dirty work for him. Only I didn't see him in the courtroom, defending what your kind did to *his* sister. You're clearly twisted around his little finger as much as that agent Caitlin Parish is.'

Jask took a step back towards her. 'You really think it's wise to stand there goading me?'

She clenched the knife handle tighter. 'Struck a nerve, Jask?'

'Brutal killer though you may be, serryn, you're nothing but a sex toy in the hands of the right vampire – just remember that. Don't tempt me into turning you into mine.'

She laughed. She wished to goodness she hadn't. 'Really? And how far are you willing to take it? Only you don't want to start what you can't finish, Jask. Not with me.'

'Does every survival instinct not tell you that tempting a preda-tor in his own territory is a really bad move? Or does that serryn arrogance make you numb to it?'

'Because you *are* tempted, aren't you, Jask?'

This time he did smile. Only this time the smile was laced with nothing but contempt. 'Sorry to bitterly disappoint, but I like my females a little more…' he raked her swiftly, dismissively, 'mature,' he said, pulling away again.

'Yeah, or maybe you don't know how to finish the job, more likely!' she yelled after him. 'You have me right where you want me and you can't see it through. Guess that comes with being able to lick your own balls, right?'

He stopped.

When he turned to face her again, her stomach jolted, a trail of expletives trampling each other in her head.

'No need to ask how it's going,' Corbin called out, approaching fast from the courtyard.

Jask remained at a standstill, despite the flare of anger still glowing in his eyes, his jaw tense. But it was the way he clenched his hands that troubled her the most. Hands that, despite concealing the talons she had no doubt had emerged, told her she'd messed up big time.

And it was made even more troubling by the concern in Corbin's eyes as he noticed too.

'As you can see,' Jask said to him. 'She's still in one piece so I haven't reached my limit yet.'

She wasn't so sure.

Neither, seemingly, was Corbin, by the urgency with which he moved in beside him. 'Not quite the quick taming we were hoping for though?'

'Temporary setback,' Jask declared, breaking from her equal glare in a clear attempt to disconnect himself from the moment. 'Due to an excessive amount of sexual frustration seemingly.'

Further mocking was the last thing she could handle right then. 'Fuck you!' Sophia snapped. 'And your boyfriend!'

Corbin exhaled tersely. 'No need to ask if you're ready to exchange rings. That's some temper she's got. What did you do to her, Jask?'

'It's more a case of what I didn't do.' He dared to look back at her. 'Isn't that right, honey?'

Embarrassment heated her face. She turned her attention to Corbin. 'I bet you know how to satisfy a woman, right, Corbin? Only your boyfriend here isn't up to the job. I'm starting to wonder who the real alpha around here is. You want to show me?'

Corbin's eyes widened. 'Wow, sweetheart, you've got some nerve.'

'You think I'm kidding. Don't worry; pretend-alpha-boy there can watch. He might learn something.'

'Is she for real?' Corbin asked, as he and Jask exchanged glances.

Jask folded his arms with a shrug. 'Like I keep saying – too long chasing vampires. Maybe you should take her up on her offer? Let her know what she's been missing.'

Her stomach wrenched at Jask's easy dismissal.

Corbin appraised her swiftly. 'She's not my type. Too much to say for herself.'

'I can silence her for you, if it's a distraction.'

'But then I won't be able to hear her scream.'

'Shall I get you boys some tea and biscuits while you chat?'

They both looked back at her at the same time.

Her stomach flipped. She tightened her grip on the knife, her arms stiff by her sides whilst resolving to add that moment to her well-established list of reasons to hate herself.

Jask looked back at Corbin. 'Do you know any other female would dare stand there and goad us both?'

'She's got spirit, that's for sure.'

Jask smirked. 'She wants *you* first. She clearly knows the difference between a warm-up and the main show.'

Corbin grinned at his jibe before they both looked back at her.

She had to tell herself it was fine. She was calling their bluff and they were calling hers. Or she was being dangerously naïve and she was rapidly getting herself into a situation she wasn't getting out of easily. Not without a massive swallow of pride at least.

Because there was *no* way Corbin was touching her.

'In that case, maybe you should go first, Jask,' she said. 'Then at least I'll have something to help me get over my disappointment.'

Jask raised his eyebrows slightly.

Something was seriously wrong with her. If she'd suspected it before, now she knew for sure – especially as the lycan eyes that glowered back at her only made her body ache more for him. The thought of what he could do, what he was capable of, evoking tingles of anticipation.

Jask was swift and efficient. He closed the gap between them in an instance – one arm sliding behind her back, locking her arms behind her in the process before he scooped her up in his, keeping her legs secured against him with his infallible grip.

But instead of carrying her behind the building, he turned around and marched back across the courtyard towards the quadrant.

'Put me down!' she demanded.

'Trust me, I'm tempted,' he said, his glower fixed ahead, his fair hair blowing in the breeze. 'In more ways than one.'

She tried to wriggle but it was useless.

'Petulant, obnoxious, irritating…' he muttered.

Turning left out of the tunnel, he marched along the path, Corbin close behind him.

Jask kicked open the double doors into the nearest building, both giving way easily to his onslaught.

As he burst inside, the echo immediately filled her with a paralyzing fear.

The darkness exacerbated her fear enough, light kept at bay by the debris covering the glass roof. But it was the dark reflective surface below that overwhelmed her with abject terror. Her pulse reached painful rates as he stepped up to the edge of the swimming pool.

'No!' she gasped.

But there was no hesitation from Jask.

Her stomach vaulted as he threw her in.

She plunged deep into the pool, the cold liquid rushing over her. Her body went into shock. Water filled her mouth. Horror consumed her as she was sucked into the depths.

All she could see were the reeds again, a flashback to the sensation of falling from the tree branch into the lake, her twelve-year-old body consumed by icy water.

In her flashback, there was nothing but her and the darkness again. Nothing but powerlessness. Nothing but the lake plants coiling around her legs, around her arm as she fought for the surface, tightening their hold and restricting her as she'd helplessly flayed.

In the there and now, she reached the surface, but failed to snatch enough air before the weight of her boots dragged her down again. She was too consumed with fear to unlace them and kick them off. Too weak in her panic to fight.

Those boots may as well have been those plants that had coiled around her as a child, and she was weak again.

And gulping water only escalated her panic, her frantic snatching at the water's surface forcing her to sink further as she tired quickly. She lost sense of time, of place, of the situation.

She barely registered something heavy slide into the water beside her.

Feeling restriction around her waist, her first instinct was to lash out. But the arm that held her, that pulled her towards the surface, was strong, unrelenting, skimming her through the water, lifting her out of it seconds later.

As her back met a hard surface, she curled onto her side, hoisted herself up onto her arms, her palms flat on the floor, her head downturned as she coughed up water.

Shivering and trembling, she gasped for breath, fear-induced tears tightening her throat and accumulating in her eyes.

As soon as she felt strong enough, she struggled to her feet, unable to look at Jask as he pulled himself out of the water beside her.

Because she didn't have to look at him to know it was Jask who'd saved her – even in her panic she knew that hold.

She brushed dripping hair from her eyes as she stumbled away, marched back towards the doors, past Corbin, yet another humiliation too much to bear for one night.

❊ ❊ ❊

Leaning back on both arms, his legs stretched out in front of him, Jask gave Corbin the nod to let her pass.

'Told you you'd try to kill her,' Corbin remarked as he strolled over to join him.

'How was I supposed to know she couldn't swim? She grew up in Summerton for fuck's sake.'

Corbin looked back towards the door where she'd disappeared. 'Summerton, huh? Bit of a comedown – privileged princess to Blackthorn serryn.'

And a bit of a comedown from an overconfident, mouthy, arrogant serryn to a shaken, vulnerable girl, from the way she'd fought back the quick onset of tears.

Guilt sliced through him with a serrated edge. Guilt he was determined to suppress. She'd had it coming. Besides, she'd got off lightly compared with what he could have done to her for her provocation.

The cold water had done them both some good.

And maybe him more than her as he'd watched her storm away – the evocative sway of those feminine hips, his sodden shirt barely covering and clinging to that shapely behind.

She had no idea just *how* lightly she'd got off.

But he wasn't going back there. He wasn't returning to being the lycan who acted without fear of consequence. The lycan who indulged his own needs rather than those of his pack. Because from the way every instinct in him was firing, if anyone was capable of inciting a setback, it was that serryn.

He pulled himself to his feet, caught a glimpse of his friend's raised eyebrows. 'What?' Jask asked.

'She had you right where she wanted you – you know that, right?'

And the fact that he *did* know it only made it worse. In a split second a battle of wills had become about pride – not just lycan pride, but male pride. She'd not just dug the knife in, she'd twisted – and she'd dared look him in the eyes as she'd done it.

And the fact she knew exactly what to say to get that reaction evoked a sense of vulnerability in him that he despised.

'I was perfectly in control.'

'She's poison, Jask. It's true what they say. If you were a vampire, you'd be dead now.'

'But I'm not a vampire, am I?'

'No. You're the leader of this pack and we need you. She pushed your buttons out there. You know how dangerous that is. I saw the way you looked at her. Worse still, I saw the way she looked at you. If this becomes about you and her and not her and this pack, you're heading for trouble.'

'She called me the TSCD's bitch, Corbin. Kane's bitch. She looked me in the eye and told me giving evidence in that court-room made me a coward.'

Corbin exhaled tersely. 'If that's what's got you so riled, you know better. She's screwing with your head. It's what they do – vampire or not.'

'Is she? Or is she saying what everyone out there is thinking – that I can't protect my own?'

'See – that's what I mean. *No one* believes that.' Corbin stepped closer. 'Everyone knows you did what you had to, to free Tyler and Malachi. And being a part of exposing the TSCD's corruption showed you're not scared of anything. It showed that we look after our own *and* that we won't be pushed around. She's jibing where it hurts, that's all. She's testing for weaknesses and you're letting her. What she thinks doesn't matter and you know it.'

He stared down at the dark water. But it did. What that serryn thought *did* matter. Reputation was everything in Blackthorn and if she believed it, others did too. And if others believed it, he needed more than ever to show he *could* protect what was his. He had to do his job. He had to protect his pack. And she was *not* going to be the one to change that focus.

'Jask,' Corbin said. 'Reassure me again that there's not another motive underlying bringing her here.'

'And like I said last time you asked – as if I'd be that obvious.'

'Really? Only your reaction to what she said proves just how much it's been eating away at you this past two weeks since Kane disappeared. This whole collaboration between you and him was supposed to be about preventing a civil war, not instigating one. So if he *has* gone soft on Caitlin Parish, you don't want to cross that line. If she's told him you threatened her outside that courtroom, he could already be baying for your blood.'

'Then he can come and face me. Because what we're dealing with now does not change the fact that he allowed those responsible to go to trial instead of killing them as we agreed. It makes us look like we have a chink in our armour. It makes it look like *I* can't protect this pack. It's bad enough that I owe Tyler and Malachi fourteen years of their lives whilst waiting, *trusting*, that Kane would see our plan through, but his letting us down at the last minute has put us at serious risk.'

'*If* he has let us down – we still don't know that.'

'But we do know our survival depends on us not being seen as an easy target in this district, Corbin, and that vampire has undone everything we have worked for to keep our pack safe. I wasted fourteen years of not enacting my own vengeance only because I trusted Kane when he said he had a better way. So Kane and I are *far* from over. But if it makes you feel better, I can assure you I'll deal with Kane only when I have time to deal with Kane. For now, he's the least of my concerns if I can't get that serryn to do what we need.'

Because as much as the prospect of sending the serryn after Kane had crossed his mind on seeing her, this *was* about far more than that, especially as his attention reverted to what he'd almost missed – something that was either paradoxically a ray of light or a pending disaster.

'You saw those tears, right?' Jask asked.

'And?'

'They weren't fake.'

'So?'

He rested his hands on his hips. 'Serryns don't cry, Corbin. That's why those little droplets are even more valuable than her blood. If this *was* a set-up by the witches, they would have sent in their best. Those tears prove she's most definitely not that.'

'So you think we *have* got lucky?'

'Or not.'

'But if she can cry, she's got a vulnerable side. That makes her more tameable, surely?'

'Or she's not tough enough to do this.'

What he needed was a hardened serryn he could meld. A complication of vulnerability, however advantageous for that, he didn't. Especially not from the way he'd felt something he had no right feeling when he'd seen those tears in her eyes.

'So which is it?' Corbin asked

Jask looked back towards the doors. 'I'll have to push a little harder to find out, won't I?'

'I know that look,' Corbin said. 'Don't make this personal. Serryn or not, physically she's still just a girl. If you lose yourself again, this pack will be lost. For good this time. Don't you forget that.'

Chapter Six

Six days previous

The agent from the Lycan Control Unit sat on the opposite side of the table from Jask. The other two guarded the exit from the compound's outer room, guns held diagonally across their chests. They stared ahead, keeping their eyes averted.

'Where's Kinley?' Jask asked as the unfamiliar agent clicked open his collection of metal briefcases.

'Agent Kinley is off sick.' The agent declared it too curtly for Jask's liking, let alone that he remained focused on taking out the various vials and foil sheets of medication instead of having made eye contact yet.

'Kinley hasn't taken a day off sick in twenty years.'

'Then clearly he deserves one.' The agent skimmed through the electronic pad he held in his hand. 'But I can assure you I know what I'm doing.'

Jask was seconds away from slamming the electronic pad from his hand, seconds away from grabbing the agent around the throat and dragging him across the table towards him. The whole system was insulting. Having to play ball with the authorities to secure what little freedom they had left was derogatory enough. But the agent's attitude was adding to Jask's building irritation, not least during what was already a bad night. 'Which is why you haven't looked me in the eye even once in the past ten minutes – a basic courtesy us lycans expect.'

The agent looked up at him. His eyes flared slightly, confirming to Jask that his glare had been appropriately interpreted. 'Agent Harper,' he said. 'With my apologies.'

Not entirely convinced on the sincerity of the latter, Jask none-theless followed the routine of laying the inside of his forearm out between them albeit whilst his glare remained on Harper's.

Every month it was the same. First came the blood test that would invariably show Jask had refused to take the issued meds, instead remaining with the pack's own concoction to control their condition. Jask would then be asked how many of his pack *had* taken the meds. He would confirm the names of those who had opted in – those who, unbeknown to the TSCD, were the rare few allergic to their herbs but who didn't want to go through morphing like others in the same situation.

Tyler and Malachi had been two of those. They'd relied on the meds. Meds that, true to the Global Council's claims, stopped them morphing. But both lycans, as well as the handful of others who opted in, still retained their hostile, argumentative and impulsive edge during the lunar phase – unlike with the lycans' own concoction – which only added to Jask's concern as to what the meds truly contained.

The fact that Tyler and Malachi had subsequently been targeted by the TSCD despite their co-operation, that the TSCD had used the volatile edge *their* meds failed to suppress as evidence against them in the Arana Malloy trial, had seemed even more cruel.

Because no lycan wanted to morph, any more than any allergy sufferer wanted to experience the symptoms, no matter how natural to their physical chemistry.

There *had* been historic warriors amongst them who had em-braced it in the past, for whom surviving the pain of the initial changes physically and emotionally had marked them as superior. Superior because it took decades to learn to manage the pain, let alone decades to develop self-control as baser urges took over. But that was back in a time when lycans were allowed to run free to develop those skills.

Now they were "managed". Now they'd be shot on sight. No-where to run. Nowhere to conceal themselves. Nowhere to safely em-brace what they were. Nowhere to hide their mistakes in the process.

Harper wrapped the strap around Jask's forearm before the in-built device punctured a tiny wound via an automated needle.

Jask didn't flinch.

He and Kinley had the system finely tuned after so many years. And Kinley understood respect.

Harper read the readings, inputted the data into his handheld device.

The exact same questions always followed.

'How many pack members?' he asked as he unstrapped the device from Jask's arm.

'Two hundred and seventeen.'

'Youths?'

'Twenty.'

'Numbers banished?'

'None.'

'All your pack are accounted for?'

'Yes.'

'Internal or external disputes?'

'None.'

And all the while, Harper continued to input the details.

'How many opting in this month?' he asked.

'The usual four.'

Then the rights would usually be read next as the meds were issued. Then would come the herb check. The agent would assess the quantity, growth and usage of the herbs and spices grown in the greenhouse. Jask would confirm none had been shared beyond the compound and that every remaining lycan in the pack was taking them to prevent morphing. Further random blood tests would then be done to ensure there was evidence of such in their systems.

Two hours later, the agent would leave.

But this wasn't just any month.

This was a month of two full moons – an occurrence every two to three years. The strength of the morphing was greater, their bodies not having had a chance to recover fully from the last. It meant an altered and more intense remedy from the norm – both in terms of their own concoction and the meds issues by the Global Council.

So of all the times Jask could have done without the newbie showing up, it was then – not least as it wasn't just any blue moon either. This was the thirteenth blue moon before the new cycle began again – the most potent time for his kind.

And things had already gone wrong. Not that he was going to give the agent any indication at all of that.

But a newbie meant the potential to be more thorough. A newbie wasn't as easy to read as Kinley had become.

Harper slid the familiar packs across to him. 'As you're aware, your pack members are recommended to start the course two days from now for exactly nine days. Any morphed lycans found on the streets will be instantly terminated. Any word of morphed lycans here in the compound will be removed, as will your herbs. Meds will subsequently be obligatory for all. You remain with the right to use your own methods, the right to manage your own condition but you do not, however, have the right to put anybody within the boundaries of Blackthorn or Lowtown at risk. Can you confirm you understand that, please?'

'Confirmed.'

'And, as the head of this pack, you confirm you are willing to take responsibility for all lycans under your domain?'

'Absolutely.'

'And you understand that should any lycans be found to have morphed, the LCU now reserves the right to remove you from this compound for prosecution as a result of…' he glanced up at him, 'previous events.'

The fact that there were *still* those who blamed his pack, his leadership, for the incident with Arana Malloy stabbed him deep. But this was not the time for confrontation. This was the time to get the agent out as quickly as he could so he could get back to deal with what had happened with Nero.

So he could work out what the hell they were going to do.

'I understand totally,' Jask said, through gritted teeth.

The agent typed into his device once more. 'Then I'll move straight on to the herb calculations,' he declared, sealing his cases again. He pushed back the chair and stood. 'Lead the way.'

Chapter Seven

Sophia burst through the poolroom doors out onto the quadrant. Cold rain snapped at her face and legs. Legs that trembled, barely holding her up as her feet slipped and squelched in her sodden boots.

She stopped only to unlace them and kick them off before clutching them against her chest, her bare feet melding with the turf as she marched back across to the main building.

She came to a standstill in the lobby, her hair dripping, her sodden shirt clinging to every curve, adding to her shame as all eyes locked on her.

It was the last place she wanted to go, but right then she had no idea where else *to* go.

She marched up the stairs and took the sharp left to Jask's room.

She slammed the door behind her and stood in the morning light, her whole body shaking from the shock, the cold.

She headed straight to the bathroom and turned on the hot water, yanking the curtains shut behind her and attempting to unfasten the shirt buttons as she stepped under the spray. Though only lukewarm, it burned and stung, prickling her skin as she waited for the shivers to subside. Her numb, trembling fingers were useless. In fury and frustration, she tore the shirt over her head, quickly becoming aggravated as it clung to her skin and got entangled in her hair. She growled in frustration as it painfully tugged at her roots until she finally yanked it off.

She let her tears fall – there in the privacy of the shower, there where they would be easily lost amidst the spray.

Recollections of the lake only brought thoughts of her sisters too painfully to the forefront of her mind again. How her older sister, Leila, was always there when she needed her – always the backup, always the calm influence, always the one picking up the pieces. Leila who'd dived into the water to save her that day, despite being the one to warn her not to be messing around on the tree branch anyway.

But Sophia didn't listen – she never listened.

There was only one thing, ironically, that kept her alive long enough that day – the very behaviour Leila had tried to curb. It was a trick she'd learned from a young age. Whenever she didn't get her own way or Leila told her off, she'd hold her breath. Hold her breath until she'd turn blue. It was cruel. Looking back she knew just how cruel.

Death had become too real to them all at too early an age. Leila had been nine when their mother had died; Sophia had been six, Alisha just two. Leila had taken it the hardest. Leila took everything the hardest – or so everyone thought. Sophia had heard her sobbing some nights in the privacy of her bedroom. She used to cry too when she heard her, not that she'd ever let Leila know, or their grandfather who had assumed the carer responsibility for the three young girls.

But then Leila had made the mistake of taking on the replacement maternal role – something that Sophia, in her grief, had resented. And in her moments of anger, she'd turn that very fear of death back on Leila. She'd hold her breath for as long as it took to get her own way whilst Alisha, their baby sister too young to understand her sister's manipulative act, would stand and scream for her to stop.

The same screams of panic Alisha had let out as she'd watched her twelve-year-old sister fall into the lake. Screams that had become muffled as Sophia was dragged deeper under the water, deeper into the darkness.

She'd always been a strong swimmer. With all the lakes and rivers in Summerton, it was a must, let alone when they'd travel through the other locales to get to the ocean.

And that's what had made the whole experience even more terrifying – that something she was so confident in was so easily snatched out of her control. Something that turned out to be stronger and more powerful than her. What had always been her safe place had nearly killed her that day, hurting like the betrayal of a lifelong lover or best friend.

But as she'd sunk to the depths, she'd felt Leila grab her.

She should have died in the seconds that had followed, but seeing the determination in Leila's eyes had convinced Sophia to hold on longer than should have been possible. Seeing her big sister defiant against the elements – seeing, for the first time, just how strong Leila was – had kept her fighting. Because Leila never gave up. As she'd yanked and tugged at those reeds with all her strength, Sophia saw just how admirably calm Leila was under pressure. Not least as Leila had switched from tugging those reeds to meticulously unthreading them – every now and again looking back at her sister, urging her to hold on, reassuring her that she'd be okay.

And she'd loved her sister in those moments. Loved her silent strength. The sister that she had jibed and resented, had proclaimed as weak, soft and a pushover, became her heroine.

But a heroine was something Leila should never have had to have been. Wouldn't have been if it hadn't been for *her*. What happened to their mother was down to her – down to Sophia. Their mother would have never been in Midtown that night if Sophia hadn't been the catalyst.

And she'd punish herself every inch of the way if that's what it took – because nothing would ever, *ever* make her feel better.

She'd been told it had been a nasty accident at the time. It had only been a few years ago that she'd searched the press and found out it had, in fact, been a vampire who'd killed their mother, despite having always been reassured that Midtown was a safe place.

The authorities had lied.

Just as the vampire royalty who had been allowed to live in Midtown were equal liars, claiming they meant no harm to humans. Because one of them had murdered her mother. Behind their shield of deceit and respectability, one of them had slaughtered Claire McKay.

And the authorities had covered it up – worried that flaws in their precious system would be exposed.

She slammed her hand against the tiled wall.

And now she finally, *finally* had the chance to do something about it – embrace the powerful blood flowing through her veins to wreak the revenge she needed. Instead, she was trapped. Worse, she was messing up any chance of getting out. All because of her stupid pride, of the stupid impetuousness that had torn her family apart in the first place.

She rested her forehead against the tiles, letting the water trickle over her as she sobbed every last tear out of her system.

She needed to be smart like her sister, not arse-kicking at every opportunity.

She would get nothing from Jask in the short time she planned on staying there if she kept throwing obstacles his way. But she couldn't help it. Something about him grated too deep. Something that made her hairs prickle just at his presence. Whether it was his reputation, the very nature of what he was, or the fact that he was so perfect as to be unobtainable whilst making her feel about him the way she did.

Something about being near him made her act stupid – like a schoolgirl irritatingly kicking the chair of the boy she fancied. But she needed to curb it. Fast. This wasn't about her. This was about The Alliance. This was about her sisters.

She'd find Rone and Samson. And if they *did* know about The Alliance, she'd tell them they were getting her out of there or she'd blow their dirty little secret.

And then, when her escape was arranged, she'd take out Jask without a moment's hesitation – somewhere isolated, somewhere where his last moments would seep by slowly enough for him to realise she'd got the upper hand in the end.

When she was done, when she was drained of all tears, she exhaled a steady breath. She switched off the shower and pushed her hair back from her eyes. Yanking back the shower curtain, she grabbed the towel she'd chucked to the floor earlier and wrapped it around herself.

She stared at herself in the mirror. Her eyes were bloodshot, the skin beneath them puffy from tiredness and tears. She hated herself without make-up – had been hiding behind it since she was thirteen. The exposure felt uncomfortable more now than ever. It would have been the perfect excuse to pile on the black kohl and dark eye-shadow – another thing Leila had always hated.

But then Leila was as much the china doll as their little sister Alisha was straight out of every teenage boy's dream. And she was neither.

She turned on the cold water tap and scooped water onto her eyes. Any sign of distress would do her cause no good. If Jask did plan to use her against Kane, he'd know he needed a skilled serryn to do it. And skilled is exactly how she'd come across. She might have only been a serryn a matter of hours, but she had sure as hell spent long enough studying them to know how they operated. In her quest to one day track one down and plead with them to join their mission, what she hadn't learned about serryns wasn't worth knowing.

Except that her sister had been one.

She towel-dried her hair, untangling knots with her fingers, noticing how much her naturally fairer roots had come through, how much the dye had faded. She was a mess – inside and out. No amount of serryn blood flowing through her veins was going to make a difference unless she got a grip fast.

She rubbed the back of her hand under her nose, rolled back her shoulders with a flick of her head and straightened her back.

She pushed aside the curtain to the bedroom, and her stomach somersaulted.

Jask was by the wardrobes, sliding his wet shirt down his arms. The sunlight graced his lightly tanned skin with an amber hue, the contrast of shadows defining every muscle on his sculpted torso and flexed biceps. She glanced at the dominating tattoo on the inside of his upper arm – the mark of his lycan clan. She'd never got close enough to see one before, but she'd heard they all had one – only to be burned off if they ever betrayed their pack, banished to survive in Blackthorn alone.

And that was the very thing she had over Rone and Samson should they not play ball – the very reason they wouldn't want to be exposed as liars to their leader.

She clutched her towel knot to her chest and looked to the window seat, locating the source of the mouth-watering aroma. He'd brought a tray of breakfast with him.

'You might need this,' he said.

She glanced back across her shoulder to accept the out-held T-shirt. Without meeting his gaze, she turned back into the bathroom – the perfect excuse to allow her longer to reduce any evidence of her tears.

She slipped the T-shirt down over her head before tugging the towel away. She looked over her shoulder to check her reflection in the mirror. At least it covered her modesty, even if not much else. Approaching the vanity unit, she leaned forward to check her complexion and eyes again, but stood abruptly as Jask emerged through the curtain behind her.

Determined not to draw attention to her still-scarlet eyes, she tried to slip past him, but his insistent forward steps backed her tightly up against the counter in a move that was as intimidating as it was proficient.

As he caught her jaw in one hand, she was tempted to slap his hand away. But she clutched the vanity unit instead, reminding herself that a change of approach was needed – along with a hefty swallow of pride. Especially as Jask too seemed to be upping his game.

He pressed his thumb under her chin, tilting her head up to him.

Teeth clenched, jaw tense, she allowed her gaze to meet his.

He stared deep into her eyes in a way she was sure no one ever had, the passing seconds painful before he eventually spoke.

'All that make-up, the dyed hair, the attitude – who are you trying to be, serryn? Or more to the point, who are you trying *not* to be? What made you dislike yourself so much that you needed to become someone else?'

Her heart pounded from the acuity, the bluntness, of the questions. That *he* had been the one to notice. 'You have no idea what you're talking about.'

'No?' His gentle grip on her jaw didn't falter. 'All this goading talk, these retorts – you're just used to striking first, putting up the defences. But those instilled deflections you have reveal far more than you want them to.'

'I'll add therapist to your lycan skills, shall I?'

'You're scared; you retaliate. You feel threatened; you retaliate. You're embarrassed; you retaliate. Because you can't handle showing any sign of weakness, can you? Anything that shows just how vulnerable you are.'

'Fuck you, Jask – there's nothing vulnerable about me,' she said, finally knocking his hand away.

But instead of backing off, he splayed his hands on the counter either side of her hips, his chest almost touching hers. 'That's your answer to everything, isn't it? So what is it now? Scared? Threatened? Or am I just too close to the truth?'

There was that scent again. *His* scent. A scent that caused a stirring deep inside her. 'You're so far off the mark I'm embarrassed for you.'

'No,' he said. 'You're just one little coil of defensive rage. So, what *is* it you're so angry about?'

'I should be out there on the streets doing my job and instead I'm stuck in here with you.'

'Out there fucking whatever vampire will have you, right?'

The disdain in his tone cut deeper than she knew it should have. 'Is that a hint of judgement in your tone, lycan? The holier-than-thou attitude that comes with you wolf-boys only having the one mate?'

'Lycan females know how to keep their males happy and vice versa – what's wrong with that?'

'I didn't say there was anything wrong with it. You clearly like to play it safe. It's sweet.'

'Sweet?'

'Don't worry. I've been with a lot of vampires, so I understand why you'd feel threatened. They may be the scum of the earth, but they sure know how to satisfy a woman. I can see why they're a notch above you wolf-boys. All that safe play with just one female doesn't quite give you the edge to know how to handle someone like me.'

'I know *exactly* how to handle you.'

'Sure of that, are you? Only I think you're so busy reading between the lines, you're missing the sentence on the page.'

He frowned a little, but the hint of a smile won. 'You've got such an attitude problem, serryn.'

'It's one of my best features.'

'I'd say it was those brown eyes. When they're not scowling at me.'

His compliment threw her for a moment, but he absorbed her silence quickly.

'How have you survived so long with such an inability to read a situation?' he asked.

'I read situations just fine.'

'Which is why you thought it okay to try and goad two lycans in a desolate part of this compound. Which is why you thought it was okay to provoke me.'

'Like I said, you need to develop a sense of humour.'

He frowned again. 'You think what you were trying to incite me to do was funny?'

'I never said that.'

'And you dared to call *me* arrogant. Is it really what you wanted? To be taken up against some dirty stone wall? By me?'

She stared deeper and longer into his eyes in a way she knew not many would dare, refusing to be intimidated by the sudden domineering silence as he awaited her response. A question to which she wasn't sure there was a right answer. If there was, she couldn't find it under the weight of his unrelenting gaze.

'That's a lot of erratic breathing for an experienced sexual predator,' he said.

'At least you can admit that's what I am.'

'I wasn't referring to you.'

Her stomach flipped for all the wrong reasons.

'Have you heard the fable of the boy who cried wolf?' he asked.

'Of course I have,' she said, her breath, to her further irritation, catching in her throat.

'You know the moral of the story then?'

'You think I'm faking?'

'Not *that* moral. I'm talking about the one whereby if you summon a wolf enough times, eventually one will appear.'

Despite her fight to stay calm, she couldn't stop her pulse from racing. A pulse she knew he could hear – something which she had no doubt was sealing his satisfaction.

'And I've whistled enough times, right?' she said, refusing to be intimidated by the look in his eyes, the proximity, his unflinching attention.

'Not quite,' he said, his gaze tracing down her throat, to where his T-shirt hung loose around her neck, exposing part of her collar bone.

'Rest assured, lycan, I have *no* intention of sleeping with anything that stinks of wet dog hair.'

His smile was betrayed by his terse exhale. 'So if I came on to you, you'd turn me down, right?'

'Not fast enough.'

'Because you've got to be the one calling the shots, right? But tell me,' he said, looking keenly back into her eyes, 'what naïve part of you thinks I'd let you?'

Her heart skipped a beat. She'd had enough threats on the street, but they'd never looked at her the way he did then. And *they'd* never stunned her to silence.

'You look surprised,' he added. 'I thought I was nothing but feral beneath the surface. I thought you said you can read situations.'

He leaned forward just a fraction, but enough to force her to lean back if their lips weren't to meet. 'Only you don't look so sure now.'

'It's called indifference, Jask.'

He almost smiled before sucking air through his clenched teeth. 'I could *so* easily prove you wrong.'

'Maybe. And maybe I'd agree to you trying, if I didn't have some semblance of taste.'

'And like I said, some of us get mistaken for sweet and honourable when we're anything but.'

'Or so you'd like people to believe.'

'I'd give it ten minutes before you're screaming my name.'

'I'd give it five before you're screaming for your mother.'

This time he gave her a brief flash of his canines through his semi-smile. 'Your reaction in the poolroom showed me everything I need to know. As do those vulnerable, bloodshot eyes.' He gave her the quick once over before he pulled away.

It was the last thing she needed to hear. The last thing she needed him to believe. Just as she needed not to have faltered the minute he'd turned up the heat. 'What, so you think a fear of water makes me weak?' she called out before he reached the threshold.

'No,' he said, tucking the curtain aside. 'The fact you don't know when to listen, that you've got to do everything your own way, needing to always be in control – that's what makes you weak.'

She frowned, unease tightening her chest. 'I make you anxious, don't I, Jask? That's why you keep walking away.'

'The only thing that makes me anxious is potentially losing my temper with you and killing you. And I can't let that happen.'

'Why, Jask? If this *is* about Kane, tell me,' she said, closing the gap between them again, her bare feet padding on the tiles. 'If I've appeared at just the right time like you said I have, why are you wasting it?'

'I'm *not* wasting time. I'm just doing what I have to.'

'Which is what? Taming me? What the fuck does that mean anyway? If you want me to do something for you, tell me now. Then maybe we can actually get somewhere.'

'We're already getting somewhere,' he said. He cocked his head out into the bedroom. 'Now get in there and get something to eat before you pass out on me. Unless you're so proud that you'd rather starve than keep up your strength.'

He'd walked away – proof enough that claiming ownership wasn't half as rewarding as earning it for him.

Round five. Round fucking five to him.

But food was good. Food was calming. Food was a break away without admitting defeat. Food was a distracter.

She stepped up to the threshold, but didn't cross it as he brushed past her and headed to the sink. Instead she leaned against the doorframe, determined not to show any sign of intimidation in the wake of his threat. 'Are you going to join me?'

'I'm going to get some sleep.' He reached for a toothbrush and applied some paste from the pot by the sink. 'The same as you are after you've eaten.'

She looked across her shoulder at the makeshift bed that was now dangerously inviting. And all the more so with the prospect of him being in it. 'With you?' she asked, looking back at him.

He glanced in the mirror, his eyes momentarily meeting hers as he started to brush.

He bent over and spat out some paste. 'Even lycans need to sleep. Or is that one of the rumours you missed?'

Her gaze raked his taut back, his tight waist, his pert, masculine behind through his wet jeans as he leaned over to rinse before standing back up to continue brushing.

She folded her arms. 'So it's true your sort sleep in the mornings then?' Met with his silence, she added, 'Dawn and late evenings are the best hunting times, right?'

He bent over to rinse his mouth under the tap again. He wiped his mouth on the towel before discarding it back onto the vanity unit. Not making eye contact, he strolled past her, unfastening his belt buckle as he did so.

Without registering what he was crossing the bathroom to do, she remained mindlessly mesmerised by the male perfection that sauntered past her.

'You planning on watching me urinate as well?' he asked as he reached the toilet. 'Or are you going to drop the curtain on your way out?'

She blushed and backed off. Stepping into the bedroom, she let the curtain drop into place.

She stared back at the bed. If he'd wanted her, if he'd meant the threat, he would have taken her. But he didn't want her. That much was clear.

The fact that serryns were supposed to be the most inherently seductive of all the species – irresistible to vampires, but with an acquired charm to affect any species on some level – seemed like a joke now. Either that or, uncharacteristic to his reputation, Jask Tao truly did have something of an honourable streak.

She sat on the window seat beside the tray – salad, chopped fruit and garnished potatoes with a couple of slices of bread. All no doubt grown and prepared in the compound. It was one thing she had to give the species credit for – they worked hard on what small fragment of land they had, avoiding, where they could, the crap that the Global Council allowed to be delivered into Blackthorn. The herbs and spices that they grew, of course, were different – they were a necessity, whereas what lay in front of her was a luxury. A luxury he was willing to share a fraction of with her. She felt a small fragment of guilt.

She took the first mouthful of food as she glanced back out across Blackthorn – not just a prison for humans but, though she hated to admit it, the third species forced to reside there too.

But they weren't her concern – and still didn't excuse the way they lorded themselves over the district. And Jask was an integral one of those.

She looked back across her shoulder as she heard movement, just in time to see Jask slipping out of his wet jeans. Distracted by thighs and a behind as toned and powerful as the rest of him, she unintentionally tipped the balancing food from her fork, the spillage irritatingly interrupting her viewing as she wiped her lap.

When she glanced back up, Jask was in bed. He eased down onto his back, one leg bent, his lax arm behind his head emphasising the strength in his torso and biceps, the blankets resting enticingly low on his waist.

She took a few more mouthfuls of food, his closed eyes allowing her appreciative gaze to linger comfortably whilst she felt another pang of envy towards the blonde in the dining hall.

'So is it true about why you lycans sleep on the floor – so you can pick up the vibrations of intruders? Some old inherited wolf thing?'

She was met with silence.

'Do you take the meds or are you one of the ones who embraces the darkness inside?'

'Because that's all our so-called shadows are to your kind, aren't they, serryn?' he said, not even flinching. 'Darkness. Never mind what we do, what we say; those shadows are our moral death sentence, in your eyes.'

'Basic law of religion.'

'This set-up is nothing about religion – it's about politics and power, nothing more.'

She took a few more mouthfuls. This was not the time to be antagonistic, and for once she'd do herself proud. Besides, maybe sleepiness made him more amenable. More open.

'Do you sleep for long?' she asked, changing the subject to one less contentious.

'A couple of hours.'

'But more sporadically and frequently than vampires, right?'

'It varies.'

She drank from the glass of water as she looked out of the window, hesitating before asking him the next question. 'So what's the love-hate relationship between vampires and lycans all about?'

'There is no love-hate relationship – only what your authorities portray. We're not as attuned to difference as you are.'

'But you have a pact of segregation.'

'An enforced segregation – your authorities' way of making sure there's some division between the third species in each district. They wouldn't want us joining forces, now, would they?'

'It's not like you're going anywhere.'

He looked across at her, his azure eyes ignited by the weak sunlight. But he didn't say anything as he rolled his head back into position and closed them again.

She pushed the tray aside and wiped any trace of food from the corners of her mouth. 'Do you have a spare toothbrush?'

'Top drawer of the vanity unit.'

She headed back into the bathroom. She brushed her teeth, smoothed down her hair, took a few steady breaths, used the toilet and stepped back over to the curtain.

She pushed it aside, sauntered across the floorboards and stepped onto the edge of the soft, plump rug. 'Where am I supposed to sleep?'

Without opening his eyes, without moving anything other than his right arm, he pulled the duvet aside to expose a space next to him.

Right next to him.

Her heart skipped a beat.

'I've had better chat-up lines,' she remarked, trampling over the cushions to slide into the place he'd reserved.

She lay down beside him and pulled the duvet to her chest. She looked up at the ceiling as she wriggled to get into a more comfortable position.

As his silence persisted, she looked back across at him. 'You're taking a big risk lying there with your eyes shut.'

'Why, what are you going to do – stab me with my spare toothbrush?'

'I'm still a serryn. I might not be toxic to you, but I'm still lethal.'

'I'll bear that in mind.'

'You're an arrogant bastard, you know that?'

'I've been called worse.'

'I bet you have.' She lingered on his stubbled jaw, the leather straps around his neck, the small platinum pendant nestled in the hollow of his throat, before sliding her gaze down his bare chest, to where the duvet sat low on his hips. 'Are you naked under there?'

'Does it bother you?'

'No. But it might bother your mate.'

It was an intentionally searching question but when he didn't answer, she gazed up at the ceiling rose.

Despite all her boasting, she'd only had five partners. For two of those, she'd been too drunk to remember much. So had they. Then there was Daniel – her friend she'd fallen into bed with too many times now. But they understood each other and it never needed to get complicated. Because the last thing she ever needed was complicated.

And now there was Jask under the covers beside her. Naked. But clearly with no intention of sleeping with her whatsoever. His silence made sharing his bed feel horribly clinical, horribly detached.

She pulled the covers over her chest.

'Have you ever been with a human?' she asked, unable to take the silence.

'They sob a lot.'

Her gaze snapped across her shoulder at him.

'I think it's the pace,' he said, not having flinched. 'Apparently it's true that we're feral. During the sex act more than any other time.'

He opened his eyes, looked across at her, his lips curling into a hint of a smirk as he echoed her jibe from earlier.

He'd taken notice of what she'd said. And this time he'd retorted with humour. It wasn't just her stomach that jolted, it was her heart.

He closed his eyes again and turned his face back towards the ceiling. 'Or I could just be bullshitting you. Must be rubbing off.'

All she could do was stare at him. Stare at the perfection that lay beside her who, more troublingly, clearly had a sense of humour after all.

'I don't bullshit you,' she said.

He looked across at her again, his eyebrows slightly raised.

He rolled onto his side in one easy, fluid movement, the blanket over him falling dangerously low – not low enough to expose himself fully, but to confirm, from glimpses below that hard, flat stomach, he was surely naked – and totally at ease with it. 'You seem to forget we're different to you, serryn – that we pick up on things you don't. Whatever words come out of your mouth, they can't hide the hitch in your breath or the telling change in your pulse rate.'

She rolled onto her side to face him, lying within inches of him. 'And what's my pulse rate doing now?'

His gaze lingered on hers in a way that felt fatally intimate.

But she wasn't going to be the first to look away – not when he was that close, not when she would have given anything for him to lean forward at that moment, to know what those lips felt like against hers.

'Turn around,' he said softly.

She laughed, but with more uncertainty than she'd intended. 'Yeah, right.'

'Scared, serryn?'

'Not scared, but not stupid either.'

'And I only ask nicely once, remember?'

She searched his eyes for the part of him that had almost seemed accessible for a brief while, but it had gone again. The lycan giving orders was back. The lycan who expected to be obeyed.

And a part of her that was unavoidably curious, that refused to show she was scared, did exactly as he asked.

As Jask spooned into her, his erection nestled against her behind, she felt an uncharacteristic surge of panic, of excitement, the intimacy stunningly disconcerting. His thighs felt strong and warm against hers, his solid chest moulded against her back, his breath caressing the nape of her neck.

But rather than seduction, all his movements seemed to be about settling down – the way he pulled a pillow beneath his head, flattened his palm against the duvet just in front of her chest, trapping her against him.

He was lying close enough to feel her every move.

He wasn't closing in for sex – he was closing in for sleep.

It was just another in a long line of insults.

'I don't need to be restrained,' she said, resentment leaking into her tone.

'And I don't need you wandering around the compound while I'm asleep.'

'You could lock the door.'

'I still wouldn't trust you.'

'So I *do* make you anxious.'

'You want to provoke members of my pack like you provoke me; I won't be held responsible for their actions, but for now I need you alive. And like I said, I need some sleep. So do you.'

She rotated to face him in the small place he had left her between his chest and arm. 'So that's it? *This* is what I turned around for? So you could sleep?'

He turned her back around, pushed her wrists together, his leather wristbands brushing her skin. He pinned her wrists to the floor with one hand as he looped his leg over hers, keeping her still as he pressed himself tight against her again.

'You sound disappointed,' he said. 'Don't worry, when I get that desperate, I'll be sure to let you know. But well done for doing what you were told.'

She stared ahead at the window, but it wasn't anger that ignited her, that she'd done exactly what he'd wanted her to. The hurt overruled it – hurt as she hung on the word *desperate*.

Her throat tightened, the final blow making her feel too sick even to retort. Instead she stared out of the window, at the dense clouds that threatened more rain – a familiar sight in Blackthorn.

Chapter Eight

Three days earlier

The knocking resounded through her dreams, stirring her from the comfort of much-needed sleep. Sophia winced, shielding her eyes from the bedside light Daniel switched on.

'What the hell…?' she groaned.

The knock resounded again, this time harder, more impatient.

'For fuck's sake,' Daniel hissed, clearly nursing as much of a hangover as hers. Drink that was no doubt responsible for him ending up in her bed again.

Sophia forced herself into a seated position. 'I'll get it,' she declared, pushing her hair back out of her eyes.

But Daniel was already tugging up his jeans and yanking on a T-shirt as he padded across the tiny Blackthorn bedsit Sophia now called home.

'Phia, open up!' The familiar voice demanded, banging the door again.

'That sounds like Abby. What the hell is she doing here at…' she looked at the clock, 'four in the morning?'

'Only one way to find out.'

Daniel yanked open the door.

Abby stood clasping a brown A4 envelope in her hand, her stout arms folded across her chest. Her narrowed eyes momentarily widened as she stared up at Daniel then into the depths of the room at Sophia still in bed. 'Exactly how long has this been going on?' she asked, striding across the threshold.

Daniel closed the door behind her. 'Morning, boss.'

Sophia pushed both hands back through her hair, clutching her head for a moment, still struggling to come round. 'Like that's any of your business.'

'Whatever happens in my team *is* my business,' she said harshly, glimpsing at Daniel now leaning back against the sink.

Sophia stared across at the envelope Abby threw down on the tiny, round dining table. 'What's going on?'

Abby yanked out a chair, her large brown eyes emanating annoyance. 'This is what is known in the trade as one almighty fuck-up, Phia.'

As Daniel lifted the envelope, Sophia pushed aside the duvet. Grabbing her dressing gown from the foot of the bed, she tied it over her sweatpants and T-shirt on her way over to join her colleagues.

The look in Daniel's blue eyes told her it wasn't good.

Sophia reached for the photos he had started to discard on the table. She frowned at the numerous shots of Jake Dehain in the bar, laughing and joking over a bottle-strewn table.

Jake Dehain – Caleb Dehain's younger brother. The Dehains who owned the most successful club in Blackthorn and ruled the west side of Blackthorn with an iron fist. Integral in the district's third-species underworld, they'd been on The Alliance's hit list for quite some time, and the night to strike had finally come twenty-four hours before.

And though Caleb frustratingly hadn't fallen for their bait, Jake had – drinking their honeytrap to death, a process that killed any vampire. And she had no doubt Jake had suffered a painful death as the dead human blood penetrated his system – Trudy having given what short time was left for her disease-riddled body for the cause. Trudy who hadn't warranted adequate medical assistance along with other humans abandoned to Lowtown. It was her way of taking down the system. Her only sense of control left – signing up with The Alliance.

'What are you showing us these for?' she asked.

'Because these were taken three hours ago. Exactly twenty-four hours after Jake Dehain apparently bled Trudy to death,' Abby announced, the tension in her voice contracting the tiny bedsit even more. 'So do you want to tell me how the hell he's still alive?'

Sophia stared at the picture, flicked through the next and then the next. Pulling out a chair, she sank onto the edge. 'But it's not possible. I saw it. I saw the footage. I saw her die. I watched her pulse rate diminish to nothing. I heard her last breath. I saw him collapse beside her. I saw it all. Right to them burning her body in the incinerator.' She looked up at Abby. 'We all did.'

'I know. So how the fuck is that vampire still walking and talking?'

Sophia shook her head, frowning in confusion. 'I don't understand. We must have missed something.'

'I put you on this job because you promised me you could do this, Phia. We had one shot.'

Phia kept flicking through the pictures in desperation. 'Trudy was dead,' she said. 'He killed her.'

She'd stood beside Daniel in the safety of the van as they'd watched Jake lead Trudy into the outer rooms inside the club, at the same time keeping an eye on Jade trying to tempt Caleb in the same way. They'd monitored Trudy's readings – pulse rate, respiration – as he'd fed. They'd watched her slip away. And they'd watched her body being cremated when the aftermath had been discovered by Caleb less than an hour later.

Just as every reading had told them Jake had consumed way above the safe quantity of blood from which there was no way back.

'Then it seems she died for nothing then, doesn't it?' Abby declared.

'Ease up,' Daniel warned. 'This isn't her fault, Abby.'

'Then whose is it? I put Phia in charge of this operation – after *she* insisted she was capable.' Her glower snapped back to Sophia. 'You should have pulled her out the minute you saw Caleb wasn't taking the bait with Jade. You should have aborted. You knew the arrangement: Both brothers or neither. No suspicion raised.'

'But Caleb did take the bait for a while. How was I to know he wasn't going to go all the way? Jake had already left with Trudy. It was all underway. We had no way to stop *without* raising suspicion.' She stopped on the photograph of Jake, his arms wrapped around a petite blonde on the dance floor, her back to the camera.

'You assured me you could do this, Phia. You've let me down. You've let the whole of The Alliance down.'

'Whoa!' Daniel said, cutting in. 'That isn't fair. Phia spent weeks planning this. And you would never have agreed if she hadn't proved herself over and over again these past few months. It should have worked. She can't account for Caleb's taste that night. And like she said, we *all* saw what happened to Trudy.'

'Just as we can all now see she gave what life she had left for *nothing*.'

'Trudy knew what she was doing; she knew what she signed up for and the risks that it might not work,' Daniel said. 'She wanted this. Not living out her last months in too much pain to care.'

'What she wanted was a dead vampire,' Abby snapped.

'Then that's what we'll give her,' Sophia cut in.

'And how do you suppose you'll do that?' Abby asked. 'Walk right back in there? Pick up where you left off? Just how many girls have we got willing and able to give their life for this? Trudy was gold dust and we wasted her. And if you think I'm letting Jade back in there only for the same to happen to her, you've got another thing coming. We had one shot and you blew it.'

'There are other ways,' Sophia insisted.

'What – put a silver bullet through both their heads; stake them in the middle of the bar? That kind of defeats the covert element in this case, right?'

'I'll find a way.'

'Too late,' Abby said. 'We couldn't afford to mess this one up. The Alliance needs to go underground for a while.'

'But we don't have time for that. We're finally making headway.'

'We *were* making headway. Which is why I'm suspending you from the next target, Phia.'

Sophia snatched back a breath. 'What? You can't!'

'I can and I will. I want your head down and you out of the way. Because if we mess up this next one, The Alliance is finished.' She looked across at Daniel as she stood. 'Two days and we reconvene. You're heading up the next one, Daniel. Unless you've got a problem with that?'

'Who is it?' Sophia asked.

Abby only glanced at Sophia before looking back at Daniel. 'We'll reconvene in two days.'

She exited the room, slamming the door behind her.

Sophia sat in the silence, her attention returning to the array of photographs.

'Bitch,' Daniel hissed quietly as he resumed his seat.

'She's right though,' Sophia said, as she rifled languidly through the photos. 'I fucked up.'

'Phia, you said it yourself – we saw what Jake did. It should have worked. And how the hell were you supposed to know Caleb wouldn't take the bait with Jade? Can you help it that he wasn't in the mood?'

'Vampires are always in the mood for a free feed,' she said, sifting through.

'Caleb's tricky. Everyone knows that. He's got girls falling at his feet all the time. I'm not having you take the blame for this. If Abby thinks–'

Sophia froze. She picked up the photo, her hand trembling.

'Phia?' Daniel leaned forward, trying to catch her attention before he craned his neck to see what she was staring at. 'Phia, what's wrong?'

'Fuck,' she whispered. 'The pretty blonde on the dance floor was now head-on to the camera, gazing drunkenly up at Jake, her arms wrapped around his neck. 'That's my sister. That's Alisha.'

Daniel took the photo off her to stare at the image.

A split second later, Sophia was on her feet. She yanked open the kitchen drawer, rooted around and pulled out her phone. She paced the room, the phone pressed to her ear. 'Pick up,' she said sternly. 'Come on!'

'What are you doing?'

'What do you think I'm doing?'

Daniel tried to snatch the phone from her. 'You know the rules, Phia – no outside contact. That's not even Alliance property. You know the risks–'

'Fuck the rules!' Sophia snapped, shoving him back. She raked her fingers through her mussed hair. 'If either of them have touched her…' she muttered, disconnecting from the pre-recorded message for the third time before re-ringing. 'Alisha, it's me,' she said to the answer phone. 'Call me as soon as you get this. Straight away, you hear me?' She disconnected and typed in their home number.

'You made contact. Phia, this is unacceptable.'

Sophia paced as the phone rang. 'Something's wrong,' she said. 'Leila always answers.' As the tone rang monotonously, she slumped back into her seat. 'Come on, Lei, where are you?'

'Phia, when you signed up, you signed up to disconnect all ties. That's how it works.'

'Pick up!' she hissed. But when Leila failed to answer, she disconnected, her hand falling limply to the table.

'Phia!' Daniel snapped.

'No, Daniel!' She slammed the photo back in front of him, her finger pressing on the image of her little sister. 'This is my sister. My little sister – right here in Blackthorn with the worst fucking vampires since Kane Malloy, so don't cite rules at me!'

'What are you doing now?' he asked as she marched to the wardrobe.

She yanked off her dressing gown and pulled out a T-shirt, black sweater and combats.

'You're going out?'

'Too right I'm going out.'

Getting dressed, she tucked her phone in her trouser pocket. 'Where?'

She met his troubled gaze. 'Where do you think?'

He grabbed her arm as she swept past him. 'No way. You are *not* going back to that club.'

'Dawn will be here in the next couple of hours. My little sister is in that club right now. And I'm going to get her.'

'Did you not hear what Abby said? She told you to lie low. Phia, this could jeopardise this entire operation. It sure as hell will jeopardise *your* place in the operation.'

'I won't implicate anyone else.'

Daniel slammed the door shut as she opened it. 'You know better than this.'

'What I know is that my sister is in trouble.'

Daniel dragged her back over to the table, picked up the picture of Alisha again. 'She looks fine,' he said emphatically. 'She's probably on her way home as we speak. You go barging in there and you could blow this whole thing out of the water. For once, think about what you're doing. Give it another twenty-four hours. Give it time until we get a clearer picture.'

'Alisha might not have twenty-four hours. I'm going to the club,' she said. 'And I'm getting her out of there. Now.'

Chapter Nine

Sophia opened her eyes to the saffron hues of the descending sun and rolled onto her back to see Jask had gone.

She pushed back the duvet and crossed to the window, the floorboards warm from the late-afternoon glow.

Jask was down on the lawn, dressed in a sweat top and sweatpants, his back to her, the breeze sifting through his hair as he ran the length of the lawn.

She kept her hands cupped around her neck as she curled onto the window seat to watch him.

He dropped to do press ups, twenty she counted, before he got back up, resuming his run. But this time he only ran half a length before stopping to unzip his sweat top, tearing it off to reveal a fitted black vest top that clung to every hard curve.

She whistled under her breath, accompanied by an ache of frustration, then a flush of embarrassment at how she had behaved a few hours before.

And the sense of embarrassment only escalated when she saw a small child run at him. She was a pretty little thing with long blonde ringlets that bore too much resemblance to the female she'd seen in the dining room – the female who now approached Jask from across the green.

Jask bent forward to catch the child, lifting her in his arms with ease, every muscle flexing as he held her above his head. The little girl giggled hysterically as he supported her by her shoulder and ankles, effortlessly easing her up and down as if weight-lifting.

The blonde female was equally laughing, her hair blowing in the late afternoon breeze. And, as she pulled level, Jask eased the child back down onto the floor only to wrap his arm around the blonde's shoulder, kissing her affectionately on the temple as the child skipped off again.

She'd never really thought about it before – having a family. But realisation panged painfully that now she was a serryn, it would never be possible, her serrynity rendering her barren. She wasn't sure the implications had sunk in yet. But then she never saw herself having children anyway. Leila was the mother figure. Alisha would nestle up with some doting partner somewhere and probably equally have an entire brood of idyllic mini-hers.

Even before her serrynity, she'd always known she'd never be mature enough to have kids anyway. She'd stick with being the irresponsible aunt always off on her adventures. If she ever lived long enough to see her nieces or nephews. If Leila and Alisha survived long enough to have them.

Now, watching Jask with the child and his mate made her feel like even more of an outsider than she always had. The Alliance claimed the third species were a freak of nature but, stood at the window gazing out, it only confirmed what she'd always believed – that *she* was the one who was the freak.

The Alliance had done something to help with that. It wasn't just about being able to do something; it was about being a part of something. And the need was only reinforced as she witnessed the community in front of her. An insular community as self-sufficient and interdependent as they appeared to the outside world.

The lycans may have been the minority species, but they were intensely tight. It's what made them so powerful. So impenetrable. And it was no easy feat keeping a naturally wild species under control – in excess of two hundred of them. But under Jask's guidance, his zero-tolerance policy, they were managed. And managed well it seemed.

She watched as the little girl now ran towards Corbin as he headed down the steps to join them. He cradled her in his arms before dousing her in kisses.

They were clearly close, Jask and Corbin. Admirably so. Both having each other's backs at all times.

Bait Jask though she may have over his decision to disclose the truth about the TSCD's set-up, even she knew he'd done the right thing. He'd done what he had no choice but to do if those responsible for the cruel murder of Arana Malloy were to be convicted – especially when Caitlin Parish's accused involvement with Kane brought the accusations into question. Jask had done what was right for his pack to secure the freedom of two of his own.

The female peeled away from Jask only to kiss Corbin lingeringly on the lips, the second-in-command's hand sliding down her waist to tap her behind.

Her heart leapt.

The blonde female wasn't with Jask, she was with Corbin. And bets were, from the way the child had responded to Corbin, she was his too.

She knew she had no place feeling relief, but she couldn't help it.

Corbin sauntered back up the steps, the blonde and the child with him, leaving Jask alone and kicking at the turf.

This time she felt a deeper pang inside – a pang at sensing a familiar loneliness.

But empathy was dangerous. Especially now.

Regardless, as Jask looked up at the sun before following them up the steps, Sophia's stomach clenched with anxiety. She hurried into the bathroom and smoothed down her hair. With little result, she grabbed the brush she had seen in the drawer and swiftly worked her bob until she got a shine. She brushed her teeth and headed back into the bedroom.

She perched on the edge of the window seat, expecting Jask to make an appearance at any point. But he didn't.

A few minutes later, disappointment hitting harder than she was comfortable with, she wandered into the living room. There, draped over the chairs by the window, were clothes – female clothes. She picked through the three tunics, before being distracted by the noise through the open sash window ahead.

Hearing yells, she slipped between the armchairs to look out.

There was a whole other patch of land behind the building, maybe a couple of acres. Surrounded by barbed wire, not unlike the rest of the compound, brick walls lay beyond.

Clusters gathered along the edge of what looked like a marked pitch of some kind. At either end, twenty-five-foot-high metal scaffolding housed jutting hoops at the top.

A game was about to start – she could hear that from the shouting and the excitement.

Jask and Corbin, amidst a group of about twenty others, were getting into position at either end.

She watched on in fascination as it all kicked off. It involved three balls the size of footballs – one oval, two round. There were two teams, both vying for top and bottom lines as well as sidelines. Some balls were carried up to the hoops, the lycans moving with admirable speed and agility as they were pursued to the top.

She didn't recognise the rules. She didn't recognise the game. At first it looked like chaos, but then what Sophia saw was the ultimate in teamwork – each team monitoring the location and position of each ball, each member having to be vigilant of what others in their team were doing – defenders, chasers, blockers. It was enthralling to watch. It was fast, ferocious and the most exquisite teamwork she had ever seen in a sport.

Because it *was* a sport – an easy-going, enjoyable sport that showed not only how close the lycans were, but just how physically impressive. She homed in on Jask in particular, open-mouthed at his speed and nimbleness – the way he climbed the frame and hooped the ball before dropping from the full height as if he were just jumping down from the bottom step of the stairs.

And as he flicked back his hair, rolling his shoulders and letting every muscle ripple as he shouted orders at the others, she let out a slow and satisfied sigh.

Until she caught a glimpse of Rone leaning against a tree in the distance.

Her heart pounded. It was her opportunity – Jask and the others distracted, Rone clearly not a participant.

Now was the time to use her escape tools. She slipped off Jask's T-shirt and pulled on one of the tunics. She hurried back into the bedroom to grab her still-sodden boots for the tools hidden in the heels and made her way over to the door. She checked the handle first and was shocked to find it unlocked.

Not wanting to waste time deliberating, she left her boots behind and hurried barefooted out into the corridor and down the stairs.

It was dead in the lobby – and she had no doubt where everyone had gone.

As she reached the bottom of the stairs, the yells and cheers echoed from her left.

She turned at the foot of the stairs, past the dining hall on her right and continued on down the hallway, past another room on her left before reaching another mosaic lobby, this one much smaller.

The door was open, the late afternoon air and cheers wafting towards her. The sun, already touching the horizon, was now a rich but dark amber glow in the distance. There were a few curious glances in her direction as she made her way down the steps but, on the whole, it was if she wasn't there.

Rone looked across from the tree, but made no attempt to approach her.

Sophia hurried over to him. 'We need to talk.'

'I have nothing to say to you,' he declared, looking back ahead at the game, his blue eyes narrowed, the curls of his fair hair wafting in the breeze.

'Good, then that gives you more time to listen, which suits me just fine. You lied to Jask.'

Rone's attention snapped back to her, his panic barely concealed. 'I don't know what you're talking about,' he said, brushing past her towards the way she had come.

She caught his arm. 'Yes, you do. You told Jask you stumbled on me by accident. We both know it was anything but.'

He glanced over his shoulder to see that, even amidst game, they had caught Jask's attention.

'Not now,' he hissed in a hushed voice. 'Later. I'll find you. Keep it shut.'

She glanced back across at Jask who had now stopped, his hands on his hips as he faced their direction.

'There might not be a later,' she said as he continued walking away. 'Rone!'

She folded her arms and turned to face the pitch. Jask had reverted his attention back to the game, but there was no doubt there would be a follow-up. Before that, she needed to make the most of the opportunity. She pulled her sleeves down over her hands and pursued Rone back up the steps.

Skimming through the lobby, she reached the bottom of the stairs. She glanced anxiously around but they were very much alone. She followed him, ascending two at a time. 'You know, don't you? You know what I'm a part of.'

He stopped. Turned to face her. His eyes flashed with concern, with shock, but not confusion.

He *did* know – and he wasn't denying it. And she needed to make the most of it while she could.

'You came to the ruins for me,' she continued. 'I know because those vampires were expecting lycan company. I heard them say it. You were going to interrogate me just like they were. Only you don't want Jask to know or you would have told him already.'

He looked around warily. 'Have you told him any of this?'

Finally the confirmation she needed. 'Of course not.'

'Why not?'

'Make sure he knows about the existence of The Alliance, you mean? Seriously?'

'But if you already knew we knew about you, why didn't you say anything when we said we were going to call Corbin?'

'I seem to remember you debating whether to just kill me outright. It hardly seemed smart to add to your reasons whilst I was chained to a wall. And I didn't exactly plan on sticking around when he and Jask turned up.' She pulled level. 'Why not just tell him?'

He tried to turn away but she caught his arm. She may as well have tried to handcuff him from the way he recoiled and wrenched free.

'I heard them talking, Rone. You'd been willing to pay for information with your herbs. That's *very* risky business. Is that why? Is that why you don't want him to know?'

His eyes flared. He lowered his voice even more. 'If you're smart, you'll keep your mouth shut.'

'If you're smart, you'll want me out of here to make sure that happens.'

'What?'

'You get me out of here or I'll tell him.'

'And expose your Alliance? I don't think so.'

'He's got to find them first. But he knows *exactly* where you are. You think I'm bluffing – you try me.'

He had another quick scan around the lobby below, wariness in his eyes. 'I'll think about it,' he said, turning back up the stairs.

She grabbed his arm again. 'What's to think about?'

'Jask finds out about this and I'm out of here. Do you know a lycan's odds in Blackthorn without their pack?'

'Exactly. So you don't need a mouthy serryn on the loose around your boss, do you? You *need* to get me out of here.'

'You think it's that easy? Even possible?' He looked around warily again. 'The longer you spend talking to me, the less likely I am to put my neck on the line.' He yanked his hand away. 'I'll find you later.'

'And a phone. I need to get to a phone.'

But he was already making his way back up the stairs.

She exhaled with impatience and made her way back down. Stopping on the bottom step, she gazed at the doorway ahead, her arms folded. Puffing out her lips before letting out an unsteady exhale, she strolled across the lobby and wandered outside.

Skirting the empty quadrant, she headed back through the arched tunnel, only this time she decided to take a left through the gate.

She stepped over the thick branches of old rhododendrons stretching onto the worn path, ducking out of the way of a few branches before opening the wooden slated door into the outbuilding. She pushed aside the rubber strips that reminded her of those found in an old hospital and stepped into the enclosure.

The comforting humidity wrapped itself around her immediately. The room was awash with greenery, heat lamps suspended from the ceiling and strung from the walls, sprays of water resounding from her left. The windows were blackened out, the plants surviving on the bright, artificial light that bathed them.

A female busily tended to the plants she was watering, her long, slender fingers gliding over their leaves as though she were dressing a small child's hair. Sensing Sophia, she glanced up, her blue eyes flashing wariness. But she said nothing.

Perspiration lined Sophia's brow as she continued through the varying plants, past the potted shrubbery. She slid back the glass doors to expose another chamber, this one filled with natural light. Water trickled somewhere in the distance, plants reaching the ceiling from their artificially created beds, a narrow laid path leading through further shrubbery.

She'd heard how self-sufficient the lycans were, but this was the proof. It was certainly true when it came to managing their condition – their response to the lunar cycle an allergic reaction managed only by a remedy of herbs that their ancestors had discovered, which counteracted their condition.

They'd been allowed to continue growing them even after the regulations, but the meds devised by the Global Council were always on standby. From what she'd heard, their intention had always been met with scepticism by the lycans. Especially as the meds were born out of research by the geneticists who had first explored lycanthropy – through experimenting on "volunteers" to devise their own version of managing the condition. The research allegedly funded by the Global Council who had once wanted to create their own breed of lycans to send into locale cores to manage vampires.

'You smell funny.'

Sophia stared down at the source of the voice.

Large, grey lycan eyes stared back up at her.

'Is that right?' Sophia remarked, turning to face the child.

The child that had giggled furiously as Jask had lifted her over his head nodded, oblivious to the potential offence of the statement.

'Maybe it's because I'm human,' Sophia added.

'What's your name?'

'What's yours?'

'You first.'

'Phia.'

The little girl's eyes widened.

'P-H-I-A,' Sophia explained. 'You can spell, right?'

The little girl nodded. 'I spell every day.'

'So what's your name?'

'Tuly.'

'Nice name.' She looked over her head. 'Where's your mother?'

'Watching the game.'

Sophia took her opportunity to be sure. 'And your father?'

'Playing.'

'Is that Jask?'

The little girl put her hands to her mouth to mask her giggle. She shook her head.

'Jask isn't your father?'

'Uh-uh,' she said, shaking her head again.

'Is Corbin?'

The little girl smiled, flashing Phia a hint of the protruding canines indicative of their kind, and nodded.

And Sophia smiled back – for more than one reason.

'Tuly, come here!'

Tuly looked over her shoulder as the blonde female closed the gap between them, her hand held out for Tuly to take – the female Sophia instantly recognised from the dining hall, and from the quadrant with Jask and Corbin.

'I'm talking to Phia,' Tuly declared. 'She's human.'

'I know what she is,' the female declared, her hand stiffening as she kept it held out in summons.

'I'm not going to do anything to her,' Sophia declared, unable not to feel affronted by the concern in the female's eyes.

'Tuly!' the female said again, her eyes flitting anxiously from Sophia to her daughter.

With a sigh, Tuly pulled away.

The female instantly swept her up to rest on her hip.

'I told her she smells funny,' the child whispered in her mother's ear.

'She smells different, that's all,' the female said. She looked back at Sophia, apology for her daughter's blatancy clear in her eyes. 'I'm sorry.'

Sophia shrugged. 'I've been told worse. Believe me.'

The lycan eyed her swiftly. 'You found the clothes then,' she said, a little more appeased by having her child in her arms. 'Jask asked me to get you a few things.'

Sophia clutched the hem and splayed it by way of acknowledgement. 'Thanks.'

'I'm Solstice,' she said. 'And you're obviously Phia.'

'P-H-I-A,' Tuly spelt out.

'Go and play on the green,' Solstice instructed the child before putting her back down on the floor.

Tuly flashed Sophia another smile before waving and skipping away.

'She's a sweet kid,' Sophia declared. 'Direct but sweet.'

'All the same, I'd rather you not talk to her.'

Clearly not *that* appeased.

Sophia rested her hip against the nearest worktop. 'I'm guessing you know what I am then.'

Solstice warily held her gaze before nodding.

'I thought it was vampires who were supposed to be nervous of serryns,' Phia remarked, 'not lycans.'

'I know enough of your kind to know you're not safe near anyone. Jask has his reasons for letting you wander around, but I just ask that you stay away from our young.'

Sophia exhaled, surprised at how offended she still felt, not least by how Solstice still looked at her like she was some kind of monster. But even she knew there was no greater monster out there than a fully fledged serryn. '*She* approached *me*.'

'We're not used to strangers here. She's going to be intrigued. Let alone a human stranger. But this is a safe environment and we would like to keep it that way.'

'Then talk to your pack leader; he's the one keeping me prisoner.'

'Not without good reason.'

'A reason you know?'

Solstice frowned warily. 'I know when to not ask questions.'

Sophia folded her arms. 'Wow, you lycan girls really are under the thumb, aren't you?'

It was Solstice's turn to look affronted. 'Not under the thumb. It's called trust.'

'You can call it what you like. I'll call it a dictatorship. Jask still has the final say on everything, right?'

'He's a great leader. A strong leader.'

'Not one who can protect you all of the time though. What happened with the TSCD only proves that.'

Solstice took a brave step towards her. 'What happened with our pack was a set-up. Jask did the right thing to protect us, but don't mistake it for weakness. I saw the way you looked at him at breakfast. You need to treat him with more respect.'

'He hasn't exactly earned it.'

'Take some friendly advice – tread carefully, Phia. Those eyes of his might be pretty but what lies behind them isn't.'

She turned away, making her way back through the plants.

Sophia knew she should have left it there, that she shouldn't have pursued. But she couldn't help it. 'You're with Corbin, right?'

Solstice glanced over her shoulder but kept walking.

'So who's Jask with?'

Solstice didn't look back as she made her way back through the sliding doors into the next room.

'Your alpha has got a mate, right? I've seen her clothes in his room.' Sophia followed her over to the front door. 'Don't tell me she's left him. Run off with a vampire, maybe?' she added, hoping her light retort would get the lycan to respond.

'She's dead,' Solstice said, turning to face her. 'Ellen's dead.'

Chapter Ten

Sophia stood outside the outhouse, uncertain whether the chill that crept over her skin was from the comparative rapid drop in temperature compared to the humidity of indoors, or a chill of a different kind.

It wasn't just what Solstice had said before walking away – it was the sadness that had leaked from her eyes as she'd uttered it.

Whoever Ellen was, she had mattered to her too.

And no matter how she had intended the remark, Sophia felt the painful stab of shame.

She wanted to ask when, how. Maybe even just to apologise instead of standing there in gawping silence. Not that any of it mattered. Not that she had any place caring at all.

But to her detriment, she did.

She curled her toes against the cold, rough stone before strolling back down to the gate. Not sure where to go, what to do in light of the revelation, she looked left at the outhouse she'd tried to explore earlier. She resolved to make another attempt – needing the distraction if nothing else.

Careful to avoid tripping over the tree roots, she reached the door. She turned the handle, only this time it gave and creaked open. She glanced warily over her shoulder at the courtyard behind, checking she was alone before stepping inside.

There was a further temperature drop inside as she closed the door behind her. What was left of the late afternoon light leaked through the small, deep-set windows left and right, igniting the glittering dust motes. But even that fragment of light was fading with the encroaching twilight.

Her pulse raced to an uncomfortable throb, her ears attuned to any sound – any indication that someone else was in there. But only silence echoed back.

She peered into the open room directly ahead, at the table and vacant chairs she'd seen earlier, before heading down the corridor to the right.

She dragged her hand along the uneven stone wall as she descended the broad wooden steps. Even less light filtered through the four high-set oblong windows – the thick branches outside blocking the diminishing light as if darkness consumed that part of the building early.

She turned the handle on the first door on the left and warily pushed it open. Half-empty wine racks dominated the periphery of the dark room within, storage boxes piled up in the centre. She found similar in the next room along only this time it was stacked not only with bottle racks, but crates and barrels too.

She turned the handle on the third door.

Her heart leapt at what looked liked upright coffins lining the walls ahead as well as to her left and right. But each lay open and empty, exposing straps within as well as what looked like the equivalent of a moulding to fit a human form.

She tentatively crossed the threshold, checking behind the door before stepping further inside.

She passed the central stone table, not failing to notice the straps that hung limply from that too.

Stopping in front of one of the coffins, she examined the soft, brown strips of leather – seemingly positioned to bind the neck, forearms, wrists, waist, hips, thighs and calves. She reached out to touch one.

'They're for punishment.'

Sophia's heart leapt a fraction before the rest of her did. She spun around, her startled gaze snapping to the doorway to where

Jask stood in the opaque light. He was still in the same clothing he'd worn out on the pitch but his hair glistened as if he'd showered.

'Lycans hate to be contained,' he said. 'We're extremely claustrophobic. Once you've been in there, you don't usually commit a misdemeanour again.'

'You put your *own* in these?'

'They're as much a deterrent as in active use.'

There was something different about him – almost as if he'd been struck with a new vigour with the pending nightfall. If it was possible, he seemed sharper, more relaxed – almost more alert to her.

She withdrew from the coffin. 'That's a somewhat tyrannical approach for someone who's supposed to care about his pack,' she said, folding her arms.

'That's a somewhat condemnatory tone coming from a serryn.'

'We do what we have to.'

He leaned back against the wall just inside of the door. 'What you *choose* to do.'

She strolled towards the table, sending a wary glance in his direction.

She wondered how long he'd been without Ellen. What had happened to her. If they'd been together long. Why he'd not found another. All questions far too personal for her to dare ask. And questions she had no place pondering.

Facing him, she perched against the end of the table nearest him and cocked her head towards it. 'A bit kinky, isn't it?'

'You want to try it for size?'

'Is that your thing, Jask? Strapping people down?'

'Does that worry you, Phia?'

Hearing her name slip from his lips for the first time sent a shiver through her.

'That is your name, right?' he said, a glimmer of amusement lacing his eyes. 'P-H-I-A, Tuly tells me.'

He seemed further amused by her silence as she struggled for a retort.

'Do you want to see inside one of the containment rooms?' he asked. 'As you're clearly curious as to how things run around here.'

'You have morphers?'

Now this *was* a useful piece of insider information. A very illegal and subsequently risky piece of information that he shouldn't have been disclosing to her.

He took a step back into the corridor, hand held out to his right.

There was something behind his eyes that spoke of a challenge – a challenge that she had the feeling was a test. He glanced down at her chest then back in her eyes, clearly having sensed the escalated pulse rate – clearly wanting her to know as such.

He expected her to say no.

'Sure,' she said. 'Why not?'

She followed him out of the room, feigning as much nonchalance as she could as he led her to the final door in the corridor. He descended the worn, wooden slatted steps into the darkness below, Sophia close behind.

There were no windows in the subterranean level. And it was cold, much colder. The silence was unearthly, the scent of damp rife.

He switched on three wall-mounted lights as he led the way, the cord still swinging as she passed, the white light only adding to the chill of the narrow stone corridor.

They passed metal door after metal door both left and right, until Jask stopped at the one in the far left-hand corner.

He pushed it open, indicating for Sophia to enter first.

As she stepped over the threshold into the darkness, she heard another click. More soft white light entered the room, but not enough to reach the corners.

What resembled a prison cell dominated the top right-hand corner of the room – maybe twenty-by-twenty-foot square. The two inner walls were stone, the two outer ones bars that were drilled into the floor and ceiling. A single door entered the side directly ahead. It was best described as a cage and she guessed that, technically, that's exactly what it was – only the entrants were voluntary.

'How many of these are there?' she asked, looking down at the double mattress on the floor within.

'Ten along this stretch. More than enough.' He indicated towards the open door. 'Try it.'

She looked across her shoulder at him as he drew level, the wariness in her eyes undoubtedly visible.

He headed over and stepped inside ahead of her.

After a moment's more hesitation, knowing only too well that he could have dragged her in there if he'd wanted to, she followed behind him.

Though only separated from the rest of the room by the bars, it felt more confined in there, even with the door open. The feeling was oppressive – as if decades of negative energy had been stored up in one tiny place.

She tried to ignore the sudden sense of claustrophobia as she stepped deeper into the cage, deeper into the darkness.

'How long do they spend in here?'

'Two days before the full moon – that's the really tetchy time – the day during and then the recuperation days after.'

'And then?'

'They sleep it off. Eat. Relax. Then spend the rest of the month like anyone else.'

'Are they the ones that refuse to take the herbs?'

'Only one. The rest are the unfortunate ones who are immune to the remedy.'

'So it's true. There are some it doesn't work for. But they won't take the meds?'

Jask leaned back beside the exit. He coiled his hands around the bars above his head, the motion emphasising the curves of his bare arms, his solid shoulders, the toned chest beneath his black vest.

She wasn't sure if the relaxed stance was supposed to create the same effect in her. From her flush of arousal, it had failed.

'If the Global Council offered you pills, but they refused to tell you anything about what they contained – would you take them?' he asked.

'Those who refuse should be declared. Those meds are obligatory for the immune ones. The LCU would rip this place apart if they knew. What you're doing is dangerous. You're putting this community at risk. What if one got out?'

'Have you ever heard of a morphed lycan on the loose in Blackthorn?'

'The two that killed Kane Malloy's sister,' she reminded him. She stepped up to the threshold of the dark recess in the top right-hand corner and peered into the tiny space that housed a metal sink directly ahead, a toilet around the corner before the room ended in a shower.

'That was different, as you well know. They *did* opt into the meds and were starved of them.'

She turned to face him. 'But you let them take them. Doesn't that go against your lycan code?'

'As opposed to forcing them to face morphing?'

'Is it really that painful?'

'For the first twenty or so times, if the body doesn't give in before then. Females of our species say it's ten times worse than childbirth.'

She raised her eyebrows slightly as her imagination filled in the gaps as it so often did, having never experienced the latter, and now never having the prospect of experiencing it. 'So what about the one you mentioned that refuses both the meds and your herbs? Why do they opt for it?'

'Because there are still some who think it is intended. I have to respect their viewpoint.'

'No, what you have to do is keep your pack in check. What you're doing here is irresponsible.'

'I'll try not to lose any sleep over your concerns.'

Now that she had seen it all, she should have left. Or at least attempted to. But she didn't want to. Instead, she leaned against the wall opposite him, her hands at the small of her back. She glanced around the cell, trying to envision spending four days down there.

'So what about you? Do the herbs work on you, or do you spend each full moon down here?'

He wandered over to the mattress against the wall and picked up what looked like a small tennis ball. He flipped it in his hand before bouncing it against the floor on his way over to her. 'The herbs work on me.'

He bounced the ball against the wall she leaned against, it re-bounding back for him to catch easily in one hand.

'Have you ever morphed?' she asked.

'Yes,' he said, throwing the ball against the wall, this time right next to her. 'When I was younger. Before the regulations changed our freedom to do so. Before I had the responsibility of this pack.'

'How old are you?'

He raked her swiftly with his gaze as if debating whether to answer. 'A century and a half, plus some.'

'You lycans get about five years to every one of ours, right? But you stay at your peak for most of it – like the vampires do.'

'Something like that.'

The repeat bounce and rebound of ball becoming rhythmic, a thud not unlike her own pulse rate, as if he was tuning into it and showing her so.

'That was an impressive performance earlier. The game,' she said, trying to ignore what she guessed was now a clever taunt – rebounding and catching, rebounding and catching, the rhythm becoming hypnotic.

'It's good for teamwork. Good for focus. It helps the young ones to channel and develop their responses. It gets them to be aware of each other and their pack. It was a game that we used to use to train for hunting.'

His rhythm picked up pace, her pulse rate ironically doing the same in the otherwise dominating silence.

'You used to hunt?' she asked, trying to stay focused.

'When I needed to.'

'Humans?'

He glanced at her. 'When I needed to.'

She felt herself prickle at the subtle intimidation. 'And why would you need to? For food?'

'Trust me, you don't taste that nice.'

'But tell me, is it true there was talk of the Global Council trying to get you on side when they first brought the regulations into being? That they wanted to develop you into being the perfect fighting machines for their cause? Faster, even better responses and the animalistic lack of conscience to rip your enemies apart – they wanted you to help keep order amongst the vampires and back up the Third Species Control Division. Like police dogs, only more expendable. But that you all refused despite the extra privileges like they offered the vampires' Higher Order?' She looked around. 'Admirable to your own maybe that you declined. But many would say stupid. Still, you secured a nice kennel here. Very cosy.'

She expected him to bite at that one. But he didn't. His calmness only added to her unease – like the steady gaze of viper just before it strikes.

'It'll do for now,' he said.

'For now? Don't tell me you're one of the optimists who believe this system is temporary? Do you believe these vampire prophecies?'

'I know it won't always be like this.'

'But surely if the vampires come into power, it'll be all over for you.'

'Sounds like more speculation to me.'

'I'm just stating the obvious.'

'We may be in the minority in this locale, but don't mistake us for the underdog.'

She couldn't help but smirk. 'Your words, not mine.'

He picked up pace with the ball, almost as if he knew the personal jibe had escalated her heartbeat a fraction more – the act in itself provoking a further increase.

Unlike humans, the third species could control their peripheral nervous system. Always had been able to. The vampires were particularly adept at managing their heartbeat, speeding it up if they chose to, or more frequently slowing it down – the same as they could hold their breath. It was used often in attack so that the enemy couldn't hear them coming. The lycans weren't as efficient at it as the vampires, but were certainly capable of it to some extent.

Just as they all had accelerated healing. Nothing near the rate of the Higher Order – vampire royalty – though, who had secured their place in Midtown with their offer to help the human race. An offer as flawed as the Global Council's intentions by writing their privileged position into the regulations – for as long as the Higher Order remained useful.

'Have you been in this area since the beginning or were you one of the ones shipped in when the regulations came into being?' she asked.

'I was shipped in.'

'Where were you from originally?'

'Western region. Like many packs, mine were separated. A collection of us were sent here.'

'Is it true that the Higher Order never consulted other third species over the outing? That they just went ahead with it?'

'Yes.'

'You must hate them. Especially with them subjecting you to all of this. I mean, it's okay for your lycan buddies in locales where they're in the majority, but you really got the short straw, didn't you?'

'We do okay.'

'But you could do so much better. Still, it was a very clever idea of the Global Council – always ensuring there was a minority group in every locale: make sure none of you rebel against the other. Civil war in one locale and the minorities suffer in another, right?'

'Ingenious,' he said, his tone laced with sarcasm as he picked up pace with the ball again.

'So, how come you assumed leadership when you came here? There must have been others vying for the position.'

'One or two. We managed to work it out.'

'Did you fight to the death? I hear that's what lycans do.'

He glanced across at her. 'Does Corbin look dead to you?'

'He fought you for the title?' she asked, unable to conceal her surprise.

'Amongst others.' He looked across at her. 'You look shocked.'

'Because you're so close.'

'We fought fairly. I won. Corbin had the option to leave the pack if he chose. Or he could be my second in command.'

'And he doesn't mind that you won?'

'It's not done for personal accolade, Phia. It's done to decide who is best to lead the pack. It's in all our best interests to choose the most suitable.'

'I bet that was quite the battle.' She paused. 'What would you have done if Corbin had won?'

He frowned, clearly never having been asked the question before.

'Because you wouldn't have stuck around, would you?' she said. 'You would have chosen to leave.'

'And what makes you say that?'

'Some want to be leaders, some are born that way. You're definitely the latter. I don't think you're capable of playing second in command.'

'Is that right?'

'Are you going to deny it?'

He bounced the ball against the wall again.

'So do *you* think the right lycan won?' she persisted.

He frowned. 'What kind of question is that?'

'I don't know. Maybe I'm curious as to why you let those lycans set up for killing Arana hand themselves in when you clearly knew the truth. Why not tell them to go to a higher authority? Why let them stay inside for fourteen years?'

'And what higher authority is that, Phia? The Global Council? Because they're the only ones higher than the TSCD, as you well know. And even if I did have the ways and means to get direct communication with them, they're really going to send one of their impartial investigators in here to interview two lycans with the sole purpose of exposing corruption amongst the very system they put in place, aren't they?'

She shrugged. 'Caitlin Parish exposed them and she worked for them.'

He continued to rebound the ball off the wall, but now he was doing so a little harder.

'Do you think it's true what some are saying?' she asked, the perfect opportunity having arisen again. 'That she's sleeping with Kane Malloy?'

'I don't know.'

'That would be really fucked-up, wouldn't it? *Really* fucked-up. Them sleeping together – with everything her father, her stepfather, let alone her boyfriend did in setting up Kane's sister. Come on, Jask. Spill. You were involved with him. You must know. What really goes on in Kane Malloy's head, huh? Putting those agents behind bars just doesn't feel right. It's not his style, from what I've heard.'

'Everyone's got an opinion on Kane's style.'

'But you *know*, don't you?'

'*You* ask too many questions.'

'I have a curious nature. It's an affliction. And this isn't your style either, is it, Jask? Tucking those responsible away with the very authorities you despise as much as the rest of Blackthorn does. I know you would have liked to have dealt with them personally.'

His gaze lingered. 'Like I said – you ask too many questions.'

She hesitated, wondering how far to push it. But these were questions everyone was asking. Everyone who had watched the court case as avidly as she did. And the more insight she got into the psychology of those self-nominated third-species leaders, the better, especially with the uncomfortable feeling in the pit of her stomach – instinct telling her Jask still wanted retribution.

'I'm right though, aren't I? This isn't over,' she said. 'Putting those agents behind bars *wasn't* part of the plan. Not yours anyway. Why do I get the feeling it's not just the TSCD who aren't happy about Kane and Caitlin's liaison? Why do I also get the feeling Kane's not the only one who wanted Caitlin dead? But that agent stuck her neck on the line for you, Jask. She turned in her family, let alone her boss, to do the right thing.'

'*Or* she did what she could purely to save the lives of those she cared about. Depends how you look at it.'

'You think she played both you and Kane?'

'I think we've discussed this enough.'

'But aren't you just a little concerned that now you've given evidence against the TSCD, now they know you knew all along about the set-up – that you disclosed the truth to Kane in the first place – aren't you scared they'll turn on you?'

'With everyone knowing where to point the finger? No one wants an inter-locale outbreak. That's what will happen if they come after us.'

'Maybe they're just biding their time.'

'Maybe.' He paused for only a second. 'What were you talking to Rone about earlier?'

Her heart skipped a beat. 'Just getting acquainted with the pack. Being friendly. Is that not allowed either?'

'It didn't look friendly to me.'

'It's very early days to be jealous, Jask.'

'Considering you talk in your sleep, not at all.' He glanced at her again, a glimmer of playfulness leaking through the only thing to ease her tension just slightly. 'So let's try again,' he said, turning his attention back on the ball. 'What were you talking about?'

'I told him what I thought of him for not letting me go when I asked him to.'

'So you won't need to talk to him again, then?'

'Is that a direct order?' she asked, finding it hard to curb her indignation that he *still* thought he could control her. 'Worried I'll start corrupting your pack? Oh no, hold on – they'd have to be desperate, right?'

She surprised herself at how heavily his comment from earlier still weighed on her mind when it had no place holding any weight at all.

And, from the look in his eyes, the unintentional exposure of hurt had surprised him too.

'I was tired earlier,' he said. 'Irritable. I shouldn't have said that.' He caught the ball as it bounced back, only this time he discarded it back onto the mattress. 'You're a beautiful girl. It's just a shame about the attitude – and the whole serryn thing.'

As he caught her eye, her stomach flipped. Stunned by the lack of mocking in his tone, struggling to come up with a retort, she dropped her gaze.

In the sudden silence, she realised just how accustomed she had come to the beat of the ball. Its absence now created a sense of flatlining and all the panic that came with it.

She looked up as she sensed his approach, the shadows enveloping him. She tensed as he pressed his hand against the wall beside her shoulder.

'Only you don't act like a serryn,' he added.

She dared to look him in the eyes. She had to. 'Met one to know, have you?' she asked, a question that hadn't occurred to her until then.

'No. You're my first. But I know enough about them to know there's *definitely* something not right about you.'

'And what *would* make me right, Jask?'

'I don't know. Maybe a little less sensitivity.'

She raised her eyebrows slightly. 'You think I'm over-sensitive?'

'I think you feel far more than you should.' He stared searchingly into her eyes. 'I don't think you've been at this very long. In fact, I'm fairly sure you haven't.'

He eased her hand from behind her back. But until she knew his intention, she didn't protest.

He held it up, palm facing him. With the same hand that held hers, he used his thumb to gently prise each of her fingers from their clenched position to expose the flesh beneath.

'I hear that the more vampires you have sex with, the stronger you get,' he said.

She'd read of it too. But she'd read many things about serryns she'd yet to test the theory of.

'So, as I'd class your attempts against me on the wasteland, in the bathroom, not least on the way to the poolroom as futile, maybe that tells me something too.'

He eased back her ring finger, just enough to make her flinch.

She kept her defiant glare locked on his, determined not to show her panic at what she sensed was the pending torture she had anticipated.

She needed to get out. And not just because of that. He was getting too close. Far too close. And if that was the real reason he'd brought her down there – to interrogate her – then she was rapidly heading towards being screwed. Not least if he decided to drop the well-behaved lycan act fast before she found an exit clause.

Because if he did decide to turn on her, if he did decide enough was enough and he wanted answers, she had no doubt he knew exactly how to get them.

'There's one way to tell, you know,' she said.

'Which is?'

Before she had time to think it through, before she had time to regret it, she lifted herself onto tiptoes until her lips were less than an inch from his – those firm and shapely masculine lips that she had longed to taste.

Her heart pounded, a shiver raking down her spine as her mouth finally met his.

She wanted to run her fingers through his hair, plaster her other hand against that hard chest as she consumed him.

But this wasn't personal.

She expected him to shove her away, to withdraw at the very least, but he didn't.

But he didn't respond either other than to take the pressure off her finger.

And she *needed* him to respond.

In the seconds that passed, as his lips gradually became more pliable, as he allowed her tongue to meet his, she almost forgot herself. His lips were surprisingly smooth, his mouth warm but fresh, his breaths enticing against her lips. And when he did finally reciprocate, her heart leapt at the connection.

She almost forgot everything as he eventually re-struck the balance, pressing her against the wall, both hands flat against it either side of her head. And as he kissed her back with perfect pressure, took control, his tongue overpowering hers, she *did* forget her intention.

But from the way she instantly sparked, from the heat pooling between her legs, she couldn't risk lingering any longer than she needed to.

Mid kiss, she bit, puncturing his lower lip.

Jask winced, his fingers instantly meeting his bloodied flesh as he recoiled, allowing her to slip past him.

She backed up towards the open cage door as he spun to face her, his shocked gaze meeting hers.

But regret and guilt were the last emotions she needed to feel, despite them consuming her.

She spat his blood from her mouth. '*I'm* not that desperate either,' she said, before turning away towards the open door.

She needed to stop shaking. She needed out of there.

But she'd barely pivoted 180 degrees before he caught hold of her upper arm.

She looked back at him as he too spat the blood from his mouth. Only there was something deeply feral about the way he did it – almost as feral as the look in his eyes.

Her stomach flipped.

He didn't need to say anything. The grip he had on her arm told her all she needed to know. There was making a mistake and then there were almighty Phia-style fuck-ups. And this was most definitely the latter.

Yet as he glared at her, all she could ask herself over and over again was why she didn't feel the slightest bit afraid.

Damn it if he didn't press every single one of her lethal little buttons.

Her arousal surged as he licked the inside of his wounded bottom lip, his gaze unflinching. But no more so than when he tutted in a way that was entrancingly sexy, not helped by his eyes betraying something behind the anger.

'Apologise,' he said softly.

'I'm sorry I didn't bite harder.'

He exhaled off the back of a fleeting smile that should have chilled her to her core. But as Jask backed her up against the bars, all she could feel was the heat accumulating at the pit of her abdomen again, let alone between her legs.

As her back met metal, he clutched the bars either side of her shoulders, trapping her. 'Apologise,' he said again, his tone lower.

Her pulse throbbed in her ears, but she didn't dare take her eyes off him. She lifted her lips to his. 'I'm *not* going to apologise and I'm sure as hell *not* going to beg for mercy. So do something about it or walk away.'

'You've flipped the lid on that self-destruct button so many times that you can't even close it anymore, can you?'

'You think you've got me worked out? Well, ditto. Twice you've walked away from me, Jask. You're all talk, all threats, but when it comes down to it, you can't come up with the goods.'

He leaned an inch closer. 'And what goods would they be?'

'We both know what I'm talking about. What is it, Jask? Can you only do it with lycans? Are they easier to please? Are you scared of me? Or is it being unleashed that scares you? Only I know the responsibility of this pack weighs heavy on you. I know it controls you. I know you're itching to break free.'

'Because you'd know all about responsibility, wouldn't you, serryn?'

'That's just it, isn't it, Jask? The real reason I get to you so much is because you envy me. I remind you of what you could be. What you used to be. A time before the regulations when you used to be able to run wild – have what you wanted, when you wanted. Only now you make everyone toe the line because it makes it easier for you to do the same, doesn't it? Because your rules aren't just about keeping your pack safe; they're as much about keeping *yourself* contained. You despise me because there's a need in you and I remind you of it. I irritate you because I take you places you don't want to go. I make you feel things you don't want to feel. It's not *me* who has self-hatred issues – it's you. So tell me, what are *you* hiding from, Jask?'

The flare in his eyes before they narrowed again, the fierce dilation of his pupils, told her she wasn't wrong.

He grabbed her wrists, pushed her hands above her head, forcing her to arch her back, and drew her closer to him, his sweatpants soft against her thighs 'Maybe you read situations better than I give you credit for after all.'

She tried to curb her shallow breaths, arousal making her stomach hurt as he held her there, staring deep into her eyes in the silence.

'But *don't* try and compare us, serryn,' he warned. 'Serryns don't feel. You switch your emotions off like a light. It's what helps you do the things you do. Perform the acts you do. The dirty, nasty, sordid little acts that define just how toxic you are.'

She couldn't deny that he was right – switching off was exactly what serryns were renowned for. And maybe that was what was happening now – maybe that was why she dared to goad him. But he was wrong that her kind couldn't feel, because she was most definitely feeling something. Something every bit as dark, dangerous and unpleasant to acknowledge as the room they were in. Something that was real. Just as Jask was real. Just as the situation was real. A situation that she knew was spiralling out of control.

But she didn't care.

Only she did care that the connection she felt in that moment was one that she should never have been feeling with a third species. She couldn't *allow* herself to feel it. But she couldn't stop it any more than she could stand on the track and stop a speeding train.

Something about him was too right. In that dark, dank cell, nothing else mattered. She refused to think about what she was doing. She refused to look beyond the haze that encompassed her.

She'd fallen from that branch again, only now the dark depths were captivating.

'So what are you going to do about it, Jask?' she asked softly, caressing his lips with her uncontrollably terse breaths. 'Are you having dirty, nasty, sordid little thoughts of your own? Only I've seen you with Tuly and Solstice. You're not the type to act on them.'

'Not with my pack, no. But as you keep reminding me, you're *not* one of my pack, are you, Phia?'

She broke from his gaze only to linger on the brown leather straps that held the pendant to his neck. A pendant that had glinted in the white light and captured her attention.

She looked back into his eyes. But to her shock, to her disappointment, he pulled away *again*.

Didn't just pull away, but exited the cell.

She felt a whole new panic. A panic evoked by a sense of loss, an excruciating sense of frustration that knotted her stomach.

She pulled herself away from the bars and turned to face the cell door, trying to work out how the hell she could summon him back without laying herself on a platter.

Because she couldn't let him walk away. Not this time.

But Jask didn't leave the room. Instead he stood there, his back to her.

Her heart pounded as she waited for him to turn around again. As she waited for him to say something – something that would give her a clue as to what to do next as they both remained shrouded in silence.

Chapter Eleven

Jask stared out of the open door – the door that led to the corridor and beyond. The door that he *needed* to walk through. The door that would lead him away from her.

More significantly, the door that would lead him away from himself – from what was resurfacing.

She'd been lucky he'd caught her looking at his pendant. The pendant that was an intentional stark reminder of what happened when he cut himself loose and thought only of the desire inside.

Because in those moments he'd wanted Phia. As she'd stared him in the eyes and fearlessly challenged him for one final time too many that night, he'd wanted to finally confront her as himself – not the sensible pack leader.

Corbin had been right. This wasn't to get personal. But damn it that it already felt that way. And licking the already healing wound on his lip only reminded him of the last time someone had left him with the metallic taste of his own blood.

He hadn't even hesitated in what he'd done to them – their broken, torn body almost unrecognisable as human by the time he'd finished, by the time Corbin had found him, inebriated, angry and unfocused, as he had so many times over those months.

That same heat now flowed through his veins again. A heat that reminded him just how liberating doing the wrong thing could be.

And there in that cocoon, for just a little while, he could unleash himself again. He could remind himself how it felt – like filling his lungs with fresh air, or a primitive yell in an empty valley.

But Phia was the last one he should have been considering it with – not just for the sake of his pack, but for the sake of himself. The way she made him spark, something he had felt too infrequently not to recognise, only increased the risk of him taking it one step too far – and he knew what that could mean for them all if it went wrong.

And that's what made crossing the threshold the right thing to do.

But for too long he'd taken the option of the right thing to do.

And the fact it *was* such a risk only incited him more. Her ragged breaths and fast-beating heart echoing in his attuned ears were already too much temptation.

He didn't have to walk away as long as he could remember who he was now. He could prove to them both that he didn't have to walk away to control himself. It was a gamble, but he'd just have to make sure that *she* backed down, not him.

It was why he'd taken her down there after all – to test her metal under pressure. To see if she really was as inexperienced at handling herself as he thought. Time was rapidly slipping away and Phia needed to accept that she was vulnerable before he could even begin to tame her. And this was the perfect place and opportunity for both.

He closed and bolted the door, slid the viewing window shut, creating a private, dark little space that would echo the one now throbbing back to life inside of him.

He walked back towards her, closed the cage door behind him and looked his prey square in the eyes.

For the first time, she took a step back.

It should have been enough. He should have walked away, having gained the upper hand that easily.

But as his tingling lip reminded him, she hadn't let *him* off that kindly.

'Backing off already?' he asked, his tone laced with taunting as he continued to close in on her.

'You'll back down before I do.'

Despite her wariness, she still had the gall to fight.

He smiled fleetingly. 'Okay, so I was wrong – you *don't* read situations as well as I've given you credit for.'

'So what's this? Your idea of foreplay?'

'Nowhere near.' He closed the gap between them, heard her pulse pick up a notch despite her efforts to the contrary. He strolled around the back of her, wondering how long she'd be able to handle it before turning to face him. 'Question is, are you going to beg me to leave?' He raked her hair back from her neck to purposefully caress her ear with his breath. 'Or invite me to stay?'

Her breaths were more ragged, his proximity behind her clearly having had the effect he had hoped for.

But she didn't turn around. She didn't even step away. 'Are you looking for a get-out clause, Jask?'

He lowered himself a little to place his palms flat against her cool, firm thighs just below the hem of her tunic. A sensual and intimate move he had not yet allowed himself.

And it felt dangerously good.

As he slid the fabric upwards, he could feel her subtle tremor, the goosebumps now swamping her skin nothing to do with the chill of the room. Stood fully again, he lifted the tunic up over her behind so her exposed flesh met the brushed cotton of his sweatpants. Wrapping an arm around her waist, he gripped one wrist to trap her against him, against his arousal, while he slid the back of his free hand down her cleavage.

'No,' he said against her ear again. 'I'm offering you a final opportunity at *yours.*'

Instead of laughing, retorting with abuse or finding an excuse to break away, she slid *her* free hand into the limited space between him and the small of her back. Easing her hips forward just the fraction that his restraint would allow, she weaved that same hand into his sweatpants and into his shorts.

His erection jerked as soon as she made contact, as soon as she dared to coil her chilled fingers around his heat.

He involuntarily caught his breath, but so did she.

'Call my bluff, Jask,' she said as she dared to squeeze, 'and I'll call yours right back.'

He loosened his hold just enough to allow her to turn around to face him, but she didn't withdraw her hand. As he kept her hand at the small of her back, she smoothed the palm of the one that still held him lightly over the tip of his erection. Spreading his wetness with an easy glide down his full length, she stopped only to grip him at the base. She even dared to press closer, her lips almost touching his.

'Is this *your* idea of foreplay?' he asked, searching deep into her dark eyes.

'I dare you to let me go down on you,' she said, her gaze unflinching.

His heart jolted, as did his erection within the confinement of her skilled hand. The sensation it evoked was raw, summoning the feral instincts that he needed so desperately to keep contained.

'*Daring?*' he asked.

She smiled – a taunting, provocative, sexy smile. 'I bite, remember?' She lifted her lips a fraction closer. 'When you least expect it.'

This was how vampires fell – the look, the smile, the coax. But he was no vampire – something she needed reminding of. Something he needed to remind himself of.

He slid his free hand up her neck, curled his fingers into her hair, and got enough of a grip to make her catch her breath again. 'You're not going to bite,' he said, his breath mingling with hers.

Her eyes flared slightly. 'What makes you so sure?'

He released her hand at the small of her back only to tighten his arm around her. He lifted her as if she were weightless, slammed her against the bars behind, his hand in her hair protecting the back of her head from the force.

Trapping her there with the pressure and angle of his groin, her thighs forced around his waist, he pushed her hands either side of her head, encircling her wrists and most of the bars they were held against with the span of his hands. And to remind her of her vulnerability, he tilted his hips a little, just enough so that his hardness pressed tauntingly against the most sensitive part of her sex – just enough to show her he knew *exactly* what he was doing.

'Because *I* bite back,' he said, his lips inches from hers again. 'Only harder and deeper. And if there's anything that's going to bring out the feral in me, it's that first taste of blood.'

Her breathing hitched, her eyes flaring slightly again. But then those enticing eyes became hooded. There was no retaliation. No fight.

Instead, she crossed her legs around his back, coiled her toes into the waistband of his sweatpants and slid them down a few inches along with his shorts, her smooth heels gliding over the curve of his solid behind, not breaking from his gaze for even a second.

Damn it, she was good. And the first inkling that he had underestimated her started to unfurl.

The feel of his freed erection against her, even though her thin tunic was still a barrier to skin on skin, sent a bolt of static through him. Even more evocative was that she was already damp. Her mouth was parted in anticipation. Her heart was pounding against her chest.

She wasn't scared, she was aroused.

And that was the *last* thing he needed.

'Come on, Jask,' she said softly. 'What are you waiting for? This isn't a guided tour. We both know the real reason you brought me down here.'

It had been as much an attempt to give her some insight into their cause as to see just how fearless and proficient a serryn she really was.

Only now she was demonstrating that she was both of the latter – which only reinforced his reason to stay in control. Because now he really couldn't afford to lose her. Now he *had* to pull back, not least because the way he was burning inside had nothing to do with her purpose for his pack.

'And what reason is that?' he asked.

'I think you like me being defiant,' she whispered. 'It turns you on, doesn't it? That's one sordid little secret you can't hide.'

And it did turn him on – the way she dared to stand up to him, to challenge him, to provoke him in a way so few ever dared. 'You're like a wind-up toy. I'm just curious to know how far I can twist before you snap.'

'Because *you're* already snapping, aren't you? The fact I'm pinned to this cage tells me that. But I'm not scared to see you for what you are, Jask. Go on,' she goaded, resting her head back against the bars to look him direct in the eyes. 'Hurt me.'

But those two words were too telling. Two words that could so easily be fulfilled had they not been contradicted by the look deep in her eyes. 'Is that what sex is to you, Phia – pain? Or do you want me to make it that way so it drowns the real feelings out?'

She frowned, but he didn't give her time to retort before he pulled her from the bars. He slammed her down onto the mattress, pinning her onto her back with effortless and efficient ease before resting on all fours above her.

It felt good to have her beneath him. And it felt good to look her in the eyes as he did so. Too good.

Keeping a grip on her wrists, he lowered himself so his lips nearly touched hers again. 'You picked the wrong one for the job, Phia.'

Because that *wasn't* who he was now. Not now his pack came first. From then on, his pack would always come first.

The pack that had, during his road to self-destruction, remained loyal against the odds. The pack that had tolerated his mood swings and outbursts. That had still respected him despite him disappearing days at a time. They'd tolerated his negligence, his lack of focus, his sullenness. And they accepted him again without question when he'd finally broken through the darkness enough to resume his full duties. Duties that Corbin had loyally assumed, before handing them back to him without challenge.

Phia had asked if he'd ever questioned whether the right alpha had been chosen. During those times he had severely doubted it. Now he'd finally prove himself wrong – and she was the test. Because she was the only one, in all those decades since, who had made him doubt himself again.

'Because I don't play that way,' he added, nearly tagging on *anymore*, before wisely pulling away instead.

He yanked his shorts and sweatpants back into position. And, as tough as it was, he turned his back on her, his frustration and unsated need berating his decision.

✳ ✳ ✳

Sophia lay there breathless, her hands lax either side of her head. But as he opened the cage door, she forced herself up onto her elbows. 'Wait!'

It was the last thing she should have said, but it came from somewhere deep, somewhere raw, somewhere uncomfortably honest.

Jask didn't turn around, but he did stop. He coiled his hands around the bars either side of the cage doorway, creating tension in every finely honed muscle of his back, shoulders and arms.

Never had someone turning their back on her filled her with such a sense of emptiness. Never before had she made the first move to stop it happening.

But never had she wanted someone so badly that she was willing to swallow her own pride.

'Then don't play,' she said, surprised how much she meant it. 'And neither will I.'

He turned to face her, his expression indefinable.

After a few seconds of contemplation, he stepped back towards her, back to the foot of the mattress, and gazed down at her.

She lay her head back down, her hands either side of her head again. Despite having never felt more exposed than if she'd lay there naked, she looked him direct in the eyes. It was a dangerously submissive pose, but one she could only hope would snag him.

'All you know is game-playing,' he said.

'You didn't have to bring me down here.' She knew it was risky – pushing things whilst he still looked contemplative. But she lifted her foot regardless, sliding it slowly up his firm, muscular thigh. As she reached his groin, pressed slightly against his hardness, she expected him to flinch. But he didn't.

Hours before, she would have taken the opportunity to draw back her leg and slam her foot hard into him just because she could – just because it would be another impulsive move that would make her feel okay for that split second.

But now, looking up into those eyes, at the perfection that stood above her, she knew this wasn't about pride – this was about self-worth. Because, for the first time in as long as she could remember, she believed she deserved not to have him walk away from her. At that moment, she wanted nothing more than him – and she was going to get him. She was going to get Jask Tao exactly where she wanted him.

Just as she knew she needed to sate whatever dark craving she was developing for him. She needed to get back on task, and her head was always clearer after sex. And if there was one thing she needed to pull her plan off, it was clarity – not the chaos she was feeling then.

'It's just you and me now,' she said. 'No one need ever know.'

But as she applied a taunting amount of pressure to his erection, Jask caught hold of her ankle. He eased it aside but, to her relief, he didn't let go. Instead he lowered to his knees. He slid his hand up the back of her calf with the motion, behind her knee, to grasp the back of her thigh as he leaned over her, his free hand pressing into the mattress beside her shoulder.

'You're a tease,' he said, his tone laced with something enticingly calm despite the look in his eyes.

'If you didn't want this too, you would have kept walking,' she said, trying to keep her breathing steady as his hand moved up her outer thigh up to her hip, pushing her tunic up with the motion.

'I'm not disputing that,' he said, before easing back on his haunches. He equally clutched her other hipbone with his now free hand in a lethally possessive move. And as he gazed down between her legs, at her exposure in the shadows, his unashamed blatancy made her stomach clench. She swallowed harder than she wanted to, the tension building in the pit of her abdomen. But she felt no temptation to recoil or cover herself despite her toes instinctively curling into the mattress.

Sliding his hand up her cleavage to clasp her throat, he leaned over her again. But there was no pressure in his hold, just a move that allowed him to glide his thumb over her lips before tucking it into the breathless parting.

'Go on then,' he said, looking deep into her eyes. 'Bite now. I dare *you*.'

The challenge sent her heart racing, but as he slowly unbuttoned her tunic at her cleavage she lay mesmerised and unflinching.

He watched every button he released reveal a little more of her flesh until he finally pushed both folds of fabric aside, exposing her fully to him.

She was lost. As his hand encompassed her breast, his thumb gliding over her already hardened nipple, she clenched her hands. And as he cupped the side of her jaw with his other hand, pressed his thumb a little deeper between her lips, as he lowered his head to take her held breast hungrily in his mouth, she let out an uncontrolled groan she never thought possible.

Her raw response clearly not having gone unnoticed, he left her breast damp and cool as he rested that arm back on the mattress. He removed his thumb from between her parted lips only for his to hover less than an inch away again. But he didn't kiss her – he kept that mouth a cruel, taunting distance away.

Instead, his azure eyes didn't flinch from hers as his free hand disappeared below their waists.

Sophia flinched as his fingers met her sex.

And as he instantly applied painstaking pressure to her tender clitoris, she gasped, jolted, her head fuzzy.

'Fuck,' she hissed, almost silently.

'That's the idea, isn't it?' he whispered. And without taking the pressure off her clit, eased a finger inside her.

She flinched again. But despite her involuntarily tensing, Jask went anything but easy, pushing deep into her in one slow but unrelenting move.

She had no idea what he was doing once he was inside her, but it evoked goosebumps all over her body, made her eyes water, her body shudder. And all the time, he kept staring deep into her eyes, his thumb simultaneously working her clit to the point she could barely breathe.

For a split second she thought she was going to have to ask him to stop, to break the intensity just for a moment. But as a dark glint appeared in his eyes, accompanied by him sliding a second finger inside her, she gritted her teeth and clenched her fists for fear of coming too soon.

❊ ❊ ❊

He *had* to stay in control.

As much as he wanted to spread her thighs further and feel the most sensitive part of him sink into her wet heat, that was one step too far across his self-imposed line.

This was about taunting and toying with her. It was about showing her how easily he could control her climax with every subtle and manipulative movement of his fingers, knowing when to apply pressure and when to withdraw, where to touch and how. She needed to know that experience had taught him *more* than enough, despite her previous coaxing. Just as instincts told him how to read what she liked and what she didn't – just how far to push and when to stop.

And Phia gave everything away so easily in each small, hitched little breath, the opening and closing of her eyes, how far she parted her lips, how much she arched her back, how deep she was willing and able to take him.

Because from the way she was responding, sex with him wasn't just about power and control as was indicative of serryns. Phia was emotionally engaged with what he was doing to her.

The serryn who arrogantly thought she could handle him. The serryn who he needed to get inside the head of to be able to tame, to persuade her to do what he needed in order to save his pack, was giving him just that. The serryn he now knew *so* much more about. And he needed to keep his focus on turning that to his advantage.

But pushing two fingers deep inside her tight, restrictive warmth set his own arousal dangerously close to the edge.

He pulled back onto his haunches again to try to ease his tension, only for Phia to lethally arch her back even further, emphasising her concave stomach.

It was a reminder that a serryn body was for two purposes only – pleasure and killing. And despite the poison that coursed through her veins, it was no danger to him. Just as he could spill inside her a hundred times to no effect but to sate his own need. And right then that was *exactly* what he'd wanted.

And he wanted to look her in the eyes as he did it – something he hadn't afforded himself in as long as he could remember.

Dare to forge that connection as he came inside her.

And it was getting harder to deny that she looked more beautiful than ever, masked partially in shadow, partially in light, arousal emanating from her glossy dark eyes, her pretty lips full and swollen. With her arched body, her arms having fallen limp beside her head, her slender, shapely thighs parted wide for him, she was more than bewitching – she was perfect.

And the sheen her arousal had created against her inner thighs, the wetness that masked his fingers, told him just how much *she* was losing herself in the moment.

He should have walked away at that point. He should have brought her to climax and left her there on the mattress – sated his own need alone somewhere else in an uncomplicated, self-satisfying act.

But he wanted *her*.

And as he firmly massaged her swollen breasts, rubbing his thumb across her hardened nipples, as she groaned in response again, it was his turn to swallow harder than he should.

This time her raw response made him teeter. Now the female who lay so openly beneath him was far more than a commodity.

He wanted to pick up the pace. Needed to pick up the pace.

In frustration, he plunged his two fingers as deep inside her as he could go.

He thought it would be the breaking point – that she'd finally fend him off. But she only arched her back more and cried out, her eyes tightly closed, her frown deep, a little flushed, lost, and never more stunning.

Her defences were truly down. In that moment, she was his. And there was no way he was walking away from that.

He looked back down between her legs, to where he fucked her exquisitely with his fingers and knew it was nowhere near enough for him anymore. He needed to be inside her. He needed to part those thighs as far as he could and compel her to take every inch of him.

He looked back at her to see she was looking at him again, gazing up at him with her molten brown eyes in a moment of complete understanding.

It was his last chance to walk away.

But he should have known he was a fool to think she was that tamed. A fool to think he'd broken her yet.

'That the best you've got?' she whispered, those full, wanton lips again curled in that defiant smirk, arousal seeping through a breathlessness that was unable to mask her intoxicating impatience.

To coax him further, she dared to further part the smooth, slender thighs either side of his hips, reminding him of the willing body that lay vulnerable beneath him.

Skilfully, slowly removing his fingers, he leaned over her again. Resting both hands either side of her head, he looked deep into the eyes that burrowed back into his, silence enclosing the room.

'Far from it,' he said. 'But *I'm* in charge here – *not* you.'

❈ ❈ ❈

It was a statement that made her stomach jolt – that and the look in his eyes.

His trail of slow, hard kisses down the length of her neck, the scuff of his stubble against her tender flesh, the coaxing rake of his slightly extended canines, had her clutching the mattress either side of her hips. And as he took her breast in his hand again only to squeeze, to suck harder than he had last time, the detectable lengthening in the talons that dug into her only reminded her of exactly *what* she was goading.

She'd almost forgotten what he was, seeing no difference in their species in the minutes that had passed.

But she knew no male of her own species matched up to him. No male ever made her spark with such a painful burning that he could have plunged those canines or purposefully extended talons into her flesh and she wouldn't have even cared.

Because those eyes that looked back into hers again *were* feral, but intoxicatingly laced with something so much more. Something that created a sense of assurance in her even as he gripped the top of her open tunic double-handed, yanking the fabric halfway down her arms. She couldn't take her eyes off him as he cupped her neck with both hands before sliding them firmly down over her breasts to her waist.

Just watching his admiration created a sense of liberation, a paradox to the makeshift restraint he had created with her tunic.

Because he *was* admiring her.

And it was the only thing that stopped her recoiling in on herself as he pressed his palms against the inside of her thighs, pushed her legs that inch further, gazing down at her with even more blatancy than last time – more than any of her other lovers had dared.

But Jask had no such qualms.

Her arousal escalated to lethal levels. The frustration of the throb between her legs left her not caring what she said or what she did.

She'd be right in what she'd said to him: No one would ever know. Whatever happened, this was between them. And it would stay between them. He wasn't going to live long enough to share it.

But this time, the very thought of killing him created a pang. The very thought of being the one capable of bringing an end to

Jask Tao. Because lying there, beneath him, she wondered how the hell she could do it.

One thing she knew for sure – there was no way she was going to be able to look him in those eyes when she did.

Even less so when he backed up, only to lower his head between her parted thighs, his mouth against her sex making her cry out again.

As he kept her thighs apart with his shoulders, there was nothing coaxing in the way he went down on her, nothing coaxing in the hand that slid up to gently grasp her throat again. His tasting of her was hungry, the workings of his tongue as he licked her and delved inside her ravenous like she'd never experienced.

She reached for something to grab but met nothing but the mattress before slamming her hands down onto his broad, strong shoulders. She dug her nails deep into his firm flesh before fisting his hair in her hand as his tongue found her clit, his mouth working her relentlessly.

It was finally one step too far – more than she could take.

As a warm tear trickled down her cheek, she felt herself peak, her climax flooding her.

Shuddering, she expected him to pull back from her release, but he didn't. His hand only slid from her throat to take hold of her breast again as his mouth still worked her sex, his tongue remaining deep inside her as she came, as he forced her to orgasm again and again until she had nothing left to give.

Body aching, extremities tingling, she'd never trembled so much during climax. Had never felt so detached from her own body.

But even that didn't seem to be enough for him.

He leaned over her again as he stayed between her thighs, slid her tunic back into place on her shoulders so he could pin both hands above her head. 'You will look at me the whole time I'm inside you,' he said. 'And you will not look away until I'm done.'

Her heart pounded. Her skin prickled.

As he pushed into her, everything in that moment stopped. Everything became a haze. Nothing felt real.

His thrust was exquisite. Steady but forceful, breaking inside her in one complete move, his breath held as tightly as hers.

She tightened her fists, her nails digging painfully into her palms, but she wouldn't look away from him even as she cried out.

Didn't dare look away from him.

Didn't *want* to look away from him.

Looking back into those eyes as he thrust again, filled her completely, revealed far too much to her. The stirring she felt inside was not one she could afford to feel. She couldn't afford to feel anything – not for him. Not there, not then.

Because it was terrifying. Her own feelings were more terrifying than the authoritative lycan who held her down and pushed satisfyingly deep into her.

She reminded herself she could handle the rules – she'd lived by them long enough. She didn't get attached. She never got attached.

More than ever she had to get used to it – now that she was a serryn, it was all her life would ever be. One encounter after another. They'd bite. They'd die. She'd move on. She had to harden herself to it.

It was just sex. Good sex. Incredible, satisfying sex. And she needed to take it for what it was. She just needed to savour the moment – some lust-filled, power-driven act on both their parts.

But something told her it was more for him too. Something that made it all too dangerously intense.

His thrusts were deep, hard and unrelenting as he consumed into her with an impatience that matched her own. And as his pace increased, it almost felt like he was punishing her.

Or punishing himself.

She lost sight too quickly of which. Either way, she didn't care. Rough, unremitting, incessant though he was, she lost sight of the discomfort amidst her own arousal. Even as he held her wrists tighter, used his free hand to hold down her hip as he dug his nails deep into her flesh, prevented her from moving even a fraction of an inch, she only wanted more.

His final thrusts were powerful. And with his eyes unflinching on hers, he came.

It had never offset a climax of her own before, but the very fact he came so hard, so fast, so powerful as he growled under his breath, had triggered her whole body to jolt with the onset of yet another climax. A climax that lasted and lasted as he purposefully prolonged the agony, the ecstasy, by staying deep inside her.

And as he spilled, as his gaze remained embedded deeply with hers, she had never felt so exposed. She had never felt like anyone had ever understood her.

Until then.

Chapter Twelve

Jask eased off the mattress and pulled up his sweatpants and shorts.

Sophia was finding it harder to get to her feet, so he caught her upper arm to help her up before she had time to protest. She stumbled a little but managed to get off the mattress without losing her balance.

'You okay?' he asked.

'Course,' she said, shrugging him off emotionally and physically.

But he knew she was anything but okay from the way she could barely make eye contact before exiting the cell and crossing to the door.

He knew he'd hurt her, but at the time he hadn't cared. He could have broken her in two for all it mattered when his climax consumed him.

Because he knew, as he thrust deep into her, that he'd let himself down.

It was the first time he'd looked a female in the eyes during the act since Ellen. All the others he'd kept turned away, or had buried in their neck or stared at the ceiling or the wall – anywhere but at them. Anything to stop that final engagement in what he was doing. Anything to ease the guilt and sense of betrayal he would always feel whenever he shared an act so dangerously binding.

He reached to his throat to clutch the small pendant between his thumb and forefinger.

He'd meant to withdraw. At the crucial moment, he'd meant to withdraw. He always withdrew, letting the toxicity inside him spill to the floor.

Now discomfort clenched his chest when he realised how weak he had been. Not just that, but how easily he'd managed to push aside thoughts of his dead mate for the first time.

He hadn't thought of Ellen at all in the latter moments. Hadn't seen her face and imagined being with her. All he could see was Phia. As she'd lay beneath him he'd thought only of exciting her, thrilling her, exploring her, of bringing her to climax to reveal the real her – for reasons he now knew were more terrifyingly personal than his mission.

She hadn't just lost *her*self in the moment; he'd unforgivably lost *him*self. Intentionally or not, in less than an hour, whatever was going on between them had turned into something else. Something that now knotted the back of his throat and made swallowing hard.

She'd got him right where she wanted him. If he'd been a vampire, he *would* have been dead.

He raked his hand back through his hair as she silently disappeared out into the corridor.

He tongued the inside of his lip again where she had bitten him.

Bitten him in more ways than one.

But her response hadn't been calculated. She was just as much in shock.

He thought about catching up with her but he realised he had nothing to say. Or more likely too much to say without a clue where to start.

He had to cut it dead there and then. However she was feeling was not his concern. His only concern was getting her where he needed her and doing what he wanted.

But as he headed out into the corridor to find she had gone, she left only a dark void behind. It was a feeling he'd promised he'd never let himself relive.

And he had no right reliving it through her.

He rested his hands on his hips and hesitated for a moment before taking the steps up into the second corridor. Something in him hoped she'd be there waiting. Even another spat, her glaring indignation and defensiveness, would be better than the silence that had consumed the space between them before she'd left.

But she wasn't there.

He marched past the storage rooms, back up the steps into the lobby. But instead of heading outside, he turned right into the holding room.

He kicked a chair across the room, kicked another before slamming his clenched hands down onto the table, his head lowered. The knot at the pit of his stomach was a heavy weight, rooting him to the spot.

He'd gone too far. And now the guilt coagulating in his veins made his heart ache.

He'd been irresponsible, selfish, self-sating. He'd broken every self-inflicted rule.

And he hadn't punished her for making him feel the way he did – he'd punished himself.

He spun around and punched the wall, grazed his knuckles, grasped the back of his head with tightly interlinked fingers as he paced the room.

He turned back around to see Corbin stood silently in the doorway. His friend's lowered brow, the concern in his eyes, negated the need for him to say he understood.

'I just passed her out on the quadrant,' Corbin remarked.

Jask's scent on her would still have been potent.

'Then you've seen she's still in one piece,' Jask replied, with a hint of defensiveness he knew betrayed too much.

Corbin stepped inside the room and closed the door behind him. He leaned back against it and folded his arms. 'Did it serve a purpose?'

'Only to confirm what her tears had told us: she's an inexperienced serryn.'

'But is she experienced enough for what we need?'

'I don't know.' He leaned against the wall opposite Corbin, his head resting back against it, his injured knuckles throbbing at the small of his back.

'So you've learned nothing new?'

Jask held his friend's gaze, as difficult as it was, amidst the silent enclosure of the room. 'You don't need to spell it out to me, Corbin.'

'I'm not, Jask. Seems to me by the smell of blood in this room that you're spelling it out to yourself.'

'Are you questioning my judgement?'

'You bet I am. That's what friends do, right? That's what your beta's responsibility is to do. And I take my responsibilities very seriously.'

'And I don't?'

'You know that's not what I'm saying. What I'm saying is that looking at you, you know you've overstepped the mark. And if you know that, then that means you have. What happened?'

Jask snapped his gaze away.

Corbin pulled from the door to take a couple of steps closer. 'Jask?' Separated by silence, he took another step closer. 'Talk to me.'

But shame prevented him. Shame in admitting to his friend, to his beta, that he'd almost lost control. That he'd thought only of his selfish needs in those moments. That he'd abandoned his pack again, shunted them aside to indulge himself with the last female he should have even been considering breaking his vow with.

'You've held it together for so long, Jask,' Corbin said. 'She sparks something inside of you. I get that. I've seen it. But the Jask we need has learned to walk away. If you need satiation, there are plenty in this compound who will willingly do that – who would see it as an honour, a privilege. You don't need her, you don't need–'

'I didn't need her; I wanted her,' he said, looking back at Corbin.

Corbin's eyes flared. 'You *thought* you wanted her. And now it's out of your system, right?' He exhaled tersely when met again with

Jask's silence. 'Of course it isn't – because we both know you too well, don't we?'

'I wanted her like I haven't wanted anyone in a long time.'

'Since Ellen.'

The mention of her name, especially slipping from his best friend's lips who had loved and respected her as much as Jask had – even if in a very different way. The sense of betrayal only escalated, forcing Jask away from the wall again, away from the truth.

'There may be similarities – even I can see that. The way she stands up to you. Her passion. Her stubbornness. But she's no Ellen, Jask,' Corbin said quietly. 'She will never even come close.'

'And what good has searching for another Ellen done me?' Jask said, spinning to face him, anger, resentment and tears knotting his throat from the truth seeping out of his trusted friend's lips to utter what he already knew.

Corbin frowned. 'Jask…'

'So I can have any female I want out there. So what? Have I not had my fill already? Does it sate the emptiness? No. Maybe for the few moments my instincts take over, when each time I think I'll come out of it cured of her, but all it does is carve another piece out of me. Because I feel nothing at the end of it, Corbin. With them or with any other female out there. And then comes Phia – and I feel anger and frustration and irritation and desire – and all of those, as detrimental as they are, are intoxicating against the nothingness I have lived with for decades. This pack might need me, Corbin, they might need me the sensible, resolute, level-minded leader, but I'm still *me* inside. And, with her, I had a short time of remembering what that was like.'

Jask pulled out a chair and sat at the table, his head in his hands for a moment.

He heard Corbin pull out the chair adjacent to his, but he said nothing.

'I looked her in the eyes, Corbin. When I was inside her, I looked her in the eyes.' He glanced across at his friend. 'I stayed looking in her eyes even as I came. And I did it because it felt right and it felt natural. And I felt connected again. For those moments, I didn't feel lonely anymore. And now I feel sick to my stomach because I know I have to rip that feeling away again or risk letting this pack down again. So just let me have my short time of self-indulgence before I do what I have to do. Because I will, Corbin. I *will* come good for this pack. So don't you dare look at me like you doubt it.'

'You're this pack's alpha,' Corbin said. 'You're alpha by proof and by choice. I never doubt you. Even those months when you were abseiling down into the darkness on threadbare rope, I still had a grip on it because I knew you'd come back. We all did. Because that darkness was never going to be stronger than you. It was never going to consume you completely. And the fact you came out of it only proves more why you deserve to lead this pack. Why every single lycan in this compound, despite seeing you at your worst, at your lowest, would never even have considered electing me over you. And that's the difference between us – that's why you deserve this position. Do you remember what I told you when you were at your lowest – that night I had no choice but to lock you in that cell until you calmed down – drunk, bruised, blood on your hands? I meant it. I would *never* have come back from what you did if I'd lost Solstice. It would have finished me. But you're still here because you're stronger than me. Than all of us. And you will come good for this pack. I know it. Then this will all be over.'

Jask held Corbin's gaze – the loyalty, the belief gazing back at him through steadfast grey eyes convincing him he meant every word. 'I'm upping the ante,' he said. 'Tonight.'

Corbin nodded. He reached out to rest his hand on Jask's shoulder and squeezed.

❄ ❄ ❄

Sophia wrapped her arms around herself and made her way across the quadrant to the main building.

The grass was damp and cold beneath her feet, the breeze chilling the perspiration that still coated her skin, her body trembling as she fought to block out what had happened.

The distant low thuds of the clubs, now revived in Blackthorn's hub with the pending darkness, brought her back to reality. One of those clubs belonged to the Dehain brothers. The very brothers who should have been dead now had The Alliance's plan not gone wrong. The club where her little sister could still be.

Damn Marid for pulling her off task that night of going to confront Caleb for herself. Damn him for selling her on. Damn them all that she'd ended up in the compound with Jask. Tempting, obstinate, delicious, pain-in-the-arse-perfect Jask Tao who had now proven himself to be as proficient in bed as he was with everything else.

Her scowl deepened.

Never would she let anyone that close, she'd promised herself.

What had happened between them didn't matter, she kept repeating over and over in her head. But the ache low in her gut, the stab in her heart, told her she'd failed the only time detachment had ever really mattered.

She ran her fingers back through her hair as she added yet *another* thing to her list of reasons to hate herself.

The very first had been Tom. She'd known exactly what she was doing but she'd still had all the fragility of a sixteen-year-old taking a step too far. She'd fallen hard, fast and deep for him as they'd shared three weeks of summer together. She'd thought she was in love, but had been in those early stages when the lines were so easily blurred. A love he'd reciprocated by boasting she'd been nothing more than a training ground.

She'd hidden away, curled in on herself, until she'd walked past him one day in the canteen and overheard him claim it was time he had a go at her little sister, Alisha. He'd almost suffocated as she'd slammed him face-first into his spaghetti bolognaise; especially as it had taken three of his mates to eventually pull her off him.

Ricky had been next. It had ended with the word "mistake" being used. He'd added that she was too complicated. What he'd meant was too much like hard work for what he wanted in return. And she was too proud to allow herself to be anyone's inconvenience.

The other two relationships started as a drunken disaster and ended as a drunken disaster.

Then there was Daniel. After a night of barely escaping with their lives, survival instincts had kicked in. It had been a one-off that had soon become an un-discussed habit.

And recollections of Daniel reminded her exactly why she was there.

She had *no* excuse for taking her eye off the ball. For letting it cross her mind that killing Jask wasn't going to be as easy as she first thought – especially as one of those reasons was unforgiveable.

Worse was knowing that he wouldn't have looked twice at her if it wasn't for those pheromones, or whatever it was that seeped out of serryns making them irresistible. It was those chemicals and not her that had eventually incited him. Clearly they were potent enough to attract even lycans, whatever legends stated to the contrary, or there's no way Jask would have looked twice at her. And once he realised that, he'd despise her even more than he already did.

She took the main steps up into the lobby. Her persistent trembling, she was sure, wasn't just down to the adrenaline rush.

She stepped up to the buffet table, poured herself a glass of water, grabbed a peach, an apple and a handful of raspberries, and headed to the back of the room to take a seat.

She should have taken a shower first, but she wasn't ready to go back to his room. Aside from the more pressing hunger, the dehydration, a small part of her didn't want to rid herself of Jask's scent just yet.

She worked her way through the peach between generous gulps of water, casting her gaze to the darkness outside. The quadrant was as quiet as indoors, no doubt many of the lycans having headed into Blackthorn already.

She couldn't help but wonder if Jask would do the same. She knew he wasn't an every-night sight in Blackthorn, but he still ventured out of the compound regularly enough. Whether that was for business or pleasure was anyone's guess.

The thought of the latter made her stomach coil.

A pack leader without a mate was free to take pleasure as he chose. And from Jask's performance down in the cell, she knew she'd been naïve to mock him for inexperience – something he had clearly intended to prove to her. Because he had no other reason to take it as far as he did, aside from the pheromones, other than to prove himself stronger, more proficient, more experienced than her.

And he'd made his point – infallibly.

She sucked her peach stone dry and dropped it in her empty cup, popped a few raspberries before twisting the stalk on her apple. She took a bite just as she looked up to see a familiar pair of large grey eyes staring back at her from across the table.

Tuly was clutching a book to her chest, her small hand encompassing a collection of pencil crayons.

She smiled, flashing Sophia those canines again – the only thing that reminded her that the child staring back at her was far from human.

Tuly eased up onto the chair beside Sophia. Placing her belongings down, she opened the book up and flicked through some of the pages.

'Does Solstice know you're here?' Sophia asked, noticing for the first time that Tuly's nails were far too long for someone so young.

Tuly shrugged, already preoccupied with her book. 'You smell like Jask.'

Sophia felt herself flush, struggled for a response.

'Are you his new mate now?' Tuly asked, glancing across at her.

The very prospect filled her with an alien sense of warmth she had no right feeling. 'No. No, I'm not. You're not supposed to talk to me,' Sophia reminded her.

Tuly sent her a hint of a mischievous glance. 'Do you do everything your mother tells you?'

Sophia couldn't help but smile at the child's belligerence, despite never having had a mother long enough to be able to answer.

Tuly looked back at her again. 'You do have a mother, don't you?' She looked back down at her book. 'Or is it different with serryns?'

'Who told you I was a serryn?'

'I heard. I listen all the time.' Tuly turned another page and started to colour a half-finished picture. 'Do you?' she asked, looking back up at her. Only this time her gaze lingered as she awaited Sophia's response.

'Have a mother? Not anymore.'

'Is she dead?'

Sophia nodded.

Tuly frowned, her eyes emanating more empathy than Sophia would have thought capable of one of her kind, let alone for her age. But then Sophia never spent any time around kids of any species. 'How did she die?'

'She was killed by a vampire.'

Tuly continued to colour as if Sophia had announced the death had been from a traffic accident or illness. The fact it was a vampire attack seemed as commonplace as any other way to die.

'So are you on your own now?' Tuly asked.

A wave of unease flooded through her. The questions seemed innocent enough, as did the stumbling across her in the communal area. But there was still that little niggle that she could have been sent there – an irresistible undercover spy.

'Yes.' The statement wasn't completely untrue. She needed a diversion. She looked at the drawing of the male and female under the tree, the male pushing the child in the swing that hung from one of the branches. The sun was bright, a lake in the distance. The grass was littered with tiny pink and red flowers. 'What's this?'

'Where we're going to live,' Tuly announced matter-of-factly.

Sophia didn't have the heart not to play along. 'You're moving?'

'One day,' Tuly announced, a frown marking her brow from the sheer concentration of her colouring.

'Somewhere like this?' Sophia asked, placing her apple aside and resting her folded arms on the table as she indicated towards the drawing.

'Summerton,' Tuly declared.

A knot forged in her throat. 'Summerton?'

Tuly nodded before swapping her blue pencil crayon for a pink one. 'This is Corbin,' she said, tapping the male figure with the end of her pencil, 'and Solstice.' And then she tapped the girl on the swing. 'And this is me.' Tuly stopped to look up at her. 'You've heard of Summerton, haven't you?'

Sophia nodded again, trying to ignore the discomfort in her stomach.

Tuly turned her attention back to her picture. 'They have trees there – proper big ones with lots of leaves, and lakes, and hills, and flowers, all different colour flowers and bees that collect their honey from them and birds…' she reeled off the list like she was reciting her Christmas present list. 'And I'll put food out every day for them so they can eat and have lots of baby birds and I'll look after all of them.'

'You like birds?'

Tuly put down her pencil crayon to flick back through the pages. She opened a double-page spread with loads of images of birds cut out and glued from magazines. 'That's a blackbird,' she said, pointing to the central picture. 'A woodpecker. A pied wagtail. A starling. One day I'm going to see them all.'

Sophia's throat constricted, but she wouldn't let Tuly see the impact her innocent hope had had. 'Where did you get the pictures?'

'In the attic. Sometimes I find things in shops – when I'm allowed to go out.'

Like her, Tuly would have been born after the regulations. Unlike her, she would never have seen green fields or breathed fresh air. She'd known nothing outside a dense world ruled by fear and control, on filthy streets with the dregs of opportunities. And still she sat there, the optimism shining through her that one day it would be better.

Tuly went back to the page she had been colouring. 'There was a blackbird that lived here once. It used to sit on the top of the greenhouse. It used to sing at dusk and at dawn. I'd sneak bread out from the kitchen when no one was looking. Then, one day, I found it dead in the bushes. Nothing pretty ever lives long in Blackthorn.'

Sophia interlaced her fingers and held them against her mouth to fight back the threat of pending tears.

'Tuly!'

The little lycan looked up at the same time as Sophia did to see Jask stood in the dining room doorway.

Her heart leapt at seeing him again, then sank as he looked to have been midway in conversation with the female he was facing – a female he just as quickly resumed conversing with as if Sophia wasn't even there.

'Uh-oh,' Tuly said, closing her book and gathering up her pencils. 'Trouble,' she said, rolling her eyes. Eyes that looked far too playful and beyond her years not to make Sophia break a smile despite feeling like doing anything but.

It was a long shot but, just as Tuly eased down off the chair, Sophia had to ask. 'Did you know Ellen?'

Tuly gathered up the last of her pencils as she shook her head. 'She's dead.'

'That's right. Do you know what happened to her?'

Tuly sent a wary glance at the door where Jask glanced across his shoulder at her again, his hands now on his hips as he continued to talk to the dark-haired female. Tuly clutched her book and pencil crayons to her chest in one hand before stretching up on tiptoes to reach Sophia's ear. She cupped her hand over her mouth. 'He killed her,' she whispered.

Something inside her plummeted.

'Who did?'

'Jask,' Tuly whispered. 'Like I said – I'm always listening.'

Sophia snapped her attention back to the doorway where Tuly hurried to join Jask. He rubbed Tuly affectionately on the back of the head, saying something before tapping her playfully on the behind.

As Tuly skipped away, he glanced back at Sophia, his eyes locking on hers all too fleetingly before reverting his attention to his companion.

Sophia still stared at him open-mouthed with shock. Tuly had to have got it wrong. She had to have misheard. It wasn't possible. Jask wouldn't do that. Jask wasn't capable of doing that.

But if that was what she had come to believe, then things weren't just getting complicated – they were a mess.

And as he moved a couple of inches closer to his brunette companion, listening intently to whatever she was saying, her jealously told her the mess was intensifying. Especially when hurt and disappointment struck deep as, instead of coming to see her, he followed the brunette out of sight, his hand on the small of her back painfully intimate.

As she stared at the now vacant doorway, she knew she needed out of there. She had to forget about gaining information. She needed away from Jask. Away from the intensity, the confusion, the constant battle of wills that left her exhausted. She needed to distance herself from the strength of feelings evolving inside and give herself a sense of perspective again. Jask was the last thing she needed and she had no doubt she was most certainly the last thing *he* needed.

Her stomach jolted as she caught sight of Rone.

He looked around warily before indicating for her to join him out in the lobby.

Shoving back her chair, she hurried as much as her tired, aching legs would allow, the muscles in her thighs already feeling overstretched.

'I've been looking for you. Let's talk,' he said, wrapping his arm around her elbow, veering her past the stairs and shoving her inside the first room on the left.

Sophia glanced around the bare confines, shelved out as what she guessed had once been some kind of library, before looking back at Rone.

He was twitchy, anxious. 'I might have a way I can get you out of here,' Rone announced, keeping his voice low despite the closed door, despite his close proximity.

Her heart skipped a beat, the prospect irritatingly not filling her with as much relief as it should have, not least, she had no doubt, following her resolve to take Jask down before she did so. 'Go on,' she said, clutching the shelf behind her for support.

'There's a tunnel. It's rarely used unless we need to get through Blackthorn unnoticed.' He stopped abruptly. 'I am literally risking my life exposing this to you. And you will owe me, do you understand?'

She nodded. But it was a risk – a huge risk, and one that made her uneasy in light of the fact he was sharing it with her nonetheless. If it wasn't for recent events, she may have been more guarded. But if a lycan leader could kill his own mate, there was no wonder the youth was frightened of the potential of Jask learning he had lied. If she wanted evidence of Jask's tyranny, it was in the youth's actions now. Just as she saw in his frown, the subtle flaring of his nostrils, that he sensed Jask's scent on her the same as Tuly had. Yet he said nothing, the threat of her intimacy with the leader no doubt adding weight to the youth wanting her out of there – fast.

'Where is it?' she asked.

'I want your word,' he said, his blue eyes wide and resolute.

'You've got it.'

'The Alliance are to have nothing to do with us. They leave this pack be. Understood?'

'Fine.'

'I mean it. I know your organisation went after Jake and Caleb Dehain. Anyone willing to go after them is crazy enough to come after this pack too. And if we lose Jask, we lose us all. We're finished here. And I've no doubt your Alliance knows that, right?'

'So why mess with us, Rone? Why get involved at all?'

'Why do you think?'

'I don't know.'

'I was going to save you. I was going to make a deal with you to leave us be. Until I saw what you were and realised it wasn't going to be that straightforward.'

'And the vampires that were holding me? What were you going to do about them?'

He raised his eyebrows slightly, not needing to answer.

'You were going to kill them? You were going to blow the truce with the vampires? No wonder you didn't want Jask to know.'

'We wouldn't have had any choice.'

'But what if they'd told someone you were meeting them there? They would have known you were involved.'

'The whole thing was undercover. And they didn't want whoever they were working for to know they were taking a backhander from us.'

'Who *were* they working for?'

'I don't know.'

She'd overheard the vampires talking of getting the job done – of finding out, from her, everything they could about The Alliance: names, locations, future plans. It had panicked her enough at the time that they'd wanted more than just simple vengeance by torturing and killing her. But this was the terrifying confirmation she'd dreaded – it wasn't just Marid and those two vampires who knew about The Alliance; the latter had been working for someone else – someone who was still out there. 'You have no idea who it is? They said nothing?'

'I didn't ask,' Rone said. 'That's your problem not mine. So if you get out of here, we've got a deal, right?'

He was taking a risk that she would keep to her word. But it seemed to be a risk he was desperate enough to take. And the very fact he *was* taking that risk sent a further laceration of panic through her. He was scared Jask would get the truth out of her. He believed Jask *would* get the truth out of her – eventually.

All the more reason for her to take whatever opportunity she could to get out of there as quickly as she could.

She nodded. 'I told you – I give you my word.'

Whether she would keep it or not didn't matter then.

'Jask's on duty at the main doors tonight,' Rone explained. 'He'll be occupied for about five hours between nine and two. That's your window. The tunnel entrance is in the greenhouse, second room in. It's hidden under a mat. I'll get the key and open it. You'll have until midnight until I lock it again. I'll leave a torch amidst the plants and the other things you need on the steps inside. You'll see a door ahead. That's the one you take, only lock it behind you. You can slide the key back under it.'

'How long is the tunnel?'

'It'll take you about forty-five minutes at a good pace. It'll eventually bring you out of a ventilation tunnel in a warehouse Jask owns on the west side.'

'Sounds straightforward enough.'

'Not quite. It's not the only tunnel down there. You have to know what you're doing. Believe me, you don't want to take a wrong turn. I'll leave a map for you to use if you get beyond the midway point.'

'*If?* Why, what's at the midway point?'

'The lagoon.'

Her stomach flipped. 'The lagoon?'

'It's an overspill from the river. An underground water supply. It's clean, so it's not going to kill you. As long as you can swim. You can swim, right?'

Her pulse picked up momentum. Water. It had to be water. 'Course.'

'The lagoon is no more than forty feet across but it goes down about a hundred. Once you're under, you need to swim straight ahead–'

'What do you mean "under"?' she asked, not even bothering to conceal her panic.

His eyes flared with concern, a sure sign he wanted her out as much as she wanted out herself. 'You said you can swim.'

'I can, but…'

'But what?'

There could be no buts, whatever her pounding heart, the sickness at the back of her throat, her clenched chest dictated. 'How far? How long will I be under for?'

'About twenty feet, then you'll come to an air pocket.'

She nodded, hoping it would abate his unease as much as hers.

'Swim upwards,' he said, 'and grab that air while you can. When you go back under, you'll need to take the tunnel to the right. It's pitch-black down there so make sure you get it right. You take the middle one or the one to the left and you'll swim about fifteen feet before you realise they're dead ends, only you won't have enough breath to get back. Once you take the tunnel, you'll need to swim another twenty feet then you'll be out. I'll make sure I leave you a knife too for that part.'

'A knife?' It was the only statement to override the fear already clenching her chest.

'Like I said, there are other tunnels down there. And things happen there that not even Blackthorn is fit to see.'

Her pulse raced. 'Are one of those *the* tunnel? The one that runs under this entire locale, even between locales? Is that *real*?'

If the urban legend was true – that there was an underground system that crossed districts, that evaded the barriers put in place by the Global Council – then the prospects truly were as terrifying as the search into finding them had constituted. A search that had led to rumours being quickly squashed by the authorities as mere scaremongering.

She remembered the newsfeeds from when she was younger – when reporters went down into the so-called tunnels with researchers and law enforcement teams. They always came up against a dead end. Just sewage or drainage systems, they'd claimed – not used for anything other than their intention. Others whispered of secret concealed doorways and tunnels, but none were found. So the tunnel had remained an urban legend. Until now.

And she'd know where it was.

'I don't know,' Rone said, though she didn't believe him. 'But I do know the network down there is a labyrinth, so don't be getting any smart ideas. Keep on the path and you'll be okay. Don't veer off course and do *not* unlock any doors. Being a serryn might save you from any vampire run-ins down there, but you come across a rogue lycan and you're going to be grateful for that knife. Let alone if you come across a con. I'm sure I don't need to tell you we're talking murderers, sex offenders – real scum of the earth.'

The cons: the hard core of the criminal underworld. The convicts deemed too much to handle for the penitentiary in Lowtown. The ones beyond rehabilitation. The ones subsequently abandoned by their authorities and banished to fend for themselves in Blackthorn as food supplies, let alone punchbags, for the notoriously less tolerant third species. It was an attempt on the authorities' part to be a deterrent. But 'out of sight, out of mind' seemed to be the Global Council's motto. Once in, they never came out – tagged so that even an attempt to cross the border into Lowtown would release a lethal neurotransmitter straight into their system. It was a brutal approach, but another so-called 'necessity'.

The cons were easy enough to spot – all marked on the inner wrist, sometimes spanning the forearm, with a sequence of numbers that specified the crimes they had committed. Many chose to hide the tattoos, some went to extreme lengths to remove them, but it was the ones who openly exposed their history who were the ones to be wary of. They wore it like a medal and, in turn, that made them the ringleaders. The fact it made them more of a target for vampires – the ones who resented the dregs of humanity invading their territory – made them even more intrepid. They lived every day on the edge and never expected to make it to the following dawn. Those who did became more arrogant each day.

They hung around mainly in the south – the parts not owned by the Dehains or Kane Malloy. On the whole they could be avoided and, up to now, she had done so successfully.

'You come across any of those and you're not getting out,' Rone added.

Suddenly his motivation for disclosing that exit route made even more sense. 'Is that what you're hoping? That I won't make it out? That your problem will be solved?'

'I'm telling you your only way out of here. It's up to you whether you take it. But if you do get through, remember our pact. And if you don't…' He shrugged.

'And when Jask finds me gone? He saw me talking to you, Rone. He's not stupid.'

'But neither will he have proof. He's not going to kill me without proof.'

'And is that what he's capable of – killing you?'

'There's nothing Jask isn't capable of.'

'Like killing his mate Ellen?'

Startled, Rone retracted like he'd been scorched. 'Do we have deal or not?' he asked, his tone now laced with hostility. Hostility that made her want to escape the confines of that room even more.

It seemed Ellen's death was a sensitive issue for everyone.

She nodded. 'We have a deal.'

But he still didn't look relieved. 'Be out in the quadrant at ten and I'll give you the nod when it's done. After that, you're on your own.'

Chapter Thirteen

Sophia pushed open the door to the poolroom, the subdued echo instantly rebounding off her eardrums.

She kept a safe distance from the edge of the pool as she headed to what she guessed, and hoped, was the shallow end.

Stood a couple of feet from the edge, she stared ahead at the sheen of still black water. Her insides twisted, her palms already coated in perspiration at the very prospect of what she was going to do.

'Come on, Phia,' she growled under her breath. 'It's water. Just water.'

The very substance she had spent much of her childhood gliding through with ease, winning trophies for her school and out-swimming the best of them.

She needed to swim again. She needed to feel control again. More than anything, she needed to get her head back under water and own it.

She stepped up to the water's edge. She'd have to feel ground beneath her feet. If she didn't, she knew she couldn't do it.

She sat on the edge of the pool and tentatively slid her legs into it, the cool darkness instantly encompassing them.

But she withdrew from the abyss as quickly as she had entered it. She recoiled her thighs back against her chest, her arms wrapped tightly around them.

There was no way she could do it.

No way.

But the other option was to stay in the compound. To be used by Jask however he saw fit. To leave her sister in the hands of Caleb and Jake Dehain. To let The Alliance work out for themselves that their cover had been blown, if it wasn't too late already.

Abby had said they were only going to lie low for two days. That time was already up.

And all she had to do to avert disaster was get into some harmless swimming pool.

She slipped her feet back into the water and clutched the pool's edge. She stared down into the darkness. No underwater plants, no fallen branches, no uneven lake bed.

She yanked her tunic over her head, took a steadying breath of grit determination and eased herself sideways into the tepid water.

She felt that same wrench of fear in her chest. Earlier it had felt as though the metaphorical plaster had been ripped off painfully fast. Now it was being dragged off an excruciating millimetre at a time.

Still clutching on to the side, she tentatively lowered herself into the water until a knobbled surface met the soles of her feet.

Her pulse raced, her breaths erratic as she rested her head on her forearms whilst she counted to three – not once, but twice before she built up the courage to let go and to turn around.

Aside from the ripples she had created, the water remained perfectly placid.

She lowered herself slowly until she was covered to her shoulders. But still she remained plastered against the wall as she crouched like a small mammal hiding.

Or an army operative under cover.

Because that's what she was. She was a soldier. A fighter. Not a coward. Never a coward. But as she stared at the dark water around her again, nothing could suppress the panic.

She needed to try and walk. She needed to face the darkness and walk through the water.

Counting to three, she moved cautiously forward whilst maintaining her crouched position.

She kept her eyes wide and wary, feeling forward with her feet before resolving whether to take another step or not. She ploughed deeper and deeper until she gradually had to stand to keep her head above water, the ripples and occasional splashes less audible than her own breathing.

When she was finally at her full height, she paused for breath.

She should have stuck to the side of the pool – she knew that. But there was no use in a safety net. She needed to get over herself and fast.

She took another step forward, and another, her eyes fixed ahead at the depths.

She was going to get there. She was going to feel nothing beneath her feet and she wasn't going to panic.

Like riding a bike. Like tying up shoelaces. Once learned, never…

She lost her footing, the incline too unexpected, too slippery, too severe, for her not too. She slipped backwards, the water rushing over her face.

She kicked, instinctively pulling herself back from the precipice, her arms flapping ungraciously, causing the water to splash down on her like rain.

She swam as fast as she could to the side, to safety.

She slammed her forearms onto the pool's edge, her head buried in her arms again, shock stealing the energy she needed to pull herself out of the water completely.

She let go only to clutch the back of her ankle, her calf – both throbbing and stinging from what she had no doubt was a nasty graze.

But she wouldn't let the tears consume her – not this time. She bit them back, she bit everything back that made her want to give up. Because she was *not* going to give up.

She'd let the shock subside then she'd try again.

She *had* to.

She pushed her hair back from her eyes and lifted her head, stared at the boots that stood less than two feet away. She flinched and looked up to see Jask gazing down at her.

'Skinny-dipping alone in the middle of lycan territory. Very brave.' He crouched down. 'Facing a few demons, Phia?'

'A girl has to find a way to pass the time somehow.'

He smiled. She wished he wouldn't. That coupled with recollections of his body pressed against hers, the magical fluidity of his fingers, the sound of his voice playing over her skin, only exacerbated the tension filling her chest at being faced with him again.

He stood up. He pulled his T-shirt over his head before unfastening his jeans at the same time as kicking off his boots.

She recoiled back from the pool side as he slid off his shorts. A split second later, he dived smoothly and fluidly into the depths of the water.

She spun to face him as fast as the water resistance would allow.

The surface rippled but he didn't come up. She couldn't see any hint of him at all. Her breaths were shallow as she scanned the surface of the water, turning left and right for any sign of where he might appear.

Only seconds could have passed, but it felt like minutes.

She spun one hundred and eighty as soon as she heard the splash behind her to see, to her relief, Jask rising out of the water.

She watched him in silent awe as he waded the few feet towards her, the water barely covering his hips, his upper chest and shoulders glistening. The shadows emphasised every curve in those powerful arms as he brushed his hands back through his hair. The same perfect body she'd had sex with only a couple of hours before. The possibility seemed unreal.

He shook his hair, getting rid of more droplets – though she wouldn't have put it past him as his mocking of her earlier jibe about shaking dry.

'So what happened earlier?' he asked, drawing level. 'You can clearly swim.'

'I panicked, that's all.'

He waded in front of her before pushing himself fluidly back into the water, far enough that she knew he was treading water above the precipice that took her under.

'Why?' he asked.

'Just something that happened when I was a kid. No big deal.'

'It looked like a big deal.'

'What does it matter?'

'Because it does to you.'

The hint of compassion in his words threw her. But she dismissed it only as him wanting to know what went on in her head.

But there was no way he was getting close again.

'I fell in a river, that's all,' she said. 'I got caught up in some plants.'

'How did you get out?'

'I just did.' She stared back into the scepticism in his eyes. More so she realised her simple explanation only exacerbated what could now be deemed as a major overreaction earlier. 'If you must know, I used to be a brilliant swimmer,' she declared to save some face at least.

'Really?'

'I could swim two lengths whilst holding my breath.'

'Not bad for a human,' he said, swimming back a little deeper.

'Easy, Jask. That was almost another compliment.'

'Another one?'

'Third of the night.'

'You're counting.'

She realised she had been – only now she had let it slip. 'I'm attentive to detail.'

He swam back towards her, barely making a splash. 'Then you would have noticed I'm also a good swimmer,' he said, stopping in front of her. 'That's one similarity we definitely share with our heritage. *Very* competent in the water.'

'I had noticed.'

'More than capable of rescuing you again should you need me to.'

'Don't flatter yourself – it's hardly the Atlantic Ocean.'

'Exactly,' he said. 'So why are you too scared to swim to the deep end?'

'I'm not.'

'No?'

'No. I'm just acclimatising.'

He moved forward from the precipice and stood up. He held out his hands for her to take.

She stared at them then back up at him. 'What?' But the look in his eyes said it all. 'Like I'd trust you.'

'If I wanted to drown you, I'd hardly have to drag you into the deep end to do it.'

She looked at his hands again, then back at him.

'I ravished you brutally in my cellar,' he said with a playful smirk. 'The least I can do is help restore your confidence in water.'

'Ravish? How very gentlemanly.'

'Oh, we both know I'm no gentleman. But I *am* more than capable of stopping you from drowning. Come on, Phia,' he said. 'You're anything but weak. And I know you're itching to prove it.'

She looked at his hands again. It was a dare she couldn't help but rise to. She reached out and let him take her hands in his, the gentle strength in them surprisingly reassuring. Hands that had so expertly brought her to the peak of climax. But, somehow, this felt even more personal.

He stepped backwards until she sensed he was standing on the edge of the precipice again.

He caught hold of her hips and pulled her close. 'Wrap your legs around me.'

'A little intimate, don't you think?'

'If you want to see it that way,' he said. 'But I'll have a better hold on you.'

He lowered in the water, his gaze unflinching.

After only a moment's more hesitation, she wrapped her legs around him, trying to ignore his arousal despite the coolness of the water.

She gripped his upper arms as he eased back into the water. But Jask treaded the depths with natural competence, one arm helping him keep balance, the other around her waist.

'I'm sorry I caused you so much distress throwing you in here,' he said.

The sincerity in his eyes, let alone his second apology of the night, momentarily took her aback. She shrugged. 'What was the alternative – being put across your knee like you threatened earlier?'

'You would have deserved it after the way you spoke to me and Corbin. You and your death wish.'

'You weren't going to do anything.'

'Know that for sure, do you?'

'Like I said, I've seen you both with Tuly and Solstice. I must say, I'm very impressed with the reputation you guys keep up on the outside, considering.'

'Everyone has their dark side, Phia. Me and Corbin no less.'

And some darker than most it seemed, if Tuly was telling the truth.

'I was still proved right though, wasn't I? You're quite the lover, Jask Tao.'

'And you were a lot more responsive than you should have been, Phia. Than your kind's reputation dictates. You should have been able to switch off in there. But you didn't.'

'Faking isn't difficult in my line of work.'

There was something that flashed in his eyes. Something that she couldn't read. 'There was nothing fake about that.'

'Had enough experience to know, have you?'

'I think you know that answer for yourself now.'

He held her gaze until she felt the need to look away.

'Tell me the truth, Phia. You haven't been in Blackthorn long, have you?'

She couldn't go down that route again, not with how dangerously close he'd started to veer towards it in the cell. And especially not now that she was on the cusp of getting out. 'You're convinced about that, aren't you?'

'I've seen the evidence of what you're capable of, but out there on the streets every night? No way. You'd be dead already.'

'You keep forgetting vampires aren't immune like you.'

'I would have heard something, Phia.'

'Why? You think people really care? You think anybody cares what goes on here in Blackthorn? Vampires die every day – there's not the time, resources or inclination to investigate them all. It's a serryn's perfect playground. And like I keep saying – I'm good at what I do.'

'You're too soft. The way you reacted when I held you down on the wasteland, when I threw you in here, your reaction in the cell – there's nothing anywhere near hard enough in you.' He paused. 'Why leave Summerton behind for this?'

'I have my reasons.'

'Reasons other than being a serryn?'

'A serryn that you clearly need. Come on, Jask – confession time. I think it's time you let me in on why, don't you?'

But this time he didn't cut her dead. This time she saw a glimmer of a smile in his eyes. 'What's it worth?' He eased her off him to encourage her to tread water for herself whilst still keeping a hold on her hands. 'Keep your eyes on me,' he said. She tried not to panic, but couldn't help but squeeze his hands tighter. Once she started to reach a controlled rhythm, he continued. 'So, what's it worth?'

'What it's worth is time. The way I see it, we've reached stalemate. Only I don't want to be here any longer than you want me here. So you tell me what you want me for, and maybe we can come to an arrangement.'

'No arrangement. No deal. You're just going to do as I tell you. *When* the time comes.'

She started to wonder if she had been way off course with the Kane Malloy theory. It would have been insane for him to go after the master vampire – a risk to his entire pack with very little gain. There was something else. Something she was missing.

Unease coiled in her chest again. 'So how long exactly are you planning on this so-called taming taking?'

'Not long.'

'And are you going to kill me when you're done?'

His silence, his steady gaze, evoked her irritation too much.

'Tell me,' she said, 'is that why you killed Ellen? Did she not do as she was told either?'

He stared at her, shock evident in his eyes. And something else. But he didn't deny it.

Only in that moment did she realise how desperately she needed him to deny it.

'I think the word you're looking for is murder,' he said. 'That's what it's called when you plan it, isn't it? When you know what you're doing?'

Panic sliced through her chest at his confession. 'So it's true?'

'Yes, it's true.'

He turned away and swam fluidly and silently back over to the side.

Only when he had exited the pool, when he had gathered up his clothes and left the room, did she realise she was treading water alone.

Chapter Fourteen

Jask stood outside the poolroom, his hair drying in the breeze as he toyed with the leather-strapped pendant at his neck.

Ellen's pendent that represented the bloodline that may as well have died with her that day.

Hearing the facts of his soulmate's demise uttered so cuttingly, so callously, had evoked only a defensive backlash from him. Not least coming from Phia. He'd wanted to shock her for her intrusion – for daring mention what she knew nothing about with such condemnation in her eyes. And clearly he *had* shocked her.

But it had been the truth.

And she'd seen as such, judging from the alarm in her eyes – worse, the repulsion. But he hadn't expected that repulsion to wound him so intensely. He hadn't expected the disappointment in her eyes to hurt.

Someone had been speaking out of turn. And he'd find out who.

But first he needed to be there for Blaise, having been in the process of following her when he'd caught a glimpse of Phia entering the poolroom.

As he looked towards the tunnel that led to the outbuilding, he knew that was where she was. She'd been so distressed when he'd bumped into her in the foyer that he'd had to lead her away, not least with Phia watching on from the dining hall.

Blaise had been building up to going down there for too long now, and despite Jask's insistence that she didn't need to face it alone, he knew that's what she would do.

He headed across to the tunnel, through the courtyard and past the tree. Entering the building, he made his way down the steps and along the passage.

Taking a left down into the containment rooms, he opened the third on the right – the one Nero always used.

Always ahead of the rest of the pack, Nero's morphing was out of sync by two weeks. His kind were rare, but a gift in terms of getting the balance right every time for the rest of the pack during those times when the concoction needed altering.

This time it had failed.

Blaise was sat against the wall to his left, her knees to her chest, her arms wrapped around them as she stared ahead at the open cage, her long brown hair almost covering her face.

'Do you want me to leave you be?' he asked.

She shook her head. 'No.'

Jask closed the door behind him and crossed the room to join her.

Slipping in behind her, she shuffled forward to allow it, before nestling back between his splayed legs as he wrapped his arms around her.

She rested her head back against his chest, her attention on the cage unflinching.

It had been filled with her screams the last time they'd been in there.

It had been routine at first – giving Nero the concoction. Only this time something had gone wrong. This time something was out with the mix. Not only had there not been a high enough dosage of aconite to help stop the morphing; there had not been enough turmeric to counteract its toxicity. So not only had he morphed; he'd been in agony – dying shortly after.

The time most likely for errors to occur was always around thirteenth moon when the balance was so volatile. But none of them had truly been prepared for it to happen to their pack – the first time it had happened since they'd been forced into the confines of Blackthorn with the regulations.

It had been a horrendous way to go. And Blaise had been stood there watching it all. Blaise who had been devoted to her soulmate for twenty years.

If it hadn't been for losing Nero, all of them would have taken the concoction in just over a week. And it would have killed nearly all of them – certainly the ones who had avoided ever morphing before.

But that was no consolation to Nero now, and certainly no comfort to Blaise. In the five days that had followed since the incident, nothing had been of comfort to her. The pack were there for her, as they always were for each other, but what she really wanted had been cruelly snatched away.

It would have been a tragic enough incident before the regulations, but now it was a disaster. In the past, they would have been able to travel far and wide to find whatever herbs and spices they needed – anything they hadn't grown for themselves. But nothing got into Blackthorn or Lowtown anymore without going through analysis at the Midtown and Summerton borders. What were once common herbs and spices were now rarities or no longer accessible beyond Summerton, not least due to the fact the TSCD had zero-tolerance policies on exchange and selling of herbs in order to keep the witches in check.

Only now he knew it was more than that – reinforced by Solstice's suspicions back in the dining hall. The authorities tolerated the lycans' ways, but only because they knew it wouldn't last forever. One day, the herbs they already monitored each month would eventually stop growing or they'd have insufficient and fail to access what they needed – like turmeric. Then it would be either the meds, or morph and be slain.

Now the herb regulations didn't feel targeted at the witches at all. Now it felt much more personal. And the authorities would already be on the road to success if Rone and Samson hadn't found Phia in the ruins.

As angry as he still was with him, he had to face the fact that Rone had come good. He felt a glimmer of pride for the first time ever – something that felt even more uncomfortable than his overly stern hand with the youth.

'I say we morph,' Blaise finally said. 'If we stop avoiding what we are, the Global Council would have nothing over us. Screw the regulations; let's run amok on the streets. Let's break down those barriers. No other species is physically stronger than a lycan morphed. Let's show them once and for all.'

'Blaise, you know this is about survival. They will shoot us dead in the streets before we even get that far – those of us strong enough to even survive the morphing. This pack has too many who have never attempted it. They won't know what they're doing, where they are, their own strength. You cannot run an army like that and an army is what it would take. The consequences don't bear thinking about.'

'And what happened to Nero doesn't bear thinking about.'

He could hear her heaving breaths, the rapid rise and fall of her chest as she started to get upset again.

He wanted to promise her that one day it would be different. That somehow they would get out of the cage that was Blackthorn and Lowtown. But he couldn't.

But he could tell her Nero hadn't died in vain. That there was some hope – at least for the immediate future.

'The serryn can get us what we need,' he said.

She was still for a moment. Then she turned in his arms. 'What?'

'After what happened to Nero, Corbin and I went to see a witch. We've got lucky. He told us there's still a supply of turmeric here in Blackthorn. That a witch has a secret stash she has kept concealed from the authorities. That a serryn can demand it.'

Blaise frowned. 'That's why you have her here?'

He nodded.

'She'll help us?' Blaise asked.

Bolshie, stubborn Phia who had no intention of playing ball whatsoever.

Yet.

'I'm making sure of it,' he said.

And as she turned back around, he held her with a renewed determination that this would not happen to the rest of his pack.

That despite the odds, he *would* succeed. No matter what it took.

Chapter Fifteen

Sophia sat on the bench, a blanket she had found in the foyer wrapped around her upper body as she stared up at the clouds, the moon an ethereal glow behind them.

The quadrant was deathly quiet, only a handful of lycans having passed her in the past hour. She scanned the barbed wire skirting the fence ahead then returned her attention to the exit tunnel where she knew Jask was on duty in the outer room beyond.

Movement to her left caught her eye as Rone emerged through the tunnel from the courtyard. He strode along the path behind her, sending her only an almost undetectable nod as he passed on his way back up the steps and into the lobby.

Sophia stared back ahead at the exit tunnel.

She should have just sloped away, but she couldn't. She had a job to finish. And before that she wanted, needed, final answers.

And in the three hours since he'd left her alone in the pool, she'd practised several lengths to rebuild her confidence. She'd also found the perfect place for their final confrontation.

Dropping the blanket, she crossed the quadrant, marched through the tunnel and to the gate.

'I need to talk to Jask,' she declared to the lycan marking it.

She was braced for persuasion, but he opened it without question, letting her through.

She stepped through the corrugated door he had equally opened for her, her attention immediately locking on the table ahead.

She hated the way he took her breath away. How he made her pulse race just to look at him.

Jask was sat with six others, all in the middle of a card game. She caught him mid-laugh before he knocked back a mouthful of beer – a laugh that seemed cold considering his earlier confession in the pool.

She hadn't been able to get it out of her head – how he had just admitted to it. Why she had been so taken aback, she had no idea. She knew his reputation. She knew the rumours. The façade of the responsible pack leader was no mask for the brutality of the creature required to make sure his own survived that long in Blackthorn. He was no different to the others – to the other third-species under-world leaders who ran the district with a merciless hand. He was of the same ilk as the likes of Kane Malloy and Caleb Dehain – eyes and looks of an angel and a core as rotten and corrupt as the district they inhabited.

And *that's* what she'd keep at the forefront of her mind to finish the job.

She hovered awkwardly until he met her gaze, his eyes narrowing slightly in curiosity before he returned to his game.

She stepped closer to the table, the lycans with him glancing at her but seemingly not daring to linger for too long.

'Something you want?' Jask asked, his attention on his cards.

'Can I talk to you?'

He threw down a card and leaned back, resting his arm on the back of his companion's chair. 'About what?'

'In private?'

A few of the lycans smirked.

They wouldn't be smirking soon.

'If you ask nicely,' he said, before taking a mouthful from his bottle.

She exhaled tersely at his taunt.

'Please,' she said, the very word grating as she uttered it, as she swallowed a jagged lump of pride.

He knocked back another mouthful of beer before discarding his cards onto the table. 'Sure,' he said, standing.

He led the way out of the door, beer still in his hand. Closing it behind him, he turned to face her. 'Let's hear it.'

She looked across at the guard ahead. 'Can we go for a walk?'

He knocked back another mouthful of beer, licked it from his lips as his eyes narrowed contemplatively on hers.

To her relief, he cocked his head towards the tunnel.

As they exited into the quadrant, she walked the path alongside him, her arms folded so he wouldn't see the tension in her hands. Fortunately he didn't press her to speak for a little while, which only granted her more time to get him where she needed to.

But it didn't last.

'Are you going to get to the point?' he asked as they passed the pool, heading towards the tunnel that led to the courtyard and out-buildings. 'Only I'm on duty.'

'I wanted to apologise,' she said, grateful that he at least kept walking.

'For what?'

They exited the tunnel and passed the greenhouse – exactly where she planned to make her escape as soon as she possibly could.

As soon as she'd said her goodbye – in more ways than one.

Her pulse rate picked up a notch. She had to stay calm – steady breaths and steady pace. She couldn't raise his suspicion one iota.

'For being so insensitive in the pool,' she said. 'I clearly offended you for you to walk away like that.'

She led the way past the oak and the outhouse before continuing to the single-storey derelict building behind it.

'You've done nothing but offend me ever since I brought you here, serryn. Why apologise now?'

'Because some things are unforgiveable.' She glanced across at him before she wandered around the back of the building. She stepped up to the chain-link fence and gazed out beyond the demolition site to the distant glow of Lowtown.

Jask moved in alongside her. 'Forget about it,' he said, as he wrapped his fingers through the wire and took another mouthful of beer.

She had to keep him there long enough. She had to keep talking. 'Do you ever go into Lowtown?'

He handed her his bottle so she could take a swig.

She would have preferred something stronger, but she accepted. 'From time to time,' he said.

She took a mouthful and handed it back to him.

'You?' he asked.

'From time to time.'

'The fact you apologised tells me you understand what family means. Do you have family back in Summerton?'

She nodded. But she didn't elaborate. Sharing her story was a no-go zone. Not even Daniel knew. But then that was part of the agreement in The Alliance – no one ever disclosed anything. It was the most essential component to prevent ever being traced.

'Is the serryn need in you *so* great that you can turn your back on your own?'

'We all have things we have to do in life.' She glanced at him before looking back ahead through the wire. 'You should know that. Besides, they're better off without me.'

He turned to face her side-on, leaning his shoulder against the fence. 'You say that like you mean it.'

'It's true.'

'Did you do something?' he asked, before taking another swig of beer.

She backed up against the wall. This was the time for *him* to open up, not her. 'I was always doing *something*.' She slid down to the floor and crossed her legs.

He settled down alongside her as they both gazed out over the darkness, the distant thrum of bass emanating from the hub from far beyond the compound behind. She rested her head against the wall and stared up at the night sky, the clouds sweeping past the half-moon, any hint of stars clouded by pollution.

It was nothing like lying on a blanket of green in the hills of Summerton, staring up at the clear sky as Leila explained all the constellations. Explanations that inevitably ended up with her talking to herself as Sophia and Alisha instead opted to roll down the hills, their squeals and laughter breaking the peace.

And all that time, Leila had been hiding a secret – if she'd ever known what she was. There was still the chance she hadn't. But too much was falling into place.

Back when Sophia had first discovered a vampire had been responsible for their mother's death, everything had changed. Like dye in a clear pool of water, the need for vengeance had polluted her veins. Her search for vampire weaknesses had inevitably led her to discover the existence of serryns – a rare species of ancient witch whose blood was poisonous to vampires. Seductresses who would hunt them down, torture them and kill them.

The prospect had excited her at the time, and she'd become fixated on trying to find one despite rumours they were now extinct. She'd openly told Leila of her intentions, but Leila hadn't shared her excitement. Infuriatingly, her big sister had told her to let things go or, worse, had met her rants with pure silence.

She'd never understood why Leila didn't have that same need for vengeance. Now all she wanted to know was why, if she had known what she was, she hadn't done anything about it.

But at the time, she'd had no reason to think anything of it. Instead, she'd ignored her big sister more and more as her trips to Lowtown became more frequent.

On her first venture into Blackthorn, she'd met Daniel. He and a couple of the others had rescued her when she'd been cornered by a vampire. They took him out swiftly, efficiently and bloodily.

She'd been enraptured by their control, their fearlessness. Less than a month later, she'd joined them. And she'd never looked back.

But now her head ached with the need for answers about her family. To find out what had been going on whilst she'd been away those past ten months.

That was personal though – this was business. And the former wasn't going to happen until the latter was dealt with.

She'd made a pact. A pact with The Alliance, who had given her a purpose, put a roof over her head, honed her skills and set her on the path to vengeance that she so desperately needed.

And here she was alone with one of those very underworld leaders that they spent weeks, months even, planning to get access to. She'd been handed an opportunity like The Alliance never had. There would be consequences, of course. Rone would know it was her – that The Alliance had been responsible. Whether he would disclose how he knew though and that, subsequently, he had allowed it to happen, was unlikely.

She reached down to the heel of her boot, where her folded blade was concealed in the opposite heel to the pins. It might have been small but it was effective. Right angle, right force, right place and he'd be gone.

She'd return to The Alliance not only as their ultimate weapon, but with one underworld leader down and only two to go. She'd like to see Abby's face then.

But as she looked across at him sat silently beside her – those beautiful azure eyes locked on the demolition site ahead, that stunning profile, that body that had made her feel like no one else had, that mind which seemed to somehow tune seamlessly into hers – she wavered again.

The reminder, the truth of what a monster he was, was exactly what she needed to make her plans easier.

'So you meant it when you said you murdered your mate? You weren't just saying it?'

He met her gaze, albeit fleetingly. He knocked back the remains of his beer. 'Why?' he asked, returning his gaze ahead.

'Did she do something wrong?'

'Yes.' He paused. 'She made a mistake wanting to be with me.'

She placed her numb hands flat against the cold, stone ground. 'How did you kill her?'

'In a blood bath,' he said. 'More blood than I've ever seen.'

She studied his eyes to try and work out if it was a wind-up – but the eyes that glanced back at her emanated nothing but truth.

'Did she betray you in some way?'

'She would never have betrayed me.' He moved to stand. 'Ever.'

But she caught his forearm, her fingers barely reaching either side, reminding her how badly a one-on-one battle could end for her.

'Then why?' she asked.

'Why are you so interested?'

'Who wouldn't be? An alpha murdering his mate – it's not exactly commonplace, is it? You're supposed to be the most loyal of all your species.'

'According to the rumours?' He pulled his arm free and stood. But instead of walking away he turned to face her. 'Your kind knows nothing. Nothing about us. Nothing about the truth. You and your Summerton education. You've no sense of the real world, just like the rest of them, serryn or not.'

She stood up, needing to be as close to eye level as she could. But she kept the wall behind her for balance. 'Don't patronise me, Jask. I've lived here long enough. I've seen what it's like.'

'Really? And yet you *still* justify your actions.'

'I can justify them *because* of what I've seen.'

'Because of what *your* kind has created. You think you know what it's like because you *choose* to live within these boundaries? Take a look around – a *real* look around at this so-called temporary measure. This was never going to be anything other than one giant experimental pod; one third-species-sized rat maze. They created this to *make* us implode – to make us exactly what they want us to be. Like a caged animal in a zoo being prodded with a stick, they stand back and justify how aggressive we are so they can give cause to keeping us contained. And then *you* come into the mix. You're not even one of them. You talk about my kind being some kind of half-breed – what are you? Human with extra skills? No, you're nothing but the second species to them. And when they've finally found a good enough reason to wipe us off the earth, they'll start on you. For as long as your kind are in charge, we're all fucked.'

'You're wrong,' she said, the breeze blowing against her already chilled skin. 'It was *your* kind that upset the balance by coming out in the first place. We contain you because we're the best species on this planet at self-preservation – and we *will* win in the end.'

He stepped up to her, pressed his hand to her shoulder, trapping her against the wall. 'Is that right?'

She held his gaze as he slipped his hand between her arm and her side, sliding his fingers down her ribcage, finding the soft flesh that would give him the easiest upward thrust to her heart.

'Like now?' he asked. 'Your arrogance, your need to be right, your need to justify your actions pressing you that one step further with a species already about to snap? Do you know how easily I could tear your heart out from you right now if I chose to?'

Her breath hitched, the feel of his now lethally extended talons digging into her flesh through her tunic. 'You need me,' she said, searching for a reason for him not to, for one moment believing, *really* believing, him capable.

He slid his hand up her abdomen, over her breast to her throat, his thumb pressing her chin up so she was forced to look him deep in the eyes. 'Keep reminding me of that,' he said.

She subtly slid her leg up the wall, her hand ready to meet her heel as he glided his thumb along her jaw line, his gaze not flinching from hers.

'And I'll remind you that if I wanted you dead, you'd be dead,' he said, 'whether I need you or not.'

She slid her fingers over her heel, pressing on the ball of her feet to create enough of a gap behind it that she could slide the hidden encasement open.

'But you *are* going to work for me,' he added.

'And then you'll kill me anyway, right?'

He slid his hand gently down her throat. 'I'd advise that whatever weapon you're reaching for right now, that you don't.' The breeze blew lightly through his hair, a sharp contrast to the steadiness of his gaze. 'Unless you want me to show you *just* how feral I can be.'

Her fingers halted on her half-open heel. Only now she realised her hand wasn't just trembling, it was shaking.

The battle drums of Blackthorn's hub now seemed a painfully long way away. Everything felt a painfully long way away, alone there, trapped between the fence and the wall, in the dark with the lycan who stared coolly back at her.

'In fact, I'll show you *exactly* what untamed is,' he said, his lips dangerously close to hers. 'Unless you hand it over.'

Less than a few hours before, she would have looked him straight in the eye and defied him. And had absolutely no doubt she would have paid the consequences. Badly.

Just as there was a time when she would have taken a punt and tried to ram that blade into his throat regardless.

A time when she thought she had nothing to lose. When she despised herself enough not to care about the consequences.

But she learned one quietly terrifying thing in that moment: she *needed* to live. What she did at that moment, the decision she made, mattered – not just for her, but for those she had left to care about.

Intentionally or unintentionally, Jask Tao *had* tamed her in some way. But she'd be damned if she'd let him know.

And there was absolutely no way she was sticking around now to give him long enough to find out.

She removed the small blade from her heel, keeping her breathing as controlled as she could as she placed it in his open palm. 'Another time,' she said.

'I'll hold you to that.'

Jask held her gaze for a moment longer before he backed away, walked away, without another word.

Chapter Sixteen

Just as Rone had promised, the trapdoor in the greenhouse was unlocked.

Inside was silent. Even the water sprays had ceased for the night.

Lifting the trapdoor, Sophia stared down the wooden slatted steps into the darkness. Hesitation cost time, and time was something she didn't have.

Collecting the torch Rone had left her amongst the shrubbery – a diver's torch in preparation for its task – she took the first two steps down. She shone the light around the depths, the vast space having far too many objects for there not to be the potential for something to be hiding behind them. Keeping watchful, she reached up to close the trapdoor behind her, sealing herself in the darkness. It was quiet enough down there to hear a page turn, her only comfort the beam of light – but even that could only ignite one corner at a time.

She sat on the bottom step and collected the taped-up plastic bag that contained dry clothes and, hopefully, the map out of there. It also had a cord, clearly so she could attach the bag to herself whilst she swam. Next to it was a knife. She pulled the heavy blade out of its encasement, the impressively sharp edge now jutting 180 degrees. Rone sure knew how to pick his weapons.

Shining the beam back around the room, she rested it on the door ahead – the entrance point to the tunnel.

She made her way over, sending the occasional wary glance over each shoulder. She should have been used to the dark, but there was no denying it was an inherent fear no matter how accustomed she was to it.

She unbolted the door and reached for the key on the hook beside it. The internal lock mechanism giving way echoed in the silence, momentarily overwhelming the blood pounding in her ears. Fortunately, the door opened silently.

She shone the torch into further darkness.

It looked like nothing more than a tunnel through rock but then, from what Rone had told her, that's exactly what it was.

She stepped into the dense chill. Closing the door behind her, she stood for a moment, her breathing ragged.

'Come on, Phia,' she whispered. 'You've been in darker places than this.'

She held the torch beam ahead.

The tunnel was no wider than four feet, no higher than seven.

'Single-file only,' she whispered again, muttering to herself as she always had when she was frightened as a child.

The temptation to leave the door open behind was immense. But she did what Rone had instructed. She locked the door behind her and slid the key back through the tiny gap at the floor.

'No going back,' she muttered as she replaced the torch with the knife, ensuring she held the weapon in her best hand, the ray of light in the other, the plastic bag tucked under that arm.

And she took her first step forward.

'There's nothing to worry about until you get to the other side of the water,' she whispered, putting one foot in front of the other. 'They don't come this way. Nothing comes this way. Twenty minutes, that's all. Just twenty minutes to the lagoon.'

She picked up pace, the beam allowing her to see at least thirty feet ahead.

At least there were no corners at that part, not for a good way in.

She swallowed hard against her arid throat. 'You're made of stronger stuff than this, Phia McKay. Much stronger.'

Keep it going. Keep it going. Only now she said it silently in her head, anxiety muting her speech.

The torch indicated she was veering right and before long she was veering left.

One way in. One way out. And nowhere to hide should something come the other way.

But nothing was going to come the other way. Rone had assured her there was minimal risk until she got beyond the water.

She picked up pace, striding ahead as fast as she could, the distance she needed to cover passing too slowly.

Five minutes. Ten minutes. Approaching fifteen at least.

As the tunnel became more twisted, she slowed down a little for fear of knocking herself out cold on a wall, before it opened up again. The walls spread, the ceiling now beyond her reach.

But she kept her pace steady. She ploughed forward, the beam bouncing off the walls, off the floor.

Until there was only a wall straight ahead, nothing but rock beneath.

No more tunnel. And no lagoon.

Her stomach clenched. She came to a standstill.

It was a dead end.

She shone the beam around more erratically for a smaller opening. Nothing but rock. Nothing but rock and a locked door behind her.

He'd tricked her. Rone had tricked her. The double-crossing…

She growled under her breath, kicked a rock against the wall ahead and turned away just as she heard the plop.

She spun back around.

Ripples spanned the small pool ahead – a pool that had been so perfectly still, it had been nothing but a mirror to the rocks around it.

Sophia warily stepped closer as the water began to still again – water that seamlessly reached the rock's edge.

Her dark and cold abyss of a way out.

Her heart leapt.

Dropping the bag, knife and torch to the floor beside her, she untied and slipped off her boots before sitting cross-legged at the water's edge. She stared down into the darkness, her heart pounding, her hands coiled around the rock. She closed her eyes, muttering to herself as she psyched herself up.

Opening her eyes again, she grabbed the plastic bag and used the cord to tie it around the small of her back. She eased herself from the edge into the cold water, shivers shimmying up through her body.

Once submerged to mid-waist, she grabbed the torch and, most importantly, the knife.

She mouthed from one to three, and slipped into the darkness.

Chapter Seventeen

As soon as the cold water enveloped her, she knew there was no going back.

Eyes wide open, she held her torch ahead as steadily as she could whilst clumsily pushing herself through the water in moves that were too erratic and energy-draining in their urgency.

She kept veering ahead as Rone had told her. But having suspected he had betrayed her once, the paranoia was now at the forefront of her mind that she'd hit a dead end – that the air pockets were a lie. She'd know in her final seconds that he'd got one over on her, his problem solved.

She couldn't expect anything less, and had been naïve not to consider it before. She'd threatened him. She'd threatened to expose him, and subsequently he'd made up some lie about her being able to get out of there to be rid of her.

But she'd taken the only chance she could. If she didn't get out of there, if she couldn't save her sisters, The Alliance, then she may as well drown.

The pain started to consume her chest at the lack of oxygen, the light-headedness kicking in, her body taking over her mind as it punched her into accepting she needed oxygen.

She kicked harder, knowing the panic that consumed her was not going to help.

Rone had said it was at the midway point.

She kicked to the surface of the darkness, slamming the back of her hand up through the water, the panic taking holding as she hit rock every time.

She clutched the knife tighter, fearful of dropping it – fearful of never getting out of the tunnel without it, even if she did get to the other side of the lagoon.

She kept slamming her hand above her head, kept finding rock, her whole body starting to jerk in desperation for air.

She slammed her hand upwards again, but this time broke into cold air.

She pushed her head above the surface, and took the deepest and most desperate breath she had since that day in the lake.

She pressed her torch-holding hand to the rock as she used it to help balance herself, to curb the panic as her legs kicked erratically beneath the surface.

Regaining her senses, she took in the small dome in the rock – the small crevice providing air from somewhere. But the regular supply didn't mean she could stay there, even if the thought did cross her mind for a split second. Her body would freeze, her stationary position already evoking blood supply stagnation further than in just her extremities.

She needed to get back into the darkness, back into the cold depths and face the final twenty feet.

She closed her eyes, took as many deep breaths as she could.

And pushed herself back under the water.

The second part was more difficult – her body working less fluidly. She knew she couldn't hold her breath as long the second time, already tiring quickly, the extra effort to make her body move consuming more energy.

But she kept the torch ahead, kept veering right just as Rone had told her, pushing through the water, her legs exerting themselves to keep her momentum going.

When she suddenly hit rock, her knuckles scraping against the stone, she took in a mouthful of water in her panic.

But her instinct was to swim upwards.

She kicked hard, sliding up the wall, seeming to get nowhere until suddenly her head pushed through the surface water into the darkness of a tunnel.

She swam forward, dropping the knife and torch onto the side of the rock. She coughed and caught her breath, her forearms pressed down onto the hard edge.

It took her three attempts before she was able to lever herself out. Even then she could only manage to flop onto her side before rolling onto her stomach. She buried her head in her forearm before her survival instincts kicked in; before she reminded herself to tune into the potential threat of her surroundings.

She grabbed her torch and shone it into the darkness ahead.

There was no sound and no movement.

Rone had explained that most wouldn't venture down that part of the tunnel. Territory ruled just as much down there as it did on the surface. But she couldn't count on it and she certainly couldn't risk taking a wrong turn.

Shivering, she eased onto her knees and unfastened the cord around her waist. She ripped open the waterproof bag and took out the dry tunic and the map, a light pair of ballet-style shoes hitting the floor.

She angled the torch so it remained down the tunnel as she hurriedly tore off the sodden tunic clinging to her wet skin. The friction was painful as she drew it over her numbing flesh before casting it aside.

She slipped on the fresh tunic, too big for her, but that was probably better out there on the streets where she was going.

She waited for her feet to dry as she grabbed the torch again and studied the map.

There was no way she'd memorise it. This required her keeping it open at all times.

She slipped on the ballet shoes and stood up, leaving everything else behind – everything but the torch, the map and the knife.

The first part of the map said straight ahead for at least fifty feet, ignoring every turn off to the left, each of those branching out elsewhere. She prepared herself for the worst as she pressed on ahead, even her quiet footsteps painfully conspicuous in the silence of the tunnel.

Not that her silence would make any difference if there were rogue lycans or vampires milling around the tunnel – they'd smell her coming from over fifty feet away. But right then, for the first time, they seemed like the least of her worries. Because what she dreaded, as much as any third species, was the potential threat of the humans that *chose* to lurk down there.

Rone had been right in saying they were the lowest of the low. The Alliance had trained her to pick out the cons and to avoid them at all costs. In the cons' eyes, *they* were the humans that owned Blackthorn and would be as resentful of The Alliance's presence as the third species themselves.

She tightened her grip on her knife as her sudden sense of vulnerability consumed her. She slowed every time she reached a recess, taking a defensive stance, the blade ready in her hand, her heart pounding wildly, the adrenaline pumping.

It had always been her weak point in combat. Zach had tried so hard to calm her down – warning her that the escalation of her pulse rate and breathing not only made her more clumsy and less focused, but also incited her third-species opponent more. It also made her seem weaker than she was – something she couldn't afford to present.

Because she wasn't weaker. She was impulsive and at times irrational, but she also had a determination that made her a relentless opponent. Some days it had been all she'd had.

She kept her back to the wall as she moved further and further along the tunnel. She checked the map, ensuring she was going the right way. But she wouldn't move her back from the wall – not with the potential of anything coming up behind her, from in front or from the sides.

She quickened her pace, stopping every now and again to read the map before proceeding.

Suddenly the compound felt like a safe place. Being near Jask felt safe. But she rejected the thought as soon as it entered her head.

Nothing about Blackthorn was safe. Nothing about Blackthorn had ever been safe. Safe was something that no one but the elite could afford to feel. In fact, under the new systems, *no* human felt safe.

That was the point behind The Alliance – to break the system. To destroy the likes of Jask.

But still she couldn't help her mind wandering to how he would feel when he found out she'd gone. If he would suspect Rone. What punishments he would inflict on him.

What punishments he would inflict on her when and if he caught up with her.

Or if that last moment with him *had* been the last moment.

Sophia took a left at the end of the tunnel and then veered right. It opened up for a while in width and height before closing in on itself again. Some sections were man-made – bricked in with cement. Others were natural rock cocoons where nature had paved the way centuries or thousands of years before. The whole place was a warren. A maze known only by those who used it.

Following the map, she ploughed on until her feet registered an incline. Her torch caught a metal grid two feet off the ground to her left.

As she crouched down to peer through it, she saw nothing but crates beyond.

She tucked the torch in her mouth and removed the grate before warily sticking her head out.

It was a warehouse just as Rone had said.

Slipping through the gap, she peered up over the top of the crates in front of it. The place was empty. Regardless, she kept alert as she crept around the side and into the open.

She hurriedly crossed the warehouse, stepping out into an alley.

She stared up at the night sky as the clouds blew past the moon, then turned to face the alley opening. She needed to know where she was – where the tunnel had brought her out. She could tell from the volume of people, let alone the noise, that she was near the hub. And that meant she wasn't too far from home.

But she couldn't go home – that she had already resolved. As much as she wanted to feel a fresh shower and get into familiar clothes, she couldn't risk it. If they knew who she was, they also knew where she lived. It was a risk she wasn't willing to take.

She knew exactly where to go instead.

Stepping out of the alley, she scanned the neon signs and the landmarks. Seeing the clock tower of the museum in the distance, she headed straight towards it.

Chapter Eighteen

Sophia climbed the familiar graffiti-stained stairwell of the tower block.

The competing thud of music, of action films, of raucous voices resounded from behind closed or ajar doors as she ascended four flights of the dilapidated building.

She clenched her hidden knife as a group of youths passed her, one knocking her shoulder, the others turning around to mock her clothing. But she kept her mouth shut, her focus on the task in hand, not on a pending assault or dying on the cold, hard steps.

Daniel's bedsit was the first on the left.

Sophia stepped up to the splintered door. Heart pounding, breaths shallow, she pushed it open all the way before looking inside.

The place was badly smashed up. No sign of Daniel. Fortunately no sign of blood or law enforcement tape either.

She knew it was as pointless as it was risky banging on doors for answers, or even requesting a phone. Just as she knew there was one more place she could look for answers if the operation had gone wrong.

She turned on her heels and hurried back down the stairs, knocking shoulders with a couple she passed, her thoughts too focused elsewhere to acknowledge their verbal retaliation.

She headed back out onto the street, the flutter of palpitations consuming her chest. If her suspicions were right, the longer she stayed on the street, the more at risk she was.

But there was no way she could even attempt to get to the safety of Summerton. There would be all the awkward questions at the security offices, not least because Leila would have undoubtedly registered her as missing. She'd have been detained for sure, and then there was no way she'd be able to help anyone whilst locked in a cell for at least forty-eight hours of investigations.

But if Leila was in Summerton, or Alisha even, then they could get to *her*.

She needed that phone. More than anything, she just needed to hear their voices. She just needed to hear that they were okay – that she'd made a terrible mistake, an overreaction, and they were both home and well.

But her instincts told her it was dangerously wishful thinking.

She marched to the right before taking a sharp left down a side street. Reaching crossroads, she took another left.

There was only one place she *would* be safe.

She'd only ever been there once. They all had only ever been there once. But the location had been engrained in their minds – each with the hope they'd never have to use it.

She passed the rows of residential houses, most of them boarded up, many front doors broken open by whatever species chose to call them home.

As she'd done on the way there, she kept her head up as she moved through the crowds. A lowered head and lowered eyes meant victim stamped on your forehead. It was about averting your eyes, but not avoiding eye contact. It was about *looking* like you had a sire in Blackthorn, even if you didn't.

Some sires, eager to climb the power chain, sent their own feeders out to look for fresh human blood to add to their brood. If you got stopped, you looked them straight in the eye and told them you were taken. It was about knowing enough names on the street to know who to claim you belonged to. Most would remain cautious if you were convincing enough.

It was how The Alliance had started finding out who Blackthorn's key players were in the first place. They'd infiltrated the furtive feeder system – finding out who the leading sires were. They'd lost some of their own along the way. Offering yourself up as a feeder was dangerous territory. But they *had* got answers.

They'd gathered the names, used them when they needed to and then picked them off one by one. The operation had been going for fourteen months – slow but steady was the fight. Each one was done a different way – each made to look like a suspicious accident. The Alliance weren't about accolade – they were about getting the job done.

Sophia crossed the street to avoid the crowd of males lurking around the steps of one of the dilapidated Edwardian terrace town houses. With vampires it was the loners to fear. With humans it was the crowds to watch for.

With the former, the sense of her new power should have been liberating but she was already starting to doubt herself. She struggled to keep her focus on the hustle and bustle as she weaved her way through the crowds. The laughter, the shouts and the jostling were as disorientating as the neon lights flashing and reflecting on the damp pavements. But not as disorientating as her nerve endings firing involuntarily, the hairs on the back of her neck alert to the potential all around her.

She had walked through those crowds countless times but had never felt more alive. More aware. Something in her had changed. Instead of wanting to avoid the vampires she rubbed shoulders with, she wanted to stop, to grab hold of one of them, lead them into one of the dark alleys, make them bite...

She forced herself out of her daze, clutched the knife she held concealed amidst the folds of her tunic.

She guessed control would become easier with practice – the very reason serryns needed some kind of training to turn them into efficient predators rather than responding to their own desires all the time. The latter never lasted long – serryns, renowned for needing the next rush, becoming more and more impulsive to their eventual demise.

She wouldn't be like that. She'd manage it.

She had to keep walking, she had to keep going. She had to keep her focus on where she needed to be.

But as she glanced over her shoulder, as she saw the crowd on the steps had disappeared, she walked a little faster.

She subtly glanced at the glass windows opposite to try and catch reflections, but there were still too many around to determine whether she was being followed or not. The only way she'd know was when she got somewhere quieter.

She tightened her grip on the knife.

She had the choice to look over her shoulder again and let them know she had noticed, or to walk on pretending to be oblivious.

As the crowds started to thin out, she opted for the former.

At a glance she guessed there were four of them.

Her heart pounded a little harder, a light-headedness trying to suppress the panic.

Four of them and one of her. Four vampires and she might live long enough once the first one took a bite. But four humans – that would come down to brute strength.

Or speed.

She pressed her lips together and quickened her pace slightly – not to get away from them just yet but to build up a steady pace.

She counted it down.

As soon as she turned the next corner, she hit full sprint.

If there was one thing she had always had on her side, it was speed – at least against her own. And when it came to four human males and her, she'd outdo them every time in nimbleness alone. They might have seen easy pickings in her, but she saw a group she was going to outrun whatever it took.

Sophia turned left and then right, slipping through the chain-link fence and navigating her way nimbly around the boxes and rubbish.

It wasn't long before her pursuers were no longer silent. Instead their whoops and yells, like hounds in pursuit of a fox, echoed down the streets behind her.

In their eyes, this was mere sport – a sadistic hunt to the finish. Her life, what may have been left of it once they'd finished, nothing more than a game. She may have been one of their own but, for them, there was no loyalty to their own species. To them she was just another piece of entertainment.

She flicked out the blade as she ran, easily clearing obstacles where-as one closing in crushed them, slowing him down for a moment.

With every amount of energy she had, she sprinted until her chest ached.

With the wind in her ears and the adrenaline pumping, she struggled to remember how long it had been since they'd fallen quiet. Since the sickening goads and whistles had stopped.

But it was enough to make her finally slow her pace and turn around.

There wasn't sight nor sound of any of them.

She leaned forward and rested her palms on her thighs to catch her breath whilst remaining on her guard.

But they didn't reappear.

She felt a sense of disquiet as she stared into the darkness ahead, like the sudden silence before a volcanic eruption.

But nothing happened.

They'd gone.

Knowing she still couldn't rest on her laurels, let alone that the route had taken her ten minutes off course, she did an about-turn and picked up pace again.

Keeping to the other side of the street, she passed the cinema on the right. It was used mainly for shows of another kind now – live performances that rumours dictated rarely ended that way.

She kept close on the heels of one group so as to look to be a part of them, veering off again as soon as she passed the dwindling crowds.

She crossed in front of broad stone steps that led to the empty shell that was once a church, before taking a right down the cobbled street that ran alongside it, past the rusted fleur-de-lis-topped rail-ings that enclosed its grounds.

The cemetery still housed a hundred or so graves – graves from decades that had long passed. Even the sanctity of burial was no longer allowed. Now, bodies, especially the third species, were mainly cremated. Human ashes, except for those of the cons, were stored in crems in Lowtown – unless you were a resident of Summerton or Midtown. Both had beautiful churchyards. Summerton and Midtown residents were allowed to be buried. Just as they were allowed the best medical treatment, the best education, the best opportunities, the best of everything.

She couldn't remember the last time she'd gone to her mother's grave. Or her grandfather's. Leila had always gone every week without fail. Every Sunday afternoon when she wasn't working at the library, she'd head there with her flowers. Sometimes Alisha would go with her too.

Sophia had accompanied them both only once – Leila having insisted on all three sisters going together for their mother's birthday one year.

Sophia had spent the whole time hovering a few feet from the graves, her arms wrapped tightly around herself as she looked anywhere but at the inscriptions on the headstones. She'd even opted out of her say in that – shrugging and saying she'd go with whatever Leila and Alisha thought.

She'd stood and listened to the wind in the trees, the irony of the peacefulness compared with the death her mother had had.

All because of her.

She'd always felt like a traitor stood there – like a criminal returning to the scene of the crime. Only this criminal had a knotted throat and barely held-back tears.

At times she'd wondered if that's why Leila had encouraged her to go – some sadistic way of making her face up to her guilt.

It was part of the reason she lashed out at Leila so much – because deep down she knew if she hated herself as much as she did, then surely Leila must hate her too. She never admitted to it, but Leila knew the cause of their mother's death as much as she did.

Leila knew her unruly, arrogant, selfish little sister was responsible for putting their mother in the position in the first place. And somewhere deep, Leila *had* to despise her for it.

She took another left and slipped through the loose board in the sealed-up doorway. It was one of a multitude of old factories that had never been claimed – one of the many abandoned buildings that didn't suit anyone's purpose.

Only this one suited The Alliance's purpose perfectly.

The sliding and scraping of the wood echoed around the vast, empty interior, but her footsteps were barely audible as Sophia made her way across the concrete floor to the elevator shaft directly ahead.

They'd made their bolthole, their safe house, in the old offices above.

If anyone was there, they would have seen her coming on the CCTV hidden in the crevices. Whether the elevator descended or not would tell her that – otherwise it would be a heck of a climb up the exterior of the girder-structured shaft.

But as soon as she'd reached the base, the metal cogs kicked into action.

Her heart leapt.

She moved from foot to foot as she waited for its descent.

She saw his trainer-clad feet first, then his loose-fitting jeans. As Daniel appeared fully in view, as he slid back the cage door, she lunged to greet him the same time he did her.

It was something she'd never done before – reach for him in any genuine sign of affection. But to see him alive and well, let alone for her to have got there in one piece, brought reality home hard and fast.

'Shit, Phia,' he exclaimed, squeezing her against him. 'I thought you were dead.'

She pulled back from his hold so she could look in his eyes. 'Same here. I've just come from your place.'

'I had word I had unwanted guests before I even got up there. Phia, one minute you're hurtling after Caleb Dehain and then you're gone. I thought he'd killed you. Where have you been?'

'Long story. Word is out there about us, right? That's why you've all come here?'

His grave blue eyes held hers, something behind them making her uneasy. He pulled the gate back across and flipped the lever to trigger their ascent. 'Let's get upstairs first.'

She watched the girders scrape past and glanced warily across at him. He looked pale and drawn, as if he hadn't eaten properly for a couple of days, hadn't seen a glimpse of sunlight. The bags under his eyes told her he certainly hadn't slept. It was all the confirmation she needed that their secret had been uncovered – let alone the fact he was there in the first place.

Daniel pulled open the gate, Phia stepping out first and heading towards the open door. As he hurriedly locked and secured it behind them, Sophia glanced into the kitchen, at the piles of tinned food and water. But it wasn't just the reality hitting her that unnerved her – it was the silence emanating from the lounge beyond.

She continued along the hallway before entering the main room. She skimmed over the empty battered sofas ahead, the vacant chairs and table to her left. There was no sound of voices in the makeshift bedrooms beyond, no echo of a shower running. There were no strewn around mugs except for one sat alone on the tarnished coffee table ahead.

Unease took a painful hold on her chest. 'Where is everyone?'

'Sit down,' Daniel said softly, resuming his place in the dip of the tattered sofa.

On autopilot, she sank next to him, her body turned to face him fully. 'Dan?' she asked again, her heart pounding.

He took a steady intake of air. 'They're gone, Phia.'

It took a moment for the word to sink in. 'Gone? What do you mean, "gone"? Gone where?'

'Some might have made it into Lowtown.'

'*Some?*'

He moved to stand. 'I'll get you a coffee.'

She grabbed his arm before he had chance to rise more than an inch. 'Dan, what the fuck is going on?'

For a moment he said nothing as he stared at the coffee table. Then his eyes met hers. 'They're dead, Phia. Nearly all of them. Dead. The Alliance is finished.'

Chapter Nineteen

Caitlin Parish stepped through the cornered-off apartment, her colleagues milling about – mainly forensics gathering up whatever evidence they could before the rest of the investigative team stepped in.

As she assessed the room, the blood splatters on the wall, the corpse strapped to a dining chair in the small bedsit, it was one hell of a way to spend her first two hours back at work.

The response had been cold enough that evening as she'd returned to the Vampire Control Unit for the first time in two weeks. For the first time since the trial that had exposed the corruption of the three agents, let alone the head of the Third Species Control Division, determined to bring down their most wanted vampire, Kane Malloy.

The vampire whose bed she had just come from.

The office, always a flurry of activity and noise, had fallen silent the minute she'd stepped into it. All eyes had been on her as she'd made her way across to the desk she hadn't sat at since the court case, since the scandal had outed.

The scandal *she* had outed.

She'd glanced around at one or two glares of disapproval – colleagues she'd had enough of a battle with over the years to prove her worth in the VCU and not just in the interrogation room.

Now they'd emanated the hateful "I told you so" look. A look she knew she'd have to get used to. Fast.

She'd sat at her desk and fired up her computer before tearing the sticky note off the screen.

Vampire whore, it had said.

Never had two words cut her deeper.

'Or just whore,' a whisper echoed behind her. 'A dirty little vampire-loving slut.'

She'd wanted to turn and march over to confront the faceless voice, to slam the paper on his desk. Instead, she'd scrunched up the note in her hand, adjusted her chair and logged into her computer.

Before marching straight to Morgan's office.

'You can't do this,' she'd said as she'd stood at the threshold to his office.

He'd looked up from his pile of paperwork, pen still poised in his hand. 'Welcome back, Agent Parish.'

'You said it,' she'd declared, closing the door behind her. '*Agent* Parish. So would you like to tell me why I've been put on shadow reading *only* for the next month?'

Morgan sighed and threw down his pen. A resolute sigh that had told her it was the precise response he'd been expecting. But he *had* been her street partner for eighteen months. And she *had* been his senior.

He'd leaned back in his chair and held his hand out towards the one on the other side of his desk.

Caitlin had promptly accepted his offer, perching on the edge, her forearms on the desk that her stepfather had once occupied almost seven days a week for over a decade. Occupied, until she'd told the court exactly what he, her father, and her ex had done to Arana Malloy under the toxic influence of the head of the TSCD, Xavier Carter.

'I can't let you back out there yet, Caitlin.'

'Why not?'

'Why do you think?'

'I did the right thing, Morgan – and you know it.'

'But unfortunately for you, ninety-five per cent of the Vampire Control Unit think you're wrong. Probably ninety-five per cent of the entire Third Species Control Division.'

'Since when did what's right and what's wrong work on a majority-decision-only basis?' She'd unscrunched the paper in her hand and smoothed it out on top of the paperwork. 'See this? Is this right?'

'People are still upset.'

'No, Morgan – this is ignorance. And I don't get bullied by ignorance.'

'It's not about what's right or wrong in this. It's about the fact I can't guarantee your safety.'

'No one wants my back, right?'

'Caitlin, I don't need to spell it out to you. They don't care about your motivations or your reasons for what happened. They don't care about what really went on. All they see is that you betrayed your unit. You took a vampire's side over the side of your own. Worse still, you chose to sleep with him. Any respect you had gained in this unit is gone. Besides, upset in the team is the last thing we need right now. I'm trying to keep morale high and the VCU united for the bastards out there who think we're broken. I'm doing what's best for the team. So I'm sorry, Caitlin, but if you want to stay a part of this unit, you have to take what I give you.'

'So you tuck me away. Pay lip service to my return to work. And what does that achieve other than you proving you're nothing but a nodding dog to every agent out there who thinks *this* is acceptable?' she'd said, slamming her finger on the paper. 'Is this *really* how you want to start your career – keeping your head down? Tell *them* that they either accept me or *they* can reconsider their place on this team.'

'And that's what you'd do in my position, is it, Caitlin?'

'Too right, I would. Because with it I would be proving to every single person out in Lowtown and Blackthorn that the Vampire Control Unit, let alone the Third Species Control Division, is not an all boys' club of scratching mutual backs and looking after your own. It's about doing what we're paid to do, which is protecting those streets with the most impartial and effective agents we have. And I was and will continue to be this unit's most effective agent,

Morgan – and you know it. You stick me down in one of those shadow-reading rooms and I will lose total respect for you. Because you will prove that this whole system, just like they're saying out on the streets right now, *is* a lost cause. You have a chance to change things, Morgan. *Really* change things. And you can start right now.'

She'd leaned back in her chair, her arms folded, her glare fixed on Morgan.

He'd held that gaze for a moment then shaken his head slightly as he'd looked back down at his paperwork.

She'd not dared move, her breath baited as she'd awaited his response in the passing seconds.

He'd slipped a thin cardboard folder out from under his pile of papers and dropped it in front of her.

'It's the eighth one in three days,' he'd said. 'All tortured before death. All totally unrelated as far as we can tell other than the fact all the victims are human.'

'Tortured for what?'

'We don't know. With no survivors, no witnesses and no one on the street talking to us, we're clueless.'

'Retaliation for the trial?'

He shrugged. 'A possibility. What's interesting though is that their fingertips were burned off to slow down identification. At the very least, whoever it is, they're buying themselves some time, which tells us there could be more to come.'

She'd flicked through the papers. 'What about dental records?'

'There were no dentures left to analyse.'

She snatched her gaze back up to him. 'So basically we have nothing until DNA results come through?'

'This is the DNA report on the first two,' he said, pulling out the yellow sheet amongst the white. 'One victim came from Midtown, the other from Lowtown.'

'Feeders?'

'No sign of it.'

'Then what were they doing in Blackthorn?'

He'd shrugged. 'That's the big question. So, are you up for the job, *Agent* Parish?'

She'd smiled and gathered up the folder.

'Just look out for yourself,' he'd said, easing back in his chair. 'Tyrell's already on this case so he'll be your partner. I don't think he'll give you any major problems, but you're still on your own now. And that's no way for a VCU agent to be.'

She'd stood up. 'I'm not quitting, Matt,' she'd said, clutching the folder against her chest. 'I know that's exactly what they want me to do, but I'm not walking out of here.'

He's sent her a weary smile. 'As if I should have expected anything less.'

Now, in the dingy bedsit, she stepped up to the chair, up to the body. She crouched down to look up at the face. It was badly beaten. She glanced down at the fingertips that had been burned off just like the others. All the teeth with missing.

She stood back up again.

'I take it we have nothing again,' she said as an open question, her attention still on the body.

When she was met with silence, she glanced around at her so-called team.

Carl, who she'd worked with in forensics for long enough, just shrugged.

They'd always had a good relationship, but now he struggled to maintain eye contact with her. She excused it as her own paranoia setting in at first, but his response was too uncharacteristic to his usual free-flowing concise and insightful analysis. It wasn't helped by him glancing at some of the others in the room, as if needing their approval.

Others who remained equally silent.

As if someone had jumped on her back, she felt the weight of their reproach.

'Do you have a problem in solving this case?' she asked, staring straight back at Carl.

His eyes, laced with resentment at being confronted, finally met hers.

'Because if you're struggling to do your job, I can organise a replacement,' she reminded him.

It was a foolhardy statement – one that wasn't going to win her or regain her any fans. Not that either were a battle she was going to win anyway. But she was going to do her job properly. And if that meant reminding her colleagues who was in charge, then that was what she'd do.

'Male, late twenties,' Harry, one of the investigators, said as he handed her a plastic evidence bag with the ID open inside. 'This had fallen down the back of one of the drawers. It's the first time anything has been left behind. We don't know if they were in a hurry, got slack or were just disturbed. His name's Mark Turner. Formerly of Midtown. Good education. Plenty of money behind him. He had no reason to be here. We've done all the standard checks. His system is clear of alcohol and drugs. There are no bite or syringe marks, so he wasn't a feeder. Like I said – he had no reason to be here.'

Caitlin scanned the information on the ID. 'I want to know more about his background. I want to know about any political influences. I want to know if he was here on a cause.'

'A cause?' Carl asked.

'These attacks are down to a third species,' she said. 'So I'm guessing Mark here, along with the others, has offended someone somehow. Until we find the link between the victims, we're not going to know.'

'Cons are proficient at staging crimes like these – shifting the blame.'

'The lab reports show from the angle, force and indentations that the victims' jaws were removed by hands, not tools. Besides, up until now this whole operation has been meticulous. From the way each of the victims was tortured, someone wanted something from each of them. This is clinical, not personal. And it's professional. This was a mission.'

'I'll see what I can find out,' Harry said.

'And flag the files up to the Unidentified Species Unit. We can't assume only vampire or lycan involvement. We might have something else on our hands.'

'Why don't you just ask your boyfriend for help?' someone piped up.

She scanned the room, detecting the smirks, before locating the officer guarding the door.

'He knows all about this kind of thing, doesn't he?' the officer added. 'Torturing, maiming, killing? Maybe he had something to do with it. *Maybe* he thinks he can get away with it now he's got someone on the inside to cover his arse for him.'

She turned to face the officer at least twenty years her senior but five ranks her junior.

'How about you produce a statement to that effect?' she suggested, biting back her aggravation. 'And submit it for consideration, if that's your genuine suspicion?'

'So you can get him into the interrogation room all over again? Oh no, you don't need to, do you? You can strap him up in your own private den now. Or is it true that you like him to strap you up?' He looked around the room and smirked. 'I think that's where we've been going wrong all these years, boys. She's not frigid.' He glowered back at her with his cold, grey eyes. 'She just likes it rough. Vampire rough.'

Pulse racing, chest tight, she stepped up to him. 'I'm *more* than capable of setting my personal feelings aside. If you're having difficulty doing the same, maybe you're not emotionally up to the job.'

The eyes of the nameless officer narrowed in hatred, despite it being the first time they had ever so much as exchanged words. He was the silent voice of everything that was wrong with the TSCD – quick to judge, quick to condemn and, typical of bullies, quick to make sure as many others as possible did the same. And he did so with a sanctimony that was the ultimate irony. 'When we're alone, I'll show you just how much I'm up to the job.'

Her stomach flipped, queasiness at the very suggestion only adding to her indignation. 'Is that a threat?'

'Not that anyone in here has heard,' he replied.

She looked around as all eyes rested sullenly on hers.

'No one wants you here, Parish,' he added. 'So why don't you go and shuffle your papers like some good little secretary and leave the real work to the men who know how to *give* it to the vampires, not roll over and *take* it.'

She glowered deep into the officer's eyes.

In the silence of the room, no one defended her. No one spoke up. No one moved. Hardly anyone breathed.

She brushed past him. 'I want everything on my desk before the end of the shift,' she said before turning to face the room again. 'Unless *you* all want to be the ones rolling over and proving everyone right who thinks the TSCD have lost their touch. I sure as hell won't be.'

She headed back to the stairs in the derelict tower block. She fisted her trembling hands and struggled to calm her breathing, not least when she heard laughter inside, even some congratulatory comments and a slap on a back.

Face flushed from humiliation, from anger, from the injustice, she headed back down the stairs, unable to stop even for Tyrell for fear of her barely held-back tears giving way.

Chapter Twenty

Sophia held her breath as if waiting on the cusp of a joke. But the punch line never came.

'What are you talking about?' was all she could utter quietly. 'What do you mean, *dead*?'

'We've been ambushed. They know about us. And they've been killing us off. Abby called an emergency meeting the night after you disappeared. She warned us to go underground. She said we were to sever all ties with each other – that The Alliance was broken. I've never seen her so scared.'

'Who?' she asked. 'Who's responsible for this?'

'We don't know.'

Marid?

Or maybe even Caleb himself.

The latter made perfect sense. If Marid knew, others knew. And if anyone knew everything that was going on in Blackthorn, it was Caleb Dehain. *And* he had Alisha. Alisha knew about The Alliance – she'd forced a confession out of Sophia months before with the threat of going to Leila.

Caleb could have found out from her. Or Alisha could have let it slip to Jake if there was something going on between them.

Her heart pounded. 'Dehain,' she said. 'The Dehains have come after us. They worked out we were responsible.'

'No. No, this is bigger than that.'

He stepped over to the dining table where the laptop was, Sophia following behind.

As she perched on one of the chairs, he turned the screen to face her.

'I'm keeping a close eye on every report, not that there's much being disclosed,' he said. 'But the VCU are involved now.'

Her gaze shot to Daniel's. 'Do *they* know about The Alliance?'

'Nothing has been said publicly. But even if they did know, there *is* no Alliance anymore.'

She flicked through the images that had been plastered over news reports. There were no images of the bodies, but there were plenty of accounts and images of the aftermaths left behind.

'We've lost at least eight in the past three days. There could be more. Like I said, we've all lost contact. Hannah, Simon, Tyrone, Cass, even Zach – they're all gone. And now Lola too. Whoever this is, they're fast. And they're meticulous. And they're covering their tracks. They pick one off, they torture them for more names and then they move on to the next.'

Sophia stared back at the screen, at the blood-splattered apartment she had known well. She'd had one or two celebratory drinks there. One or two discussions putting the world to rights through to dawn. Lola had been a quirky little thing – tiny but lethal. And Sophia had always had a soft spot for her.

Originally from Midtown, Lola's parents had been forced to move from Midtown into Lowtown after her father failed on his employment scores. A bout of severe ill health for his wife had had him exhausted and underperforming. Instead of looking to support him, he'd become an inconvenience to his employers. They'd turned up the pressure and he'd been destined to fail. Her mother's ill health and inability to go out had subsequently lowered all their social contribution scores. The worry meant Lola had started to struggle in school.

Their move to Lowtown meant they didn't have enough credits to be entitled to free health care anymore. And there was no way they could afford the long-term payments for the medical care her mother needed. Her father looked for work but failed to find anything legitimate. All the decent jobs went to those with the right cohorts. But being in with the right cohorts meant you didn't own yourself anymore – let alone your house or your family. When they'd offered to take Lola as payment, it had been the final straw.

Her father's visits to Blackthorn had become more regular – his only source of income becoming a feeder. One night, he never came home. Less than two months later, Lola's mother passed away in her arms – the two of them alone in the dingy, damp, run-down bedsit Sophia now stared at on the screen.

Lola was one of the first to join The Alliance. She was determined, feisty and efficient in their cause. She wouldn't have gone down without a fight.

Sophia felt her throat clog with suppressed tears, pleading that they wouldn't surface.

'I thought they'd got to you too, Phia. What happened? How are you still alive? Where have you been?'

Even now her heart pounded with a mixture of anger and fear. If it hadn't been for the serryn line jumping, she would have been dead just like her Alliance colleagues. That was the simple fact: her serrynity had been the only thing to save her. Her sister, Leila, knowingly or unknowingly, had saved her again. 'Marid took me. I didn't even get inside the club.'

'Marid?'

'He knows about us. He found out that I was after him.' She hesitated. 'He kept me for a couple of days before selling me on to two vampires. They were planning to question me about The Alliance. They must have been a part of this.' Rone had said the two vampires had been working for someone else. Someone who clearly intended to make The Alliance suffer as much as possible. She looked back up at him. 'But some of these have happened in the last twelve hours. I killed the ones who came after me, Dan, so how many are involved in this?'

'You killed them?'

She nodded. She couldn't tell him about her serrynity. Not yet. She had too many things she needed to get her own head around first.

'Did you get their names?' he asked.

'I didn't get the chance.'

'But why didn't you come back? Why didn't you warn us? If you got away, where have you been?'

Awkwardness coiled through her – a new sense of guilt, though why, she wasn't sure. 'The compound.'

Wide-eyed, it was his turn to stare at her for a moment. 'The compound?'

'A couple of lycans found me. They took me back there.'

The shock emanated from his face. 'You've been with *lycans*?' His frown deepened with concern. 'You've been in the compound all this time?'

'The last twenty-four hours.'

'How the hell did you get out?'

'By doing what we're trained to do – making the most of what opportunities I had.'

'Do they know about us too?'

'One did – but he's saying nothing. He's the one who got me out.'

'A lycan acting against the pack? Against Jask Tao's pack? This doesn't sound right.'

'It's complicated. What matters is I'm out.'

'Did you meet him? Jask Tao?'

She looked away at that point, resolving it was time she did get herself a coffee. 'We had one or two encounters.'

Daniel followed her to the kitchen.

She flicked on the kettle and grabbed a mug from the cupboard. She scooped two spoonfuls of coffee from the oversized tub before resolving to scoop in another. She rested her palms on the worktop as she waited for the water to boil.

Daniel pulled away from the doorway where he'd been watching her and placed his stained mug next to hers.

'Sorry,' she said quietly for not thinking of him. She scooped a couple of spoonfuls into his mug too.

'It's okay. I know this must be a shock. Are you all right?'

She shrugged, sending him a sideways glance before staring back down at the mugs.

But she wasn't okay. She was far from okay. The plan to take down the Dehains had failed because of her. And if this *was* down to Caleb, the fact he was still alive to wreak that retribution was down to her. Just as if Caleb had somehow got the information from Alisha – Alisha who, she was sure, wouldn't have been in Blackthorn if it wasn't for her – was also down to her. One way or another, The Alliance was dead because of her. Those were the facts.

'Did he hurt you?' Daniel asked with the irritatingly soft tone of a therapist.

Sophia exhaled tersely. The very prospect of it seemed ludicrous, and that's what shocked her the most. Her instinctive response was to defend Jask, like being asked if a lifelong faithful partner was capable of infidelity. 'No, he didn't,' she said, lifting the boiled kettle and pouring its contents into the mugs.

Daniel moved closer and slid the powdered milk towards her. 'You can talk to me.'

She looked Daniel in the eye. 'Trust me, Jask Tao has more to worry about than a scrag like me.'

She scooped in the milk powder and stirred.

But he *would* be looking for her.

More than ever she was sitting on a ticking bomb surrounded by landmines. Now it was whether she could be quick enough and efficient enough to get to her sisters before everything went off.

'I need a phone,' she said, remembering herself. 'I need to call home.'

'There aren't any. I destroyed mine in case they caught up with me and traced the others. It was the first thing Abby told us to do.'

'Then I need to get back out there,' she said. She swallowed a couple of mouthfuls of hot coffee, burning her tongue, on her way back through to the lounge. 'Are spare clothes still kept here?'

'In the women's dorm. Phia, we need to lie low for a few days. We'll be okay here for a while. We can't risk going out there.'

It was a question she hadn't thought to ask. 'Why are you still here, Dan?' she asked, heading down the hallway, taking a left. 'Why haven't you tried to get into Lowtown for yourself?'

'Why do you think?' He leaned against the doorframe as she flung open the wardrobe doors. 'I wasn't going to leave without you. Leave you here alone.'

She looked back at him. 'This isn't how it's supposed to be, Dan. No attachments, remember?'

'I'm still your friend, Phia. As little as you want them. As little as you think you need them. Besides, someone had to warn you in case you did reappear. I knew you'd come here if you failed to contact anyone.'

'Yeah, well I'm not lying low anywhere.' She rooted through the bags at the bottom and picked out underwear, checking the labels for the right sizes before tearing the price-tags off. 'I need to get to a phone, then I'll get back here and we'll talk about what we're going to do. We need to find out who's responsible for this.'

'What does it matter? It's too late anyway.'

'It's never too late,' she said. She slipped the knickers on under her tunic before tearing the fabric over her head to pull on and fasten the bra.

'Phia…'

'We can sort this. Whoever is responsible, be it Marid, Caleb or whoever, this doesn't end here.'

'Phia…' Daniel said again, but he may as well have been white noise for all she tuned in.

'They need to know who they're dealing with…'

'Phia, it was a vampire.'

She reached for the combats. 'That's what I'm saying. And they're not getting away with it.'

'Phia…' She'd barely registered his hesitation. 'It was a vampire who paid us. A vampire *paid* us to do the Dehain job.'

Her gaze snapped to his. She clutched the waistband of her combats, barely mid-hip. 'What?'

Daniel slumped onto the edge of the nearest bed. He lowered his head for a moment, his forearms on his thighs.

She fastened the top button and took a step towards him, the sweater loose in her hand. 'What are you talking about?'

'After you disappeared, Abby came to see me. She was in a really bad way.' He looked back up at her. 'The new equipment – all the stuff we used that night for the Dehains – it came via a sponsor, a sponsor who paid us a lot of money to go after them. That's how they got to the top of the hit list so quick instead of being our crescendo along with Malloy. We were paid to take them out – by a vampire.'

'No,' she said. She yanked on the sweater and stormed into the bathroom.

He followed behind her. 'I knew how you'd feel about it. I didn't want to say anything.'

She brushed past the hospital-style mint green shower curtain, the mould on its base betraying the years it had been there. She opened the cupboard beside it and grabbed a new toothbrush, ripping open the packet as she marched across to the sink, the bitterness in her mouth, the dryness, too much to bear. She turned the creaking chrome tap, the spray spluttering before letting out an inconsistent flow of water.

'Phia…'

Toothbrush loaded with paste, she brushed too vigorously for her gums. She spat out blood before continuing.

'Phia, Abby told me. That's why she was so stressed that night when she knew it had gone wrong.'

She spat out another mouthful. 'No. There is no way,' she said, pointing the toothbrush at him before resuming brushing again. 'That's fucking absurd. We hunt them. We don't fucking work for them.'

'They made Abby an offer she couldn't refuse. We kill vampires, but it doesn't mean we can't take funding from them. The end result is the same–'

'No!' Sophia snapped, chucking her toothbrush aside in the sink, rubbing the back of her hand across her mouth as she turned to face him. 'I do *not* work for vampires. I did not sign up to work for vampires. They do not pull my strings. I do *not* do their dirty work for them.'

She grabbed the threadbare towel and wiped her mouth properly before marching past him back into the dorm.

'We did. And we failed,' Daniel said. 'And they know it. And now they know *us*. And they're hunting and tracking us down like wild animals. I'm only telling you this because I cannot let you step outside those doors. We don't know what kind of influence they have, only that they don't want to risk even one of us leaking word back to Caleb Dehain that this was an inside assassination. They will be hunting every corner of Blackthorn and Lowtown for us to make sure that doesn't happen. So we *have* to stay here.'

'And what if the vampire was Caleb himself, huh? Maybe Caleb was the sponsor. Maybe there wasn't a third party in all this. Maybe he set us up – one giant double bluff. It would be perfect: using his own brother as a honeytrap to bring us out into the open. That's why he turned the girl down that night – he already knew. And maybe he had someone on hand to cure Jake–'

Discomfort wrenched through her.

A witch skilful enough to do it. The most powerful witch there was. A serryn.

But she pushed the thought out of her head – the ramblings of a panicked mind.

There was no way Leila was in Blackthorn too. No way *both* of her sisters were with the Dehains.

'Phia, you know that makes no sense.'

No, it didn't. And that's what she'd cling too.

'Neither does some vampire who wants Caleb Dehain dead hiring a group of human vigilantes instead of doing it themselves. Who would waste that amount of money, take that kind of risk?'

'I don't know.'

As much as she wanted to deny his words, she couldn't deny the look in his eyes.

'Well, we're not going to sit on our arses in here whilst we wonder. You said it yourself – they're coming for us. There's only one way to stop that: get to them first.' She headed back out into the living space. 'What the *fuck* was Abby thinking?'

'About keeping our heads above water,' he declared, following her. 'About getting the job done.'

'Paid by *vampires*?'

'One who wanted Caleb dead too. The way Abby saw it, it was a mutual and lucrative cause.'

'But we've both seen that equipment. Who's got access to technology and resources like that here unless they're top of the food chain?' She stared at the floor, hands on her hips, before she snapped her attention back up to him. 'I'm making that call. Then we're tracking down who did this. Someone out there's got to know.'

'No one is going to talk to you, Phia.'

'I'll *make* them.'

'And where the hell do you start? All you'll do is draw attention to yourself.'

'I don't care.'

'Well I do. I didn't risk my life sitting here on my arse waiting for you when I could have been long gone across the border.'

'And that's my fault because…?'

He glared at her. 'You ungrateful…'

'What?' she asked, slamming her hands on her hips. 'Say it, Dan – selfish, unappreciative, stupid, impetuous. I've heard it all before. A hundred times. I know it. You know it. We all know it. And it changes nothing. The Alliance may be gone, but *I'm* not.'

'Listen to yourself – waging a one-woman war. We lost. We tried and we failed. We're lucky to be alive.'

'Alive for what? What do we have? Stuck in this place, in Blackthorn – at best Lowtown. We fight to the bitter end on this, Dan.

I'm taking down whoever did this. They want us to hide and there's no way I'm giving them that.'

'You're not going out there alone. Not like this.'

'I'm better alone.'

'With whoever this is looking for you? With Jask Tao looking for you? Maybe Caleb too if he *does* know about all this?'

'Is the kit still here?' she asked, marching down to the kitchen.

'Did you not hear what I said? You're getting nowhere out there.'

'We'll see.' She ploughed through the cupboards before finding the box masked as a first-aid kit. She carried it back through to the living space and placed it down on the coffee table. Sitting, she pulled out the packets of syringes they used to fill with garlic and silver – a concoction that would slow down their vampire victims or a useful tool to get them to talk.

'What are you doing?' he demanded.

Sophia wrapped the bandage around and around her arm before pulling it tight. She took the lid off the syringe with her teeth before slipping it into the crook in her arm.

'What the fuck, Phia?'

Sophia drew back the blood, sticking the cap back on the syringe before reaching for another. 'There's one simple reason I got away from those vampires – I poisoned the bastards.' Sophia glanced up into wide eyes. 'Nutshell,' she said, returning her attention to the next needle she slipped it into the crook of her arm, 'is that my sister was a serryn. I emphasise the word *was*. The line's capable of jumping.' She glanced up at him again. 'I'm sure I don't need to explain the rest.' She looked back down to check how much blood she was taking. 'Let's just say her timing was perfect or I *would* be dead by now. Just like the others.'

The silence between them was unavoidable.

'A serryn,' he finally said. 'Your sister's a serryn? You never said.'

'No disclosures, remember?' She swapped the syringe for another. 'No background information.'

'But a *serryn*? You know what that could have meant to our cause. The power it would have given us.'

'And if I knew, maybe I would have. But I didn't have a clue. Trust me, no one's more stunned than me. But if it's jumped, then something is wrong. Very wrong. And that's why I'm getting back out there.'

She placed the lid on the third syringe before reaching for the fourth. Once she'd finished, she unpackaged some plasters to cover the pinprick wounds.

'One way or another, what has happened to my sisters could be down to me,' she added. 'I'm not turning my back on them.' She gathered up the syringes and stood, despite how light-headed she felt. 'You stay here. But if you do decide to head out, and any of them come after you, you stick one of these in them,' she said, handing him two of the syringes. 'You'll watch them sizzle like a steak on a barbecue before they implode if you stick it in hard and fast enough.' She tucked two of her own in the thigh pocket of her combats.

'Does Jask know what you are?'

She nodded. 'I'll come back for you when I've contacted them.' She headed back into the kitchen and opened the tallest cupboard. She took out two of the handguns. She checked the ammo before sliding one into the back of her combats, the other in the loop on the thigh of her trousers. 'And they'd better be alive and kicking,' she said, as she swept past him to the main door, 'or all hell is going to break loose in Blackthorn by the time I've finished.'

But Daniel slammed his syringe-holding hand to the door, grabbed her arm with the other. 'Have you not listened to anything I've said? If you are what you say you are, it's even more important we keep you alive.'

'Don't make this into a fight between us. I don't have the time.' She stared deep into his eyes as she yanked her arm from his grip. 'I have to do this, Dan. Try and stop me and I'll kick your arse, and you know it.'

He stared right back, a steely silence between them that squeezed the air from her lungs.

'Then I'm coming with you,' he said.

'No. You'll slow me down.'

His eyes narrowed in indignation. 'Since when? I'll keep you in check. We both know how much you need that.' He held her gaze for a few moments. 'I mean it, Phia.' He stepped back into the kitchen, picked a handgun of his own. 'We're a team, right?' He tucked the gun and syringes into his pockets, then faced her.

'More like you're too valiant for your own good,' she remarked, opening the door.

'I'm no hero,' he said. He drew back the cage to the elevator shaft, letting Sophia enter first. 'And I hate you for making me do this.'

'Add it to the list, Dan,' she said as they descended. 'But whatever is going on out there, we have to know. We can't let them beat us.'

He pulled back the cage as they reached the bottom, the cool night air leaking into the warehouse a sharp contrast to the mustiness of the room they had just left.

'You're going to a phone first, right?' he asked as they strode across the concrete.

'Then I'm paying Marid a visit,' Phia declared, her breath like smoke in the air, the temperature seeming to have dropped even in the short time they'd been inside. 'He knows what's going on here. *And* he'll talk. I'll see to–'

They both flinched simultaneously as they saw movement in the shadows ahead.

Sophia snapped her gun into position, directly on the dark figure.

Daniel was a fraction too slow.

Another figure had already appeared behind him – swift, forceful, strategic. A split second later, Daniel was slammed against the wall.

Her heart pounded as the six-foot-two-inch male slid Daniel a foot up off the ground, Daniel swiping at the hand that rigidly clasped his throat.

As she stared back at the figure ahead, she understood why every instinct had stopped her pulling the trigger.

'Long time, no see, Phia,' Jask said as he emerged from the darkness.

Chapter Twenty-One

Twelve hours previous

Jask had fallen asleep waiting for Sophia to do so first.

Now he'd woken to find her sleeping soundly, the glow of the descending afternoon sun warming them both. Her body was enticingly soft against his, the heat of their bodies having melded in the couple of hours they'd lay there.

He lifted his head from the pillow to look at her face, but it was too masked by her hair to see her eyes – only her delicate nose and slightly parted curvaceous lips visible.

It had been a long time since he'd woken next to a female – since he'd allowed himself that luxury. He'd almost forgotten how it felt, let alone the stirring sense of intimacy it evoked, not least from sharing his bed.

Only mates shared beds. That was an understanding amongst their kind. It prevented complications and misconstruing one intent behind a sexual act from another.

But taking the serryn to his bed had been nothing about sex, though the thoughts had irritatingly slipped into his head too many times over the few hours before. And no more so than when he'd cornered her in the bathroom, provoking his resolve to get some much-needed sleep before acting in a way he'd regret.

She was too intense, too unrelenting, too provocative for him to deal with her when his irritation levels were that high. Besides, she'd looked on the edge of exhaustion herself – getting more and more irrational in her choices. Trying to provoke both him and Corbin outside the holding room had proven that. They'd both needed downtime.

And he'd needed to calm the frustration inside.

But gazing at her sleeping only reignited the thoughts again – how he could so easily lay her beneath him, find the core of her heat, sate himself for a short while at least.

And thoughts of her submitting, of her letting him take her amidst the comfort of her hazy sleep like familiar lovers, only aroused him further. He felt himself harden as he thought of tasting every inch of her smooth skin before sinking as deep into her as he could.

But what he wanted and what he needed were two entirely different things. What he *needed* was to head out to Rone and Samson – to see if time in the caskets had drummed sense into them.

Because this time, he wasn't leaving without answers.

Carefully he pulled away.

Rather than stir her, he'd enjoy the refreshing outdoor showers after his training session, after their afternoon game out on the pitch.

He pulled on his sweatpants, vest top and jacket and sent one more glance at the feminine curves that lay beneath his duvet, before heading out of his room.

Corbin was already down in the foyer when Jask nodded his head out towards the quadrant, indicating for him to follow.

'We'll get them out now,' Jask said as Corbin drew level.

'Earlier than planned?' Corbin remarked, keeping up with Jask's strides as they crossed the green towards the tunnel.

'Like you said, we don't have time to waste.'

Jask unlocked the outbuilding, Corbin sealing the door behind them before they made their way down the steps, taking a left into the room where Rone and Samson were held.

Opening the casket was worse than closing it, Jask knowing the trauma, disorientation and exhaustion that would be in both the youth's eyes after their experience. But he pushed it to the back of his mind as he opened the casket, met Rone's startled gaze only fleetingly before releasing him from his binds.

Trembling, Rone all but fell out of his enclosure, the glazed look in his eyes sign enough that it would take him a while to reacclimatise.

A luxury Jask had no intention of supplying.

Rone bent double, his hands on his thighs before he stood upright again, stretching his neck to the ceiling. He paced unsteadily, as did Samson, needing to move their aching limbs and flex.

Jask leaned back against the stone table, Corbin beside him, both their arms folded as they allowed them a minute.

'How are you feeling?' Jask asked.

Rone looked across at him mid-pace and nodded.

'You've got fifteen minutes,' Jask said.

Rone stopped abruptly, Samson mirroring him.

'For what?' Rone asked.

'Until you go back in there.'

Samson's troubled gaze shot to his friend before it flitted between Jask to Corbin.

'Back in?' Rone said, as if saying it would make it any less true.

'Unless you're planning on telling me what really went on down in those ruins.'

Rone and Samson exchanged glances, but neither spoke.

'Your choice,' Jask said. 'But we can keep doing this until you break. Because you *will* break.'

'Jask…' Rone said, his tone laced with a plea.

But Jask remained staid, despite hating the look of cornered panic in youth's eyes. 'One way or another you are going to tell me the truth. I've got all day, all night and all day again tomorrow if that's what it takes. Who is she? How did you *really* come across her? And what went on down there before we arrived?'

Rone stared back at the floor.

'Just tell him,' Samson said quietly, shooting him a troubled glare.

It was the exact confirmation Jask had been looking for. He knew Samson would break first. But it was Rone he wanted to hear it from. Rone was the decision-maker. And Rone needed to

242 ❋ LINDSAY J. PRYOR ❋

learn that decisions came with responsibility. It was *essential* that he learned the weight of responsibility.

'Eleven minutes,' Jask said, reminding them of the ticking clock.

Rone looked at Samson, the pleading in the latter's eyes not waning.

'We overheard two vampires talking,' Rone finally said.

'About?'

'They were collecting a girl for questioning.'

'The serryn?'

Rone nodded.

'Questioning about what?' Jask asked.

Rone glanced back at Samson, the latter's wide eyes urging him on.

'About working for The Alliance,' Rone added.

Unease clenched Jask's stomach. 'What's The Alliance?'

'Remember talk of Jake Dehain drinking a girl to death and nearly killing himself a couple of days ago? Apparently it was a set-up – a suicide mission by the girl he drained. She worked for The Alliance. That's what they're calling themselves.'

The hairs on the back of Jask's neck stood on end. 'Go on.'

'The serryn works for them too. Not that the vampires who'd held her said that's what she was. I don't think they even knew. Neither did Marid or my guess is he would have sold her for more. They were paid to collect her from him and interrogate her for information about other Alliance members.'

'You're telling me you suspected that serryn had something to do with a covert attack on Jake Dehain, Caleb's brother?'

Rone nodded.

'And we brought her back *here*?'

Though he tried to maintain a steady gaze, Rone faltered as the implications sunk in. 'I didn't know what else to do, Jask. When we went down there and saw what she was, I panicked.'

'Why would a serryn be involved with a covert attack on the Dehains?' Corbin asked Jask. 'That doesn't make any sense. She could have gone in there and taken them out by herself.'

'Caleb Dehain is the best serryn hunter there ever was,' Jask said. 'She had to have known that. You've seen how unskilled she is. My guess is she knew it would have been suicidal to take him on. But still, serryns don't work as a team. Something still isn't right here.' He looked back at Rone. 'So you overheard them talking. Why did you get involved?'

'Because I overheard them saying The Alliance's aim was to kill off the key players in Blackthorn. That had to make you and Corbin on the list, right? I wanted to know if our pack was at risk.'

'And you didn't think to come back here and tell me any of this?'

'Once we'd overheard them, I didn't have much time. I had to persuade them to let us in on it before I lost them. It took a lot of persuasion, but they agreed.'

'Because you offered them our herbs.'

'We weren't really going to hand them over.'

'Then what *were* you going to do?'

Rone looked to the floor again.

Jask exhaled tersely. 'You were going to kill them?'

Rone looked up at him from beneath his lashes. 'We would have had no choice. If they were right about her, we were going to strike a deal to keep The Alliance away from the pack in exchange for saving her life. Then we saw what she was and it all went wrong.'

Jask stood from his leaning position. 'That's the stupidest fucking plan I've ever heard.'

'It all happened so quick. We cut in or we lost them. They weren't exactly happy that we'd overheard. Whoever they were working for wanted this kept quiet, which we turned to our advantage.' His blue eyes widened as he dared to take a step closer to Jask. 'Jask, I was looking out for the pack. Looking out for you. For Corbin. I had an opportunity and I took it.'

'And how do you know those vampires didn't plan the exact same for you? Did that cross your mind? They were working for someone who, as you said yourself, wanted all this kept a secret. Did you seriously think they were simply going to let you walk out of there?'

'It was two on two.'

'There could have been more.'

'But there wasn't.'

'*Fuck*,' Jask hissed, walking away from them, not wanting to even think about what could have happened to them. He turned to face Rone again. 'And did she talk about The Alliance? Did you ask her about it?'

Rone shook his head. 'We walked in on them mid-feed. It was over within seconds. She asked us to let her go but I was frightened of what she'd do if I did. But I couldn't kill her. And I knew I couldn't leave her there either – not once she'd seen us. If others did turn up and she told them about us, they could have thought we were a part of it.'

'Which is why you should have got me involved from the very beginning.'

Rone looked back at the floor again. 'And I nearly did.' He glanced back up at him. 'When I came to get the herbs. But I thought I could handle it myself. I wanted to handle it myself. I wanted to prove I could do this. You're always telling me to learn responsibility, so I took responsibility.'

'Not for the entire pack!'

'Then how, when, where? I honestly thought I was doing the right thing. I *tried* to do the right thing.' His blue eyes were wide, glossy. 'And I know I failed. I know I messed up.'

The thought of the youth needing Jask's approval *that* much as to do something so risky caused frustration with himself to lodge in his chest.

'I wanted to come back here and be able to tell you I'd sorted it,' Rone added. 'That's all I wanted. Because…'

Jask frowned at the youth's hesitation. But he was glad he hesitated. He wasn't ready to see any more of how much he had failed him, not amidst the weight of too many other things.

'But why not tell me the truth earlier, Rone? Or even when we were down in the ruins?'

Rone's heart rate escalated as he exchanged glances with Samson. 'Rone!' Jask said firmly.

'We were at Hemlick's when we overheard them,' Rone finally confessed. 'We were in one of the booths.'

He could barely believe it. 'Hemlick's?'

Rone nodded.

'Deal central?' Jask snapped. 'That hovel of a bar? What the *fuck* were you doing there?'

'Because I was looking for a solution,' Rone said, glancing up at him warily. 'I was trying to get my hands on some turmeric. I thought going to Hemlick's would be the best place find out if there was any way we could get hold of it. I was trying to strike a deal with a witch, but they said turmeric is inaccessible now.'

'So now word might be out there that we're looking for some? Rone, I can't believe you've been so reckless! As if offering our herbs wasn't bad enough, you could now have evoked questions about our supplies. Did you not think I'd been out there asking my own questions?'

'I had to do *some*thing.'

'By going to that infested black-market den? You were lucky to get out alive!'

Rone's eyes flashed with something more than panic. He seemed momentarily taken aback by Jask's concern. Taken aback enough to remind Jask he'd never shown it to the youth before.

If being dictatorial had become more commonplace than just authoritative, he truly was failing his pack.

'So what now?' Rone asked. 'Now that you know everything. Are you going to banish me? Banish both of us?'

Jask exhaled tersely through his nose before leaning back against the stone table. He may have been as much the cause of Rone's stupid decision as the youth's naivety, but that still didn't excuse what he'd done. And it still didn't excuse the guilt the youth had managed to evoke. 'You'd deserve it.'

Rone's lips quivered at the injustice. 'How many times do you want me to say I'm sorry?'

Jask glanced at Corbin.

Corbin raised his eyebrows. He wouldn't vocalise what they both knew was the right thing to do, but it was enough of a silent, albeit respectful, rebuke should Jask not put him out of his misery quickly.

And put him out of his misery he could, as a thought struck him.

A thought that could not only save their pack but give the youth every chance at gaining the self-esteem and approval he clearly so desperately wanted. The only thing he could offer him as some sort of consolation right then.

He fixed his attention back on Rone. 'That is if fate hadn't been kind to you. Seemingly to us all.'

Rone frowned. He exchanged a swift glance with Samson again.

'I *had* been out asking questions,' Jask said. 'And you're right – turmeric is impossible to get your hands on in Blackthorn now, unless you're in the right circles. There's a witch who still holds some. And I was told by another that the only way she'll be open to persuasion to part with it is if she gets commanded to do so by one more powerful than her.'

'A serryn?' Rone asked.

Jask nodded.

Rone's eyes widened. 'That's what you meant down in the ruins, when you said she couldn't have come at a better time. But this is great!'

'*If*,' Jask continued, 'I can get that serryn to walk into a coven and demand the turmeric be handed over without giving even a hint that I've been holding her hostage to make her do it. Because I don't need to tell you what a raging coven of angry witches could do to us should they suspect. Only, thanks to you, now that's going to be even more complicated if word *has* leaked back that we're looking for a supply.' Jask looked back across at Corbin. 'Looks like we're going to have to move quicker.'

'Do you think you can get the serryn to do it?' Rone asked.

Jask looked back at him. 'You said the serryn didn't talk about The Alliance. You said in front of her that you stumbled on her. Is that what she thinks? Does she not know about your deal with the vampires?'

'Only if they said something to her about it before we got there. But she didn't mention it.'

'So it's possible that, as far as she's concerned, we know nothing about The Alliance.'

Rone shrugged. 'I guess so.'

'Perfect,' Jask said. 'Let's keep it that way.'

'What are you thinking, Jask?' Corbin asked.

Jask folded his arms again. 'If this Alliance theory is true, our little serryn has a pack of her own. And you know what that means.'

'Leverage,' Corbin said.

Jask nodded. '*Possible* leverage. There's only one way to find out.'

Corbin raised his eyebrows. 'You're going after them? You're going after The Alliance?'

'I think we should pay them a visit.'

'She's not going to lead you to them, Jask.'

'Not knowingly, no. But what she *does* know, thanks to those vampires, who I think it's safe to guess started to question her before Rone and Samson got there, is that her covert operation isn't covert anymore. My bet is that she wants out of here and fast, to warn the rest of them – let alone get out of here before I find out. I say we give her that opportunity.'

He looked back at the youth – his eyes finally hopeful.

'Looks like you could be about to redeem yourself, Rone,' Jask said. 'If you're up for the job, that is.'

Chapter Twenty-Two

Sophia kept her gun locked into position on Jask despite hearing more movement behind her.

The place was surrounded – that much was obvious. She shouldn't have expected anything less.

'You set me up,' she hissed quietly.

Jask took another couple of steps towards her so he was only a few feet away. Stood there in his jeans, plain shirt and jacket that skimmed mid-hip.

She held her gun directly at his chest, trying not to be distracted by Daniel's gasps for breath, forcing herself not to panic, to restrain her pounding heart – and not just from the adrenaline of the situation, but from seeing *him* again.

'That's not very hospitable,' he said, glancing at the gun.

'The bullets are even less hospitable, so I suggest you stay where you are.'

Jask broke a fleeting smile as he continued to gradually close the gap between them.

'Tell Corbin to let him go,' she warned, even impressing herself with the steadiness of her voice despite the tremor in her hands.

'Drop your gun first, Phia,' Jask said.

'Not going to happen.'

Daniel gasped desperately for air, Corbin no doubt having tightened his grip to make a point. He slid him another foot up the wall. Any more pressure and he'd snap his windpipe.

She looked back at Jask, his calm gaze burning through whatever sense of control she thought she might be able to gain. But she kept her arms outstretched, her finger poised on the trigger.

'You came here for leverage, right?' she said. 'That's what you meant when you said you'd be able to get me to do what you wanted. Well, he's *it*. You kill him and I do nothing for you.'

Jask's eyes narrowed slightly. He glanced at Daniel but not long enough to take his attention off Sophia. 'How many are in there?'

She subtly licked her dry lips. 'Tell Corbin to let him go.'

'How many?'

Ironically she knew the truth of their vulnerability would be the only thing to save Daniel. Besides, they'd find out soon enough. 'None.'

Jask's eyebrows knitted together.

'Have you not seen the news lately?' she asked. 'It's making for very colourful viewing.'

Some unspoken exchange passed between him and Corbin.

'It's the truth,' she said. 'It's just us left. Me and him. So if he dies, you've wasted your time. Send your brood in to check if you don't believe me.'

Jask took another couple of steps towards her and this time she purposefully lowered her gun to point at his pelvis. He knew she wasn't stupid enough to attempt to kill him, but she had no doubt he wasn't quite so sure she wouldn't permanently wound him.

Regardless, he closed in on her enough for the gun to make contact with his hip.

He put his hand over hers, sending a jolt through her as he guided the gun down towards his groin, to an artery. 'It's more effective there,' he said, his gaze lingering tauntingly on hers.

'I know how to shoot,' she said, his proximity unsettlingly distracting. 'I'm aiming to wound you, not kill you.'

'You pull that trigger and you'd better hope for the latter.'

She could just squeeze the trigger for the hell of it. The Phia she had been twenty-four hours ago would have. But she knew this was not the time for impulse. Too much depended on her making the right choice.

And as he stared deep into her eyes, their connection renewed, she couldn't. She couldn't even look away despite Daniel kicking at the wall in desperation.

Jask guided her hand the rest of the way so the barrel pointed to the floor, equally allowing him to move another inch closer. 'Drop it.'

She defiantly held his gaze as he squeezed her hand.

'Drop the gun and Corbin drops your friend,' he added.

'You're lucky I don't permanently damage the only thing you've got going for you.'

He almost smiled. 'And what would be the fun in that?' But as his hand crushed hers against metal, she could tell his patience was waning as much as hers.

Daniel's flaying was getting weaker. Any longer and the damage to *him* would be permanent.

He'd believed what she'd said about them being the only two left. If he didn't, he would have given Corbin the nod to kill Daniel just to prove his point.

Just as them both still being alive proved he really did need her.

And with that proof playing out in front of her, suddenly the enemy that stood before her – the unexpected inconvenience, the threat – morphed into something else entirely as her strategic brain kicked in.

'Shall we do this inside?' she asked. 'So you can see for yourself?'

'Saves me huffing and puffing and blowing the doors in.'

She laughed tersely. 'We both know this is no fairy tale.'

'No?' he said, finally slipping the gun from her reluctant hand as Corbin simultaneously lowered Daniel to the floor. 'Hansel and Gretel weren't set up to be murdered? Beauty was never held captive by the beast?' He took hold of her upper arm and led her back towards the entrance. 'The ugly duckling wasn't victimised just for being different? This sounds like the perfect fairy tale to me.'

Led over to the elevator shaft, more lycans swept past her in the shadows as they assessed the periphery.

'What level?' he asked her.

'Penthouse, of course.'

She glanced past him at Daniel who was just about being held upright by Corbin. A couple of times he stumbled, but his consciousness was, at least in some way, reassuring. She should have dropped the gun sooner, but immediate surrender would have done neither of them any good. Daniel would understand. Though she wasn't so sure he'd be quite as understanding of her next move.

As they reached the shaft, Jask guided her in first, Corbin and Daniel alongside them, another couple of lycans bringing up the rear.

Jask moved in close behind her, his chest hard against her back, his breath combing through her hair. There was something odd about being around him away from the compound, but he still had that same characteristic composure – oozing that same sense of ownership of whatever space he was in.

One of the lycans slammed the gate behind them as Jask pressed the button to trigger the elevator into ascension.

'Using me as a human shield – how chivalrous,' she remarked.

'Just acquiring my preferred position with you, honey,' he said tauntingly against her ear.

She glanced at Daniel again, who frowned across at her. She immediately broke from his penetrative stare, suddenly feeling uncomfortable with his presence.

Jask slipped the second of her guns out of her thigh holster, handing that and the other to the lycan behind before tapping down Sophia's behind.

'Hey!' she snapped, trying to pull away, before seeing Corbin mid-frisk of Daniel too. 'Have you never heard of just asking?'

Jask smiled against her ear. 'Try not to take it personally.' He slid his hand down her thighs, delving into her pockets. He pulled out the two syringes. 'Nice.'

'They're mine,' she said sullenly.

'What's yours is mine, darling. Isn't that how it goes?'

He slid his hand into the pocket at her hip to find it empty, only to have Corbin hand him the keys from Daniel's.

As the elevator jolted to a stop, Jask swapped his grip on her from his left hand to his right as he pulled out his own gun.

Corbin did the same, poised and ready like his pack leader.

'Metalwork,' she remarked. 'How disappointing. Did you boys forget to file your nails this morning?'

But this time Jask didn't respond, he was too focused on what potentially lay ahead. Obviously he'd believed her enough to investigate without a full-on raid, but not enough to let his defences down. She wondered if he'd have been so quick to use her as a shield if he genuinely thought they were in danger. For some reason, she believed not.

He pulled back the gate, metal sliding against metal echoing in the silence. Jask exited first with Sophia, Corbin close behind with Daniel.

She flinched as Jask pointed his gun at the CCTV camera to the left of the door before accurately blowing it out. It fizzed before dying like a dropped sparkler.

Then all four lycans came to a standstill.

She knew what they were doing. They were listening, let alone assessing airborne scents undetectable to humans. With next to no breeze, they'd be able to pick up on human scents still lingering from hours before. Not just that, but the subtleties between those scents would give them some indication of numbers.

His nod towards Corbin told her he was satisfied with what he had found so far, but he was remaining guarded. He guided Sophia to the door, caught the keys Corbin threw at him and turned them in the locks.

The door clicked open.

'After you, honey.'

She knew it was his final test to sense any hesitation.

She cast him a taunting smile. 'Coward,' she declared, before pushing the door open and stepping inside.

❄ ❄ ❄

He wasn't letting Phia out of his sight despite the silence emanating from within; despite the fact that the only scents he could detect were those of the two humans they held; despite her casual stroll being a clear indication that she was telling the truth.

His gaze wandered down to her behind regardless of it being concealed by her unflattering clothing. It was the same style of uniform he'd seen her in when he'd first laid eyes on her – a stark reminder of what she was.

He looked into the kitchen to the left and the dumping ground of a room to his right.

'Wait!' he called out as she reached the threshold ahead.

He signalled for Phelan and Connor to check the rooms he'd just passed before closing the gap again between him and Phia.

Surprisingly, she'd done what he'd said, albeit like a child prevented from crossing a road. She folded her arms in weary resentment before she leaned back against the doorjamb, her eyebrows slightly raised, her tongue thrust into her cheek.

There was a time when a stance like that would have irritated the hell out of him, but now it was overshadowed by her compliance. Another small triumph on his part.

He moved into the doorway alongside her, slid his hand to the small of her back to guide her in, a move he could tell was dangerously intimate from the way she stiffened. But, surprisingly, she didn't protest.

He indicated for Phelan and Connor to check out the hallway on the far side of the living room, only to catch the glare from Phia's companion. A glare directed at his lingering hand.

He could almost smell the territoriality leaking from the human's pores – a clear indication that the relationship between Phia and her companion wasn't purely business. The evidence was potentially fatal enough, not least if he continued to look at Jask the way he did.

Phelan and Connor returned with the all-clear.

'Told you,' Phia said, breaking their physical contact as she backed away.

'Do another full check of the building with the others,' Jask instructed Phelan. 'Give me the heads-up when you're done.'

Phelan nodded, and exited the room alongside Connor.

Jask indicated for Phia to join him at the dining room table, Corbin following behind with her sour-faced companion.

Jask pulled out a chair at the head of the table for himself and the adjacent one for Phia.

Corbin took the head of the table the opposite end, sitting the male alongside Phia.

'So what happened to the rest of your comrades?' Jask asked.

She leaned back in the chair, those folded arms still betraying her petulance. 'Look on the laptop,' she said, indicating to the centre of the table.

He reached out and slid it towards him. He flipped the lid to reveal the last page it had been on. He flicked forwards and backwards through the news reports – sketchy at best, the authorities struggling for leads.

'Eight in total,' Phia announced. 'In less than three days. With me and Dan and another four missing, that accounts for at least fourteen of us. A further four are unaccounted for as yet.'

'So The Alliance has been uncovered,' Jask declared.

'You already know that,' she said curtly. 'I've no doubt Rone would have told you that was the reason I was down in the ruins in the first place. Because it was Rone who told you about me, wasn't it?'

He looked back at the images. The thought that Phia could have ended up the same way made him feel deeply uneasy, when he had no place letting it. It seemed her serrynity had been the only thing to save her. That and Rone being in the wrong place at the wrong time. Or, from the way he was feeling being near her again, the right place at the right time.

She was in deep. Too deep. But also, now, was the ever-growing sense that so was he. And subsequently his pack.

'Who's responsible?'

She shrugged. 'Fuck knows.' She tried to look self-assured, composed. But he knew those eyes too well now. She was screwed and she knew it – which made the fact she'd left the security of the factory too irritatingly rash for his liking.

He slid the laptop along the table to Corbin.

'Well, well,' Jask remarked, leaning back in his chair and folding his arms to mirror her. 'Aren't *you* in the thick of it? But then again, you did *try* to take down Caleb Dehain. That constitutes you as not just insane, but suicidal.'

'Depends on your perspective.'

'You took on Caleb Dehain and you were lax enough to fail.'

'On the first attempt, maybe.'

'So you and your army,' he cocked his head towards who he now knew to be Dan, 'were heading out for round two, were you?' He leaned forward, resting his arms on the table. 'Are you so arrogant that you have no comprehension of who Caleb Dehain is? How much power he has around here? What he's capable of?'

'Exactly,' she said.

'So your group – The Alliance – really were picking off all the key players then?'

She kept her gaze solemnly on him.

'Who the *fuck* do you think you are, Phia?'

His venom seemed to momentarily shock her, but she masked it quickly.

'If you're so proud of what you're doing, why are you hiding?' he asked. 'Why a covert operation?'

'It makes us more effective.'

'You *seriously* think doing this will help anyone?'

'What alternative is there? People have a right to live without fear. Humans forced to live here because their own kind have turned their back on them. Humans in Lowtown and Blackthorn should feel safe – those who have no choice but to be there at least.'

'So you're taking out the key players because that'll help?'

'We're bringing down the underworld and restoring human control.'

He laughed from an uncomfortable place in his gut at the naivety and ignorance of her belief. 'The third-species underworld is the only thing holding this place together. Do you not see that? Do have *no* idea how it works here? And who would step into their place instead? The cons that roam the streets here?'

'I *know* what the likes of Caleb Dehain are capable of.'

'Exactly – and so does anyone in Blackthorn and Lowtown who thinks about overstepping the mark. This place is ruled hard and mercilessly because that's what is required. Mainly to keep in line the dregs your authorities deem aren't fit to share the same air as them. This was supposed to be *our* space, not a dumping ground for your unwanted. Do you seriously think this place will be better if you put your kind in charge? Are you really that arrogant? We have a balance here, a balance we have fought to maintain, so who the fuck do you think you are, coming in here and trying to unsettle it?'

Her gaze dropped to the table, but she soon glared back at him.

But she knew he was right. He could see it in her eyes. Hear it in her lack of argument.

He leaned back in his chair, his arms folded again. 'Was I on your hit list? Was I next?'

'Lycans weren't on our radar.'

'Why? What makes us so different, in your eyes?'

'I never said you were.'

'But you see differentiation even within the third species, right? What gives you the right to pass judgement on us? To make decisions about who lives and who dies? You're no better than the authorities who have failed you, and you can't even see it.'

'We're nothing like them. They're about money and power and–'

'And what are *you* about if not power? How do you justify *your* actions?'

'We cannot let the vampires rule.'

'And this is how you go about it?'

'We have to do something.'

'So you invade our district, our homes.'

'It's a carefully targeted operation.'

'Full of judgemental bigots. Excuse me if I'm not bowled over in admiration and reassurance. Where does it stop, Phia? Where will you draw the line? Because the way I see it, anything that is a risk to the vampires is a risk to my pack. One third species, all third species.'

Her eyes flared. 'That's not how it is.'

'So *you* say. But do what's left of your so-called Alliance agree?' He looked across at Dan. 'You're quiet. Where do *you* stand?'

He could sense the hairs on the back of the human's neck bristling as their eyes locked. Dan didn't quite have Phia's edge of defiance, nor the balls to look him in the eyes and say what he thought. In fact, Dan caved relatively quickly. Clearly his reputation *did* precede him.

'Never mind where anyone stands or stood,' Phia said, recapturing his attention. 'Let's face facts here – whatever has happened, and despite what you know now, you still need me.'

He raised his eyebrows slightly. 'Is that right?'

'I'm still alive and he's still alive,' she said, indicating towards Dan. 'That's proof enough for me. Whatever your plan is, I'm still a part of it. Just as the minute you took me from those ruins, you became involved in whatever I'm involved in. You *and* your pack. I might have failed to protect mine,' she declared. 'But you'd better hope you can do a better job with yours.'

She'd echoed his very thoughts, not least now he'd seen the extent of whatever her Alliance had become embroiled in.

'We were paid to take the hit on the Dehains,' she added, out of the blue.

Her companion's eyes flared in disapproval at her disclosure, only giving weight to the truth of her words.

Words that escalated the complication of the situation to a whole new level.

'They were on our list, but not for a long while,' she explained. 'They were our crescendo along with Kane Malloy. But they got jolted forward.'

'So much for vigilantism.'

'It was a one-off.'

'Paid by who?'

'We don't know. What we do know is they're wealthy, powerful, don't like getting their hands dirty and they don't give a fuck about your so-called Blackthorn code. And it seems they're responsible for wanting The Alliance silenced so that word doesn't get back to Caleb, just as I'm guessing they'll want you silenced if they find out you have me. You've got another player in town, Jask. And I'm certain it's in *both* our interests to find out who.'

Her gaze didn't flinch, which was as impressive as her decision to negotiate. In fact, every decision she'd made since he'd stepped out of the shadows had been

smart. Petulant though she still was, this was a whole other side of Phia – the side to Phia that he needed for his own cause. And, as much as he resented finding yet another appealing trait in her, this new attitude was most definitely topping the list of reasons to like her.

It wasn't helped by knowing that beneath the disclosure was her acknowledgement, her acceptance, that she was now vulnerable. That she needed him. Not only was it perfect in getting her to do what he wanted; more to the point, it was potentially binding them on a whole other level.

'Are you bartering for your life, Phia?'

'The same someone who wants me dead could also be a risk to you. And I'm your perfect honeytrap to find out who that is. So yes, I am bartering. If you want me to do what *you* want, you help me get the answers *I* want. Help me take this player out and then I'll help you.'

'What?' Daniel said under his breath, unable to conceal the shock.

'I was taken off the street by a vampire called Marid,' Phia added, ignoring him. 'He sold me on. We track him down and find out if he knows where the money came from. Failing that, we find out who those two vampires were who collected me and we find out from them. We'll trace it back to the source somehow. We'll kill whoever destroyed The Alliance and *then* I do what you want. It's the only deal I'm offering you.'

He folded his arms, making her wait for his response. 'So, basically, you're asking for my help.'

She frowned, betraying her umbrage at the new dynamic between them, let alone that he was toying with her over it. But still she managed to keep herself contained, adding to his admiration of her new self-control. 'I'm not stupid. I know I'm not going to get any answers out there alone.'

'You want me to help with your vengeance tirade.'

'I want justice. You understand that, right? Better than most.'

He looked down at the table, traced his fingers over the dented surface. 'And what makes you think I'm not a part of taking your Alliance down?' He looked back up at her, liking the startled look in her eyes. 'What makes you so sure you weren't taken back to the compound for that very reason?'

Chapter Twenty-Three

Sophia's heart jolted.

Jask didn't flinch. His eyes gave nothing away.

Her ears thrummed in the silence of the room. She felt Daniel stiffen beside her.

Jask leaned forward, looked deep in her eyes. 'In fact, how do you know it wasn't *me* that paid you to kill the Dehains?'

'Because we were hired by a vampire.'

If Dan was right. If Abby had been telling the truth. Her stomach wrenched, every iota of her being hoping they had been – and not just because her newfound plan had just imploded if not. But because she couldn't accept that Jask would be so cruel as to have played her like that.

He raised his eyebrows slightly. 'Is that right?'

She nodded, uncertain if she should have made the further disclosure. 'So I know you're screwing with me.'

His smile was fleeting. 'But you *don't* know, do you, Phia? You run around here with your judgements and your principles and your fully loaded gun and you have no idea what you're up against.'

Her stomach was so tight it was painful. She didn't bother to try and take deep breaths to calm her racing pulse. 'I'm up against someone who has destroyed my pack and will inevitably come after yours. We need to team up, Jask.'

He knew she was holding up her hands – not in surrender, but in an attempt to strengthen her resources. She could only hope Jask was a smart enough leader to at least consider it.

More than that, she hoped he'd look for a reason *not* to kill her.

'Can I talk to you, Phia?' Daniel asked, his tone anything but a request. His eyes flared with warning, a look that grated more than she knew it should have – like being berated by a parent in front of new friends.

'Open forum,' Jask remarked, giving Phia's permission on her behalf – a move that evoked a disgruntled glare in his direction.

'In private,' Daniel said.

Jask exhaled tersely. 'And would you like waiter service as well?'

'Five minutes,' Daniel said. 'That's all.'

'We need five minutes too,' Corbin cut in, his eyes equally grave as they locked on Jask's. 'Don't you think?'

Jask glanced from Daniel back to Phia again. He stood and headed across to the coffee table. He searched through the contents of the open box before returning with a couple of rolls of plaster tape. He threw one to Corbin, kept another for himself. He moved in behind Sophia and eased her arms behind her back.

'Is that really necessary?' she asked, but knew it was futile protesting physically. 'I'm not stupid enough to do anything.'

'I've seen you in action, remember?' he said dangerously close to her ear. 'So forgive me for not trusting a word you say.'

'Likewise,' she said, wincing as he wrapped the tape around her wrists, securing them to the spindles at the back of the chair.

Corbin did the same with Daniel.

'Five minutes,' Jask said, before leaving the room to head down the hallway, Corbin close behind him.

'Teaming up with Jask Tao?' Daniel hissed as soon as they were out of sight. 'What the *fuck*?'

'I don't have much choice, do I? Weren't you the one who said I don't stand a chance of getting answers out there?'

'What happened to you being able to handle this alone? Jask Tao turns up and you surrender your war cry?'

'That's not how it is. I'm making the most of the advantages we've got. It's called being strategic. I'm trying to keep us both alive. He's going to use me anyway, so we may as well get something out of it.'

'Use you for what?'

'I don't know.'

He frowned. 'Like hell you don't.'

'I don't.' He didn't need to know all her Kane Malloy theories – especially now she wasn't so convinced herself. 'But this is the only way I'm going to find out.'

'I don't like this. I don't like any of this.'

Neither did she completely. Not when teaming up with him also meant putting off her call to her sisters. 'Then what else do you suggest?'

He stared at her then exhaled with impatience as he looked away.

'Jask is one hell of a force out there and we both know it,' Sophia reminded him. 'I've seen those lycans in action. They're one hell of an ally, Dan. So, loathe as I am to say it, we *do* need him – at least until we know who we're up against.'

'So we team up with the third species. Doesn't that break our entire code? Isn't that what you went off on one about earlier? A bit hypocritical, isn't it?'

'I either let him force me into doing whatever he wants or we strike a deal now and make sure we *all* get something out of it. We owe it to The Alliance, to those we've lost, to see this through.'

'And how do you know he's *not* a part of this? What makes you so sure he was screwing with you when he said that? He's right – we know nothing about third-species politics. What if they've all teamed up against us? What if they just want the other four? I can't believe you let that information slip, Phia. Maybe *that's* the only reason we're alive right now.'

'What happened to The Alliance isn't down to him.'

'How can you say that with such conviction?'

'Because I know him.'

Daniel frowned. Something flashed behind his eyes. 'What *exactly* went on between you two in that compound?'

'Nothing.'

'No? I'm not blind, Phia. I've seen the way he looks at you. The way you look at him. The way he handled you back there. I heard the banter in the shaft. The rest of us may as well not have been there.'

She broke from the accusation of his glare, but his words burrowed deep. She didn't think Jask looked at her in any particular way. No way she'd seen, at least. The prospect of it made her insides flit. 'You're talking stupid.'

He raised his eyebrows. 'Is that right? You both sitting there, staring into each other's eyes, a hundred silent messages passing between you. Come on, Phia.'

Heat flushed to her cheeks, her stomach flipping. She kept eye contact fleeting. 'I never knew you were so poetic, Dan.'

'And I never knew you were so gullible. It seems his charm really is quite the killer. I expected more from you. Have you slept with him?'

It was her turn to exhale with impatience as she looked at the wall. The use of *gullible* was too insulting, too plausible for her not to take a moment before forcing herself to look back at him. 'I'm playing the game,' she said, as much to convince herself as him.

'With Jask Tao? You're making a big mistake, Phia,' he said, disappointment in his eyes. 'I'm your friend and that's one lake you don't want to be dipping your toe into. Those lingering looks, the snatched smiles – you're already wading too deep.'

'And I'll go as deep as I need to in order to see this through,' she said quietly. 'Because I *am* doing this.'

❄ ❄ ❄

'You're not seriously considering this,' Corbin said. 'We don't have time.'

Jask folded his arms and leaned back against the kitchen counter. 'I need her on side, remember, not digging her heels in.'

'Then call her bluff – turn up the heat on her boyfriend in there.'

'It won't work. You've seen her in action. She's just not the type to cut her nose off to spite her face; she'd kill herself just to make me suffer – especially if she thinks she's lost. And now we know there's definitely another player in town, we need her even more.'

'A player who's already going to be asking questions about what happened to their henchmen, let alone their missing hostage. Someone who has potentially dared to go up against Caleb. Is that someone you're sure we should be taking on? And if it is a vampire, you know we could be seen as taking sides here. You know what that could evoke. And going out there with her is only going to draw attention to the fact we have her.'

'And what if it wasn't a vampire who paid them, Corbin? What if we were right in the beginning – only it's not the witches being used by the TSCD but The Alliance? What if they're using them as a scapegoat just as we were, only to get to Caleb this time instead of Kane? And knowing what another court case could do to them, they're destroying the evidence this time.'

Corbin looked across his shoulder at the boarded-up window before staring back at Jask. 'And what about us keeping ourselves to ourselves? It isn't our priority. Caleb Dehain is more than capable of looking after himself.'

'If this is the TSCD fucking with this district again, we need to know. We all need to know. This is just as much about protecting each other's backs to protect our own. And there's only one way that's going to happen.'

'And what if it's *her* who's double-crossing you? We don't know those deaths were The Alliance. We only have her word for it. How do we know they're not alive and well and ready to take you out?'

'I believe her.'

Corbin raised his eyebrows. 'That unequivocally?'

'I know when she's lying. And I know when she's scared. And she's scared right now, Corbin. You saw those images. You read what's happened to the rest of them. She's screwed and she knows it. If I get the name she's looking for, I'll have even more to bargain with.'

The look in Corbin's eyes was too telling. 'You care about her, don't you?'

'I care about our pack. I care about what goes on in Blackthorn.'

Knowing him too well, Corbin raised his eyebrows. 'I warned you. I warned you not to let this become personal.'

'I'm not doing anything to jeopardise us. I can handle this. I can handle her. We'll get the answers we need and then we'll get what our pack needs.'

'Then I'm coming with you.'

'No. I need you to be my eyes and ears back at the compound. Take Phelan and the others back with you. And Dan. I'll sort this with Phia alone,' he said, pulling away.

'I haven't seen that for a long time,' Corbin remarked.

Jask turned to face him. 'What?'

'That look in your eyes. The one that's there when you mention her name.'

'Do you have a problem with it, Corbin?'

Corbin pulled himself away from the counter. 'Not if you're adamant you know what you're doing,' he said, stepping past him. He sent him a glimmer of a smile. 'I just never thought I'd see it again.'

❄ ❄ ❄

Daniel looked away, oozing disapproval at her decision despite knowing there was no alternative.

But justify it to herself all she wanted, there was an equally strong underlying reason to make a deal with Jask. A reason evoked by the feelings reignited the moment she'd seen him again.

Because though she hated it more than having to make a deal with him in the first place, she wasn't ready to let him go. Seeing him again hadn't just brought shock; it had brought relief. It had brought a strange and alien sense of security, even as his pack had surrounded her.

And as he re-entered the living area, as he stopped on the other side of the table, Corbin beside him, she held her breath in the hope that a fraction of him felt the same way. If not, she knew things were about to become painful and messy.

'You've got yourself a deal,' he said.

Sophia's heart leapt, but she forced herself to remain composed as he crossed the room towards her.

'Smart move, Jask,' was all she could bring herself to say.

Corbin skirted the table to stop behind Daniel. Taking a knife from his pocket, he sliced through the tape before yanking him up as if he were nothing more than a child.

'What are you doing?' she asked, looking first at Corbin then at Jask.

'He's going back to the compound with Corbin,' Jask declared.

'No way!' Daniel protested. 'We come as a team.'

'Phia and I will handle it alone. Won't we, Phia?'

As Jask's gaze burrowed into hers, nerves curdled her stomach. She and Daniel had worked together for months. They trusted each other, were seamless. Being on the streets of Blackthorn alone with Jask was a whole new territory.

'I want him to cross into Lowtown,' she insisted.

'He's going to the compound. I'm not risking him getting caught. And I'm not arguing about this, Phia.'

She glanced at Daniel – at the concern and despondency in his eyes. He knew as well as she did that arguing was futile. She lowered her gaze.

The next time she looked up, they'd gone.

The silence of the empty apartment, the isolation of being alone with Jask, suddenly seemed oppressive. It wasn't helped by him remaining stood in front of her, his powerful arms folded as he assessed her.

She shrugged her shoulders to remind him she was still secured to the back of the chair. 'Whenever you're ready.'

He pulled out the chair he'd previously been sat in, put his hand on the seat between her legs and tugged her square-on to him as soon as he sat down. 'Let's lay down some ground rules first.'

She scanned the length of his finely honed arm, now brushing her shoulder as he clutched the side of the chair.

'You do as I say, when I say, how I say.'

She raised her eyebrows. 'That's it?'

'I mean it, Phia. You present even a hint of being a liability and I call this off and take you back to the compound. Do you understand me?'

'Naughty step – yeah, yeah, I get it.'

He narrowed his eyes, reminding her how dangerously uncompromising he could be. And also reminding her he was only agreeing to her plan because it made sense, not because he wanted to.

The latter hurt more than she knew it should have.

'This isn't a joke, Phia.'

She frowned. 'Tell me about it.'

He held her gaze for a moment longer before he stood, reminding her of the same strength of presence she'd felt when she'd looked up at him from the floor of the ruins. A presence she was sure would help get the truth out of Marid, let alone the other two vampires they might need to track down.

'So how long *have* you known,' she asked, as he stepped behind her, 'about all of this?'

'About your involvement with The Alliance? Since Rone decided to tell me the truth rather than go back into containment.'

She felt him slice through the first band of tape. 'Before I saw him out on the playing fields?'

'Before you woke up this afternoon, yes.'

That was a long time before. What now felt like a lifetime ago.

Before she'd had sex with him.

Which meant he'd had sex with her whilst knowing he was setting her up. No doubt her swimming lesson had equally been a part of his plan to ensure she saw it through. All the time she'd thought she was playing him, he'd been playing her.

Anger sparked deep – not just that he'd tricked her, but that she'd dared start to feel something for him in the process. It was a sharp wake-up call to what she was dealing with. He was out for what he could get as much as she was. And she'd remind herself of that every time she felt her heart skip a beat when their eyes met.

'How did you find me, Jask?'

'A little something sewn into the hem of the tunic Rone gave you.'

She frowned. 'You sniffed me out?'

'I was right behind you from the moment you stepped into the tunnel.'

'It was you, wasn't it? You were the one who took out the men pursuing me earlier?'

He sliced through the last piece of tape. 'That makes it three times now that I've saved your life.' He pulled level with her again as he pressed the blade back into its encasement single-handed.

She glowered up at him. 'I don't remember ever asking.'

He folded his arms again. 'Except now.'

'Only because I have no choice. There's something bad out there, Jask.'

'I know.'

She stared deep into his eyes, not liking the fact she detected worry behind them.

'And we've only got a few hours until dawn to find out what,' he added.

Their sudden sense of understanding, of agreement, felt too alien for her to handle.

She stood up. 'Then let's get on with this.'

Chapter Twenty-Four

'We'll head out past the old church,' Sophia said, leading the way back across the factory grounds. 'There's a backstreet bar down one of the cobbled side streets that's Marid's main hangout, especially for business deals.' She glanced across at Jask, sensing he was impressed. 'I know a lot about what goes on in this district – it's my job, remember? Besides, he was next on my hit list.'

'You were going after Marid?'

'That vampire's the scum of the earth. And I'll be having a quiet word of my own when we catch up – not just for what he did to me, but all the others who weren't quite so lucky.'

She turned left, heading back down the street that brought her there. It would mean passing through the hub again, but there was no other way to get there unless they took the more time-consuming detour.

'Is that how you see what you do – as a job?' he asked.

'How would you see it?' She raked him swiftly. 'I take it you know what Marid does – buying and selling humans off the street like they're commodities?'

'Amongst other things.'

'Do you agree with it?'

He frowned. 'You're even *asking* that? Most of the third species despise him.'

'So why doesn't anybody ever do anything about him? Why doesn't anyone do anything about what goes on here?'

'Each to their own – that's the rule in Blackthorn.'

'But the line has to be drawn somewhere, surely. There has to be rules, a basic moral code or any society will implode.'

'This society has survived without a civil war for over eighty years since the regulations came into being. That is the code.'

'Hear no evil, see no evil, speak no evil. Or, as I like to say, burying your head in the sand.'

'It's called survival, Phia. Some of us don't have an opt-out clause. Which reminds me – you never did answer my question. Why do this? Why give up your life in Summerton for this? Serryn or not, you had everything.'

She kept her attention ahead, her strides purposeful. The vibrations from the numerous clubs and bars were already echoing through the distant streets.

'My mother was killed by a vampire in one of the districts that's supposed to be safe.' She stepped down from the pavement and crossed the street. 'She was in Midtown, on her way home from my sister's school performance when she had her throat torn out.'

A place her mother would never have been if her daughters had remained educated in Summerton. If Sophia hadn't scuppered that.

'How old were you?'

'Six. But I only started looking into the facts a few years ago. And it didn't take long to work out the Global Council are as corrupt and self-seeking as the Higher Order they mutually scratch backs with. The authorities claimed they never found the one who was responsible. But a vampire in Midtown means only one thing – either they were Higher Order or useful in the labs. Either way, my mother's life was second priority to keeping the lid on it all. So it was covered up, only proving that those so-called borders don't mean shit if you have money and influence. And we all know the Higher Order have plenty of the latter when it comes to the authorities.'

'You're one of the ones who believe the two are embroiled?'

'I *know* the two are embroiled. It's as transparent as glassless windows. They slither into the Global Council, convincing them they're no threat. A few examples later of what their precious and pure healing Higher Order blood can do and suddenly labs get built and our so-called authorities are making compromises. It's not because they're royalty that they're allowed to reside in Midtown – it's because they're useful. And for as long as they're that, we all lose.'

As they reached the crossroads, she took a left down the partially lit street, the breeze blowing back through her hair and chilling her face.

'You don't agree with the research?' Jask asked. 'Don't you want cures as much as the next human?'

'Like fuck I do. Not *their* way, anyhow. Their coming out wasn't for our benefit, whatever lies they spout. They just know that even the enemy can become an ally if they're indispensible enough. And what better way to get humankind on side than by offering cures? It's about controlling us. They know our weakness. They know that the irony of all of this is that we want to *be* you. They know the authorities are hiding behind all this third-species morality crap when all they want is your prolonged life, your youth, your vitality, your strength. And until the authorities can harvest whatever magic gene you have, whatever it is that *really* sets us apart, they'll keep the third species contained and the Higher Order on side. And all the while, too many humans will be caught in the middle – forced to reside in Lowtown because they don't quite meet the standards. Those that are nothing but the expendable waste of a system they enforce not only to limit the threat of this prophesised vampire uprising, but to have the available finances to keep their research going. Anything can happen to those people as long as, one day, the powers that be no longer have to look in a mirror and see the signs of their own vulnerability.'

'That's a damning summary. Just whose side are you on, exactly, Phia?'

'Not the Global Council's and not the Higher Order's, that's for sure.'

'And do you believe in these vampire prophecies?'

'I don't disbelieve them. But neither do I believe the Higher Order are going to sit around and wait for what might not happen for centuries, if ever.'

'You think them coming out is part of a plan?'

'Right now the cures are only being developed for the really sick, or so they claim. But how long before they progress on to minor ailments, cosmetic, even life extension? Soon everyone will want a piece of it. And then what grounds will there be for segregation? Where will the line be drawn when our DNA is so interwoven that we won't know who are third species and who are human? New constitutions will have to be drawn up, that's for sure – and that's when the Higher Order will *really* come into their own. Prophesied leader or not, they're planning to get on the inside one way or another. And then they'll destroy us.'

'But that's why the segregation is based on the grounds of shadows and souls. Nothing can change that.'

'No? I'm not so sure. Especially as the curing research isn't the only type going on in those labs.'

Jask came to a standstill. 'What do you mean?'

She'd probably already said too much. She shrugged. 'I'm just saying I don't trust them.'

He caught hold of her arm. A hold that was as uncompromising as the look in his eyes. 'You said more than that. How do you know so much?'

She subtly tried to tug her arm free, but Jask wasn't giving.

'You want to waste what little time we have in your mission on standing here arguing?' he asked.

She sighed tersely. 'My mother was a haematologist at The Facility. I stole one of her diaries after she'd died. It was just a random book of my mother's at the time. But then I got old enough to read it. Let's just say there are a lot of closed-door activities going on in those labs.'

Jask's frown deepened. 'Like what?'

'I don't know. I probably never will. But whatever it is, your third-species shadows have caused as much interest as the Higher Order's blood.'

'Why?'

She shrugged again. 'Maybe because they think there's a greater significance to the difference between our species. Maybe because the whole "we can be redeemed because we have souls and you're beyond morality because you have shadows instead" is a tired concept.'

'You don't believe in that?'

'Oh, I think you're damaged goods all right. But I'm not so ignorant as to believe it's all as simple as that. I'm guessing others are of the same belief. Why, what do *you* believe, Jask?'

'I believe you need to accept that just because something is different to you, it doesn't make it bad, a threat or the enemy.'

'Sweet,' she said. 'Very sentimental.' She freed herself from his grip and kept walking. 'We'll forget the threat of the prophecies that leaked out then – how vampires are going to rule us. How you and all the other third species will be their lapdogs.'

'And you thought The Alliance could change that,' he said, catching up with her again.

'You've got to swim deep to find the sharks, Jask,' she called across her shoulder as she turned the corner. 'It's no good paddling on the shoreline.'

She came to a standstill as she surveyed the milling crowds ahead. The renewed buzz reverberating through her was undeniable. She clenched her hands before she noticed he'd held his out for her to take.

'It's not a proposal,' he said, his eyes taunting. 'It's a safety measure.'

'I don't need it.'

'I'm not thinking about you.'

She almost smiled, but managed to refrain as she accepted. But his fingers lacing with hers only added to the stirring deep in her abdomen. 'A bit intimate,' she said, glancing up at him again.

'A more secure hold,' he declared.

But the glint in his eyes turned the stirring into a flutter.

She looked back at the crowds, and took his cue to walk towards them.

They'd be at the bar in under ten minutes. She had to stay focused. She had to keep her attention ahead and not on the burning sensation as she brushed shoulders with the crowds. There were several occasions when heads were turned, several times when she was met with some questioning frowns, but she refrained from eye contact, keeping her focus on the security of Jask's hand.

A hand that abruptly led her left into a clothing shop.

Weaved through the rails, Phia glanced over her shoulder, wondering what Jask had seen to necessitate the prompt detour.

She ploughed into the back of him as he stopped abruptly, letting her go.

He turned, took a dress off the rail to examine it before showing it to her.

'What?' she asked.

'We need to get you changed.'

Her eyes snapped to his. 'For what?'

'You're in the clubbing capital and you're walking around in black combats, army boots and a sweat top. You need to blend in – especially considering the attention you might get walking around with me.'

'But we're *not* going clubbing,' she said, her voice hushed as she snatched the dress off him to return it to the rail.

He slipped his hand around her upper arm, encircling it as he led her deeper into the shop. 'Remember the rule about doing what I say?'

She tried to wrench her arm free without attracting any more glances. But it wasn't 'them' who were on the receiving end of the glances, she realised – it was most definitely Jask.

Suddenly, as pretty eyes flashed in his direction, as shapely bodies brushed past him a little too closely, Sophia felt a prickle of resentment.

And he did have a point.

'Okay, so what about this one?' she asked, reaching for a navy dress – a round neck, long sleeves, knee-length. Practical in a fight.

A girl brushed between them, but Jask moved out of the stranger's way without even looking at her, his full attention remaining locked on Sophia. A small knot formed in her stomach, one she told herself not to read into.

'Stick to black. It suits you.' He searched the same rail and pulled out a knee-length, halter-neck dress. 'But show off your shoulders. They're one of your best features.'

Her eyebrows lifted involuntarily, her stomach flipping again. 'What's wrong with my face?' she asked, her humour a weak attempt to ease her awkwardness at the compliment.

His eyes met hers before he stepped away again. 'Nothing,' he said. 'Absolutely nothing.'

Her grip on the hanger tightened. She looked down at the dress. He'd even got her size right. She scanned the shop again, catching a few curious stares, before hurrying behind him.

Her pace quickened when she saw him heading to the lingerie section.

'I have this covered,' she said, taking the bra off him and slamming it back on the hook.

'I didn't have you down as a prude, Phia,' he said with a smirk as he wandered around the other side of the display.

She folded her arms as his taunting blue eyes met hers. 'Fine,' she said. 'Choose away. And how exactly are we supposed to pay for any of this?'

He lowered his eyes as something caught his interest. 'I've got it covered. Unless you want to waste time arguing about that too?'

She stepped around the display to be greeted with a matching lingerie set. She wasn't sure why she'd assumed it would be something tacky, but the black lace strapless bra and high-cut shorts were anything but.

She looked up at him. 'What makes you think you've got my size right?'

He sent her a knowing smile as he indicated towards the cubicle behind her. 'Get yourself changed. We're on a time limit, remember?'

She watched him saunter back through the store towards the counter where a female lingered despite clearly already having paid.

Sophia reluctantly turned on her heels, stepped into the dressing room and pushed back the curtain on the nearest cubicle.

She removed her boots and tore off her comfortable sweater, combats and underwear. She'd always been a tomboy. There was no point being anything else with Leila, let alone Alisha, to compete with. She was popular from scuffling with the boys, not dating them.

She pulled on the lace shorts and fastened the bra before slipping the dress down over her head. She stood back to look at herself in the mirror as she fastened the clasp at the nape of her neck.

She'd worn plenty of other dresses in the past few months – all to blend in just like Jask had pointed out. But they were cheap. Nothing like the one Jask had chosen for her.

The prom was the last time she'd put on a dress of that quality. A dress she had ended up tearing in half in frustration at her lack of feminine curves, despite having spent months earning enough to pay for it.

Subsequently she'd never made it to the prom, even when Leila had offered her an alternative dress. Instead, it had been another night of slamming her bedroom door and locking herself away rather than deal with the pain.

What she knew was that her frustration was nothing to do with her tomboyish appearance – it was because she'd wanted her mother there. She'd wanted her mother to see her and be proud. Because once the excitement of the prom was over, she'd still be left with the truth – her mother was dead. And nothing would ever change that.

She flinched as Jask pushed back the curtain, holding it open just enough for him to block the gap he had created.

He handed her a pair of dainty heels. 'Might complement the dress better than the boots.'

She accepted the shoes off him. She perched on the edge of the stool and fastened the straps over her feet and around her ankles. She stood back up, liked the extra three inches the heels gave her. 'This do?' she asked, arms out at her sides, palms exposed.

She hadn't meant her tone to sound confrontational, but she knew it was inevitable as she stood there feeling as vulnerable as she did.

'Almost perfect,' he said – the "almost" being the word she hung onto rather than the "perfect".

She opened her mouth to retaliate, but he held up his hand, spun what she could see was a garter around his forefinger.

She raised her eyebrows again. 'Kinky.'

'I'd say useful,' he declared, stepping into the cubicle and letting the curtain drop into place behind him.

She instinctively took a step back, the cubicle suddenly feeling very enclosed with him joining her. Her pulse picked up a notch, her breathing terse.

He crouched down – the only thing to reduce his imposing presence in the small space – to reach behind her knee and lift her foot onto his lap.

Sophia held her breath as he slid the garter over her shoe to her ankle. With his thumb looped over the outside of the lace band, his palm flat against the back of her ankle inside it, he slowly slid the garter up her calve, over her knee, making her shiver as he reached her lower thigh.

But he didn't let either the garter or her thigh go as he stood again. Instead he guided her foot up onto the stool beside them, her inner thigh brushing against his jeans as he finished sliding the garter into position mid-thigh.

'You've done that before, haven't you?' she said, her back pressed to the wall.

'A couple of times. But never with the added extras though,' he said, his lips dangerously close to hers.

Her heart pounded. Her mouth turned dry.

She felt something cold against her thigh and glanced down to see him slipping the two syringes he'd removed from her combats earlier into the inside of her garter.

Her eyes snapped back to his as he rested his forearm against the wall beside her head.

'It's smart to have a backup,' he declared.

'Being bitten works just the same,' she said, sensing the tremor in her voice.

'I don't want you getting bitten.'

Her heart jolted. 'I didn't have you down as the jealous type.'

His gaze remained on hers. 'You'd be surprised.'

She involuntarily parted her lips slightly – not just for extra air but because she was sure, positive, that he was about to kiss her.

But he didn't.

He pulled away, stepping back out of the cubicle.

Sophia dropped her head back against the wall and cursed silently. As soon as she'd caught her breath, she followed swiftly behind him.

She caught up with him at the door, pulled on his arm to take a left, only to have Jask pull to the right.

'But the place Marid hangs out is this way,' Sophia said, indicating left.

'We don't have time to waste on hoping he'll be there,' Jask replied, winning the strength battle and walking her to the right.

'Then where are we going?'

'Have you ever been to The Circus?'

Her stomach flipped. As their eyes locked briefly again, she knew her silence said it all.

The Circus, as it was nicknamed by the cons who squatted in that part of the south, was nowhere any sane human being would ever voluntarily go.

It seemed that was about to change.

Chapter Twenty-Five

Jask would have nothing to do with most of the human convicts – not being able to be trusted was reason above all else. But he and Travis had an understanding, formed in Blackthorn, that was too rare not to maintain. It didn't mean he liked him. He didn't like him at all. But there were times he proved useful. And now was going to be one of those times.

Holding Phia's hand, keeping her close, Jask led her through the run-down building that was once a row of town houses.

It was just one congregation area of many more. Some cons mixed with the third species, but on the whole the cons were as resentful of them as humans outside of Blackthorn were and so stuck with their own kind.

Jask led Phia down the dark, claustrophobic corridor. Cigarette smoke, as well as the stench of other smoke, fogged the air. The whole place was disorientating enough without the conflicting battle of musical tastes spilling out from various rooms.

A lot of the cons' places were notoriously like mazes. They'd take over a row of properties, knocking through walls and corridors, interlinking one building with another. They were fairly simple to get into for those who dared – but not so easy to get out of. And especially not in a hurry.

He felt her grip on his hand tighten as they passed open room after open room of the sordid activities the cons were renowned for. Those that couldn't be seen could be heard coming down through the ceilings, or could be added to the scents in the air.

Finally they were in a situation she was far from comfortable with and, ironically, it was with her own kind.

He hoped, at the very least, it was a wake-up call about the point he'd been making earlier – that *this* was exactly why they needed the strong third-species leaders in Blackthorn: to keep places like they were in now from spilling over. Those outside of Blackthorn talked about the so-called underworld leaders living off the misery of the humans forced to reside there and in Lowtown – but there was nothing worse than what humans were capable of doing to their own. He'd seen enough of it first-hand to know.

'Where's Travis?' he asked, grabbing the arm of a familiar face he saw brushing past him.

The con cocked his head over his shoulder. 'Next floor up. Usual room.'

The subsequent few cons cleared out of his way as Jask led Phia further through the poorly lit space. A couple of males dared to eye her up as they passed, their lascivious looks causing Phia's grip on Jask's hand to tighten.

He glowered territorially at the cons who, fortunately for them, instantly resolved it wasn't worth the effort.

But her anxiety was still painful. The need to reassure her, to protect her, overwhelmed him in a way that pulled him out of his own comfort zone. And he did what he knew he never should have done – he interlaced his fingers with hers and squeezed.

It felt too instinctive not to.

And to his shock, she squeezed back.

The simple act, a silent message passing between them, struck him deep. Phia clung to him in that corridor like she believed he could protect her. And he would. He would never have taken her there in the first place if he thought he couldn't. And now that he knew he'd finally gained a little snippet of trust, he wasn't going to let her down.

Jask ascended the stairs and took a right through a knocked-through room.

He didn't need to look in the direction of writhing bodies amidst gasps, grunts and cruel laughter to know exactly what was going on. And neither did Phia from the way she kept her head lowered. She wasn't just uncomfortable now, she was frightened. She knew as well as he did, as well as everyone who glanced in their direction knew, that the only one standing between her and the dubious attention of each of the cons they passed, was him.

As they reached another hallway, passed unnervingly quiet rooms, shadows playing disturbingly on the walls through the ajar doors, he could hear the escalation in Phia's heartbeat.

'Fuck,' she hissed under her breath as they finally entered an empty hallway.

He glanced across at her. 'I take it you've never been anywhere like this before?'

'By the looks of it, you have.'

'A necessity sometimes.'

'I didn't think lycans had anything to do with the cons.'

'Like I said – a necessity sometimes.'

'Why do they let you just walk through here? Do they not have a problem with you being a third species?'

'If I'm here, I'm on business. Most of them know not to interfere in that. Socially, they'd have a problem.'

He stopped outside a door and knocked on it. He unravelled his fingers from Phia's and guided her against the wall opposite. 'Keep it zipped,' he warned her. 'And leave this to me.'

Travis semi-opened the door and peered out. His hazel eyes widened as soon as he looked at Jask. He craned his neck to catch a glimpse of Phia. He raked her up and down swiftly before turning his attention back on Jask. 'What's up, Jask?'

'I want to talk to you.'

A naked Travis glanced over his shoulder. 'We're a bit busy in here.'

And the bunched-up shirt he held over his groin told him exactly what with.

'Do I look like I give a fuck?' Jask asked.

Travis glanced over his shoulder again before looking back at Jask. He reached up behind the door for a key, handing it over. He indicated to the room directly opposite. 'Give me five,' he said, and closed the door again.

❋ ❋ ❋

Jask pushed open the door to reveal a dark room inside. He flicked on the light, but it only ignited a handful of wall lights in the twenty-by-thirty-foot room. It wasn't helped by the fact that the glass shades were red, adding to the sordidness – not least when the first thing Sophia saw was an unmade, metal-framed bed up against the wall to the left. The thin curtains were drawn, not that she had the feeling much light ever got in anyway.

She followed Jask to the two facing sofas in the middle of the room.

Like him, she opted for the sensible choice of the sofa facing the now closed door. She wanted to wipe down the sunken leather seat first or at least lie a towel down. Instead she perched on the edge and kept her hands in her lap as she continued looking around. 'This place is a dive.'

'What were you expecting?'

She could barely hold back on her lip curling in disgust as she looked over at the worn, mahogany sideboard where an array of adult toys and contraptions were cast aside. She was no prude but they made her stomach coil – the ones that she could work out the purpose of at least. 'It had better be worth our while being here, Jask.'

As he placed his arm along the back of the small sofa, his knee touching hers, she felt her stomach tighten again.

She had to trust him. There in that den, he was the only way she was getting out. More to the point, if whatever he had planned went wrong, she wasn't getting out at all. The reality of just how *much* she needed him made her as uncomfortable as the room itself.

'You'd better be able to get us back out of here,' she said, needing to vocalise it – needing to hear him say it would all be fine.

'Not losing your nerve, are you, Phia?' he asked, a glint of a taunt in his eyes – no doubt equally a glint of triumph at having found a weak spot.

'I'm just saying you'd better know what you're doing.'

He lifted the foot furthest away from her to rest it on the edge of the coffee table before leaning closer. 'Is that because you know your serrynity isn't going to protect you in a place like this??'

'If he touches me, I'll kill him.'

'If he touches you, *I'll* kill him,' he said, gazing deep into her eyes.

Her stomach flipped for one time too many that night. 'Are you planning on protecting my honour?' she said glibly.

'For as long as you're useful. For as long as we've got a deal,' he said, the response seeming cold compared to the look in his eyes.

The click of the door made her flinch, her full attention snapping to the con that slipped inside.

She had a proper view of Travis now as he stepped over to the sofa opposite.

He had a swagger that had never failed to irritate her in his kind. He wore nothing but an old pair of grey sweatpants that were a size too big, hanging low on his crotch. His shaved head matched the harshness of his over-exercised body – every muscle and sinew showing through his lean frame. His arms, neck and torso were littered with a multitude of tattoos – some a harsh black, some multicoloured. A naked, large-chested woman sat sensually in the centre of his abdomen, splayed for both of them to see as he stretched his arms out across the back of the sofa, a burning cigarette nestled between his thin lips.

But it was the numbers tattooed along his inner arm that gave him away.

He sniffed crudely before scanning Sophia, her skin crawling as he lingered too long for comfort. 'Who's the bitch?' he asked, looking back at Jask.

Sophia's stomach tightened, as did her throat. Her eyebrows lifted involuntarily. The turn of phrase, let alone the lascivious look is his eyes, would have, under any other circumstances, had her smacking him right in the mouth without even thinking about it. And she probably would have caused him equal damage between his splayed legs – rendering him permanently useless from the activities she had no doubt he liked to indulge in.

But she contained herself. She clenched her hands and controlled herself, taking slow and steady breaths as she counted to ten in her head.

Jask, on the other hand, hadn't even flinched. 'The fewer questions you ask, the better. I'm trying to get hold of Marid.'

Travis looked back at her. He scratched his stubbled chin as he examined her more closely. 'If you're selling, I might be interested. I'll want to test her out first though.'

The mist kicked in before her common sense did. She lunged forward. 'You fuh–'

But knowing her too well, Jask was quicker. He pulled her back against him, locking her arms in front of her chest, one hand firmly gripping her wrists as he slammed his other hand over her mouth.

She kicked at the table, jamming it against Travis's knees, making him jolt to his feet, shoving the sofa back with the force.

'Smart,' Jask whispered curtly in her ear.

She tried to steady her breathing again, to feel the reassurance of Jask's hold. To look at the wall instead of Travis whose very presence in the room was now enough to make her blood steam.

'Shit,' Travis hissed, kicking the table back into place before slamming himself back down into the middle of the sofa. Only now he wasn't so relaxed. Now he had his legs planted firmly apart on the floor, his elbows on his knees. But when his anger had subsided he laughed – a laugh that both infuriated and unnerved her.

She counted to ten again.

'Oh, she'll be fun,' he declared. 'After I get a bit of work done on her first,' he added, glancing at her chest.

This time she closed her eyes. She had to. She clenched her jaw and tried hard again to relax into Jask's reassuring hold.

'I want you to find out where he's hanging out lately,' Jask said. 'But you know how it works – if I ask questions, questions get raised in return, so I need someone else to do the asking for me. You're the man for the job, right?'

Jask loosened his grip on her slightly, but he kept his hand firmly over her mouth, clearly not trusting her not to explode again.

'Have you been to the usual place?' Travis asked.

'This is a private affair. I either want to know where he is or where to meet him. And I want him to know it'll be worth his time.'

Travis frowned, looked back at Sophia again, his eyes narrowed questioningly. 'What are you getting me into here, Jask? Only this ain't your style. She agency or something? Only I'm not fucking with the TSCD. You know I'm not having them sniffing around here.'

'She's not agency.'

Travis rubbed his stubbled jaw again, sliding his thumb and forefinger to a point at the base of his chin. 'I don't know,' he said. 'This don't feel right.'

'I'm not asking you, Travis. I'm *telling* you.'

Their gazes locked long enough for Sophia to look at Jask and then back to Travis.

This was a mini-showdown. This was a con who wasn't used to being told what to do and this was a lycan who always got his own way in the end.

But Jask had some kind of hold over him – everything about the situation told her that.

Travis sniffed again before taking a few curt inhales of his cigarette. 'How will I get the information back to you?'

'We'll wait here,' Jask said.

Her heart skipped a beat.

'You want it done *now?*' Travis asked.

'I'm in a hurry.'

'Shit, Jask. I told you – I've got stuff to do.'

'And I told you I don't give a fuck. You get the information I need, you come back here and if I'm happy with the answer you can get back to it.'

Travis shook his head but he didn't put up an argument. 'Fuck,' he muttered under his breath as he stood, making his way back over to the door and semi-slamming it as he disappeared outside.

Jask immediately dropped his hand from Sophia's mouth and let her go.

She swivelled in the seat, turning to face him again. 'Don't you *ever* do that again!' she warned. 'Silencing me like the little woman.'

'As opposed to what? Drag you off him? You overreacted.'

'Did you hear what he said? Did you see the way he looked at me?'

'For someone who works the streets, you make some stupid choices sometimes.'

'Stupid?' she asked, narrowing her eyes. 'Did you just call me stupid?'

'I said your *choice* was. What happened to the smart and strategic Phia? It's about thinking three steps ahead. It's about not reacting to every little thing. It's about being selective and keeping your eye on the goal. He would have expected me to contain you – either that or allow him free liberty to deal with you the way *he* chose. Is that what you wanted?'

'I would have shown him *exactly* what I'd thought.'

'You would have lasted seconds. And I would have lasted even less if he had so much as touched you. And then I think that would have blown our cover, don't you?'

She stared at him, momentarily stunned by the sincerity of the revelation. 'I don't need you to defend me.'

'In these four walls you know *exactly* how much you need me.'

'Then why the hell keep us here? Why not meet him somewhere else?'

'Because here we're out of sight. He'll be back soon enough.'

'Even that's too long.' She stood and headed over to the curtains. She pushed them aside and looked down onto a back alley, more brick buildings less than fifteen feet away. Even outside was like a maze.

She pulled away again to see Jask stood at the sideboard.

'At least we've got a few things here to keep us entertained while we wait,' he said, hands on his hips as he glanced across at her, a playful glint back in his eyes.

'That's not even funny,' she said. She marched away, rubbing the tips of her fingers back and forth across her bottom lip, her other arm wrapped tightly around her waist.

'I thought you were the liberated type, Phia.'

'Liberated with some self-respect.' She stepped up to the bed. 'This whole place is sick.'

'They're *your* species.'

'The worst of my species. Not representative of them.'

'These are the ones your Alliance defend though, aren't they?'

'No,' she said, turning to face him again. 'I told you – we protect the ones caught in the middle.'

'Oh, so you're capable of making judgements on your *own* kind now as well as the third species – deciding who lives and who dies, who's good enough and who isn't? Wow, it must be a very dizzying height from that pinnacle you've built yourself.'

'You tell me there's anything right about this set-up, about the way he looked at me, the way people like him treat women, treat anyone. It doesn't take any judgement to work out he's scum – and if you say anything to the contrary, then you are pitifully low in my esteem.' She stepped up to the camcorder focused on the bed. She switched it on, watched a sordid two seconds before recoiling and switching it off. 'I want out of here,' she said, striding back towards the door. 'Tell him to meet us somewhere else.'

Jask stepped in front of her, blocking her way. 'We're staying here until he comes back. I told you – you're perfectly safe as long as you stay with me.'

'Because it's not as though I'm questioning why you'd have anything to do with him anyway. What kind of a hold you've got over him to make him jump like that.'

'There are some things you're better off not knowing.'

She warily held his gaze before glancing across the room that now felt like more of an enclosure than the cage had.

Because she didn't know him. Not at all. She'd seen what she'd wanted to see – a decency beneath the reputation – because she'd needed to see it. A conclusion she'd made based on his actions with her – actions that were necessitated out of his need to get her on side. But none of it changed the fact that she did know of his reputation. That he'd obviously had dealings with Travis before. That he'd been *there* before. There where opportunities were aplenty if he liked to indulge his dark desires. Her stomach coiled unforgivably in jealousy at the thought of it. More than that, in disappointment.

This was why she had to keep a distance. This was why she couldn't let herself feel the way she did. Because of the *very* way she was feeling right then – insecure, anxious, disappointed, jealous even – were all emotions she couldn't handle.

He'd said she'd be safe. But paradoxically, there at her most vulnerable, she didn't want to feel safe with him.

She didn't want to feel safe with anyone. When she let her guard down, that was when bad things happened – that was when things went wrong. She didn't feel safe *feeling* safe.

Least of all with a third species.

Least of all in that place.

Least of all with Jask.

❉ ❉ ❉

Phia perched back on the edge of the sofa. She stared down through the glass table she was hunched over, her arms folded, her elbows on her knees.

She looked painfully on edge. And a far cry from the girl who'd first glowered up at him from the floor of the ruins. This was Phia with the mask slipping and whom he'd made feel a hell of a lot less secure with what he'd just said.

But he'd said it because it was true – he was anything but a saint. Not that she needed to know the details any more than he needed to revisit them.

And he hadn't expected the place to have that much of an impact on her. She was bound to have rubbed shoulders with the likes of Travis on plenty of occasions if she worked the streets like she claimed she did.

She'd even convinced him his instincts were wrong when she'd shown a completely different side of herself during the ambush. Back when she'd been calm and methodical, strategic even, to get him on side. When she'd weighed up the advantages of doing so and swallowed her own pride to put the suggestion forward. He'd seen the more mature, the more responsible, let alone the smarter side of her. And he'd admired her for it.

Most of all, he'd seen the side of her capable of doing what he wanted.

Only now her clenched hands, her tense body and her furrowed brow filled him with doubt again. It wasn't only hard to believe she was *part* of such a vicious vigilante group, but that she'd had any experience *at all* out there on the streets, seducing and slaying vampires as a serryn.

Because she should have marched down those hallways and through those rooms like she owned the place. She should have played Travis like the pliable instrument he was in the right hands. She should have laughed off the insults, depersonalised the threats.

Not unlike he'd had to.

She'd been too wrapped up in her own anger to feel his seeping through – to sense that he'd been seconds away from knocking Travis out cold for the way he'd dared to look at her, not least what he'd said.

And under any other circumstances, he would have.

But that sense of protectiveness over her, a need to defend her, was crossing the line. And, fortunately for them both, for their cause, reacting on impulse and lashing out wasn't him anymore. Because, personal feelings aside, he still had a job to do.

A job he still needed her at her best for.

And now her exposed vulnerability was too useful a way in for him not to use it to test if his instincts were right again. Not to check if he'd made a huge mistake agreeing to her terms. Whether he needed to get her back to the compound and deal with it himself from there on.

He took the seat beside her again. 'Travis has good connections. He's also swift and efficient. And they're both attributes we need right now.'

'He's also a repulsive tosser.' She glanced back at him, her eyes laden with concern behind the defensiveness. She looked back down at the table again. 'Nobody looks at me like that, Jask.'

'I got that impression.'

She sighed heavily, her whole body lifting then dropping with the motion.

At times he'd forgotten that beneath the serrynity, she was still human. She'd barely slept, barely eaten, was probably surviving mainly on adrenaline.

'You must be tired,' he said.

She shrugged. 'I'm fine.'

But she wasn't. And that's what he needed to tap into.

'You must have met plenty of vampires who looked at you like that. Isn't it too much a part of the vocation to get that worked up about it?'

Her gaze snapped warily to meet his before she looked away again. 'I'm prepared for it with them.'

He stared at the mop of dark hair now covering her profile and leaned forward to rest his elbows on his knees so he could get a better look at her. He felt a bastard for the line he was taking, but he had to keep his eye on the task. 'And how do you feel about how *I* look at you?'

She glanced at him. He was sure he saw her blush, but couldn't be certain in the scarlet glow. 'I haven't noticed any particular way you *do* look at me.'

'Liar,' he said. 'I know I make you uncomfortable sometimes. Like in the changing cubicle.'

She glanced guardedly at him again. 'I'm claustrophobic.'

'And I'm much better at reading you than you give me credit for.'

'After two days? That's quite a gift.'

'How many vampires *have* you killed? As a serryn, not a part of The Alliance.'

'I'm not one to boast.'

'But you must be used to dives like this. Being up close and personal with the enemy.' He purposefully looked across at the sideboard, drawing her attention to it. 'Doing whatever they want you to do as long as you get your kill.'

She held his gaze, her eyes narrowed. 'What's your point?'

'My point is how does such an emotionally vulnerable serryn last this long?'

'I'm not emotionally vulnerable.' Her narrowed eyes turned into a scowl. 'Fuck you, Jask,' she hissed under her breath, moving to stand.

But he caught hold of her forearm, keeping her seated. 'Why do you keep doing that: talking to me like that and thinking you can get away with it?'

But he knew what she was doing. She was doing what she always did – creating safe distance every time something he said or did caused a spark in her that made her feel something she didn't want to feel. The same as every explosion of hers caused an implosion between them. An implosion that would force them further apart.

This time she tried to prise his fingers away. 'Let me go.'

'Where? Out there? Without me? Seriously?'

Her glare was unflinching. A glare he needed and wanted to push a little further.

'I said, let me go,' she warned.

'And if I don't?'

Her eyes flared.

'It gets to you every time, doesn't it?' he said. 'That I might think you're useless to me.'

'I'm not useless to you though, am I? Or I'd be dead already.'

'You don't believe that.'

'Why not?'

'Because you lied when you said you don't see the way I look at you.'

'And how's that, Jask?' she asked, her eyes boring into his.

He didn't know if he was irritated by the interruption or relieved, but as Travis stepped back into the room, he was forced to release his grip on Phia's arm.

Travis slumped back into the worn leather and threw a piece of paper on the table. 'Marid's not been seen for two days. Not that that's unusual. That's one of his collectors. He should know where he is.'

Jask reached forward and picked the paper up. He looked back up at Travis. 'Zee? He works for Marid now?'

'Apparently. He knows where his lockup is. He's your best bet.'

'If this lead proves right, you owe me one less,' Jask declared, standing. He indicated for Phia to follow him out.

Fortunately she did so without any fuss. Just as she managed to keep her mouth shut until they reached the end of the corridor.

'You know this Zee?' she asked, as he led her back down the stairs.

'I've heard of him, yes. And I can't say I'm surprised.'

'Bad news?'

'Bad enough.'

'*I've* never heard of him.'

'Let's just say he's working his way up the ranks. Or trying to.'

'Vampire or human?'

It was as if their conversation had been forgotten, along with his near proclamation. Her focus was back on task. So too did *his* need to be.

'Vampire,' Jask said, looking across at her. 'In *every* sense of the word.'

Chapter Twenty-Six

The chill in the air had intensified since they'd been inside, albeit having been no more than an hour at most.

'Where are we going?' Sophia asked, keeping up with Jask's purposeful strides.

'A bar called Hemlick's.'

A place that was only one step down from The Circus. 'I know it.'

'Is there any part of Blackthorn that you *don't* know?'

'I told you – I work this place. I know all the main bars. Though even *I* don't venture into Hemlick's.'

'Then clearly you do have some sense.'

'Enough that I'm still operational.'

Though by reason of fluke more than any other, it increasingly seemed: fluke that the serryn line had jumped just when she needed it; that Rone had overheard the vampires talking about her; that Jask needed her alive.

Away from The Circus, now that she was calmer, she wished she hadn't become defensive so quickly back in Travis's room. That she'd asked Jask what he meant by "the way" he looked at her.

She wondered if that was the "look" Daniel had been referring to too.

She glanced across at him to see his gaze fixed ahead, his fair hair blown back by the breeze revealing all his chiselled perfection. Because he was perfection. Everything about him was painfully perfect.

As was the way he'd handled Travis. The way he'd got her in and out of The Circus safely. The fact they'd left with the name they needed.

As much as she'd convinced herself she was adept on those streets, she was clearly nowhere near as adept as Jask. And a huge part of it, as she could now see, was down to his self-control. A self-control that had infuriated her since the moment she'd laid eyes on him because it reminded her of her biggest weakness. The weakness that always got her into trouble.

The weakness that had come into play with her fury at seeing Jake Dehain alive – not only seeing him partying with *her* little sister, but for the wasteful loss of Trudy too. And the subsequent tirade had been an almost fatal error on her part. Instead of warily looking over both shoulders as she had been trained, her attention had been too fixed on getting to the club – allowing her to be swiped off the street by Marid.

But now she knew that falling into Marid's hands had been preferable to entering the Dehains' club. Caleb would have taken one look at her and that would have been it.

But she hadn't seen that at the time – she never saw anything when she was in a rage. Her most instinctive defence mechanism ironically made her at her most vulnerable.

And she had to keep remembering that. She had to learn to keep it contained. And there seemed to be no better teacher than Jask. More than anything, she had to trust his decisions if she was going to succeed.

They headed down the cobbled street. Melancholic music spilled out, cold light embalming the shiny bulbous stones outside the bar.

Jask opened the door, but this time he entered first. He scanned the dense, smoky room before veering left into the far corner. He took the seat opposite Sophia's in one of the few uncurtained booths.

Even he looked guarded this time, and she knew why. Hemlick's was implosion central. Vampires, rogue lycans and cons all mixed in the same space – but not for pleasure. They all went there to do deals with each other, to gamble and to barter. And everyone wanted to leave with the upper hand.

Laughter – loud, brash, and maniacal – emanated from one of the booths across the smoky room.

'As soon as he's on his own, I'll take him aside,' Jask said.

Her pulse raced. 'He's here?' she asked, moving to slide to the edge of the booth seat so she could peer over her shoulder in the direction of the laughter.

But Jask slammed his foot on the edge of the seat, blocking her way. 'You stare and you're going to get noticed.'

'Isn't that the whole point?'

'The point is we get him on his own.'

'Who's he with?'

'There's a small group of them – Zee, two other male vampires and a female too. There are also a couple of cons who've got a feeder with them by the looks of it. Seems there's some kind of deal going on.'

'What does Zee look like?'

'Five ten. Cropped fair hair. Pale skin. Black vest.'

'What if he sees you? Or saw you come in?'

'No one asks questions in this place. It's one of the rules.'

'What happens in Hemlick's stays in Hemlick's, right?'

He glanced back at her. 'Something like that.'

The barman brought a tray of drinks over, sliding it between them.

'They don't take orders around here?' Sophia asked, rooting through the collection as the barman stepped away again without a word.

'Flat price,' Jask said. 'No one drinks here for pleasure.' He browsed through the bottles himself before taking the two off Sophia that she had selected, placing them back on the tray and pushing them all aside.

'Spoilsport,' she said.

'You need to be on top form, not inebriated.' He poured them both half a glass from his chosen bottle, before returning it to the tray.

'I'm quite capable of holding my drink.'

'Then you're equally capable of taking it easy. This is work, Phia. Not a night out.'

'You don't mix business with pleasure much, do you?'

He scanned the bar, ignoring her question.

'What do you even *do* for pleasure, Jask?'

'I thought I made that clear earlier today.'

She pressed her lips together at what could have been mistaken for another compliment. 'So that *was* pleasurable for you?'

He looked back at her. 'Are you fishing for flattery?'

'Was it pleasurable enough to deserve it?'

'I'd consider a repeat performance if the mood took me. Is that compliment enough?'

She would have been more insulted if the playful glint hadn't glimmered in his eyes. 'You can be such an arrogant git sometimes, Jask Tao.'

'And I've no doubt that practice will one day make you perfect, Phia.'

She exhaled tersely, but refused to bite. 'I've never had any complaints before.'

'Like you said, you've never been with a lycan before. We have high standards.'

'And like I keep telling you – you can only ever learn so much perfecting the art with one mate, Jask.'

'I beg to differ. As your response down in the containment room earlier clearly demonstrated. So tell me – what is it about monogamy that you find *so* threatening?'

She lifted the glass to her lips, avoiding eye contact. 'There you go – reading between the lines again.' She knocked back a mouthful, it almost making her cough with the burn.

'And there *you* go – deflecting every time I get too close again. Is that what it is? Does monogamy scare you? The commitment of it? Or giving too much of yourself? Making yourself vulnerable? Have you ever been in love, Phia?'

She swallowed harder than she'd meant to. 'I'm a serryn. It's not an emotion that's exactly conducive to my condition.'

'You're evading again.'

She dared to meet his gaze. 'No, Jask – I've never been in love and I don't ever plan to fall in love, either.'

'Is that what you told Dan? Only he looked like a shunned puppy back there.'

'Dan and I are friends.'

'Looked to me like he really cared about you.'

'Did you care about Ellen? Is that why you killed her?'

He laughed curtly under his breath as he looked away. She had no doubt both were an attempt at containment. He knocked back another mouthful, but this time there was a hint of a sneer behind his smile.

She felt a brief stab of guilt, let alone annoyance that her question had slipped out so curtly. Worse was the disappointment she felt in herself at her hostility. But the feelings inside were too frightening, too intense, for her *not* to be hostile. Feelings that she needed to face if the question was still burning so inextinguishably inside her.

Because she'd seen enough to know that whatever had gone on with Ellen, it was an integral key to the real Jask. And she needed to know the Jask beneath the surface, the snippets of insight he'd allowed her nowhere near enough to sate her curiosity.

And she wondered if she was flattering herself to think he was as curious about her as she was him, especially as questions about her views on monogamy had nothing to do with strategy as far as she could see.

Neither could commenting on what he'd noticed about Daniel's responses to her.

Her stomach knotted as she reached for the bottle. She scraped her thumbnail over the label, peeling the paper away. 'Sorry. That didn't come out like I meant it to.'

She looked back at him, but he only met her gaze fleetingly this time.

She continued to scrape at the label as he reclined in his seat, his attention back on Zee's table. His eyes were narrowed, focused. Like a predator monitoring its prey, it was unwavering.

'I'd hate to be on the end of that look,' she declared.

His gaze snapped to hers.

'I bet you're quite the hunter, Jask Tao.'

But he didn't answer as he looked back across the room again.

'Do you kill swiftly or slowly?' she persisted.

This time he frowned. This time she'd captured his attention fully. 'What kind of question is that?'

'Just curious. Kane Malloy is renowned for the long game. Caleb Dehain for his swift ruthlessness. I want to know what the other great Blackthorn leader is renowned for. Do you *really* tear?'

'I protect my pack. Whatever it takes.'

Like he'd protected her. Kept her alive.

'Something could have happened to me back in that tunnel, Jask,' she said as she remained focused on her busy thumbnail. She glanced back at him guardedly from under her eyelashes. 'What would you have done then?'

'Nothing was going to happen to you.'

'I know what those cons can be like, rogue vampires…'

He smirked.

'What?'

'It's not *the* tunnel, Phia. Well, there are access points but they're well and truly sealed from our side. I just wanted you to stay on your guard. Keep the tension going. Though I was worried I might have pushed too far from the second thoughts you were having sat on the edge of that pool.'

She frowned, thinking back to the terror she had felt moving through that dark passage. 'You were watching me the *entire* time?'

'Of course I was watching. Me and Corbin had placed bets on whether you would do it. I knew you would. A little bit of water between you and freedom? The way I scared you before you left?'

'You didn't scare me.'

'So why else didn't you see through your plan of killing me before you left?'

She met the taunt in his azure eyes, her heart having skipped a beat not only that he'd known of her intention, but that he referred to it so nonchalantly. She looked back at the label she'd been massacring. 'It's a good thing I didn't, with how useful you're now proving to be.'

Leaving the bottle alone, she picked the label from beneath her thumbnail as she plotted a change of direction.

'So is it always about your pack?' she asked. 'Don't you ever do anything just for you?'

'What happened between us in the containment room was hardly for my pack's benefit, Phia.'

As his gaze lingered, she reluctantly looked into her glass to break the intensity. 'So what *was* it for?' she asked, glancing back up at him a few moments later.

'The reason matters to you?'

It did – more than she'd admit to. But the fact he'd asked her so directly made her flounder. 'If I hadn't been useful to you, *would* you have killed me down in those ruins?'

He knocked back a mouthful before lowering the glass swiftly back to the table, his eyes narrowing again as he followed movement somewhere across the room.

Sophia followed his gaze to the bar. She knew from the description Jask had given that she was staring at Zee.

But there was someone with him. Another male.

They both stepped past the bar, pushed aside a heavy curtain and disappeared beyond.

Her heart skipped a beat. 'Where's he going? Should we follow?'

'There are only toilets down there.'

'But they're on their own.'

'I said *him* on his own.'

She sat up straight, poised and ready. 'Come on, Jask, we can take two of them.'

'And kill the other? If he recognises me, that's what I'm going to have to do.'

'So?'

His eyes narrowed with disapproval. 'You don't just go around randomly killing, Phia. Death has consequence, even in Blackthorn.'

'Then let me handle this one. Alone.'

'No,' he said, looking back towards the curtain.

'Why not?'

He looked back at her. 'Where do I start?'

'They're vampires and I'm a serryn. This is what I do, remember?'

'And I know of him,' Jask said. 'You're not going in alone.'

Her stomach clenched, something behind his eyes telling her his reason was far more than fear of her messing up. 'I can handle this, okay? That way you might not even need to be involved. I'll get the information we need. We're a team, remember? You handled Travis; I'll handle Zee.'

And she needed to prove she could do it – not just to herself, but to him. The look in his eyes when he'd quizzed her about her serrynity back in Travis's room was a worry. If he worked out she hadn't even made a kill as a serryn other than those in the ruins, he'd send her back to the compound. Her hunt would be over. This was her chance, once and for all, to throw him right off the trail.

Besides, she needed to know what she was capable of – to stretch her fledgling wings. And though she hated to admit it, there was something reassuring about the security net of having Jask as back-up should it go wrong.

'And what if he recognises you?' Jask asked. 'What if he was one of the ones who helped Marid get you?'

'Then he's going to be even more curious, right?'

'No,' Jask said. 'It's too risky.'

Her heart beat a little faster, her question as self-seeking as it was tactical. 'Are you worried about me, Jask?'

He held her gaze for a moment. 'I'm worried about you messing this up.'

Her heart slumped. She folded her arms on the table and leaned forward. 'I'll say it again – *this* is what I do. I'm made to do this and I'm damn good at it. If you're not going to use the resource you have right in front of you to get this done, then it's *you* who's taking your eye off the ball. Unless that little speech you gave me back at Travis's place applies to everyone but you.'

Jask stared her down, but she stared right back.

'He's going to be back any minute, Jask. This might be our only window.'

He contemplatively looked back at the curtain.

'No one's going to take any notice of me slipping out there,' she insisted. 'His defences are going to be lower seeing me than seeing you. You know it makes sense. Make the smart choice, Jask.'

The seconds ticked past, Sophia moments away from putting forward another plea when he looked back at her.

'If I don't see the second one come out in under five minutes, I'm coming in there,' he said. 'I've giving you another ten minutes with Zee and that's it. And you do *not* leave the building, do you understand me? I can only pick up your scent from limited distances in places like this.'

Her heart pounded. He was conceding. He was actually conceding. Only she wasn't entirely sure now that she'd wanted him to.

But it was too late for second thoughts.

She reached for her glass and knocked back the remains. She slipped out of the booth and stood, her gaze lingering on Jask's for a second longer.

'Be careful,' he said.

She never would have thought two words would have made such an impact.

She nodded. 'Always.'

❊ ❊ ❊

Jask could hear her heart pounding as she crossed the room towards the curtain, but he couldn't tell if it was with adrenaline or fear. Maybe both.

As she slipped behind the curtain, he stared down into his glass.

It didn't feel right – sending her in there alone. But he needed to curb the macho protectiveness. It was insulting to her and unnecessary for him. She'd been right – it did make more sense her going in alone. Just because he chose not to see the serryn traits didn't mean they weren't there. Just because he saw her vulnerabilities didn't mean he couldn't see her strengths.

And if she *did* know what she was doing, he'd finally have the evidence he needed that she was ready for her task.

But the thought of her being alone with Zee… the thought of the vampire touching her. The thought of him sinking his teeth into her. The thought of him hurting her. The thought of him taking it one step too far before Phia could gain control.

He knocked back another mouthful.

He'd wanted to say more before she'd left, but he was as comfortable with her seeing his weaknesses as she was with him seeing hers. He wasn't even sure she'd understand. She only ever searched for differences between them – the differences she was conditioned to see, rather than the similarities that were becoming increasingly apparent. Because more and more, he was sensing that neither of them wanted to start feeling about each other the way they were.

A feeling he couldn't afford – not just for the sake of his pack but because he couldn't have his heart torn open again. And that's what would happen if he allowed his feelings for a serryn to develop. Because the way the disdain for him in her eyes had serrated too deep too many times now, told him he already felt more than he should.

As the curtain moved, his heart skipped a beat. He'd almost wished he'd have an excuse to go in there. Instead, the vampire who had accompanied Zee made his way back across to rejoin his companions.

Now Phia was alone with Zee. Alone in that dark, dingy corridor. Seducing him.

He slammed his empty glass down a little harder than he'd intended.

He smelt her before he caught her in the corner of his eye.

She was barefooted, her denim shorts barely clipping the tops of her shapely thighs. Her white sleeveless shirt was buttoned low, revealing her absence of bra beneath.

He looked up into her young eyes as she raked him slowly, her lips curling into a smile behind her heavily made-up face, her contrived curls cascading over her shoulders.

She leaned forward, rested her hands on the booth table and cocked her curvy hip to the side in preparation to slide in opposite him.

Jask rested his head back against the wall. 'Don't even waste your time,' he said, his gaze tearing through her.

She didn't wait a second longer, slipping away as silently as she had appeared.

❋ ❋ ❋

Sophia pushed aside the musty navy curtain. The few steps down were as narrow as the corridor they led to. The unadorned brick walls as unwelcoming as the concrete floor and exposed light bulbs dangling twenty feet above.

The music suddenly seemed distant, the heavy curtain muffling everything in what now felt like another world beyond. And it was cold down there, the tiny hairs on her arms standing on end. But she knew that was about more than just the chill. Her palms were clammy, her pulse racing, a light-headedness taking over.

As she reached the bottom step, she thought of turning around and heading straight back into Jask's arms.

Into the arms of the lycan who let her go down there in the first place? Who agreed to her putting herself in that situation?

To her detriment, she had insisted too much, put forward too strong a case. All in an attempt to seem strong, to gain control, to deceive him into thinking she was useful. To impress him.

And running back to him now would not only be humiliating, it would raise his suspicion.

She *could* do it. That's what she had to tell herself as she stood frozen at the base of the steps. She *was* made for this. And it was about time she had some practice. If she was going after Caleb De-hain and Kane Malloy, if she was going to face whatever vampire had taken down The Alliance, she had to learn fast.

And she sure as hell didn't need a lycan holding her hand to do it.

She pushed her fingers back through her hair and rubbed her hand across her mouth before smoothing down her dress. She took steady breaths.

But jumped as the door opened.

Someone else exited first, laughing, but Zee was right with him.

Her heart skipped a beat as their eyes met. His were blue too – but unlike the vibrancy of Jask's, Zee's eyes were cold, cruel, dead.

As both males sized her up, she felt the walls close in on her, any self-assurance she'd manage to build up now instantly plummeting.

'The toilets are down here, right?' she asked as nonchalantly as she could.

Zee gave her a swift once over. 'That's right.'

Clearly neither intended to move despite the female toilets being further along the corridor behind them. Whoever designed it that way was either thoughtless or knew exactly what they were doing.

'Thanks,' she said. And instead of waiting for them to part, she stepped between them, her back to the other vampire, her eyes meeting Zee's as she rubbed her body past him.

His eyes widened slightly in curiosity, his smile telling her he liked her blatancy.

As soon as she made it through, she wanted to duck into the toilet. Instead, she did what she needed to. She glanced over her shoulder, making eye contact with Zee again. And she smiled, bit tauntingly into her bottom lip as she raked him slowly and purposely with her gaze.

If that hadn't told him she was interested, nothing would.

She pushed open the toilet door and let out a deep and shaky breath as it slammed behind her.

She hadn't needed to go before, but now she sure did.

She slipped into one of the cubicles. Did what she had to. Over the top of the flush, she heard the door squeak open. And slam again.

Her heart pounded uncomfortably, her breaths uncontrolled. He'd sense it. But that wasn't such a bad thing. Come across too calm and it would raise his suspicions.

Male footsteps – steady, purposeful, taunting – strolled past her cubicle. Then fell silent.

She knew his type. Anyone who followed a female into toilets had only one thing on their mind. She had the feeling it was going to get physical quickly. If he reached for her inner thigh, the game was going to be over before it began.

She lifted her dress and slid out the syringes before removing her garter, placing them on the back of the toilet. She reached for the door, looked at the plaster on her arm, and looked back over her shoulder.

There was caution and then there was being unprepared. She grabbed one of the syringes, ripped the plasters off her arm and used them to attach one of the syringes to the underside arch of her shoe.

She took a steadying breath. A face-off with a vampire had never really bothered her when she'd felt she had nothing to lose, but now her queasiness was not only about *needing* to survive but, more so, of *wanting* to.

She pulled open the door and sure enough he was there – leaning back against the vanity unit, his arms folded.

He was good looking enough – if you could see past the dead eyes – and he clearly knew it.

'I didn't realise this was an open house,' she said, concealing her trembling hands under the flow of water before reaching for a squirt of cheap-smelling soap. She rinsed and stepped past him for a paper towel.

'It's open house for anyone who looks like you.'

She feigned a smile, despite her stomach curdling. 'Is that a compliment?' she asked, discarding the paper towel into the bin.

'It's a fact,' he said, moving to face her directly, standing between her and the way out. 'And that's quite a body I felt under that dress as you squeezed past.'

If he did recognise her, he was giving nothing away.

'A gentleman would have moved out of the way.'

'We both know no gentlemen hang out here. Which makes me wonder what kind of lady you are?'

'Who says I'm any kind of lady at all?'

She was used to the banter. The banter she could handle. Even if, for the first time, she didn't have other members of The Alliance to back her up if it went wrong.

This time her backup was Jask. Jask, whom she firmly believed *would* appear in under ten minutes if it went wrong.

But she wouldn't let that happen. Wouldn't prove him right.

Zee grinned – a perfect, toothy grin that flashed his extra set of incisors. She'd had plenty of near misses with bites, and others that had managed to penetrate when things had gone too far – but never long enough to feed before The Alliance intervened.

Zee backed her against the cold, tiled wall. 'Then let's not waste any time,' he said, looping his finger over the side of her halter-neck dress. He eased it aside to reveal the upper curve of her breast.

As he lowered his mouth to taste her before sliding his lips up her neck she involuntarily stiffened, repulsion flooding through her.

He sensed it but he lifted her anyway, parting her thighs around his, spinning her to plonk her on the vanity unit between two sinks. He grabbed her behind, sliding her forward tight against his groin, his mouth inches from hers again.

'Are you not a feeder?' he asked.

'Not yet.'

He smiled.

Her skin crawled.

'Looking for a sire?' he asked.

A crippling sense of revulsion snaked through her. And as he slid his hands up her parted thighs, she decided he'd touched her quite enough. 'I want to see Marid.'

His eyes flared, his thumbs pressed deep. 'Is that right?'

'You can take me to him, can't you?'

'And who told you that?'

'He has my friend. That's why I'm here. I want you to take me to him.'

He smiled again, but this one was as theatrical as it came.

He took a step back, looked at the floor as he rubbed his hand beneath his nose, giving a sniff as he did so, before looking back at her. 'Are you trying to play me?'

She eased down off the vanity unit, purposefully letting her dress rise up with the motion. 'Have I got it wrong? Only I was given your name.'

He grabbed her by the back of her hair, the brutality of the grip seemingly familiar to him. 'Are you with the authorities?'

She snapped back a breath but forced herself to stay calm. 'Do I look like I'm with the authorities? I told you – I want to know where my friend is. I'm willing to pay a lot of money. A *lot* of money.'

'And what makes you think Marid's got her?'

'I know what questions to ask.'

He smiled a toothy smile again. His grip switched from the hair to her upper arm as he yanked her back to the door.

'Where are we going?' she asked, trying to constrain her worry as he led her down the corridor, away from the bar, deeper into the shadows.

'I don't talk Marid business in here,' he said, glancing over his shoulder before taking a sharp left.

He shoved open the fire doors, leading her out into the back alley. Her stomach wrenched, not least at leaving Jask behind. But she knew a protest would only evoke more suspicion.

He took a sharp left at the end of the alley.

She looked over her shoulder. At least it remained just the two of them.

And she had to handle it alone. She had to prove to herself that she could handle it alone.

They passed the metal slatted steps of a fire escape, water droplets already gathering on the rusted metal from the light spray falling from the darkness above.

He backed her against the wall opposite it.

'So, you want to be taken to Marid.'

'That's right.'

'And you've heard of Marid? You know what he's about?'

She nodded.

'Who was it that gave you his name?' he asked.

'I can't tell you that.'

'Come on, sweetheart,' he said, placing his hands either side of her shoulders. 'We both know I'm not going to take you to him. But we *do* know I'll get *that* out of you.'

Her pulse raced but not, she realised, with fear. His proximity, the underlying threat, was inciting her in a whole other way. Something was happening inside, something beyond her control. Her pulse was racing out of *excitement*.

'And how are you planning to do that?' she asked, the even edge in her tone surprising even her.

He laughed, giving her another flash of his incisors as he glanced left and right down the alleyway.

A second later he grabbed her hair again, yanking her head back even harder than last time so she was forced to arch her back as he pulled her into him, forcing her to look him in the eyes as he loomed over her.

Pain shot through her scalp, but still she felt no panic. 'That tickles.'

He exhaled curtly. 'Girl, you've got some guts.'

She should have been pleading. She should have been begging him to let her go. Instead she gazed deep into his eyes. Her breathing was far from erratic; instead, it was as steady, focused and rhythmic as her heartbeat.

She slid her hand up his hard chest to cup the back of his neck, to seductively rub her thumb along the nape. 'Feisty, aren't you?' she whispered.

A glimmer of uncertainty crossed his eyes. But there was also something else. He seemed to be losing focus. His grip loosened and he frowned, seemingly unable to tear his gaze away. Suddenly he didn't look too sure of himself.

'But you've got it wrong,' she said. 'You're going to be the one telling *me* what *I* want to know.'

He closed his eyes and shook his head sharply before letting her go. 'Fucking witch,' he hissed, shoving her away from him. He stumbled but quickly regained his balance. He wiped the back of his hand across his mouth as if ridding himself of the traces of some invisible drug. 'Did you have something on your skin?'

She smiled as she proceeded to slowly close the gap between them. 'I'll ask you again: Where's Marid?'

She could tell his masculine pride was preventing him from walking away, but more than that, he *couldn't* walk away.

She'd not been looking for the signs down in the ruins. Down in the ruins she hadn't seen it coming. They'd taken a bite hard and deep and it had struck them fast – too fast for her to work out what was going on until it was too late.

But now she was curious. Now she wanted to watch. Now she wanted to see the effects of whatever chemical was exuding from her skin continue to consume him, leaking into his system, intoxicating him.

'Come on, Zee,' she said, sliding her hand up his chest as she took her turn to push *him* against the wall. 'Don't let playtime be over already.'

His move was swift, his hands grabbing her wrists before he forced her backwards against the wall opposite.

She caught her breath as he pinned her against brick.

His kiss was eager, hungry as he consumed her lips, her tongue; his hands grabbing her behind as he ground himself against her.

And she did nothing to retaliate as he swept kisses down her neck, her chest. Instead she clutched the short hair at the back of his neck, urging him on.

She realised she felt nothing, not even repulsion now – just flesh on flesh. She was becoming hazy herself just like she had read. When in her serryn state, her human body responded differently. And, in that moment, she didn't care as long as she got what she needed.

She turned her head to the side as he slid his wet kisses back up her throat.

'Hungry?' she whispered breathily.

But instead of biting, whatever self-preservation was fighting through had him grabbing her hips and turning her away from him, slamming her face first against the wall, scuffing her cheek.

But this wasn't how it was supposed to work. And as he ground himself against her again, slid his hand up under her dress, she lifted her knee against the wall and shoved backwards.

She'd only given herself a momentary advantage though. One that he quickly regained as he shoved her face-first onto her knees on the cold metal steps. He grabbed the back of her neck to hold her there as he moved in behind her.

Her patience snapped.

As he fumbled under her dress again for her underwear, she drew her foot to her behind so she could reach for the syringe.

She lost her grasp as he found the top of her shorts.

But he wasn't getting off that lightly.

As he freed her neck to unfasten the buttons on his jeans, she flipped around. She lifted her knee to her chest and slammed her heel sharply between his legs. She struck him for a second time – this time directly in the throat, right on his Adam's apple.

Zee fell backwards onto the concrete, momentarily stunning himself, his hands clutching his throat as he gasped for air.

'That is *not* polite behaviour,' she said, getting up and adjusting her clothing before lifting her foot behind her to tear off the syringe.

She stepped over him and slammed her heel down into his groin again.

Zee curled into a ball, his breaths short, shallow clicks. 'Bitch,' he hissed.

'Worse,' she said, with a smirk. 'Serryn bitch.'

His eyes widened as he stared up at her.

Flicking the lid off the syringe, she slammed her heel into his chest, distracting him enough to plunge the needle into his neck. She inserted just a little of her blood before stepping away again.

Zee slammed his hand to the wound and recoiled against the wall despite still fighting for breath, his eyes wide with panic as they fixed on her. 'What… the fuck have… you done to me?'

'You'll see,' she said. Knees splayed, she crouched down, just a few feet away. 'Let's call it the starter before the main course.'

Perspiration dripped from his brow, his entire body already trembling.

She tilted her head to the side as he remained clutching his throat, his other arm already in a tension spasm.

'Where's Marid?' she asked.

'Fuh… fuck you,' he exclaimed, dribbling spittle from his numbing mouth.

'You tried that,' she said. 'As I'm sure you've tried it with many before me. Only you picked on the wrong one this time, didn't you, Zee?' She held the syringe up between them. 'Or would you like me to prove the point a little more?'

He flinched, pinning himself tighter against the wall.

'Or I could *make* you bite,' she said. 'You have worked that out, right? I can override that fear and make you sink your teeth deep into me and drink. Make you feed to death. But,' she said. 'I get the strong feeling you're the type to peak too early – and I need information. So we're going to do this nice and slowly.' She glanced over each shoulder. 'For which you picked such a perfect place. I really am *very* appreciative.'

'You stay the fuck away from me,' he warned, as she stood up to step back over him.

He tried to bat her away, but she pinned his only working arm to the wall as she sat astride him. He tried to buck beneath her as she held the tip of the syringe to his lips.

'Don't be a spoilsport,' she said.

He turned his head away, his mouth tightly sealed as she squeezed a few droplets onto his lips.

He quivered, clearly using all his willpower not to lick it off.

'Where's Marid?'

He shook his head.

'One little taste, vampire,' she said. 'That's all you've had.' She slid her thumb into the inside of his lip. 'Can you feel yourself weakening? I know you want more. Much more. And I'll give it to you – slowly, painfully. Because you *will* tell me.'

He tried to let her blood dribble out of the corner of his mouth as he pressed his head back against the wall, every sinew in his neck straining.

But he couldn't stop himself swallowing.

He jerked as more of her blood penetrated his system.

'Marid, Zee. I want to know where he is.'

But still he stayed silent.

She held the syringe up in front of him again. 'Do you know what a full syringe of this will do?'

Hyperventilating, his eyes widened again, sweat trickling down his temples.

'Last chance,' she remarked.

He shook his head.

'Fine,' she said, slamming the syringe into his heart. She pushed the plunger down a little.

'Drake's corner!' he said, his speech slurred, his eyes clouded with blood. 'Drake's corner,' he repeated, as if uncertain he'd said it aloud.

'Which building?' she asked.

He glazed over, every limb stiffening.

'Don't you pass out on me yet,' she warned, grabbing his jaw and making him look at her. 'Come on, Zee – it's a big estate. Which building?'

He gasped for air. 'Regency.'

'Good boy,' she said. And pushed the plunger down a little more.

His eyes widened again. Then he shuddered just like the other two vampires had down in the ruins – convulsing and jolting like some insane wind-up toy, the strained grimace on his face too telling as he tried to swipe her away.

'Stop making such a fuss,' she said. 'You can't expect me not to see this through.'

She pressed the plunger down a little further, until a hand grabbed her wrist.

Chapter Twenty-Seven

Phia stared up at him across her shoulder. But it wasn't Phia's eyes Jask was staring back into. Like staring into a mirror for too long, he didn't recognise the face staring back. Because, right then, the eyes he thought he had come to read so well he didn't recognise at all. There was no longer vulnerable chaos behind them – just pure, driven, dark intent. She had tortured the vampire for information. Now she was torturing him for pleasure.

It seemed to take a moment for her to register it was him who had grabbed her but, as soon as she had, she turned back towards the vampire and attempted to push down on the plunger again with her free hand.

Jask was behind her in a second, lifting her off Zee in one simple move. He slipped in behind the vampire as soon as he'd moved Phia away, and broke Zee's neck with ease.

Phia glowered at him – frustration and disappointment emanating from once warm eyes that were now sub-zero. 'What the fuck did you do that for?'

'You've got your information.'

'You had no right to interfere.'

'You *got* your information.'

There was even something different in her stance now – her hands on those shapely, slender hips. Hips that were now emphasised by her cocking one higher than the other, those rolled-back shoulders thrusting out her chest. Everything about her exuded something sultry, seductive. And lethal.

This was the serryn he had yet to see.

But, as she stared at him from under those eyelashes with a look that was far too evocative, he wasn't entirely convinced how intentional it was.

'We're going,' he said, taking her by the arm and turning back down the alley.

'What's the rush?' she asked, pulling him to a standstill and stepping in front of him, blocking his way.

He looked down at her hand – at the slender fingers now splayed against his chest, before looking back into her eyes. Eyes that now smiled at him.

Lascivious eyes.

She slid her hand down to his groin. 'No one's going to come down here,' she said, moving in close enough for him to feel her breath on his neck. 'Not for a little while.'

She unfastened his belt, all the while guiding him back against the wall.

His heart jolted as she slipped her hand inside his jeans, inside his shorts, coiling those slender fingers around his instantly stirring erection.

'What do you say, Jask?' she asked, her lips curled into an intoxicatingly wanton smile as she lifted them to his. 'How about you try and make me scream like you once promised?'

She tightened her hand, rubbed her thumb under his sensitive ridge.

He jerked, breathed deeper than he meant to, his whole body stiffening involuntarily. He closed his eyes for a split second – something he had never done when faced with a predator. And right then that was exactly what Phia was – an unsated, frustrated predator.

That was all.

He took hold of the wrist that held him. 'Neither the place nor the time.'

'As if either matters,' she said, lowering to her knees.

He snatched back a breath as she exposed him fully before taking him into her mouth without hesitation. Pressing his head back against the wall, he stared up at the dense clouds above.

The warm wetness of her mouth, the depth with which she took him into it made his lower spine ache. He looked down at her as her tongue played around his tip before she consumed him again, taking him deeper, deeper still, until he clenched his jaw with the sheer pleasure of it.

Maybe this was it. Maybe he was finally seeing the real her. This was the serryn who roamed the streets. This was what she did.

And better that she let off that frustration with him than some vampire.

His hand instinctively grabbed the back of her head, his fist coiling in her hair.

This was a serryn in action.

And damn good she was in action – lost in the moment, lost in pleasuring him and, with it, herself.

He pressed his head back against the wall again as she grabbed his behind, taking him into her mouth again – hot, silky, hungry for him.

Her enjoyment was intoxicating, the way she lingered over tasting him, one hand now pressed to his abdomen, keeping him against the wall.

He'd had enough encounters to know how to switch off his emotions. Only this time he couldn't disconnect. Not from her.

He couldn't do it. He closed his eyes again. He couldn't let *her* do it.

He cursed under his breath. It wasn't right. It was Phia, but it wasn't Phia. Not Phia in her right mind. Like some drunken act, she was intoxicated by the serryn blood that coursed through her. Like a split personality, the temptress going down on him was not his Phia.

But she wasn't *his*, which made the fact he was considering stopping her even more unpalatable.

Too many times he would have let her continue, but he had to remember who he was now. More importantly, he had to remember who *she* was. And the damage this could do *them* if he let her continue.

He pulled himself from her, grabbed her arms and lifted her to her feet. He let her go only to force himself back into his shorts and jeans. 'Enough,' he said.

She reached for his jeans again just as he'd fastened them. 'Don't be a tease.'

He grabbed her wrists, spun her and pressed her back against the wall, pinning them either side of her shoulders.

Instead of being startled, her eyes flashed playfully. '*Or* we can play it this way of you want.'

He stared into her brown eyes – glossy, tempting, dangerously seductive, viciously alluring.

'I know you want me,' she whispered.

'Not like this,' he said.

'Then how?' she asked, yanking her hands free, reaching for his jeans again. 'Are you going to wine me and dine me, Jask?' She unfastened the top button again before tearing open the rest. 'Are you going to get down on one knee and propose? Hmm? Or are you going to punish me like you keep promising and fuck me on the naughty step?'

His heart jolted again at the enticement of her words. Only this time there was more than mocking behind her eyes. This time there was sadness. Tears were starting to form. Whatever emotions were inside, the floodgates were beginning to open.

'Let's not pretend this is anything else,' she said. 'Let's just do this. You want me and I want you. I want that lycan out, Jask. I don't care if it hurts. I want it to hurt. You're capable of that, right?'

He caught hold of her hands again, this time both of hers in one of his as he refastened his jeans.

'I said stop,' he said firmly, his stomach wrenching.

She wasn't just vulnerable; she was positively fragile.

Only right then he wasn't sure he was strong enough, could contain the heritage flowing through his veins enough, not to consume every inch of her regardless.

'We're leaving,' he said, breaking from her penetrating gaze as he yanked her from the wall, tugging her back down the alley.

'What is *wrong* with you?'

'There's nothing wrong with me, sweetheart. Be grateful for it.'

'You're *seriously* turning me down?'

'I'm turning the serryn down, Phia. Not you.'

'And what's that supposed to mean?' she asked, yanking free.

'What do you think it means?' He reached for her arm again but she recoiled.

'You have no right to do this!' She snapped in frustration, her eyes wide with fury and desperation. 'If you're not male enough, I'll find someone who is!'

'Not male enough, huh?' he said, stepping up to her, his temper fraying. 'Maybe it's because I *am* male enough that I know when to say no. Do you know how many out there would willingly take you up on your offer? Not even wait for you to offer?'

'But not you, huh? Am I really that detestable to you, Jask? Do you not like what you see? Do you not like the real me?'

'This *isn't* the real you, Phia.'

'Oh, and you'd know that, would you? Less than two days and you know all about me.'

'I know more than you're comfortable with. More than you want me to know – and that in there is *not* you.'

'Yeah, well I know you too, Jask.'

'Then you'll know that, unlike you, I'm not taking my eye off the ball for a quick fuck in some dirty, backstreet alley. You deserve better than this. And you're worth more.'

Tears clouded her eyes. 'No, what I deserve is to know how it feels. To have one moment – just *one* moment of knowing what it feels like to have one of those vampires exactly where I want them. Not whilst I'm chained to a wall – I mean for real. I want to know I can do it. I *need* to know I can do it. And I almost did until you ruined it!'

His heart could have flatlined. 'What did you say?'

Her eyes flared in minor panic – a reaction that told him everything he needed to know.

And it was a confirmation that sickened him.

He took a step towards her. 'How long have you been a serryn, Phia?'

She stepped back as much in regret as avoidance and wariness.

He closed the gap between them as her back hit the handrail of the steps. He caught her jaw and stared deep into her eyes. 'I asked you a question.'

Her eyes darted between his, her cheeks flushed, her lips parted. In the shock of it, she was starting to return to herself – and with it, the guardedness was coming back.

He tightened his grip on her jaw. 'How long?' he demanded quietly.

He knew he was tightening his grip out of his own frustration, from the realisation of what was staring back at him. But not purely from anger that his plans for her were ruined – more from the fear of how the situation with Zee could have turned out.

'Since the night you found me,' she said quietly.

'And before that?'

'Just human.'

She may as well have punched him.

'How?' he said. 'How did you change? Why?'

This time, as she stared back at him in silence, he knew he was getting nothing more out of her unless he *did* hurt her. But right then he had the feeling not even that would make her talk.

It was over. His hope to use her was over. A less-than-two-day-old serryn would be useless up against an established witch. She'd know in an instant.

His pack was lost.

He felt sick.

But even sicker knowing that, by not trusting his instincts, his instincts that constantly told him something wasn't right about her, he'd let her go out there alone. The thought of what could have happened to her, what he could have found, made his chest burn.

'You're a fucking liability,' he said, grabbing her wrist. 'You're going back to the compound and I'm handling this myself.'

'No! You can't!'

'You watch me,' he said, all but dragging her down the alley.

'No!' she said. 'We came into this together!'

'I *saw* you,' he said, spinning to face her. 'I saw you unable to stop. Serryn or not, that's all it ever is with you, isn't it? You never know when to pull back, when enough is enough. You lack discipline, you lack control, you lack foresight and you lack the common sense to know how to play the game. So yes, that makes you too much of a liability to work with me. And now that I know you're not even a proper fucking serryn…' He hissed before marching them both towards the main street.

'Then I'll work on my own,' she said. 'You are *not* making me go back to the compound. Marid is *my* issue. And I am not being shoved out of it now because I'm some kind of inconvenience.'

He stopped and stared at her again, raindrops glistening on her hair like a tiara, her eyes wide with frustration, her now free hands clenched with resentment.

He had to understand her.

He *needed* to know what the hell was going on inside the head of the female who he dared care enough about to ask the question in the first place.

'What is it with you, Phia? Why this fight? Because of your mother? Some vengeance tirade? Do you think *this* is what she wants for you?'

'I have to.'

He stepped closer. 'Why?'

When he was met with her silence he raised his voice to a level he hadn't used in a long time.

'*Why*?!' he demanded.

'Because it's my fault!' she said. 'It's *my* fault she died. *I* killed her.'

She stood there trembling – and not just from the cold, the shock, or from whatever was now waning from her system. But because everything was finally spilling from inside her. The hurt in her eyes was painful.

'But you said she was killed by a vampire.'

'In a place she *never* should have been.'

'Phia, you're not making any sense.'

She clammed up again, her gaze dropping from his, those hands tightening to fists.

He had to strike before he lost her.

'Fine,' he said, reaching for her again. 'If you won't talk, you're going back to the compound.'

She recoiled from his grip. 'She was in Midtown because of me. She *shouldn't* have been there.'

She stared at him in the silence, tears accumulating behind the raindrops. Her breathing became laboured as she gasped to repress her tears. But she didn't seem to care enough to wipe them away when they finally did emerge.

'Have you any idea how that feels?' she asked, her brows knitted tightly together, her eyes wide despite it. 'To hate yourself *so* much? *Really* hate yourself, to the point you can't even look in the mirror? You stand there in judgement of me and my behaviour. Go ahead. You can't judge me any worse than I judge myself. Because it's all *my* fault. My *stupid* fault. And I despise myself that I'm still here and she isn't. You want to know why I have a self-destruct button? Well, it's because I don't care. I don't care what happens to me as long as I wipe every one of those things off the face of this planet. So don't you dare tell me now that I can actually, *really* do something about it that you're going to stop me – because *no one* is stopping me from doing this.'

She stood motionless aside from the subtle tremble in her lips, the shallow but rapid heaving of her chest, all the while glowering at him like he was clueless.

Only he knew *exactly* how it felt. He knew every one of those emotions spilling over from inside her. And the self-loathing he knew better than anything.

If it hadn't been for his pack, he would have been dead years ago. If Corbin hadn't dragged him out of every fight, every confrontation, every drunken assault – anything where he could feel pain, feel just an inch of what he had inflicted on Ellen. Back when he'd wanted nothing but to spit on the world around him and spread the disease of his anger.

And now the Phia glaring back at him was a reflection of how he'd once been.

He saw it all behind those wild eyes as she'd condemned herself.

Her life was just one incident after another in a long line of defiance, of disorder, or rebellion. Though she had survived that day in the lake, Phia had never stopped drowning. Every day she was grappling, gasping for air and reaching out for something to grab on to. All the while she was sinking deeper, pulled under by her own wild ferocity – kicking away anyone who tried to save her, mistaking them for a further threat amidst her panic. In Phia's head, she was *still* fighting for the surface.

Only now he saw far beyond the irrational, arrogant and petulant girl to the true one, who was lost, alone and scared. The one who carried a burden too heavy of guilt and self-hatred and regret. A plight that had since been worsened by a curse coursing through her veins. A curse that was beyond her control. A curse that had taken hold of an already vulnerable soul.

But there was no way that self-destruct button was going off in his presence – not now he'd dared to feel something for her. Not now that he saw more than ever how his polar opposite undeniably had more similar traits than he could ignore. Not now that the female who stared back at him with that unrelenting chaos back in her eyes was far too deeply embedded.

He'd help her. His first instinct was to help her. But not until he got his head around what the fuck he was going to do about it all.

'This downward spiral tirade you're on will get you nowhere,' he said.

'You can't stop me.'

'I fucking well can. And I will. Which is why you're going back to the compound.'

She recoiled further. 'No! *Please,* Jask. I can do this. I need to do it. Keep me with you and I'll do what you want. Tell me what you want me to do. We'll do that first if that's what it takes. *Please.*'

The desperation in her eyes tore through him. The pleas as she stood there with her defences down, the mission so important to her that she didn't care he saw it, gave him a power over her that he hated.

'You're not ready.'

'You don't know that.' She stepped closer to him, her eyes painfully searching his for hope that only he could give her. 'It's about more than my mother, Jask. It's about all I have left. I fucked up the mission with the Dehains. Whoever came after The Alliance came after them because of me. I need to find who's responsible. I *have* to put this right. You do understand that, don't you, Jask?'

'I can find Marid without you. I can get answers.'

'No you can't. You must know how big Drake's is. You might be able to sniff him out eventually, but I bet he sees you coming first. Only I kept my eyes open when they led me out of there. All I needed was the name of the estate and the building. Now I can lead you right to his room. You need me for this. Neither of us can risk losing our only lead.'

He stared up at the sky, at the pending storm, the indecision between wanting to protect her, wanting to keep her close, and needing to do what was right for their mission all winning their own battles in the seconds that passed.

'Come on, Jask. You know it makes sense. You're smarter than this. I promise I'll be on my best behaviour.'

He looked back at her, into those wide and expectant eyes, as she bit into her bottom lip.

Eyes that he swore could melt even his most rigid resolution.

'I'd better not fucking regret this,' he said, taking her hand a little too sharply before frogmarching her back down the alley.

Chapter Twenty-Eight

They ploughed through the spitting rain, through the crowds. Sophia tried to maintain her focus, but something was stirring inside again – something provoked by rubbing shoulders with so many vampires. Like a gambler stepping into a casino, temptation was all around her.

Only the pull felt even stronger than before. Even stronger than when she'd headed to Daniel's place and to the safe house. Even stronger than when heading to Hemlick's. Her encounter with Zee had unearthed something. Something that was fast becoming harder to control than she'd conceived.

Her hand loosened in Jask's as she felt herself being drawn back into the crowds. But sensing it, he only held on tighter, pulling her closer, proving that fate really had thrown her a lifeline in the shape of the lycan. A lycan who now led her purposefully through the darkness and density ahead.

Every instinct of self-preservation resented it, but for the first time in years she needed someone. The very feeling she had tried to avoid, to shut out, for all that time, was inevitably rising to the surface.

And it was only proven more when someone pushed between them, her heart jolting as their hands were pulled apart.

But they only lost contact for a second before Jask had hold of her again, this time tighter, this time his fingers interlaced with hers to secure his grip.

Only when the crowds gradually dispersed, as they left them behind, did he finally release her.

As they picked up a steady pace along the quieter streets, as her head became clearer, so too came a flush of embarrassment as recollections of pinning him against the wall, of lowering to her knees, of taking him in her mouth, came flooding back. And the persistence… the pulling at his trousers… let alone the words that had slipped from her mouth.

At the time she'd felt like an outsider looking in on herself. She'd felt so distant, not there in the moment at all – conscious of what she was doing, but unable to stop herself. She'd wanted him so badly. *So* badly.

And he'd said no.

She lowered her gaze to the pavement, the humiliation taking full hold as they turned down another street.

She wondered if he sensed her awkwardness, but he didn't say anything. Just as he didn't say anything further about her serrynity. She could tell he was annoyed – annoyance that was only suppressed by a sense of purpose.

'Are you taking me up on my offer?' she asked. 'Are we going to do what you need me to do first?'

'No,' he said. 'I need you completely level-headed and at ease for that. And I don't think you're going to get to that stage until we get answers.'

'Taking a risk, aren't you? How are you going to persuade me to do what you want if you've done everything I want first?'

He looked down at her, but this time he didn't answer.

Jask took a left down a lane, led her through concrete forecourts before heading across a short patch of wasteland.

They stopped at the periphery of the abandoned housing estate. The multi-storey blocks loomed down at them – the regimented windows and concrete balconies reflecting more an abandoned institution than a once thriving residential area.

Jask led the way through the buildings, weaving through block after block, the overgrowth, the litter, abandoned cars and household items.

Her heart skipped a beat as she saw the play area in the distance, tucked behind rusted, buckled railings.

Children were now few and far between in Blackthorn, most of them kept locked away – mainly from the cons. Vampires had even fewer young than the lycans. They rarely chose to reproduce and usually vampires did so only much later in life when they wanted to continue their line. So the play parks remained abandoned and damaged. It was a haunting sight but no more than the emptiness that loomed from the vacant apartments that surrounded them.

But the park, the faded pink elephant rocker with the broken ear, told her they were there.

'This is the Regency,' he said, before she had time to say the same. 'But there are several ways in.'

She looked ahead at the doorway. 'That's the one,' she said. 'That's where they brought me out.'

'Are you sure?'

She nodded, a chill creeping over her. 'Oh, I'm sure.'

It had been the first thing she'd seen as she'd been led out of the building. That was before she'd nearly fallen face first into the wall after she'd managed to wrench herself from their grasp. The graffiti face that had loomed back at her in partial shock and distaste was one she would never forget.

And it stared across the park at her now, right next to the doorway.

'I kept my eyes open so I could find my way back,' she said.

As she felt his gaze burning into her, she looked back at him, his eyebrows raised slightly.

She shrugged. 'You don't think I was going to let him off that easily, do you?'

He looked back at the building and scanned the windows. 'Then let's be quick about it.'

Marching over, Jask yanked open the door, instantly tucking Phia behind him.

'I don't need your protection,' she whispered.

But his swift glower was enough to silence her as they stepped inside.

Jask was perfectly still for a moment, and she knew he was listening out for the slightest sound as well as taking in scents in the air.

The fact he stepped further into the confines reassured her all was okay.

Dust motes lingered in the air, glistening in the weak moonlight as they made their way along the empty corridor, deeper into the darkness.

As they stopped at the stairs, he indicated upwards but Sophia shook her head, cocking it to the right instead. She remembered the elevators ahead, the corridor that spanned to the right.

As they turned the corner, Phia pointed towards the metal balustrade cornering off a stone staircase. Steps that descended to another level. Steps that led to the basement.

He frowned.

She nodded. 'Definitely,' she mouthed.

He led the way down the steps, down to the door below. But it wasn't locked. It wasn't even properly on its hinges.

He looked back at her and she could tell he was contemplating leaving her behind.

She shook her head in warning, giving him her best stubborn glare. He seemed to pick up on the fact there was no way he was going in there without her.

Clenching his jaw, he turned his attention back to the door. Deftly, silently, he eased it aside.

It was a tight space, poorly lit other than a hint of light coming from an open door to the left.

A room Sophia remembered only too well.

Seeing it again flooded her with anger and resentment, with renewed humiliation, not least as Jask stood alongside her and finally saw for himself what she had been through.

Three single metal beds sat along the wall opposite. Beds that were bolted to the floor, housed only with stained mattresses. Up above them, the barred and partially boarded-up window barely let in enough moonlight let alone daylight – something she had remembered well as she'd slipped in and out of consciousness during the time she'd been there.

In the far top right-hand corner behind the door was the camera she had no doubt Marid used for more than just monitoring his captives' wellbeing. A single metal toilet and sink were tucked beneath it.

Jask glanced across at her, unease in his eyes. He knew as much as she did that she'd been lucky to survive.

'Like I said,' she whispered, 'he should have been wiped out a long time ago.'

Jask stepped back out of the room to turn his attention to the only other door down there – this one at the end of the corridor. This one firmly shut.

She looked up at Jask, at his narrowed eyes.

'What is it?' she whispered.

'Stay here,' he said, holding his palm up to her as he proceeded cautiously ahead.

'Like hell I will,' she whispered curtly, following behind him.

But as his eyes locked back on hers, flashing disquiet, discomfort tightened her chest. 'Jask?'

He continued on down the corridor.

And stopped a couple of feet away from the door.

He reached out and turned the handle.

The back of his hand went to his nose instantly.

The stench was overwhelming enough for her, let alone him. She instinctively took a step back, barely having glanced at the blood-stained walls before recoiling.

She spun away, facing the corridor again, and gasped for air.

When she turned back around, Jask had stepped inside the room, just a foot, but enough to take in the full extent of the slaughter.

And slaughter was a kind way of putting it from what she had glimpsed.

'Marid?' she asked across her shoulder.

He nodded. 'What's left of him.'

She cupped her hand over her mouth – not with sorrow, not with regret, but a pure physical response to the stench of his remains. 'Recent?'

'Last twenty-four hours, I'd say.'

She turned around, composed herself and stepped into the doorway behind him. She always thought she'd be able to handle it – could never understand why on movies so many vomited at the first crime scene. And it never irritated her more than when it was the woman who ran out first.

But right there and then, she knew that was exactly what would have happened if she had had anything in her stomach *to* spill. Instead she wretched dryly, gulping back the acidic taste it generated in her mouth.

He'd been torn limb from limb to the point the room looked like nothing more than a deranged butcher had been left loose in an abattoir, cleaving up whatever he could find.

She pulled away again, taking a few steps back down the corridor. 'What the fuck…' she whispered, her body cold, her hands numb against the heat of her face.

'Let's get out of here,' Jask said, grabbing her arm and leading her back up the steps.

'Who's done this? That's got to be a third species, right? I mean he hadn't just been hacked up – they literally tore him apart. Do you think it's them? The ones that came after The Alliance? I mean, what the fuck is going on here, Jask?'

He led her back up the steps, back out into the corridor above, his eyes alert, his tension unsettling her even more.

'What are we going to do?' she asked, struggling to keep up with his pace as he burst through the door, marching back past the play area.

'We're out of here,' he said, checking over both shoulders, scanning every section of the estate they passed back through.

'This *must* be something to do with The Alliance. The coincidence is too great. But why would they go after Marid too? Just how desperate *are* they to cover their tracks?'

'All we know is we just lost our best and only lead.' He frowned as he looked across at her. He stopped, Sophia doing the same. He wiped some damp hair from her cheek in a move that was surprisingly tender. 'You're trembling.'

'I'm cold,' she said. 'What do you expect?'

'You're also in shock.'

'I'm fine. I can handle a dead body or two. Especially vampires.' She rubbed her hand across her numb nose before folding her arms. 'Who doesn't care about the code? Who's willing to come in here and take on The Alliance as well as tear one of their own limb from limb?' It all seemed too obvious. 'This has to be down to Caleb, right?'

'This isn't his style.'

'Murder, mutilation and torture? Are you kidding me?'

'Marid did his job. He delivered you. It makes no sense for Caleb to want to kill him. Besides, if Caleb wanted you he would have come after you and he would have found you, not hired someone. Marid is the last vampire Caleb would get entangled with. And he would also have been down there in those ruins handling things personally. Hiding behind others isn't his style.'

'Caleb's a monster and everybody knows it. Say what you like, that's proof enough to me.'

'It's not proof of anything.'

'It's proof enough that I have to get my sisters out of there. That I–'

'Your sisters?'

She slammed her eyes shut as if it would take away what she'd said.

When she opened them again, she expected to be greeted by a Jask-style grilling. Instead he was staring across her shoulder into the darkness beyond, his eyes narrowed, watchful.

'What's wrong?' she whispered, her heart pounding painfully.

'Vampires,' he whispered back.

Chapter Twenty-Nine

Jask picked up three different scents. Intense scents.

'Trouble?' Sophia asked.

'They're keeping quiet – three of them from what I can detect.'

'An ambush?'

'Taking me on, there's something more to this.'

Much more to it if there were only three of them. Even inebriated vampires weren't that stupid. In a space like that, with such little interference from any other scents or noises, they were easy to detect and locate.

Sophia stared out into the darkness. 'Do you think they followed us from Hemlick's?'

'Maybe.' He glanced back at her. 'Do you still have the other syringe?'

She hesitated for a moment then shook her head. 'Fresh from the source it is,' she said with a shrug.

He looked back into the darkness. 'We need one of them alive. For questioning.'

'Then I guess that'll be down to you.'

He scanned the darkness for movement, for shadows. He could detect outlines as easily as humans reading a heat sensor. And they were hiding. 'They're not striking.'

'Just watching?'

He caught a glimpse. Not just watching – backing away.

And he knew why. Just as he'd suspected, they weren't out to get them – they were informants. Informants that realised they'd been spotted.

'Fuck,' he hissed.

He didn't want to leave her, but he'd never catch them with her alongside him.

He pulled off his jacket and handed it to her.

'Stay here!' he demanded. 'Anything comes near you, you don't play the heroine, you just scream – you understand me?'

He didn't have time to wait for her response.

Jask sped into the darkness. Vampires were fast, but not as fast as lycans. And very few lycans were as fast as him.

They knew to split up. One took an abrupt nine o'clock turn to the left. The other two, further ahead, split up with less of a distance between them – one taking a one o'clock turn, the other three o'clock.

Nine o'clock vampire was hightailing it back into the density of the estate whilst the others were heading off site. If he lost him, nine o'clock would not only be harder to trace but had the potential to give a few nasty surprises along the way.

Besides, Phia was back there.

He'd have to take him out swiftly and cleanly if he stood any chance of catching up with the others.

The wind swept through his hair, the drizzle masking his face as he kept his focus fixed ahead, his feet barely skimming the ground as he pursued his prey.

He vaulted one-handed over the railings before leaping over the discarded crates and household items in his path like hurdles. All the time, he navigated as if he were in familiar territory – assessing risk, height and depth before he even reached the obstacles.

He was already closing the gap between him and the vampire despite the latter moving at an admirable pace.

Until nine o'clock took a sharp right and ploughed into one of the abandoned buildings.

Jask didn't bother to be slowed down by the door that had clearly done so to his opponent. Seeing the pane-free window beside it, he lifted his legs, curled forward and swept through, landing nimbly beyond.

Catching sight of nine o'clock slamming through the double doors at the other end of the corridor, Jask used the wall behind him as a kick-off and sprinted ahead. He cleared what was left of the corridor in seconds, bursting through the doors to outside.

The vampire had barely reached the bottom of the stone steps.

Jask used the top step like a springboard, twisting mid-air, aligning himself perfectly with his target.

He wrapped his arm around nine o'clock's neck, using it as a pivot, snapping it with ease, before landing nimbly again, his feet and fists hitting the ground simultaneously.

He looked back up the steps.

He was cutting it fine. But it wasn't impossible. He'd covered greater distances, pursued even faster prey in equally short times. It had been a while, but his heart was pounding, his senses tuned, adrenaline fuelling him with all the energy he needed to work his inherent skills to full effect.

Jask ploughed back up the steps three at a time.

They'd head back to the hub. They'd know it was the only chance they stood of escaping him if they mingled with as many other scents as they could. Anything else – anything into the more sparse or lower populated areas that time of night would be suicide.

And to best take advantage of distance and time, to put his predatory skills to best effect until he could pick up their scent trail again, there was only one way *he* could go.

Jask sped back along the corridor but instead of ploughing back through the window, he took a sharp left. He ascended the stairs three at a time again, his powerful thighs enabling him to clear floor after floor as if aided by a fast-moving escalator. He burst out of the fire doors onto the rooftop. He scanned the route to the exit from the estate, calculated the number of flat roofs that he had detected on their way in there.

It was a trait of every lycan – wherever you were, for whatever purpose, know the territory, know the threat points and know the quickest exit route.

He allowed himself three minutes to make up for lost ground, for lost time.

He lowered into the sprint position, his knuckles flexing against concrete. He rocked back twice before feeling his energy peak. And, with only a few bounding steps before reaching the edge, he cleared the twenty-foot space between the buildings with ease.

Like boulders across a river, he leapt onto roof after roof, using disused cables, discarded scaffolding poles, anything he came across that would prove useful for leverage. He navigated pipework and external fire steps with nimble ease before landing as far as his route would allow.

They'd gained more distance than he'd anticipated, but they'd also made the mistake of re-finding each other, both knowing the route that was the best option for their survival.

Jask crouched, his eyes darting between one and then the other in the distance.

It didn't matter which one he took out first, only that the other saw it.

He leapt off the building, landing on the roof below and then the next, then an outbuilding before finally grounding. He leapt over the skip, cleared the upturned, burnt-out car and pounded the concrete like it was made of rubber.

One o'clock was his target. And, as he glanced over his shoulder and realised just that, the vampire picked up pace.

But not pace enough for the lycan leader, who had no intention of letting him escape.

Jask sprung off the ground, closed the gap, took the vampire down onto the rough terrain with him, rolling and scuffling until he finally wrapped his solid forearm around his neck and wrenched.

Bones cracked.

The vampire's body fell limp.

Jask's sharp gaze locked on three o'clock who had made the mistake of stopping to look back, just as he'd hoped he would.

Three o'clock had the sense not to run, but to just take a few wary steps backwards as Jask got back to his feet again.

Even from twenty-five feet away, he could hear the vampire's heartbeat race at almost human rates from his exertion. Now, no doubt, equally in panic.

'Who do you work for?' Jask asked, steadily closing the gap between them.

The vampire's eyes narrowed. He knew he was onto a loser, but the pride indicative of his species was still there.

'Whoever it is isn't going to help you now,' Jask exclaimed. 'And we both know it.'

The vampire glanced across his shoulder to the nearest cluster of buildings – all only one-storey. Even though he knew Jask would outrun him, his powerful sense of self-preservation wouldn't allow him to roll over just yet.

'Are you anything to do with what happened to Marid?' Jask persisted.

The vampire genuinely looked confused at the question.

'Why are you here?' Jask asked. 'Why are you following us?'

Still the vampire remained silent.

'You were spying on us,' Jask said. 'You were spying on *her*. So I'll ask you again, who were you reporting back to?'

The vampire cut his losses. He turned and ran towards his only hope for cover.

Jask brought him to the ground seconds later.

He got to his feet and lifted the vampire with him. He slammed him to the wall, one hand around his throat as he slid him two feet off the ground.

'Talk,' Jask said sternly.

The vampire inhaled and exhaled deeply through his nose, his eyes locked in defiance on Jask's despite his fear.

Jask tightened his grip. 'There's a lot I can do to you before your death,' he reminded him. 'And you know it.'

'There's a bounty on her,' the vampire finally said. 'You'd be best to cut your losses.'

'So why not try to claim her now? Because I was there?'

'Cut your losses, Jask,' he repeated.

'Who set the bounty?'

The vampire glowered back at him.

Jask pressed a little closer. 'Protecting them? Or protecting yourself?'

The vampire looked away.

His reticence was insulting enough, but to be more fearful of whoever set the bounty than him was one step too far in light of recent circumstances.

Jask pulled the vampire from the wall and threw him down onto all fours. He moved in behind him, jammed his knee into the small of his back. He drew back the vampire's arm so it was extended painfully behind him, and slammed his fist into his shoulder blade to hold him in place before yanking the vampire's arm with the other.

The vampire cried out as his wrist broke, as his shoulder shattered.

Jask stood back as the vampire slumped to the floor, sneering in pain into the concrete before forcing himself up with his good arm.

Jask circled in front of him. 'There are a lot more bones left,' he said, before circling around the back of him again as he rolled up his sleeves. 'And you've got a lot of blood to lose. So, who set the bounty?'

'Fucking…' the vampire hissed before sensibly stopping himself, instead spitting at the ground.

'*Who* set the bounty?'

'Someone you do *not* want to be fucking with,' the vampire declared, glowering behind at Jask.

Jask stepped up to his side, kicked him hard and precisely in the stomach and then in the jaw.

The vampire collapsed to the ground, squirming on the concrete and spitting out blood.

Jask grabbed him by the throat, lifted him off the ground and slammed him against the wall again. 'You should know I'm not known for my patience. Now who the *fuck* do you work for? Or do I have to start making you bleed properly?'

The vampire's attention shot past Jask's shoulder.

But even in his distraction, Jask had already sensed movement. Had already picked up on the approaching scent.

❋ ❋ ❋

Sophia had hesitated less than a couple of minutes before she'd pursued Jask.

As she hurried in the direction he had headed, she knew her chances of catching up with him were minimal. But it wasn't just because he might need her – her own common sense told her the shorter the distance between them, the quicker he could get back to her if she *did* scream.

She scanned the darkness, checking three hundred and sixty degrees in occasional steady spins as she ploughed on through the estate. All around her was silent other than the distant beat from the hub resounding and echoing through the avenues between the buildings.

She couldn't see Jask. She couldn't hear Jask. And as only the partial moonlight led the way, the sense of isolation crept over her skin.

She clutched his jacket tighter to her chest.

It could have been a ploy on the ambushers' part – to separate them.

But Jask would have had that in his calculations. He wouldn't have just run off and left her if he believed that. Jask had been thinking something else. The urgency that he'd sped off with had emanated purpose – a purpose she had to trust.

She should have stayed behind. She should have waited like he'd told her to.

But the thought of all three vampires turning on him had wrenched her stomach. It could have been a trap for him. Jask might have been strong, he might have been fast, he might have been powerful, but taking on three vampires?

It was a never-ending area of debate amongst the humans – as to who really was the most powerful out of vampires and lycans. Lycans were faster. Lycans were more nimble. Lycans were unmatched in their strategy in numbers. But vampires were more calculated. And, as for sheer physical strength, one on one it came down to the opponents.

And Jask was alone with three of the bastards out there.

Sophia checked across each shoulder as she kept moving ahead. There were so many things to hide behind, under, in. She couldn't switch off for a second. She couldn't let her guard down for even a fraction of that.

She'd kill them. If they hurt Jask, she'd kill them.

Her fists clenched as she strode with more purpose, hugging Jask's jacket tight to her chest, her need to protect him overwhelming.

Let them take a bite out of her if that's how they chose to play it. She'd take a bite out of herself if that's what it came to, and force her blood down their throats.

She picked up her pace to a trot, a sense of urgency overriding her fear.

They could already have cornered him. Be taunting him. Torturing him. She knew what they were capable of. She thought of Marid. If they were a species that could do that to their own, then it was unthinkable what they could do to a lycan at their disposal.

She ran, avoiding the debris around her as nimbly as she could.

She ploughed ahead, having no idea if she was even heading in the right direction. The buildings loomed over her. The emptiness of the place echoed back. She needed a clue. Something. She was on the cusp of screaming his name but knew how idiotic it would be.

She kept running. Running as fast as she could in her heels that irritatingly clicked on concrete. The stupid heels Jask had bought her. She was tempted to run barefooted but with the litter, let alone broken glass, her guaranteed cut feet would attract vampires even more than her feminine footsteps.

Perspiration coated her forehead, her palms and her back, despite the chill in the air.

She couldn't lose him. She couldn't *bear* to lose him.

She stumbled to an abrupt standstill.

There was something on the ground twenty or thirty feet ahead. Something still. But something that wasn't like any debris that she had passed.

She caught her breath as she stared at it, expecting it to move.

It didn't.

She looked across both shoulders. Checked behind her. There was no movement anywhere.

She looked back at the mound, headed slowly and cautiously towards it, all the time checking every angle within her visible field.

It was a figure. A hunched-up figure. A motionless, hunched up figure.

Her heart pounded, her legs leaden.

Jask.

Jask.

She stumbled forward, barely able to breathe. She was moments away from throwing herself to her knees to turn him over.

But as she drew closer, her stomach flipped. The clothing was wrong. It wasn't him.

The vampire lay dead, his neck at an impossible angle, clearly broken sharply and efficiently.

She stumbled past him, noticed movement against the building off to her right.

She hurried towards the scuffle. Heard a cry of pain. Heard the crack of bones.

Jask lifted the vampire off the ground and slammed him against the wall single-handedly in one swift and powerful move.

This was the warfare that was always potential between the species. This was what they were trying to avoid. This was how it would be if they were pitched against each other. This was lycan versus vampire.

She had no doubt he'd been responsible for the other vampire, probably the third one too. And he seemed to be planning exactly the same fate for this one.

Her relief to see he was okay was intense.

Her instinctive reaction after that was immoral. More than that, she knew it was unjustly immoral under the circumstances. The vampire was still a living, breathing creature, however she felt about them. A creature on the cusp of being throttled. But all she could do was trace her gaze slowly up the back of Jask's jeans, where his stance tightened the otherwise loose fabric around his strong thighs, to where it also now pulled tighter over his solid, pert arse. The narrow but masculine tautness of his waist was partially exposed by his slightly uplifted shirt. The power in his shoulders, the strain of his biceps against the sleeve of his extended muscular arm that effortlessly held the vampire against the wall.

The vampire almost surely equated Jask in height and weight, but that seemed to make no difference. Jask was angry. Angry enough that when he glanced across his shoulder, obviously having sensed her presence, even she took a wary step back.

'I *told* you to stay put,' he said.

And the impatient edge to his voice, the command in his tone, did nothing to abate her flutter of arousal.

She closed the gap between them. 'I thought you might need my help,' she said, folding her arms. 'Which clearly you do.'

He exhaled tersely at her attempt at humour. 'I'll let you know,' he said, before returning his attention back to the vampire struggling for breath.

He tightened the grip on the vampire's throat, Sophia watching on as she saw the brute determination in Jask's eyes.

'Enough time wasted,' Jask said. 'I want to know who has put the bounty on her and why.'

'A bounty?' Sophia echoed. This was why the vampire wasn't dead yet. Jask was after information.

'We were being spied on,' Jask said, his glare not flinching from the vampire who was turning a peculiar shade even in the shadows.

But the vampire was staying silent. Moments from his own potential death, it was obvious that whoever he was working for wasn't anyone he wanted to grass on – further confirmation that this was someone big.

'Is it Caleb Dehain?' Sophia asked.

Jask glowered back across at her for her interruption.

But Sophia took a step closer anyway. 'Is it?' she demanded of the vampire.

The vampire licked his dry lips. His attention shot back to Jask.

'No,' Sophia snapped. She dropped her hands to her sides, clenched and unclenched them, her proximity to the vampire already sending her hazy. 'Don't look at him – look at me. You think he's the bad cop in this? I haven't even started. He can snap your neck in seconds. I can let this take hours. Did whoever's paying you tell you you're hunting a serryn?'

The vampire frowned. He looked confused, disbelief evident in his eyes.

'No, I didn't think so,' she said. She looked back at Jask. 'We've got a little bit of time to play with, haven't we? I could start feeding him my blood now. Or dawn will be here in a couple of hours. We could wait until then. And when the sun's properly up, we could strap him to one of the rust buckets of a car back there – bake him for a little while until he's ready to speak.'

Jask looked back at her, his eyebrows slightly raised. She couldn't tell if he was genuinely surprised by her suggestion, but he seemed to be willing to play along. 'That's quite the imagination you've got there, honey. Remind me never to cross you.'

She shrugged. 'I have more invasive procedures for situations like that.'

He smirked. A genuine smirk. But then he looked back at the vampire. 'So do I,' he said, yanking the vampire away from the wall. He glanced back over his shoulder at Sophia. 'And this time, you *stay* here,' he commanded, before dragging the vampire over to the nearest door, kicking it open and forcing him inside.

Sophia checked over her shoulder at the desolate housing estate behind her, listened to the distant sounds of Blackthorn caught on the night breeze.

She looked back at where Jask had disappeared. She flinched when she heard the first of the gut-wrenching yells, more intermittent ones soon echoing from inside the derelict apartment.

Nervous of someone else hearing and coming to investigate, she looked over her shoulder again as the minutes passed, as the yells kept coming. Until, placing one foot in front of the other against her better judgement, she stepped up to the window to peer inside.

Moonlight from the temporarily dispersed clouds created a seamless shower through the broken roof of the abandoned apartment. Jask stood in the shadows to the right of it, the vampire splayed on his back on top of a kitchen table.

She squinted but couldn't see exactly what he was doing – only the shudders of the vampire's body as Jask loomed over him. She flinched again as the vampire jolted.

A conversation was happening – a conversation she felt she had the right to hear.

She pushed open the door and stepped inside, approaching the table just in time to hear the vampire splutter, 'Caleb. It *is* Caleb. He's the one who wants her.'

Sophia's heart skipped a beat.

'Why?' Jask demanded.

But, for Sophia, whether it was confirmation that he knew what The Alliance had done to Jake or whether it was because he knew there was a serryn loose in Blackthorn, it was irrelevant – Caleb was coming for her.

'I don't know,' the vampire gasped. 'He… he put a call out on the streets. Anyone who sees her is to report back.'

'He wants her alive?' Jask asked.

'Yes,' the vampire said.

Jask withdrew his left hand, the one nearest to her, from the vampire's throat. A split second later, he rammed it into the vampire's side, up under his ribcage. The vampire jolted violently, the shock transparent in his eyes.

Sophia jolted too. She instinctively took a step back as she stared at Jask's now retracted bloodied hand, at the mound of muscle that he held there – the vampire's torn out heart black in the moonlight.

She held her breath waiting for Jask to acknowledge her. Waiting for something, anything, to happen next.

But he didn't look at her. He didn't speak as he dropped the now defunct organ to the floor, as he walked into the moonlight shower.

Instead he turned his back on her, crouched down, dunked his hand in the water-filled bucket, shaking off the excess water like some ritualistic cleansing as he stood again.

She looked across at the vampire corpse that now resembled a limp and abandoned macabre toy. Proof of what the lycan leader was capable of.

And she *had* to take a closer look.

Her hand shot to her mouth as she stared at the purposeful bloodletting, at the severed and torn tendons and muscles that demonstrated Jask knew all the vampire weaknesses. That he no doubt knew a human's too. The torture had been the work of a craftsman – a swift, efficient and experienced craftsman.

This was why Jask was the alpha in his pack. *This* was why Jask could be the alpha anywhere he chose to be. Because when it came to it, Jask did what he had to do. He'd done exactly what he'd once warned lycans do – he had torn in *all* the right places.

And had succeeded in getting what he wanted as result.

The heat inside, the heat building inches below her stomach, scorched. The blood spilling had incited something in her just as much as it had incited the wolf in him. The serryn was resurfacing again – summoned by the scent of vampire blood in the air, her survival instincts kicking in at witnessing the slaughter. She felt herself become hazy, felt the dark room closing in on her so all she could focus on was Jask and his moonlit backdrop.

He remained with his back to her, his interlinked hands holding the back of his head, his talons, still partially extended, caught by the moonlight. His legs were apart in a soldier-type stance, his sleeves still rolled up and revealing his powerful forearms, his breaths slow and laboured as if he were calming himself.

Or trying to.

Because he was *trying* to be a soldier; his acts had been those of a soldier looking out for his pack. And she now felt a part of that pack – in his purpose for her at least.

His clinical act to get what he needed from the vampire gave her a sense of belonging she hadn't felt in a long time. The comfort of a family unit she had felt she had no place being a part of ever since she had been responsible for tearing her own apart.

Only now she sensed she was on the cusp of losing it again.

Her pulse raced, perspiration coating her palms.

Hearing that Caleb wanted her had changed things. Jask knew they were both in way over their heads now that the notorious vampire's involvement had been confirmed. That it was only a matter of time before they were cornered – no doubt a catalyst to Jask's anger. And from the way he ignored her, she guessed he was holding her responsible for the raised odds.

But if this was his rejection, if he'd resolved Caleb wasn't worth tackling, then he was going to tell her to her face. Because they had become a team in those past few hours and she wasn't walking away from that yet.

Because now Caleb was after her, she needed Jask more than ever. More to the point, her sisters needed him. They needed the lycan she had just caught a glimpse of.

And she was going to fight her corner to keep him.

'You're angry, I get it,' she said, her mouth dry, her numb hands clenched. 'But if you want to back out on me now, whatever plan you had for me, then you turn and you tell me to my face. Because I did warn you, Jask. I did tell you this could involve Caleb. It's not like–'

She detected his curt exhale in the silence. He dropped his arms to his sides and turned to face her.

A spark of electricity shot through her – something visceral, something instinctive, something too evocative awakened right then. Her stomach curdled, his eyes as hypnotic as they were fatal.

This was the monster. *This* was what they all feared. This was Jask on the cusp of unleashing his true temperament.

His eyes, from what she could see from the few feet away, were consumed by his opal pupils. His canines glimmered behind the gap in his sensual lips. Lips that had gone down on her, tasting her shamelessly, taking her beyond what she thought possible in the cell.

And he most definitely *was* trying to calm himself. His still-laboured breathing told her that much – his hard chest, revealed even more by the top buttons lost from his shirt in the struggle, rising and falling non-rhythmically.

Despite the coolness of the night air, she felt hot, flustered as those eyes remained mesmerizingly locked on hers.

She didn't know if she was consenting to suicide, staring right back at him – every instinct compelling her to pull away.

Because Ellen came to mind. That this was how she had met her end. That for some reason Jask had lost it – killed her by accident, not murdered her as he claimed.

But she remained rooted to the spot – armed only with the hope he was still focused enough to remember that he *did* need her alive.

And rooted to the spot because she wanted him. Stood there oozing all that was powerful, the untamed glint in his eyes, she *wanted* him. Badly.

And he sensed it.

As his eyes narrowed, her instincts took over. *Her* instincts, those of the serryn suppressed in the wake of what could be about to happen.

She dropped his jacket and took a wary step back.

He turned his head slightly, watching her out of the corner of his eye.

She snapped back a breath. Realising her nerves were inciting him further, she froze.

Nowhere to run. Nowhere to hide.

He closed in on her in seconds.

He pushed her forward over the dilapidated kitchen counter nearby and kicked her legs apart with ease.

Her breaths became short gasps as his fingers coiled in her hair, as his powerful legs pressed against the backs of her thighs, his arm across her shoulder blades holding her down in the submissive pose he clearly craved.

❋ ❋ ❋

All he could see was her – Phia bent forward over the counter, ready for his taking, her futile attempt at a struggle only inflaming him more.

All he could smell was the scent of vampire blood in the air mingled with her arousal. His heart pounded, the fast-flowing blood in his veins setting every nerve alight. He was breathless, the sense of liberation more powerful than he had felt even since their encounter in the cell – the liberation he had felt when, instead of withdrawing, he had succumbed to the thrill of spilling inside her, her serryn womb enticingly ineffectual at any semblance of creating life. Ineffectual of condemning him.

And he resented her for creating that sense of instability in him again. Stability that he had worked for decades on maintaining. A stability more necessary than ever, with disaster looming for his pack. Tempting him with a sense of liberation he'd not dared feel for decades.

And it had felt good, despite still having had to choice but to force himself to be restrained.

But it didn't have to be like that this time. Not if he chose to shrug off the weight of responsibility. Do what he wanted. Let

Corbin take the reins. They still had Dan back at the compound to bargain with.

And there was no great temptation as he held her helpless beneath him, on the cusp of using her to sate his anger, his pleasure, his craving for freedom. Not now Caleb wanted her too. Wanted *his* serryn. And no vampire was taking what was his, his need to claim her firing him up even more.

This time he wouldn't hold back at all. This time he would take her every way he wanted. The only thing he had to concern himself with was keeping her alive.

He looked up through the caved-in roof – catching the moon as the clouds swept past, the silence all-encompassing.

He was running through the fields again, the woodlands, the breeze in his hair and fresh air in his lungs. A time when there were no borders and barriers. Where alphas chose their territory and ruled it.

A time when he was fast becoming the most powerful in his pack, on the cusp of challenging his then pack's alpha.

He had morphed on seven blue moons and he had survived – screaming in agony in the caves where he had taken himself. A place away from any towns where the smell of prey would draw him on a rampage. Instead, he'd been learning to control the wolf inside – his decision not to take the herbs even during those potent cycles the greatest test of all.

And he would have reached his potential if the regulations hadn't come. If he hadn't been forced into a cage. Forced against his instincts.

Still been forced against his instincts.

But now that could change.

And he had nothing to stop him.

He lowered his head, his nails scraping through the wooden counter, leaving splinters in their wake.

Every temptation was laid out in front of him.

But he couldn't do it.

He didn't *want* to do it.

The power was in the pulling away. The power was in the self-control. The power was not in commanding others but in commanding himself.

He was *not* that uncontrollable lycan anymore – and his very hesitation was proving that to him. He *was* in control of himself.

He *did* deserve his alpha status – and this was why. What he had once lost, in those moments, he had now earned back. His deepest fears that he would lose it again were finally overridden.

He hadn't tamed Phia – Phia had tamed *him*.

Because he couldn't hurt her. No matter how much the wolf inside summoned him to act on his most basic instincts, he was *incapable* of hurting her.

Taking a steady breath, he leaned over her, his lips brushing her ear as he said, 'We need to talk.'

Chapter Thirty

Caitlin Parish sat in her car, her forehead against the steering wheel, rain smattering the windscreen and beating rhythmically on the roof.

Too many times in the last few days she'd questioned whether she could go back to the unit. Whether she could face it again. Now, as she dried her eyes, she couldn't help but question if she'd been wrong to be so belligerent as to believe she could cope.

Arguing with Kane for the three days leading up to her return hadn't helped. And they'd argued fiercely. He'd stormed around and glowered and told her exactly what he'd thought of her wanting to go back out there, her resentment at his possessiveness only tempered by the concern in his eyes.

Because even in the short two weeks since the trial, so much had evolved between them, not least Kane gradually having become increasingly open emotionally. And it was when they had those moments, when he'd let her in, or even when she'd catch him secretly looking at her and he'd respond with a playful smile or wink, that she'd questioned whether she was willing to risk renewing a division between them that rejoining the VCU could potentially cause.

But her job was a part of her – part of her identity, her independence, her values. And not just that. Facing the aftermath was a matter of principle – not only for her, but for the very reason she'd exposed the corruption in the first place.

And she would not be intimidated out of doing that. As shaken as she felt, as humiliated, as repressed, she was not going to be beaten by a bunch of bullies who were still too opinionated to see beyond their own ignorance.

And it was because she was still so shaken that she knew she'd chosen right to stay at her own apartment for that first night back. She couldn't let Kane see how she was – the effect the day had had on her – not least the implications it could have for the relevant members of her unit if Kane worked out *why* she was upset.

More so she knew that after a day like that, once he held her again, she wouldn't want to leave his place at all. Not ever.

But she was used to dealing with things alone. Had spent too many years since her parents' death dealing with things alone. And she couldn't risk losing that part of herself. It was still early days with Kane. And no matter how intensely she felt for him, she'd still had enough moments of doubt not to give herself completely yet.

Because no matter how close they'd become, parts of him were still closed. He still didn't talk about what he knew about the vampire prophecies. He still didn't tell her why, back in the warehouse during his standoff with Xavier Carter – the now ex-head of the TSCD and mastermind behind the slaughter of Kane's sister – he'd been so concerned by Xavier mentioning the name Feinith. Let alone what the vampire secret was that Xavier had claimed that same Higher Order vampire had disclosed to him. Instead, it seemed that when it came to vampire business, it stayed vampire business.

And the VCU, let alone this latest case, was *her* business. Those deaths were all linked. She just had to work out what that link was. Because if she messed up, it would be another reason too many for those same bullies to shake their heads and revel in their condemnatory smug smiles.

She looked across the car park as dawn encroached on the darkness. She'd have a shower, get some sleep, maybe get some food, and think things through in her own space and time.

Grabbing her rucksack from the back seat, she slammed the car door and took the back exit into the apartment block, ascending the stairs up to her floor two at a time.

She unlocked her front door.

And retrieved her gun from the back of her trousers a split second later.

She pointed the barrel directly at the intruder.

It took her a split second longer to assess there was another in front of her kitchenette to her right.

Another facing her in the sofa chair directly ahead of him.

Three males. All suited. None showing any reciprocal sign of hostility.

'Caitlin Parish.'

Her attention snapped to her sofa chair – at the source of the dulcet male tones.

'Or should that be Agent Parish? Where are my manners?' He stood, his wrinkled grey eyes gleaming as they rested calmly on hers. 'Please. Do take a seat. You've had a challenging first night at work from what I hear.' He resumed his seat again. 'Though I've no doubt it appears somewhat impertinent me offering you a seat in your own home. But as your home is nonetheless paid for from your salary, a salary that I pay, I guess we could argue it's just as much mine as yours.'

Despite recognising him, though never having met him, she couldn't bring herself to lower her gun. Instead, she warily assessed his silent companions. Companions she now understood were there to protect the older man who sat reclining in her chair again, one leg casually crossed over the other.

He took off his glasses, rubbed them with the handkerchief he'd taken from his top pocket, before tucking it back in again. He replaced his glasses and smiled. 'Come now. You're letting the cold air in.'

'Sirius Throme,' she said, though she could hardly believe that the head of the Global Council, the overseer of every Third Species Control Division in every locale, was sat in her apartment.

The suit to her right held out his hand towards the sofa as an indication, more so an instruction, for her to step inside.

'Come, come,' Sirius said again, as if ushering in a dawdling child. 'Bates,' he said, addressing the suit by the kitchenette, 'make Caitlin a coffee. Milky. No sugar. That is still your preference, I assume?' he asked jovially as he looked back at her.

But it was a joviality she found unnerving, let alone the fact he knew such a basic fact about her.

But then the Global Council knew everything. Or certainly everything about anyone they were interested in.

'There's really no need for the gun,' Sirius added. 'As effective as you are with it, the two gentlemen either side of you are equally as effective and would have already proved it. But, as you can see, that's far from my intention. So, please,' he said, indicating towards the sofa opposite him, '*do* sit down.'

With one more glance at the suit to her right, she reluctantly lowered her gun. She stepped inside only to have the suit hold out his hand to remove it from her. Resentfully, she relinquished her weapon.

'Lovely little place,' Sirius declared.

She sat down on the edge of her sofa, placing her rucksack, her spare gun within, at her feet. Heart pounding, she wasn't willing to let her guard down for a moment. As pleasant as he was trying to be, Caitlin's well-honed instinct was screaming it wasn't going to last. 'What are you doing here, Dr Throme?'

'I've come for a chat, Caitlin. It is okay if I call you, Caitlin, I assume? I feel like I've known you such a long time. And what with all this unpleasant business of late, I feel like I know you even more.'

'Well, Dr Throme, I don't know *you*, so you'll have to excuse my wariness.'

'There's no need to be wary.'

'You've broken into my apartment.'

'It was the best place for us to chat in private.'

'Chat about what?'

Bates placed the coffee on the table between them.

'Tell me,' Sirius began, his fingers steepled at the base of his thin lips as he examined her gaze unflinchingly, 'what was it like returning to work today?'

'Fine.'

'Fine?'

'Fine.'

'Many thought you wouldn't appear.'

'Many don't know me very well at all.'

'I think your recent actions clarified that.'

'Am I in some kind of trouble, Dr Throme?'

He laughed lightly, but it didn't reflect in his eyes. 'In trouble for telling the truth?'

'Isn't that usually what gets people in my position into trouble?'

'Oh, you are delightful,' he said, his smile fleeting. 'Tell me, how are things with you and Kane?'

Her stomach somersaulted, her mouth dry. 'Now it's my turn to excuse *my* manners, Dr Throme, but I don't believe that is any of your business.'

He pressed his lips together, creating a more forced smile as he swiftly scanned the room. 'You're clearly as direct as they say you are'

'I've never been one for small talk.'

He unbuttoned his suit jacket at the same time as dismissing his companions from the room. As they closed the door behind themselves, he eased back into the chair again, one elbow resting on the arm whilst he tapped his forefinger against his lips.

She struggled under the steadiness of his gaze, the silence oppressive.

Until he stood abruptly, thrust his hands into his trouser pockets and strolled around the room.

'I know it was hard for you,' he said, 'after your parents' death.'

'Is there anything you don't know about me?'

He glanced across at her. Sent her another fleeting, insincere smile. 'I'd say not. At least I thought not, until you threw me the Kane Malloy curveball. I never quite saw that coming. Just as I never quite saw you standing up in court to testify against your own. But then I know how persuasive Kane can be.'

'I did what I had to do.'

'Oh, of course you did,' he said, turning to face her. 'Absolutely.'

He stepped up to the threshold of her bedroom and peered inside, the intrusion escalating her indignation. He turned to face her again, with another faint smile. 'This is where Kane took you from, isn't it? Right out from your bed.' His eyes flashed. 'Under the cloak of midnight. What woman in her right mind *wouldn't* be swept away by such a debonair action?'

'Dr Throme, either you get to the point or you're going to have to start excusing my manners even more. See this apartment as equally yours or not; I'm going to kindly ask you to get the fuck out of it if you don't tell me why you're here.'

He smiled again. 'My, my, Kane *has* rubbed off on you. You're even starting to sound like him.'

'Somehow I don't think *he* would have tolerated your intrusion as much as I have.'

'Yes, he really is quite the law unto himself, isn't he?'

'Dr Throme…'

'I want him once and for all, Caitlin,' he said. 'And you're going to help me.'

Her pulse picked up a notch, her hands clenching in her lap as Sirius's steady gaze seeped coolly into her. Every part of her that felt a fierce sense of protectiveness towards Kane sparked. 'Don't you think it's time you left Kane alone?'

'That's just it, I can't. Especially now. Especially with what you've shown us.'

The coldness that had seeped inside her converted to an icy grip. 'What are you talking about?'

'I'm talking about what happened that night in the warehouse a couple of weeks ago,' he said, tucking his hands in his pockets as he strolled over to the window to gaze out into the dawn light. 'When Kane met with Xavier Carter. I'm talking about the footage I saw

– at least until the soul ripper got too close and the electromagnetic interference temporarily screwed up the recording. I'm talking about the fact that my soldiers, the ones the soul ripper dragged the souls out of, still remember a great deal of what happened that night.' He turned to face her again, now just a dark outline. 'Most of all, I'm talking about the fact you're still alive.'

Caitlin didn't move, didn't flinch, didn't utter a word despite her pounding heart thrumming in her ears.

'Vicious, aren't they?' he said. 'Those soul rippers. I use the plural as I'm assuming there *is* more than one still out there. Just as I've no doubt there are countless more of the time-shifting, dimension-hopping, intangible-when-they-want-to-be blighters we've come to call the fourth species.' He continued his stroll around the room. 'Arana Malloy certainly knew what she was doing setting one of those on your family. My hat is off to her at having acted so lucidly under pressure. Strapped to that post by your father, watched on by your now stepfather, let alone your charming ex boyfriend. Seeing those lycans scratching at their cage, itching to get to her.'

He fell silent for a moment as he stopped to gaze out the next window.

'But that appears to be a Malloy family trait – calmness under pressure,' he added. 'Getting even in the end. I really am brimming in admiration that Kane bided his time these past fourteen years, let alone the poetic justice of doing so to use the very creature his sister's killers' actions evoked, to get back at them.' He turned to face her again. 'Or should I say "us"?' His fleeting smile told her all she needed to know, all that she'd expected from his presence: that there was always another above pulling the strings. Or casting a blind eye. Both were the same in her opinion. 'Do you know why we really turned up the heat on finding Kane Malloy? Has he told you that yet?'

'Why don't *you* tell me?'

'Clearly not,' he said with a smirk – one that grated deep into her insecurities about Kane's lack of disclosure. 'I didn't think so.

And tell me, do you question why you're still alive? Have you asked him that little gem?'

'Why don't you get to the point, Dr Throme?'

'For decades we've dabbled in these blood experiments, tried every way we know to bind the Higher Order's blood with our own. Ploughed countless resources into the promise of a stronger, fitter, healthier, immune human race as a result. Yet more than seventy years later, still we cannot find the adhesive to make the binding permanent. Every time, the human body eventually rejects it like a bad transplant. An act of nature some would say, or an act of God – keeping that divide between them and us.'

'I am more than aware of the problems with the research, Dr Throme.'

'But do you know how fearful the Higher Order are that we'll go back on our deal with them and abandon them to Blackthorn with the rest of their kind? Which is why, some decades ago, they disclosed that a master vampire would know how the bloods could be bound. And, of course, we *all* knew who Kane was by then.'

Kane had said nothing. Nothing at all. And if that was the secret Xavier had been referring to, the secret Feinith had disclosed, it made no sense why he wouldn't have mentioned it. 'And you believe them. Which is why there has always been a no-kill order on him.'

He stepped back over to the sofa chair. 'Can I let you in on a little secret?' He drew his trousers up his thighs slightly before perching on the edge of the seat. 'That's not why *I* want him at all. You see, I think *much* bigger than just the Higher Order's blood. Because even if we did find the adhesive, what then? And there's always that risk that we *are* dabbling in the sacrilegious. We've all got to meet our maker one day. *If* you believe in that. Personally, I'm not sure I want to run the risk. No, I don't want to be like them, Caitlin, I want to be *more*. And then came Arana – the curse she inflicted on your family opening up a whole new possibility.'

The ache in her chest intensified under his gaze – a gaze that caused her to question the rationality behind those stony eyes.

'I've always been fascinated by this whole soul and shadow difference,' he continued, 'ever since our psychics first picked it up as a core difference between our species. Then, when they read your parents' dead bodies and claimed that their souls had been removed and held *alive* in some other dimension, I have to admit I was rather excited.'

Her stomach clenched, a little spark of anger igniting. But she held it inside, even if not from her tone. 'I'm glad one of us was.'

She needed to hear him out. She needed to hear everything he had to say. Everything that could explain the maniacal look in his eyes as he dared to utter such cruel words.

'Whether you believe in faith or science, an afterlife or a dispersal of energy, the existence of the fourth species, what happened to your family, proved that soul removal can be *controlled.* More importantly, as I sit here looking at you, after what Kane did, I see the evidence that you can have your soul removed and *survive* on this plain. It was the link I was looking for, and here you are.'

Flashbacks of the monster that had killed her family, that had come after her, wrenched her gut. 'You want to find a way to summon the fourth species?'

He laughed. 'No, no, I'm not insane, dear girl. But I do want to know how Kane did it. Because I want to make use not of the Higher Order's blood, but of what *we* have. Our bodies are weak, are our burdens, whereas our souls are our strength. A fact proven by the latter potentially outliving the former by centuries, even longer, *if* we can make it happen.'

'You want to remove souls?'

'I want to transfer them – just as Kane did for you. Imagine, the minute our bodies become weak or damaged, being able to transfer ourselves – every memory, every thought, every piece of knowledge – to a younger, fitter, healthier duplicate of ourselves.'

She frowned. 'Clones?'

He nodded. 'Clones. Clone after clone after clone until eventually we just fade into the ether – even avoiding the very concept of heaven and hell, should either exist. We have the science all worked out, Caitlin, but souls can't be generated in a lab like bodies can. Yet what happened to you at Kane's hands proved they *can* be transferred safely. Imagine being able to do that again and again and again. Imagine centuries of preserving the greatest minds of this globe.'

'And not least the Global Council itself,' she added, knowing exactly where he was going.

'That too.' He smiled again. 'You,' he added, leaning forward, his elbows on his casually splayed thighs, 'are our walking miracle, Caitlin Parish. Kane is the key to that miracle. Who would have thought that he would be the one to show us how to save the human race once and for all?'

She stared at Sirius, at first unable to speak as the implications trickled through her mind. Trickles that became increasingly coagulated with unthinkable possibilities. 'But this isn't about saving the human race, is it, Dr Throme? The very system you have in place already shows us exactly how you would go about this.'

He leaned back in the chair again. 'Obviously there would have to be some selection process,' he said, with an indifferent flip of his hand. 'This planet can only sustain so many human beings.'

She swallowed against her arid throat. 'And you want me to get Kane to help with this insane idea?'

'It's either that or I give up. My dreams, my aspirations, my hopes.'

'Then I suggest you do that, Dr Throme.'

He smiled. 'You say that with such conviction.' He leaned forwards again. 'Tell me, does the conviction remain if I tell you that if I *do* give up those dreams, the third species are no longer of use. In fact, there are many who are looking for any excuse to return this world to how it was before.'

The blood rushed from her head, a subtle disassociation taking over. 'Meaning?'

'Meaning a mass cull, Caitlin. Meaning I send in the biggest, most powerful armies to wipe every single one of them out. Like rats under a house, we'll cleanse Blackthorn and, of course, Lowtown, just to be sure. And every other locale across this globe will do exactly the same thing.'

She could barely breathe. He wasn't just talking of war; he was talking of a Global Council-incited apocalypse. 'You can't do that!'

'The chosen one, Caitlin. I only have to spread word that the prophesied chosen one has arisen and I will have every ounce of support I need from the residents of Summerton and Midtown and all their equivalents. I'll make them believe what I *want* them to believe.'

'And those humans caught in the crossfire – what are they? Collateral damage?'

'A side effect of every war, Caitlin. I guess how many we lose is down to Kane and how long it takes him to mull things over. Because either he surrenders himself to avoid all this or I will turn every resident of Blackthorn and Lowtown against him until he does. One flick of a switch and I can cut off their water supplies, their electricity supplies, their food supplies. I can have the whole place on lockdown *and* I'll tell them why. We'll see how loyal they are to him then. Especially the cons.' He sucked air through his teeth before tutting. 'No, those cons aren't going to like it at all.'

Despite the amber dawn glow, the room became unnervingly dark. 'You're insane.'

His gaze didn't flinch. 'You'd better fucking believe it, little girl. If you think I'm bluffing, you keep a close eye on those lycans. They'll let Kane know I do *anything* but bluff.'

Her chest clenched. 'What have the lycans got to do with this?'

'Jask Tao's not too happy about Kane letting you off the hook, is he? I saw the footage outside the courtroom that day. And as I can't have any threat to Kane or you now either, I thought the lycans would be as perfect a place to start as any. It'll add a little time pressure. After all, I can't have Kane mulling for too long. Besides, those hounds had it coming. They should have got on the right side when they could have.'

'What the hell have you done?'

'Be a good messenger. Go to Kane. Persuade him to hand himself in, because if you fail, or if you utter one word of this to anyone, you will personally be responsible for the mass slaughter of thousands of third species, let alone humans, that you so reverently claim to protect. You tell Kane it's D-Day for him and his kind. You tell him it starts tonight and the clock is already ticking. I want him, Caitlin – and this is one mission you're *not* going to want to fail.'

Chapter Thirty-One

They made their way along the street, the puddles mirrors to the flashing neon lights that shone from shop frontages and bars.

Jask looked far from amused, his grip on her hand echoing his mood.

'Where are we going?'

'Somewhere we can talk properly,' he said. 'In private.'

He turned down a dark, dank, graffiti-emblazoned side alley. Ahead, a single fly-riddled light nestled above a door marking the stone steps that led up to it.

They ascended the steps into a tight vestibule before emerging into a lobby.

The low-wattage lighting, the threadbare rug, the worn armchairs in front of the windows that stared out onto the grimy alley, let alone the female groans that emanated from the sofa facing the wall to her left, told her exactly what kind of establishment it was.

Even more disturbing was the swollen-faced middle-aged male who sat in the armchair facing the sofa, his eyes snapping from whatever he was watching to look directly at her.

Her skin crawled, despite the connection being brief, and she stepped forward to be as close to Jask as she could.

The male receptionist stood behind a glass window – a reasonable precaution, she decided. Few words were spoken between him and Jask. The receptionist slipped the key off the hook and slid it through the gap beneath the glass without any exchange of payment, just a quick glance in Sophia's direction, his wrinkled eyes narrowed behind his thin-rimmed glasses.

'And a bottle of your good stuff,' Jask added.

The guy reached under the counter and unlocked and slid open the glass panel between them to hand Jask a label-less bottle.

Taking the bottle by the neck, Jask led Sophia to the stairs immediately to their left, Sophia grateful for their exit as the groans from the sofa became louder.

'You know this place?' she asked as they turned the hairpin corner to face more narrow stairs.

'I've done some business here.'

She kept her hands away from the peeling wallpaper, off the handrail, despite the steep incline. 'When you say business…?'

'Things that needed sorting.'

She knew it was the best she was going to get.

They stepped into another hallway, passed three doors on the left before he led her up another set of stairs. The place smelt of mould, of damp, of decades of cigarette smoke and moral decay to the point it seemed to be the only thing holding the place together.

Reaching the top of the stairs, Jask led her to the end of the dim hallway. The only hint of air came from the breeze leaking through the cracked window ahead – and she knew it came to something when even Blackthorn air smelt fresh in comparison.

He unlocked the door to the left and indicated for her to enter first.

She stepped inside the dark room, lit only by the neon lights flashing through the window in the far top left-hand corner. Lights that encompassed the bed jammed into the corner and against the wall beneath it.

If the wattage of the single shadeless bulb above bared any relation to the power of the rest in the building, it was pointless putting it on, which is why she guessed Jask didn't bother.

At the foot of the bed, to her left, was an open door into a tiny bathroom. A small kitchenette was tucked in the corner to her right. Further along the wall and nestled in the narrow gap between the wall and bed was a small wooden table with two mismatched wooden chairs either side.

As Jask closed and locked the door behind them, Sophia headed over to the bed. Kneeling on the pillows, she slid the sash window up to let in some much-needed air.

The thin, worn curtains fluttered in the breeze as she pushed them as far back as she could before sitting side-on to the window, her forearms partially on the headboard, partially on the sill.

Groups passed on the street below, piling in and out of the bars along the stretch. The lit windows in the buildings opposite displayed what could only be described as peep shows – whether unintentionally or intentionally. She had the feeling it was the latter.

She unstrapped and kicked off her heels and nestled in the corner of the bed, her back against the wall. 'I guess you don't find this place in the travel guide.'

'Not exactly.' He placed the bottle and a glass he'd retrieved from the kitchenette on the single bedside table. He quarter filled the tumbler. 'But it's useful if you need to be left alone.' He handed the drink across to her.

'What is it?' she asked, accepting it.

'It's drinkable,' he said. 'And good for shock.'

'I'm not in shock.'

The look in his eyes told her he begged to differ. He pulled the chair out from the table and sat down, resting his feet on the edge of the bed not far from hers.

At least it was a drink in her hand, so she wasn't going to argue. One way or another, she needed it. She knocked it back in one before wincing, the liquid burning all the way down to the pit of her stomach.

'Wow,' she said, momentarily widening her eyes. 'That *is* good stuff.' She leaned forward to hand the empty glass back to him. 'Fill her up, barman.'

Jask filled it another quarter. 'Sip it slowly,' he said. 'I want you in your right mind.'

'Sorry,' she said, 'but that opportunity passed by years ago.' But this time she did take a steadier mouthful, the vapours already leaking into her senses. 'Are you not joining me?'

He shook his head before leaning back in the chair, his elbow on the table, his jaw on his knuckle. 'Tell me what's *really* going on, Phia.'

She took another mouthful before drawing her knees to her chest. She brushed her hair back from her forehead and glanced back out of the window before looking back at Jask to see his attention was well and truly fixed solely on her.

'I was picked up by Marid on the way over to the Dehains' club,' she said. 'I was going there to get my sister, Alisha.'

'What makes you think she's with Caleb?'

'I saw evidence. Photos.'

'Go on.'

'We thought we'd killed him: Jake. We sent two honeytraps into the club that night – one for him, one for Caleb. Only Caleb didn't take the bait. But Jake did. And I *know* he did. We had Trudy all rigged up with the equipment we'd been given. We're talking proper, high-tech stuff – scalp patches, tiny inbuilt receivers monitoring her heart rate, her respiration, her temperature. We watched her die. From a van outside, we watched Jake drink her last drop – something no vampire survives, as you know. But he *did* survive. The boss woke me in the early hours of the following morning. She came with photo evidence of Jake alive and well and partying it up in his club. And there, in the evidence, was my sister partying with him.' She knocked back another mouthful.

'When you say *partying*, clearly not against her will?'

'Clearly.'

'So what's the issue?'

'The issue is he should have been dead. But he goes and recovers.'

'Vampires don't recover from dying blood.'

'Not unless you have a powerful witch at your disposal.'

Jask frowned. 'Your sister's a witch too?'

'Not Alisha, no.' She sucked her bottom lip into her mouth as she glanced back out of the window. 'As far as I know, she's a regular human.' She needed to tell him. To get his help, she had to. She looked back at him. 'Our older sister, Leila, on the other hand, appears to have been harbouring a secret for a long time. The serryn line jumps down the age group, Jask, not up.'

'You're telling me Leila's serrynity jumped to you? How?'

She shrugged. 'There's only two ways – falling in love with a vampire and consummating that love, or suicide. Neither are probable as far as Leila's concerned. But it seems I'm walking evidence to the contrary.'

'Go on.'

'Which is what got me thinking – what could have saved Jake? What could have cured that bad blood? What kind of witch is powerful enough to break all the lores of nature?'

'A serryn.'

'And not just a serryn, but a gifted interpreter underneath it all – an art that's as academic as it is skilled. My sister knew her stuff – spells, concoctions, medicines. Even if she didn't practise, she sure studied enough to pull it out of the bag if she needed to.'

'So you think Leila came to Blackthorn. That she saved Jake's life. But serryns don't save vampires; they kill them.'

'You think I don't know that? But don't you also think it's too coincidental that I see pictures of Alisha in that very club, her arms wrapped around Jake, whilst I fail to contact her, whilst I fail to contact Leila?'

'You tried?'

'The night after Jake was saved – before Marid took me. I called at half four in the morning. Trust me, Leila would have been there and she would have answered. Somehow Alisha got Leila into Blackthorn. Somehow she persuaded her to save Jake. Or they were forced into doing it. Either way, I think Caleb's not just after me because I work for The Alliance – I think there's a chance he knows I'm a serryn too.'

'But if you're right, Alisha would have been signing your sister's death warrant knowing what she is.'

'I didn't know. I had no idea. Why would she? My guess is Leila's kept it secret from us both. But we both knew she was an interpreter – and something made Alisha spill that to the Dehains.'

'You're seriously telling me you didn't have a clue about any of this?'

She shook her head.

'How is that possible? Was she never active?'

'Not that I know of. She never left Summerton except to go to Midtown. I don't know whether she was avoiding temptation or was just scared.'

There was something in his eyes she couldn't read. Something in his frown. 'That must have taken quite some willpower.'

She exhaled tersely. 'You don't know my sister.'

'Still, with what happened to your mother. It obviously evoked you into a vengeance tirade. Why not her?'

'We deal with things differently.'

'Like how you blame yourself, even though you were nothing more than a kid at the time.'

Sophia watched the rain sweeping horizontally past the window, the streets outside suddenly falling quiet except for the force of the storm. 'I wouldn't toe the line enough for Summerton school standards. Even as a six-year-old I was stroppy. They wanted my behaviour to improve and I couldn't handle being told what to do. When they said they wanted me removed, that I'd have to be schooled in Midtown, my mother decided she wasn't going to have that division between her daughters. So she made sure me and Leila went to the same school. Nine months later, she was coming home from Leila's school performance when she was attacked.'

'So you hold yourself responsible.'

She looked back at him, back into those calming eyes that watched her pensively. 'She would never have been there if it wasn't for me.'

'She wouldn't have been dead if it hadn't been for the vampire that preyed on her.'

'And it shouldn't have had the opportunity in the first place.'

'That's quite the burden to carry, Phia.'

'Deservedly so,' she said, picking at something imaginary on her dress. She looked down at the covers at her feet as she dug her toes in deep. She knocked back another mouthful, finishing the contents. 'That's it,' she said. 'Now you know everything.'

When met only with his silence, his eyes downturned on the table, she reached forward for the bottle.

'You've had enough,' he said. His glance in her direction told her he meant it.

She had a feeling he was right. She placed her glass upside down beside the bottle and withdrew into the corner again, knees to her chest. A gang whistled and yelled outside. A strong breeze billowed through her hair.

'Your turn,' she said. 'What really happened to your mate, Jask? Because I don't believe you murdered her. You might have killed her, but I think it was an accident and for some reason you hold yourself responsible.'

The lights flashed on his skin, illuminating him in pink, red and amber before following the sequence again as his gaze remained unflinching. 'You say that with such conviction.'

'Because it's what I believe.'

'You don't know me.'

'I know honourable people don't murder their mates. Was it like tonight, when you nearly lost it with me?'

'What makes you think I'm honourable, Phia?'

'I've been amongst your pack – I see the way they look at you, the way they talk about you, how they respond to you and re-spect you. And because I've seen you keep making the honourable choice when you've every reason not to. Out on the wasteland, in the bathroom that first time, when I was goading you and Corbin, down in the cellars, in the alley earlier, let alone what happened less than half an hour ago. I know how badly they could have ended for me.'

He held her gaze, but only for a few seconds, before he rested his head back against the wall. 'Well it wasn't an accident, Phia – I *did* kill her, knowingly and willingly.'

❋ ❋ ❋

Of all the times he wanted her to keep talking, she didn't.

Phia stared at him, waiting for him to elaborate, only the rain overflowing from the gutters breaking the silence.

He hadn't spoken of it in as long as he could remember. He wasn't sure why he was contemplating it. Why he should be considering sharing anything so intimate, so deeply personal – and with Phia of all people.

But from the troubled look in her eyes, the pensive furrow of her forehead, her unflinching gaze, it wasn't a question motivated by power, one-upmanship or malice – she was interested in *him*.

And in the isolation of that room, of having seen her laid bare out in the alley, he wanted to do the same for her as much as for himself. He wanted her to not feel alone in her self-directed anger. He wanted her to know he understood.

More selfishly, he wanted her to delve into the deepest, darkest part of him just to see if that look in her eyes would still be the same when she came out the other side. Because, from the way she was looking at him then, her emotions for him were as mixed up as his for her.

But it was a risk telling her. She'd want the complete story and would learn that he was anything but the honourable leader she would be willing to help. The truth could cause a division between them at the crucial point – just when he was detecting he was starting to get her on side.

But she still needed him for her own cause – that much wouldn't change.

'How?' she eventually asked.

'By loving her too much. More than I ever should have.' He reached for the bottle. He upturned the tumbler and half filled it, before leaning back in his chair. 'You blame yourself for what happened to your mother and you were nothing more than a kid. A kid who had no idea of the implications. It was impossible for you to know. Only *I* knew exactly what I was doing.' He knocked back a mouthful, the liquid burning his throat as much as the pending confession. 'We met after the regulations. I tried not to fall for her, but I did.'

And he'd fallen deeply. Painfully deeply. Deep enough to have only ever fallen once, and never again.

Or so he thought.

Because telling Phia as such didn't feel right. Because what he'd come to realise was that the pain of a lost love he'd once thought unsurpassable had inexplicably finally started to ease in just the short time Phia had been with him.

The serryn who was everything Ellen wasn't and vice versa.

Except they both had one thing in common – in their own way they'd both sparked something in him. And it was a spark he could no longer deny.

'What was she like?' Phia asked, her gaze unflinching.

'Beautiful. Smart. Kind. Compassionate. Wise. And she was good for my temperament.'

'You said you didn't want to fall for her. Why?'

'I have a condition. A part of my lineage. I suppose those of a more superstitious nature would call it a curse. I'm very much in belief of the latter.' He finished the remains of his drink, but kept hold of the glass as he rested his head back against the wall. 'I can't have a family. Which I told her. Though, at the time, Ellen didn't care about that. She loved me regardless. Said being with me was enough. In time, though, it wasn't. She wanted young. Desperately. And one night, I lost myself. I got her pregnant.'

She frowned. 'But you said you *can't* have a family.'

'I didn't mean physically – I meant morally.'

She dropped her legs into a cross-legged position so she could lean forward. Never had she looked more attentive, more focused. Instead of being repelled, his confession only seemed to be drawing her closer. 'Why?'

'The rule of three. That's the curse. I was destined to have twins.'

'Why is that a curse?'

He looked into his glass before looking back at her. 'That's not the curse; the fact that only one can survive is – either the mother or one of the young. But never more than one. And never all three.'

Phia was sat upright now, her body tense, her lips slightly parted in shock. But still she didn't look away. 'And Ellen knew this. Ellen knew the risk but she still wanted to try?'

'Yes.'

'It was guaranteed to happen?'

'Not guaranteed. But a high enough risk that she shouldn't have even contemplated it.'

'She didn't survive,' Phia said.

'She died during the birth. She lost too much blood. I've never seen so much. The pain she was in…' He took a deep, unsteady breath, fighting back the tears as he lowered his gaze, remembering how helpless he felt just stood there, watching, her grip on his hand so tight, her glazed eyes staring up into his during those last moments.

'And you blame yourself,' Phia said quietly. 'That's why you said you killed her.'

'I did kill her. If I had been strong enough to say no that night, she'd still be alive,' he said, his throat tight. 'Maybe with someone else. Maybe with a family. If I loved her, truly loved her, I would never have got involved with her in the first place.'

'If only the choice of whom you fall for were that easy. None of us choose who we love, Jask. If it were about reason and logic and choice, it would be science, not emotion. It would stop being magic.'

He held her gaze, stunned for a moment not only by the sensitivity behind the words, but the tenderness in her eyes as she uttered them. Thoughts that were beautifully naïve, beautifully innocent. Thoughts that were cracks of light beneath the rubble of her grief, fury and fear.

'But we *do* choose what we do about how we feel,' he said. 'She's dead because of me. If I'd had more control, if I hadn't been so selfish as to fear losing her to someone else, if I'd said no, if I had been stronger, if I'd loved her enough to let her go, she'd still be here.'

He stared deep into eyes that no longer brimmed with the anger and confusion and resentment he'd come to know, but with compassion. Compassion and empathy he didn't deserve.

'You think I'm honourable?' he asked. 'I was so scared of losing her, so selfish, that the minute I found out she was pregnant I told her to get rid of them.' And he'd never forget it – how easily the words had slipped from his lips. How, in his fear of losing her, he'd become someone he didn't recognise. 'But that was the difference between us – because she said no. She'd accepted her decision and her fate. She even wished that one of them would survive *instead* of her. And that made me so angry. For a short while I hated her for putting our unborn young first like that. For choosing them over me. For not fighting any way she could to stay with me. For leaving me so helpless that all I could do for the months that followed was to stand by and count down the days whilst hoping my wish would come true.'

He glanced back down into his empty glass as he blinked the tears away.

Phia didn't move. She didn't speak. But she'd turned her head away from him slightly, despite her gaze not flinching, her frown deep, those brown eyes penetrative. Eyes that he now felt ashamed to look back into.

'Did either of the twins survive?' she eventually asked.

'Yes. And every time I looked at him, all I could see was her. And I couldn't handle it. Couldn't handle knowing she had died so he could live. My beautiful, strong, amazing mate, whom I loved with every breath I took, was replaced by a weak, demanding, selfish little stranger who cared nothing for what he had caused. So I shunned him. That's how I held up her memory – by ignoring all I had left of her.'

'If our actions in grief define us, Jask, we're all fucked. No one reacts rationally to loss. You couldn't help being angry.'

'My son's still alive. Her only legacy. But all these years later, I still treat him like he's dead to me. I ignore him, or I make him work harder than anyone else. He looks for my approval every day and all I do is stare back at him with disdain. Is that what he deserves?'

Feeling too much shame to hold her gaze any longer, he looked back out of the window, the curtains now whipped by the breeze.

'But you feel guilt because you *do* care about him,' she said.

'And I've got a great way of showing it.'

'You said he seeks your approval every day. Is he here? In Blackthorn?'

He nodded.

'Then it's not too late to tell him. It's never too late.'

❋ ❋ ❋

She could never have anticipated seeing so much pain behind a third-species' eyes. The pain of self-loathing, of guilt, of a burden too heavy to bear. And she didn't know what to do to lighten it. Had no way of lightening it but to give a piece of herself in return, to somehow show she understood.

'From the morning my grandfather sat us all down and told us our mother was dead, I shunned all that was left of my family,' she explained. 'I wouldn't even let them comfort me. Instead I ran up to the bathroom, locked the door, wrapped myself in a towel and hid beneath it in the bathtub. I lay there all day and all night, ignoring their pleas, their distress. Not once did I offer to comfort either of my sisters or my grandfather in return, thinking only of my fear, my pain, my loneliness.

'And whilst Leila had kept going, kept working to get the grades, to get a good job to keep us in Summerton, to make up for the social and academic pointage where I was lacking, I responded with tormenting her with years of anger I couldn't deal with.

'You asked me why Leila wasn't filled with the same vengeance as me? I think losing our mother gave her the strongest survival instinct of us all. She knew that surviving isn't always about fighting back. Being the heroine isn't always about kicking arse just because you can. Only I mocked her for doing the contrary. Whilst she was holding it all together, I ran around with a torch on my head and a stake in my hand, threatening to force-feed our little sister garlic. And look at me now – no different. Because how did I repay Leila? I came here – to the pit of her worst fears and left her behind to suffer and feel that loss all over again. So if you're asking me to sit here in judgement of you, you're asking the wrong person, Jask. Only when I see her again, I'm going to make it up to her. And you can do the same with your son. Because it's not our mistakes that define us, but what we do about them.'

He rested his head back against the wall, frowning contemplatively at her confession.

Even she was taken aback by how easily it had come out – insight she'd never shared with anyone. She wiped away her tears with the heel of her hand and stared back down at the duvet.

She knew it was wrong – her empathy with this third-species leader. And she couldn't cope with what was stirring inside of her now she'd finally seen inside of him. She couldn't afford to care – not for him, not for Jask. Not for the third-species leader who, despite his hostile front, looked at her like he completely understood everything that had spilled from inside her.

Because, despite what he'd said, he *was* honourable – honourable and good and decent and everything she wasn't and everything she would never be.

Just as she would never replace Ellen. Just as she could never give him what he wanted, what he needed, what he was owed. Because having seen him on the lawn with Solstice and Tuly, she knew that he deserved another chance at happiness. That maybe one day fate would be kind and grant him a family of his own. Surely not even fate was so cruel as to strike him twice.

But she'd never be the one to give it to him. She was tarnished now. Ironically, the serrynity she'd craved for so long now weighed heavily on her in its cruelty because, as she looked at Jask, she would have given anything to have been the one.

But instead of fantasising, she needed to focus on what really mattered – what was left of her own family. The family she needed to get to before she lost any more time. Jask would move on when they were done. He'd go back to his pack. And she'd go back to nothing. Not unless she did something about it.

'Jask, please just tell me why you want me. What purpose do I serve? Then we can both go back to what we should be doing.'

Her chest ached as he held her gaze. And as he glanced out of the window, retaining his silence, before looking back at her with equal reticence.

But it wasn't anger she felt – it was hurt. His lack of trust tore through her more deeply than she could handle, not least after he'd shared such an intimate confession, let alone after she had.

She'd dared to think for a moment that they had connected. Now she felt a fool.

But no more so than when panic struck her.

Up close and personal just wasn't Jask's style. Because it *had* been a confession. A confession that she had the gut-wrenching feeling he'd uttered only because he'd known it would remain safe.

That's why he wouldn't tell her why he needed her. She'd already proved herself useless. Worse, his involvement with her was a risk now that Caleb was involved. More than that, he'd known she'd intended to kill him.

He'd brought her to that dive, that reclusive room, for one reason only.

The betrayal lacerated her heart and squeezed her lungs.

Something inside her snapped.

'Fine,' she said, as she slid to the edge of the bed. 'Keep your secret, but I don't have time for this.' She pulled on her heels, fumbling with the straps with trembling hands, before standing.

Jask stood up at the same time, blocking her only exit. 'Where do you think you're going?'

Her instinct was to push him away, but she didn't – and not just because she didn't have the energy for a futile battle on her part, but because even in her anger, she couldn't strike him. Not now she'd seen him for what he was.

Instead she allowed herself a moment to read the situation. A moment to read the concern in his eyes, the lack of aggression in his stance.

But then the most proficient predators always were the composed ones. And she had the feeling she was desperately searching for signs that weren't there.

'Where do you think?' she said. 'My sisters are here in Blackthorn because of me. Just as whatever has happened to The Alliance is because of me. This is *all* down to me. And I need to get to them and find out what's going on. Because if something *has* happened to them, then Caleb's at the core of it. And I'm going to sort this out.'

'Have you any idea what you're contemplating?'

'I don't care,' she said. 'They're my sisters, Jask. They're all I have. If I lose them, what's the point in any of this?'

She tried to slip past him, but he grabbed her arm.

'You seem to be forgetting something,' he said. 'Before you go on your suicide mission, we had a deal.'

She dared to look him in the eyes. 'Like you said, all our leads are gone. And I don't have time to find another. For the first time in my life, I need to put my sisters first. I'll find whoever is responsible for The Alliance *after* I've saved them.'

'And where do I fit into this plan?'

'You're going to let me go.'

'And I'd do that because…?'

Finally her patience waned, the knot in her chest too tight. 'Then end this, Jask. Don't toy with me.' She nearly choked on the tears already constricting her throat. 'Clearly you don't think I'm capable of doing whatever it is you want me to do. Clearly I'm not meeting your expectations. Clearly I'm not the serryn you'd hoped for. So either we call it quits and solve our own problems, or you finish this.'

Chapter Thirty-Two

It was the first time he'd seen it.

Plenty of times she'd glared him down, enticed him to hurt her, not cared what happened to herself in the process. It's what made her so lethal to his self-control – that she wanted the lycan in him to out.

But whatever had happened in the past twenty-four hours, Phia had gone from reckless, impulsive and suicidal to *wanting* to survive.

Because now, as she glared back at him, he could see she *did* care what happened. She was frightened. More than that; she was hurt. He could see it in her eyes: she felt betrayed by him. And that meant she'd learned to trust him.

And because of that, as her eyes flared, glossy and expectant, he wanted to make her a promise that he was the last one who would ever let her down. But he couldn't. She needed so much – so much containing, so much care, compassion and protection. Not least now he knew Caleb was coming for her. And he had to question if he could do it – if they survived long enough, whether he could do it night after night. If he could manage her and still be there for his pack.

Or whether he should let her go. Make her do what he wanted and then let her walk away to solve her own problems like she'd suggested.

Until she walked into Caleb Dehain. Or Kane Malloy. Or an unruly gang of vampires. Or a group of cons. Ones who wouldn't see what he saw. Ones who didn't care what was beneath the surface.

Ones who would only see the attitude, the challenge, the bolshie female looking for trouble. Not one who, deep down, was desperately trying to escape her pain in the only way she knew how.

They wouldn't see his Phia the way he saw her. *His* Phia.

'You don't believe that,' he said. 'You don't *really* believe I'll hurt you. Because not only do you believe I'm honourable – you trust me. Or you did. That's why you're angry now – because you don't think I trust you in return. And you want me to. You need me to. Because if I trust you, you've finally got your self-worth back, right? And you need your self-worth back so you have the strength to go and get your sisters. To find a way out of all of this.'

She tried to yank her arm from his grip, but his hold was unrelenting.

'You can keep pushing me away all you want, Phia, but we both know what's going on here.'

'And what's that, Jask?' she asked, her lips already quivering.

'You've fallen for me as much as I've fallen for you.'

Just seeing the flare in her eyes filled him with a warmth he hadn't felt in as long as he could remember.

A feeling that equally filled him with terror because she didn't deny it.

Instead she exhaled tersely. 'Fallen? It's been less than two days.'

'How long does it usually take?'

'A lot more than two days.'

'I knew the minute I saw you, Phia. The minute I looked into your eyes down in those ruins. And I have *never* felt a connection like I did then. And I hated you for it. Hated you for making me feel that way when I didn't even know you. But now I do know you, I know it was right to feel that way. My instincts knew what my heart and head weren't ready to accept. Trust me, denial is the preferred option for me, too, but I want you to know how I feel.'

She frowned. 'Let's not do this, Jask.'

But he finally had her – her defences almost down, the real Phia almost fully laid bare. And he wasn't letting her go easily.

'No, Phia. *Let's* do this. Here and now.'

'Why? What's the point?'

'And what's the point of keeping some kind of barrier up between us?'

'Because it makes it easier.'

'It makes it easier for you, you mean.'

'Yes, it makes it easier for me. I prefer it that way. So let me go.'

❋ ❋ ❋

She could barely breathe, the intensity in his eyes, the sincerity of his words throwing her off guard more than she could handle.

'It wasn't easy saying no to you in that alley,' he said. 'Don't think for a minute it was. I wanted you then like I want you now. Just like I wanted you only an hour ago.'

Her heart skipped a beat, a cool perspiration breaking out in her clenched palms.

'And despite what you think, it's nothing to do with you being a serryn. I know you think I'm too good for you. I see it in your eyes. Well I'm not good, Phia. Not underneath it all. I have to fight all the time to make the right choices. Just like now – trying so hard to make this about my pack and not about you, not about us. Because you have no idea what I did in the years following Ellen's death. I was on a downward spiral and dragged my pack with me as I immersed myself in my own contempt, caring for nothing but inflicting whatever pain I could on myself. They were hard times for them, something I cared nothing for at the time. And yet they still stand loyally by my side. For them I should be walking out of this room right now. But I can't. Which is why I can't let you leave either. Not until I've broken the last of those barriers of yours. And I will break them, Phia. Not for what I have to do, but for us.'

Her heart pounded painfully.

'Because you're going to acknowledge the way you feel too,' he said. 'You're going to make yourself vulnerable to me. And you're going to face it. Just as I am.'

She could no longer see anything but him. Hear nothing but the pounding rain. Feel nothing but the cool night breeze.

She instinctively tried to yank herself away again, but his grip tightened, his gaze still locked on hers.

'Has no one ever warned you about cornering a serryn?' she asked breathlessly.

'Has no one ever warned you about being cornered by a lycan? One on one, we both know who'll win.'

Everything that exuded from his eyes, his tone, his touch told her to stop fighting back. And she didn't want to fight anymore. If he thought he could break her, she needed to see him try.

She lifted her lips to his, needing, wanting to face the consequence should he succeed. 'Then prove it.'

❄ ❄ ❄

Her final submission unleashed every primal instinct he'd had to contain and suppress. Instincts he now knew he didn't need to fight anymore. Not now he had finally proven to himself just how close he could get to the edge and that he could pull back – something he could only do with her.

Could do because he loved her.

He'd grown since all those decades before. He'd become stronger and not even he had known it. Had not dared to test it to know.

But now he had.

He didn't have to fear himself with her. He was too conscious of her. More aware of her than he was of himself – her scent filling his senses, her warm body trembling against his. And now he understood her, now he knew he finally had her trust, he was aware of her even more.

He no longer needed to fear himself. She'd liberated him. And now he'd liberate her.

They *both* needed to finish what they'd started.

He heard the hitch in her breath as he spun her around, as he lifted her onto the bed with ease. He pinned her onto all fours, slamming both her hands together on the windowsill, contained them in one of his as he pushed his thighs between hers.

She didn't move, didn't struggle, didn't utter a word as he ran his free hand up her spine to her neck. Brushing her hair aside to reveal the clasp of her dress, he unfastened it with one deft flick of his thumb and forefinger.

She shuddered as he kissed the base of her neck, her grip on the windowsill tightening.

'What? No struggle this time?' he whispered against her ear.

'If you want to exhaust yourself, go ahead,' she said, echoing his words from the wasteland.

He smiled, nipped her lightly on the earlobe before sliding his hand all the way down her bare spine, down over the curve of her behind before taking the hem of her dress back up with the motion to expose the lace shorts he had chosen for her. They suited her curves perfectly, just as he'd imagined they would.

He rubbed his thumb under high arch of lace that exacerbated the fullness of her behind – a feminine roundness enhanced by the contrasting slenderness of her small waist. A femininity he couldn't help but revel in. Because she *was* painfully feminine. Painfully beautiful.

A femininity he needed to feel as he tucked his thumb into the crotch of her shorts to stroke her sex.

She gasped. A gasp that sent him reeling. Her pulse picked up a notch, indicating the adrenaline rush she thrived on. The same adrenaline rush he'd sensed down in the containment room – not one of fear, but one of arousal.

He nudged her thighs further apart, the feel of her warm bare legs through his jeans only escalating his arousal to the point of pain, and no more so as she continued to surrender.

Finding her clit, he applied just enough pressure to make her flinch.

She moaned almost silently, lowered her head onto the windowsill. But still she didn't resist him, his arousal surging as she pressed back against him slightly, as if urging him inside of her.

She was giving herself to him again. Locked away there in their cocoon, just like when he'd taken her on the cell floor – when he'd first seen the real her – the fight in her was subdued, her defences were down. She was accepting what she wanted. *Really* wanted.

Him.

And giving herself to him was all he needed. He *would* protect her – somehow. He had to.

But that moment was about more than just that. She may have started to feel safe enough with him to allow him to get that close, but under it she thrived on the potential danger as much as he did. It was a part of her very nature. She liked him being in control, she liked him drawing the line. Because that's *how* she felt safe: when he set the boundaries. Her retaliation all along, ever since meeting him, had been about getting that as much as anything else. She needed to be contained. She needed to be held. Because she might have trusted him, but she didn't trust herself.

Keeping the pressure on her clit, he slipped his middle finger inside her, watched as she dug her fingers into the windowsill in response, aroused further by her lack of resistance.

He let go of her hands to unfasten his jeans, relishing in his freed straining erection as he locked into the hypnotism of her quiet groans.

He unhooked her strapless bra before clutching the windowsill again, his hand inches from hers. Lowering his lips to her bare spine, he licked, kissed and nipped along her bare vertebrae as he pushed his finger deeper inside her.

As his mouth met the very base of her spine, she shuddered, instinctively arched her back, lifting her behind in a way that was far too provocative for him to ignore.

He pulled himself upright, gently withdrew his finger, his hand. He closed his eyes, bit into his bottom lip to prevent him tearing off her underwear there and then.

Because her sudden stillness told him that was exactly what she was anticipating. He could hear her heart rate escalate, her breath held between its shallowness. She was expecting him to take her quickly.

Instead he clutched her neck again, keeping her in position as he gently eased her shorts down to her knees. As he slid his fingers back down over her now wet sex, she let out a groan, lifted her head a fraction only to slam it back down onto her arms. And as he pushed two of his fingers back inside her, she took the deepest inhale he'd ever heard.

He leaned back slightly, revelling in watching her tremble, his own arousal peaking as he watched his fingers disappear inside the moist, sensual folds of her sex.

She cursed indefinably under her breath, her head still buried in her forearms as he pushed as deep as he could go.

His erection twitched and throbbed at her tightness, her involuntary moans, the sensual whimper that accompanied them diminishing his resilience. She was lost in him, taken to his world, where he was all she could think about.

The power of it surged through him. Only empowered him more.

'Good girl,' he said, as he leaned over her. He nipped her tenderly on her ear again. 'Tame now, aren't you?'

He knew it would evoke a reaction, albeit laced with a playful retaliation as she pushed against him. But they both knew the game they were playing – the unspoken rules as if they had been lovers for years.

He grabbed both her hands again, slamming them back onto the windowsill, trapping them there as he yanked her shorts off the rest of the way.

He pressed the tip of his erection just an inch inside her before coiling his fingers in the hair at the nape of her neck.

She held her breath, her nails scraping into the windowsill, her whole body tensing. She knew he wasn't going to hold back. She'd already worked out that the position he had put her in would allow him deep and unbridled penetration.

She had summoned his lycan instincts yet again, only this time she'd finally get what she asked for.

❋ ❋ ❋

Jask did what only Jask could do – perceptive enough to read her and reckless enough to act on the signals.

Sophia clutched onto the windowsill, her head lowered.

Just as she'd expected, his thrust was unbridled, deep, intense.

This time her groan was almost pained as he tightened the grip on her hair, his other hand clenching her wrists as he pushed himself even deeper, unrelentingly, until he filled her to the hilt.

The discomfort was just enough to sate her – to convince her of his honesty, as, instead of picking up pace, he slowed down, thrust deeper, more lingeringly, making her feel every inch.

She knew he'd be watching. She knew he liked to watch. She'd seen that for herself down in the cell. And it only enthralled her more – his sexual confidence a painful aphrodisiac.

As he lowered his chest onto her back, his hand spanning the back of her thigh so she couldn't move, her cries echoed out onto the empty street below, ripples of pleasure moving from the back of her neck where he held her, down her spine, to pool where they were joined. Her limbs tingled and became numb until she felt nothing but him buried inside her.

'Does this feel good?' he whispered against her ear. 'Do you like the feel of me inside you? Is it liberating, Phia, having someone else take control. *Dare* to take control?'

And as he picked up pace, as he freed her neck to grab her hip, she could feel herself slipping away.

She was giving herself to him willingly and unrepentantly. It didn't feel like her – not the her she had come to know. Instead, it felt like a part of herself that she had once known had now returned – the liberated part of her that had been free and unrestrained and untroubled, back when life seemed simple and there was nothing to worry about.

Because the very submissive position she had allowed him to get her into, her helplessness beneath his control, should have had her worried, should have had her panicked.

No less than as he tugged her back against him, forcing her onto his lap, her thighs spread wide either side of his as he continued to thrust into her.

But not even as he clasped her breast with one hand, wrapped the other possessively around her throat to keep her back against his shoulder, as he raked her neck with his canines, did she feel a moment of fear.

She should have been troubled at the lack of connection both positions could have evoked – a position void of eye contact and an inability to read each other's expressions. But it felt even more intimate – a physical and emotional understanding where all the normal cues weren't required; where he was listening to and watching for cues another way – a lycan's way – whilst she relaxed into his consuming of her.

And consume her he did. Because never had she felt so much during sex. Not just physically. Far more than just physically.

So when he withdrew only to flip her onto her back, the resumed eye contact with him as he pushed back inside her only made the act even more powerful.

She couldn't look anywhere but at him. The neon lights bounced on his skin, glimmering in his eyes, igniting them one moment and darkening them the next – like the civility versus the visceral that fought inside of him.

He slid her wrists together above her head, holding them there with one of his as he freed the other to cup her jaw, keeping her head tilted up towards him as he lowered his lips to hers.

A kiss would be a painfully intimate act to perform during sex and, at that realisation, her heart jolted.

'Lust, Jask,' she said, before his lips touched hers. 'Nothing more. Just like before.'

'Lust doesn't make your heart beat that fast,' he said. 'Lust doesn't make me feel the way I do about you.'

As he cupped her neck, as his thumbs rested beneath her jaw, as he claimed her with a tender but possessive kiss that made her lose contact with her body, something clenched deep inside.

She should have pulled away because she knew he was right – this was anything but a lust-fuelled kiss from the way she churned inside. Lust didn't make her question what she was doing. How deep she was getting.

Instinctively, she lifted her thighs either side of his, wrapped hers legs around his back, allowing him deeper penetration as he pressed his hand against the small of her back to meet her halfway. This time his thrust was more urgent, his stubble brushing against her already sensitive skin as he buried his face in her neck.

Images of what she had done to him back in the alley flashed behind her eyes. But now, instead of embarrassment, she felt arousal. Because those images told her just how difficult he *had* found it to say no.

The sigh he'd let out as she'd taken him in her mouth still haunted her. As she'd looked up to see his head stretched back against that alley wall, eyes shut, his masculine neck exposed, it hadn't just been about her own satiation – she'd wanted to please him too.

It had made taking him deep into her mouth as natural as it could be. As she worked his tip with her tongue, the base of his erection with her fingers, as he'd jerked and twitched in her mouth, she had revelled in her power over him. And never had it been more exciting.

Jask *was* attracted to her.

And the way he'd kissed her told her he *did* care.

The combination was more lethal than she'd ever imagined.

She struggled to take the full force of his next thrust, let alone his increased pace, but he held her firmly, keeping her in position.

She held onto his upper arm, her fingers barely spanning the extension of his biceps, her other arm wrapped tight around his neck as she held him close, felt the powerful onset of her own climax as she felt him not just come, but explode inside her.

And something inside her gave again.

She cried out, felt him shudder, heard him groan. But this time it was not a groan of anger or frustration, but of satisfaction. More so, with contentment. And as she shamelessly gasped with pleasure, she finally gave in to a connection that was never going to go away.

Chapter Thirty-Three

Sophia lay on her side, facing the wall.

Jask lay silently curled in behind her, one arm above her head, the fingers on his other hand interlaced with hers as it lay on the covers, his thumb gently rubbing hers.

'What's your name?' he asked. 'Your real name?'

She hesitated for a moment. 'Phia *is* my real name. Short for Sophia. Sophie to my family.'

'Sophie,' he repeated. 'It suits you.'

Her heart leapt at it slipping so easily, so sensually, from his lips. 'Phia suits me better.'

'No,' he said. 'Phia makes you *feel* better. There's a difference.'

She eased onto her back so she could look at him. 'What changed it?'

'What changed what?'

'The downward spiral you were on. What changed it?'

'Having someone who cared enough.'

There was a knot in her stomach. 'You met someone after Ellen?'

'Before. I'm talking about Corbin.'

She lifted her eyebrows slightly, playfully. 'Something you need to tell me?'

His smile made her stomach churn all over again.

'He's a good friend,' he said. 'The best kind of friend. The kind who's there when you need them. Who sees you at your worst and works hard to get you back to your best.'

'He pulled you back?'

'He more or less kicked my arse into pulling me back. He dragged me back to the compound one night. Locked me in one of the containment rooms. Gave me more home truths than I wanted to hear. And he wouldn't let me out again until I started to see sense.'

'How long did it take?'

'A month.'

'A *month*?'

'I didn't want to hear what he had to say. And he wasn't going to let me out for as long as I continued to be a threat to our pack. Luckily, I'd kept my head beneath the LCU's radar. Only because of my own covering my back.'

'But you did listen eventually.'

'Actually it was Solstice who got through to me in the end.'

'What was her secret?'

'Making me realise how much Corbin cared, how much she cared, how much the pack needed me. What a selfish bastard I was being. And how I was entitled to brood – but only for a little while. Apparently almost a decade was pushing it. I put my pack under a lot of risk in those early years – not being there for them.'

'Corbin took the reins for you?'

'When he needed to.'

'But you're together now. I mean, you've pulled yourself together?'

'I still have my moments.'

'Like with me.'

He smiled. 'Darling, you'd push a pacifist to the limits.'

She smiled back. But she stared into his eyes, eyes that didn't flinch. 'Have I met him?'

He frowned. 'Who?'

She eased herself up slightly, rested her head on her palm. 'Your son.'

He glanced back at the ceiling. 'You could say that.' He looked back at her. 'You could say he's the one who brought us together.'

She knew she was gawping, but she could do nothing about it as only two possibilities came to mind. And there was only one who resembled Jask. 'Rone? Rone's your son?'

'Not that I have any right to call him such.'

'From what you've told me, something tells me he begs to differ. Jask,' she said, gently catching the side of his face to force him to look at her. 'If you need me somehow, and he's helped you get me, then he's been a part of far more than us meeting. This could be the breakthrough you both need. You need to tell him he's done good, Jask. You need to tell your son you're proud.'

And he could. She could see in his eyes how much he wanted to. And to make that happen, she needed to prove she could do whatever he wanted her to. More than that, she *wanted* to help him.

'Tell me what you want me to do, Jask,' she said. 'Trust me enough to tell me.'

He averted his gaze for a few moments. Eventually he eased onto his stomach, looked into her eyes again. 'You know how the lunar cycles work, right? Every two to three years there's a thirteenth moon – a second full moon to appear in a single solar calendar month. Some call it a blue moon.'

Sophia nodded. She understood as much about lycan lore as anyone else. Though she wished she'd taken the time to learn more.

'A thirteenth moon appears seven times in total in the Metonic cycle of nineteen years,' he added. 'That seventh thirteenth moon is make or break for lycans, our allergy to that moon particularly potent. We have to alter the ingredients we take, let alone the dosage. One of the herbs we take is aconite. We manage to grow it back at the compound under special conditions. It's the base herb to all our concoctions. Not only does it contribute to suppressing the morphing, but it works like an anaesthetic – effective in paralysing the nerves to the sensation of pain, touch and temperature, acting on the circulation, respiration and nervous systems. The only problem is, if it's not processed properly, it's fatal. It needs to be steamed with a very specific dose of ginger first. A very distinct type of ginger – turmeric.'

'But?'

'We had someone in our pack – Nero. He's always morphed before everyone else. We gave him a dosage that should have worked.'

'*Should* have?'

'Not only was the morphing barely suppressed, but he died in agony shortly after. Such an event is rare, but it's always a risk when the concoction changes. We now know we need a stronger dose of aconite, but with more aconite, we need more turmeric. We have enough of the former. The problem is, we don't have anywhere near enough turmeric that their calculations showed we need.'

'How do I come into this?'

'Next to us, the next best source for herbs and spices is the witches. Your kind. I've traced a source down where there could be enough turmeric for our needs. But, as you know, liaising with anyone in the exchange of herbs and spices is prohibited – so the authorities can manage the witches and make sure they don't become too powerful. Just as they stopped importing particular herbs and spices into Blackthorn and Lowtown decades ago, knowing our supplies would run out one day.'

'And they have the meds on standby. Meds you'd have no option but to take.'

'Exactly.'

'You want me to go and get it.' She frowned. 'That's what all this was about? But why don't you go in and take what you need? You could take down witches any day.'

'Why do you think? Charge in there and we're not only going to have some very angry witches baying for us, we would have broken one of the regulations. If word leaks out, the Lycan Control Unit will work out we don't have what we need. They'll close the compound down and they'll incarcerate us.'

'Which is why you want me to go in instead.'

'A serryn is top of the witch chain. You can walk in there and ask for whatever you want from them, and they have to give it to you without question.'

'But I could also expose what you're doing. I could get away and send the authorities after you.' Now it all made sense – not least why her impulsivity, her recklessness had caused him so much frustration. 'That's why you needed me on side. This is what this has been about – you needed my co-operation for it to work.'

'I either get my hands on that turmeric or my pack turns in less than a week – and if that happens, one way or another, they're not going to make it. Those that do, those strong enough to survive the morphing, will be too many for me to safely contain. And if they get out of here, they'll be shot at the hands of the TSCD. The only alternative is the meds – and I trust the Global Council even less than I trust the TSCD. One ingredient, Phia, stands between my pack's downfall or its survival.'

And the survival of countless others. She'd never seen a lycan morphed, but she knew what had happened to Arana Malloy in explicit detail – their thought processes and their conscience suppressed by their baser urges.

She'd seen just a glimmer of the potential of it in Jask back on the estate, and he hadn't even been morphed.

Tens of them let loose on the streets of Blackthorn, free to roam across the border into Lowtown, didn't bear thinking about.

And what would happen to Jask as a result didn't bear thinking about either.

'I can do this, Jask.'

She *would* do it.

'But I have to send you in there alone or they'll suspect. You need to walk in there like you own the place, like you've been a serryn for years. You don't answer their questions, nothing.'

'You want me to go in there arrogant, stroppy, defiant, confrontational and unrelenting?' She smirked, despite her nerves. 'I think I have this covered.'

'It's not that simple. Sending you in there brings with it another risk. Rone let it slip that we were looking for turmeric. Word could already be out. If you don't play it right, they could know you're involved with us. Worse, the witch you need to go to meet is called Tamara – she's rumoured to be linked with Kane Malloy. She could expose you, Phia. Not only will Caleb know there's a serryn in Blackthorn, but so too could Kane. And if he works out you're involved with the pack, this could lead to vampire retaliation against us.'

She raised her eyebrows slightly. 'No wonder you needed me tamed.'

'I'm letting you know what this involves.'

She frowned. 'You don't believe I can do this, do you?'

'I'm saying if this goes wrong, it's all over for my pack.' He hesitated for a moment before gently cupping her face. 'It could be all over for you. And I don't want to face either.'

Her heart soared. 'It isn't *going* to go wrong. I can do this. I swear. You said you trusted me; now's your chance to prove it. Just give me your word that once I bring back what you need, you'll help me get my sisters.'

After studying her gaze for a moment longer, he nodded. 'I give you my word.'

'Then it's a deal,' she said. 'So what are we waiting for?'

Chapter Thirty-Four

'That's it?'

'That's it,' Jask said, as they both looked from the shadows of the alley across at the shop. 'She lives beneath it. The steps are down the side.'

Sophia nodded. As she moved to step forward, Jask grabbed her arm.

'I'll be here waiting,' he said.

She held his gaze for a moment. 'I'll do this.'

'I know.'

It was all she needed to hear.

Sophia crossed the road and headed down the alley that ran alongside the shop. She descended the narrow stone steps, her hand clutching the wet handrail to prevent herself slipping on the smoothness of the worn stone.

The windowless door was nestled in the tiny recess at the bottom.

She straightened her shoulders, steadied her breathing and knocked.

Tamara, if she was in, took her time. Long enough for Sophia to lift her clenched hand ready to knock again, until she heard the sliding of bolts on the other side.

The door opened only a fraction before a woman, maybe in her late thirties, opened the door. She frowned, then her eyes widened. She opened the door fully, revealing the line of salt that marked the inside of the door.

'Tamara, right?' Sophia said.

Tamara stood there in her oversized sweater and jeans, her sharp, kohled blue eyes raking Sophia from head to foot.

'Are you alone?' Sophia asked.

Tamara nodded. 'Are you what my spidey-sense is telling me you are?'

Sophia folded her arms and cocked her hip to the side. 'Do I have to invite myself in?'

Tamara stepped back, clearing the doorway. 'It's not every day a serryn turns up on your doorstep.'

'Then I guess you can put this down as one of your lucky ones,' Sophia remarked, stepping inside.

A door lay ajar at the end of the short hallway, the flickering flame light beyond the only source of light.

'Sacrificing late into the night, huh?' Sophia asked.

Tamara almost smiled, albeit still warily. 'Go on through.'

The heavy curtains were drawn over the small windows, the fire kicking off heat from inside the log burner directly ahead, the flames reflecting on the stone grate and surround.

Tamara indicated towards the left of the small double sofas that sat either side of it.

Sophia sank into the middle one whilst the witch took the one opposite.

Now, in the glow, she could see the true brightness of Tamara's eyes, sharp against her dark hair. She could also detect the telltale signs of her age by the crow's feet and faint lines around her mouth.

Tamara stood up again almost immediately. 'Can I get you a drink?'

'Sure,' Sophia said, by instinct. 'No, actually…' She needed to keep a clear mind. She needed more than anything not to let Jask down. Not to let herself down. 'I'm fine. Thanks.'

'I'm hoping you don't mind if I get myself one.'

'Feel free.'

Tamara returned only moments later, resuming her seat and taking a sip from her cut-glass tumbler, her eyes unflinching from Sophia.

Aside from her sister, it was the first time she'd looked into the eyes of a witch – or interpreter as was the politically correct term. Her stomach clenched under the intensity, as if Tamara could read her very thoughts.

Something on the fire cracked and Sophia flinched.

Tamara frowned, only momentarily, but enough for Sophia to know she needed to get a grip. The witch was waiting for her to take the lead. Expecting her to take the lead.

'I need some turmeric,' she said, getting to the point.

Tamara raised her eyebrows just a fraction. 'Turmeric?'

'Word has it that you have a source.'

Her eyes flashed with concern. 'Word from where?'

'Nowhere for you to worry about. So is it true?'

'You must know how rare turmeric is. Blackthorn isn't exactly the best environment to be growing it – in terms of temperature that is.'

'I know you don't just grow things yourself, Tamara. I know you have links. And one of those links told me you have a supply here.'

'How much are you needing exactly?'

'I'll take whatever you've got.'

'What do you want it for?'

'That's not of your concern.'

'Oh, on the contrary – it's very much of my concern.'

Sophia's stomach flipped. There shouldn't have been any question at all, let alone any confrontation.

'You must know the exchange, sale or giving of any plant, herb or spice in Blackthorn and Lowtown is strictly prohibited,' Tamara added.

Already it was going wrong. She needed to pull back control. She needed to take charge – but smartly, calmly. She needed to keep Jask at the forefront of her mind. She needed to remember how he had handled Travis. She *had* to keep her eye on the ball. 'Who's going to know?'

'My business is all I have,' Tamara declared. 'It's my lifeline. I lose it, and I may as well become a feeder in this district.'

'That's not going to happen.'

'You can guarantee that, can you? Serryn you may be, but this is a whole other world now. You ladies can't go around lording it like you used to. None of us can.'

'I beg to differ. I'm here to collect and I'm assured you're the witch to collect from. And I'm guessing my blood will be as useful to you as your turmeric will be to me.'

Tamara took a sip of her drink, her gaze unflinching on Sophia's.

There was a time when such reticence amidst her own desperation would have pressed every impatient button and made her explode.

But not this time. She wouldn't let it overrule *this* time – not with so much at stake for Jask if she lost. Because this *had* become as much about Jask's plight as seeing things through for her sisters.

He'd trusted her. He'd trusted her to save his pack – a trust that came hard to him. She wouldn't let him down.

'*Very* useful for lining bullets,' Sophia added. '*Very* effective protection.'

'Turmeric is rarely on anyone's list. It's very specific.' Suspicion glinted in the witch's eyes. 'What did you say your name was?'

Sophia crossed her legs, stretched her arms across the back of the low sofa. She glanced into the flames. 'You're an associate of Kane Malloy from what I hear.' She looked back at her. 'Do you really expect me to disclose who I am to you?'

Tamara's eyes narrowed. 'You *have* been asking around.'

'Is he why you're asking so many questions? Are you planning to disclose there's a serryn loose in Blackthorn?'

'My loyalty to Kane has no bearing on my loyalty to my own.'

'And I *am* one of your own. So how about you try remembering that before I start getting upset?'

Her eyes flared. 'Like I said, it's not how it used to be anymore. Questions get asked now. I'm monitored all the time because of the nature of my shop.'

'But you do have a *secret* stash somewhere. Something that doesn't get monitored.'

'How do I know I can trust you?'

'You don't. But you can. And I *will* make it worth your while.'

Tamara took a steadier sip on her drink this time. And a second. She gazed into the flames for a few moments.

Finally, to Sophia's relief, she stood. She indicated towards the door in the alcove to the left of the log burner.

Sophia followed her out into the flagstoned hallway, down a narrow flight of stairs immediately to the left. Stairs that were treacherous in their steepness, proven by Tamara clutching onto the roped handrail as she descended them with caution. Reaching the bottom, she opened another door and switched on the light.

Sophia stopped herself from entering, her doubts about the witch's intentions creeping into her mind. But although a witch, Tamara was still just a human physically. And Sophia hadn't forgotten how to handle herself. Tamara may have had the advantage in height and weight, but so had many others Sophia had taken down.

Besides, she knew her hesitation would only raise questions in the witch's mind – could have her having second thoughts about issuing her with the turmeric, if that's what she actually intended at all. Instead she'd remain on her guard, reminding herself of that as she glanced once more up over her shoulder before following Tamara inside.

As they passed through a cold, dark chamber and another door, Sophia expected to find a cavern at the end of it. Instead they entered a clinical whitewashed room. Herbs, plants and unidentifiable specimens were contained in row upon row of jars, vials and boxes that aligned the ceiling-high shelves. Various apparatus including measuring jugs, scales, test tubes and conical flasks adorned the white worktops that were fitted to the periphery of the room, all of it spotless under the powerful lights that shone down from the ceiling.

Indeed, the last thing she'd expected to find was a full-blown laboratory but that, in essence, was exactly what it was.

Not that she could show Tamara she was surprised. Tamara, who was now on her hands and knees at one of the under-worktop cupboards, emptying its contents.

At first Sophia assumed she was just looking for the turmeric supply. Then she realised what the witch was actually doing was clearing the cupboard out. A few minutes later, there was a clunk.

'I'm assuming you're not claustrophobic?' Tamara asked without even glancing over her shoulder as she crawled inside.

As it so happened, small spaces were another of Sophia's pet hates – probably a part of a drowning-evoked claustrophobia – and part of the reason she had recoiled in such horror that Jask had the casketing procedures he did.

Nonetheless, Sophia stepped up to the cupboard and eased down onto her haunches to peer into the entrance Tamara had created. A door had been opened, obviously on some kind of concealed latch system. The tunnel ahead was less than a foot long. Another glow, this one amber, emanated from beyond.

Getting onto her hands and knees, she crawled through behind her.

This time she did enter a cavern – a cold but dry cavern, the recesses stacked with more jars, vials and boxes and sacks upon sacks of leaves and herbs.

Tamara was busying herself at a recess on the other side of the twenty-foot space as Phia pressed her hand up onto the low ceiling. The sooner she got out of there, the better.

'Turmeric,' Tamara announced as she came back across the room with three sealed plastic bags, each the size of a standard paperback book. 'I don't need to tell you how valuable this is. This is the rarest spice there is now – at least here – thanks to the powers that be.'

'How did you get it?' Sophia asked, accepting the packets off her.

'Most people owe someone something in this district. I held these as safekeeping for someone who lost a lot of people to obtain it. They never made it back to collect it. Once this has gone, I don't think there's any chance of getting any more. It was one of the first spices the authorities put a ban on being imported here. It obviously has some significance to a concoction for something.'

And she knew exactly what concoction – and that the authorities picking turmeric of all spices to put a ban on was no coincidence.

'They know about things like that?' Sophia asked.

'You think The Facility is just used for medical experiments into healing research? You think when witches, lycans and vampires, let alone others, miraculously vanish from this district that it's only those in-house who are responsible?'

She knew only too well. 'Of course not.'

'Whatever you want it for, use it wisely.'

Sophia nodded, before turning back towards the exit. 'Thanks for your help,' she called over her shoulder, the weight of the packets feeling good in her hands. 'I won't forget it.'

'I won't have to say anything to Kane,' Tamara stated. 'He'll find out you're here for himself – if you're not discreet.'

She turned to face her again. 'I've been discreet so far.'

'He's one of the good ones. I know you won't appreciate me saying it, but he is. And we need him here in Blackthorn. You'd do well to leave him be.'

'Depends what he does *if* he does find out about me, doesn't it?' she said, turning away again, not wanting the witch to see any glimmer of hesitation in her eyes.

Getting down on her knees, she crawled back through the gap, carefully cradling the packets against her chest.

'There's a lot I'd like to learn – spells, medicines, manipulations,' Tamara called from behind her as she followed her back out into the lab. 'I'd like you to come back. To impart your knowledge. To teach me. I've always dreamt of meeting one of you. Of learning what I can.'

For that, she was most definitely asking the wrong sister. But maybe it was time she did learn – not just about her serrynity, but the other innate skills it brought with it.

If she survived long enough.

'Maybe,' Sophia said.

'Then make sure you do stay discreet,' Tamara said. 'Kane's the least of your worries in this district.'

Sophia turned to face her again. 'Meaning?'

'Caleb Dehain's here too. You must have heard of him. He runs the west side.'

'I thought Kane was the ultimate bad boy in this district?'

'Not when it comes to serryns.' Her eyes narrowed in concern. 'You do know about Caleb, don't you?'

'Know what exactly?'

'I thought you all knew? Caleb's the most prolific serryn hunter the Higher Order ever hired. If he casts his eyes on you, you're not making it anywhere, let alone back here.'

Her pulse rate sped to a painful rate, making her light-headed as her face flushed before the blood plummeted from it, leaving her cold on the inside.

She turned away before Tamara saw it. Before Tamara sensed anything.

Sophia ploughed back through the door, ascended the steps, taking a sharp left back into the living room.

'The exchange you promised,' Tamara reminded her. 'Unless you promise to return.'

'I'll return,' she called back as she headed back along the hallway, back out the front door and up the steps.

The world blackened in on her as she crossed the street without looking, as she ploughed back into the darkness of the alley.

As soon as Jask stepped out of the recess, she slammed the packets hard against his chest before drawing back her fist ready to punch him in the face.

But Jask was too quick, blocking her easily, keeping a hold of her wrist as she swiped at him with the other hand. This time she managed to catch his face before shoving him in the chest, but only because he had no choice but to let her unless he dropped the packets.

And it made her feel sick. It made her feel sick to her very core that she could lash out at him. Made her feel even sicker to know *why* she felt sick.

'You knew, didn't you?' she said. 'You knew Caleb was a serryn hunter. You knew and you didn't tell me.'

His azure eyes widened.

'She told me,' Sophia all but hissed. 'The witch told me. You fucking *knew*. Deny it. Deny it!'

'Yes, I knew.'

She wrenched her wrist from his grip. 'If I'm right, if Leila did go there, she's dead, isn't she?'

He held her gaze, his brow furrowed. 'You don't know that.'

'No,' she said, fighting tears of panic, of anger. 'But I will. Take your fucking turmeric, Jask,' she said, abruptly turning away. 'We're done.'

He caught up with her, grabbed her arm, pulling her to a standstill. 'Where are you going?'

'Where do you think?'

'No,' he said. 'You're not.'

'You got what you wanted,' she said, trying to free herself. He'd got *exactly* what he wanted – and her heart tore at the acknowledgement of it. 'You got your precious spices. So go and save your pack, Jask. I'm saving my sisters. Or *sister* if that's all I have left. And I'm fucking killing Caleb Dehain if he has touched either one of them.'

She yanked her arm free again, but Jask caught hold of her again as he shoved the packets in his coat pockets.

'You're not going anywhere near that place,' he said, pinning her back against the dank, graffiti-emblazoned wall. 'Even if you could, look around – it's nearly dawn. The Dehain club will be on total lockdown. So unless you can penetrate armoured steel, you're going to calm down and get that insane idea out of your head.'

'And would it be insane if it was someone you cared about in there?'

'There will be someone I care about in there if I let you do this.'

Sophia exhaled tersely, it already hurting too much to hear more of his lies, his treachery.

Like everyone else, he had used her.

She pushed against him but was forced to relent as he only held her tighter against the wall.

'We will get to your sisters,' he said. 'But we'll do it together. Later.'

'I don't need your help.'

'The fact you say that tells me that's exactly what you need.'

'Get over yourself, Jask. Who saved your pack, huh? You? No. Me. You needed me, remember?'

'I know,' he said. 'And I still do.'

'For what now? You got what you wanted, Jask. We're done,' she said curtly, finally shoving him away.

'That easily?' he called after her.

'Yes, that easily,' she said. 'That's what happens when people lie to me.'

'I didn't lie to you.'

She spun to face him. 'You didn't tell me the truth because you wanted me focused so you could get your job done. Fuck me, fuck my sisters, this was about you – you and your precious pack. You *used* me.'

'I didn't even know about your sisters being there until a couple of hours ago, remember?'

'But before, you made me believe you cared, before those lies slipped from your lips. Because if you *did* care, you would have told me then. You would have made my sisters your priority. We could have gone around there straight away before letting me waste a whole other day. Your pack has time. My sisters don't.'

'It was too late by then. We would never have got there in time. And I saw no point in giving you another day of distress. I was going to tell you tomorrow night.'

But she wasn't going to hear it. She wasn't going to stand by and listen to his excuses. She turned away again, her clouded vision focused only on the exit ahead.

'Have you any idea what it took me to trust you to do this?' he called after her. 'Do you think it was easy for me handing over that kind of responsibility?'

She clenched her jaw, kept marching with no idea where she was going to go, what she was going to do next – as long as it was away from Jask and away from the pain of his betrayal.

'You really can't see it, can you?' he called out.

Just as she reached the exit, she spun to face him again. 'See what, Jask? What seems plainly obvious to me?' She took a steadying breath, clenched her hands before splaying them, composing herself. 'Do you know what hurts most? I went in there to prove I was good enough for *you*, do you know that? And I was proud – *proud* with the way I handled myself. Do you know how many times I've been proud of myself, Jask? Not once.' She pressed her lips together and exhaled through her nose, fighting back the tears. 'And for once I didn't feel like a fake hiding behind a selfish tirade of vengeance whilst pretending it's for some other cause. What I did in there, I did for *you*. And that's why I'm walking away, Jask. I'm walking away with my head held up because I'm *not* going back to what I was just because *you* have hurt me more than I would have thought possible. You ask me if I know what it took for you to trust me – well, do you know what it took for me to trust *you*? Because if you do, I've not just been a fool, *you* have.'

She turned away again, only a few more steps from getting away, fighting her tight throat with every shallow breath.

'I love you, Phia.'

She snatched back a breath.

He silently closed the gap between them, until she could feel the breath on her neck, sense that scent of earth and rain exuding from him.

'Is that not obvious to you?' he asked, catching hold of her arm again.

His touch made her falter again. The reassurance of his strength. The comfort of his proximity.

'Let me go,' she said, breaking free as he relaxed his grip.

'I can't do that,' he called after her as she walked away. 'Because I do love you, Sophie. I meant what I said back in that room. I knew it from the first moment I saw you.'

She stopped again. But she couldn't turn to face him.

'Damaged, chaotic, stubborn – and I love you,' he added. 'And I'll keep telling you until it seeps in. You keep walking and all you're doing is walking away from that. But that's what you always do, isn't it? You walk away when it really matters. When something *really* matters to you. You *know* I'm telling you the truth. You just hate yourself too much to believe it.'

She pressed her lips together, her throat constricting as she fought back the tears.

'What happened to your mother is *not* your fault,' he said. 'And you need to forgive that unruly kid if you're ever going to get over this. However misled your actions have been since then, you tried to make it better.'

As a tear trickled down her cheek, she let it roll, refusing to wipe it away for fear of him knowing she was crying.

'Because you're a fighter, Sophie,' he added. 'You're strong and you're fiery and you're brave. You're beautiful and you're funny and you're compassionate. And you deserve better than this. Than all of this.

'I know you're not ready to believe it,' he added. 'Just like I wasn't. Until I met you I thought I could never love again. But here I am, yelling it down an alley because I am not letting you go without a fight. You said you're not the same, so prove it. Prove you're not the scared little girl anymore and turn and face me like the woman I know you are. Because that woman has changed me too, Sophie. That woman has made me fall in love again. So *don't* you dare walk away from me.'

She stared ahead as the dawn light reflected in the puddles, the breeze lightly caressing her face. His words were too powerful, too overwhelming for her not to question his motivation. 'Then why? Why didn't you tell me about Caleb?'

'I told you: I tried to do what was best for you.'

'It wasn't your decision to make.'

'You don't just walk into the Dehains' club. It takes time, planning. Neither of which we had by the time you told me. If your sisters are in there, and you want them out alive, if *you* want to stay alive, then it's going to take more than storming in there with a bad attitude. Battles aren't always about bloodshed or being the most brutal or the loudest. Some of the best battles are strategic. About being smarter than your enemy.'

She rubbed a tear away with the heel of her hand before she turned around. 'But why me? Why, when there are countless of your own kind who would gladly give themselves to you?'

'Because you're what I want.'

'Why?'

He stepped up to her. 'Because you're petulant, irritating, hard to handle, impulsive, naïve. All of the above – and I *still* want to be with you. Because no one else makes me feel more like myself. No one makes me feel more alive.'

She shook her head. 'But there's no way we can be together, Jask. Me just being with you is putting your pack at risk. More than ever now. I'm not worth it.'

'I'll decide that.'

'No,' she said. 'Because I'm making the decision for you.'

'Because you care about me too, don't you? And that means I will protect you whatever it takes. You're part of my pack now, Sophie. You're a part of me. And your sisters are too important to you to make a snap decision and go ploughing in there.' He stepped in front of her and cupped her face. 'We'll do this together.'

'But nothing ever lasts with me, Jask. I'm bad on the inside. I always have been. You don't deserve to have your world torn apart by me. And that's what would happen. I tear everything apart in the end and tear another part of me by doing it. I can't do that to myself. And I can't hurt you. What happened back in that alley was just the start. And even if I save my sisters, we'll never get back into Summerton. Not as the family we were. I can't join them – not with what I am now. It'll be Lowtown at best. And it's only a matter of time before the proximity makes the cravings too much.'

'You still have a choice.'

'I *don't* have a choice, Jask,' she said. 'Any more than you do over what you are. And there's certainly no medication to contain *my* condition – only to get as far away from vampires as I can. Only now that'll be impossible. I'm tired, Jask. I just want this to be over. I want my life back.'

He held her gaze for a moment before reaching into his pocket. He pulled out his phone.

She stared down at it before looking into his eyes.

'Call them,' he said.

She didn't know whether to cry in relief or punch him. 'You've had the phone this whole time?'

'If you need to call them, then call them. Maybe I was wrong to protect you. And yes, part of my reasoning was that I was scared I'd lose you if something had happened. But be quick – the battery is nearly dead.'

She took the phone off him, shocked at how much she trembled, how much her stomach wrenched. The truth was on the end of the call. Another night without Leila answering would be proof something had gone horribly wrong.

She stared down at the screen then looked back at Jask. 'What if neither answer?'

'You need to know.'

It took her a moment to recall it then she typed in Leila's number.

The phone rang. And rang.

She glanced up at Jask then leaned back against the wall for support, her fingers knotted in her hair. She was all ready to try Alisha's mobile number instead, when the phone clicked.

'Hello?'

Sophia slammed her hand over her mouth, anything to hold back the tears. She took a deep breath, the knot tightening at the back of her throat.

'Sophie?' Leila asked. 'Sophie, is that you?'

'Lei.' It was all she could say – all she could bring herself to say.

She heard Leila gasp at the end of the phone – her big sister clearly not as reluctant as her to contain her tears.

'You're okay!' Leila exclaimed.

'I'm okay,' she said. 'You?'

'Okay,' she said, 'doing okay.'

'Alisha?'

'Alisha's fine. Sophie, where are you?'

'I'm in Blackthorn.'

'Where?'

She looked at Jask. He shook his head to her disclosing her location. 'Safe,' she said. 'Lei, I don't have long. Is Alisha with you?'

Silence was the last thing she needed.

'Lei? Is she still at the club?'

There was another moment of silence. 'How do you know?'

'You saved him, didn't you? You saved Jake Dehain.'

'And you were the one who tried to kill him.'

Sophia ran her fingers back through her hair as the pieces fell into place for both of them. 'What happened? Did you escape?'

'He let me go.'

Sophia glanced at Jask. She frowned in disbelief. 'He let you go? And Alisha? Please tell me she's with you.'

There was a moment's hesitation. 'She's still there.'

Sophie stood upright from the wall. Her heart wrenched. 'You left her behind?'

'Because I had no choice. Sophie, this is more complicated that you know.'

Sophia rested her head back against the wall. It was all the con-firmation she needed that it was all down to her. 'Alisha was in

Blackthorn because of me, wasn't she? Just as you came to Blackthorn because of me.'

'Soph, that's not important right now.'

She heard the first of the beeps, telling her the battery was fast waning.

'Why didn't you tell me, Lei? Why didn't you tell me what you were?'

'I'm sorry.'

But she couldn't be angry. She was not going to turn the blame on Leila this time. Leila who was still alive. Both of them still alive because Leila had fallen in love with a vampire. Leila who, for some reason, somehow, against every principle she had ever known her to have, had consummated that love.

But coils of discomfort tightened inside her. She'd only been in Blackthorn a couple of days at most. She would have gone straight to the Dehains' club. She could have only been with Caleb and Jake.

The implications were only just beginning to take hold. The very thought of her big sister even looking at one of the monsters that were Caleb and Jake in that way…

Another beep resounded in her ear.

'How did you lose it, Lei? How did you lose your serrynity?'

'It's a long story. Sophie, you need to listen to me. Caleb knows about you. He knows what you are now and he will be looking for you.

She'd been right to suspect his hunt for her was about far more than being responsible for trying to kill his brother.

And now she had the most prolific serryn hunter on her heels for more than just personal reasons.

'Soph, you said you're safe. How safe?'

She looked back at Jask. 'As safe as I can be in Blackthorn.'

'Then stay there. There is something I have to do. I'll be returning to Blackthorn in the next couple of days.'

Another beep.

Her heart skipped a beat. 'Returning? Why?'

'I'll explain everything when I see you. But you must listen. You must not be on the streets. You cannot let Caleb find you. You cannot let anyone find you, do you understand me?'

'What's wrong?'

'I can't explain over the phone. But I need you, for once in your life, to do as I ask. You can't even imagine the consequences if you don't. Tell me you understand.'

'Lei, you're freaking me out.'

'Please, Sophie, *please* tell me you'll do as I ask.'

'Lei, I might only have seconds of battery left. I'm going to go and get Alisha.'

'No! Sophie – listen to me! Alisha's all right. I promise you. I would not have left her if I didn't believe it.'

'She can't be all right! She's alone with Caleb and Jake Dehain!'

'And I am telling you there's more to it. Sophie, promise me, please. Prom–'

The air went dead.

The tears welling behind her eyes.

Eventually she reluctantly dropped the phone from her ear.

'They're alive?' Jask asked.

She nodded. Her tears finally gave way.

Jask instantly took her into his arms, Sophia willingly burying her face in his chest, accepting his comfort, anyone's comfort, for the first time in too long to remember.

'I'll help you,' he said softly as he clutched the back of her head. 'You're not on your own anymore, Sophie. We're in this together. Not because I *have* to be anymore. Because I *want* to be. And we'll sort this. I promise.'

Chapter Thirty-Five

Jask knew there was something wrong, something horribly wrong, as soon as he approached the compound.

But seeing the open door, the corrugated metal buckled and splintered, was like waking up from a nightmare only to see the monster still crouched at the foot of the bed.

Even Phia's hand felt distant as he marched down the corridor as if on automatic pilot.

He pushed through the next buckled door to find the usually permanently occupied room empty. The security-coded door ahead equally lay open. But it was the bloodstains on the floor at the table, against the wall to his left, let alone to his right, that made his gut clench.

Fresh bloodstains.

'What the fuck?' Sophia whispered.

She echoed what he couldn't even bring himself to think.

Pulled between ploughing on and protecting Phia, he froze to the spot. 'I need to find you somewhere to hide.'

'No way,' she said curtly, tightening her grip on his hand. 'I'm not leaving you.'

He glanced across at her – at the determination in her brown eyes. 'You'll do as I say,' he said, his tone laced with impatience.

But movement at the door ahead made them both flinch.

The look in his fellow lycan's eyes sent an icy stab into his heart.

'Jask,' Caspian said.

Whoever it was, they were long gone. That much was obvious. What he had walked into was the aftermath.

He clenched Phia's hand and ploughed forward, glancing at the dismantled security panel as he passed.

'The alarm didn't go off,' Caspian explained. 'We didn't get any warning.'

Jask picked up pace. He let go of Phia so he could shove open the first gate, sending it ricocheting back at him before he slammed it back against the wall.

He passed through the tunnel in seconds. He came to an abrupt halt, his heart racing like he'd never known.

The bodies were laid out on the green – thirty easily. Bloodstains marked their makeshift shrouds. The atmosphere was dense with the pain and mourning of the distraught survivors.

He looked across the quadrant to see Corbin picking up pace to meet him halfway. From the way he clutched his side, a side Jask then saw was bloodstained, he knew Corbin was struggling to contain his own pain. His face was bloodied, grazed, as were his hands. He'd taken a beating. A beating he had thankfully survived.

Jask instantly wrapped his arms around his friend, the relief of seeing him alive the only consolation.

'Corbin?' he asked in need of an explanation as he eased his friend away again.

'At least forty of them,' Corbin explained. 'They disarmed the alarm systems somehow. They ploughed in here and didn't hold back on the fire.' Tears were already glossing his eyes – tears of fury, tears of sadness. 'No reason that we know of. No explanation.'

Jask looked back out across the quadrant as something dark, something dangerous, something long suppressed coiled inside of him.

'We tried to take them down but they'd gathered a small number of us,' Corbin continued. 'They threatened to kill them if we got in their way. Whoever the fuck they were, they were professional. Uniformed. Silver neck cuffs. Helmets. The works. But not uniforms I've ever seen. We didn't stand a chance. Not unless we sacrificed the ones they held.'

Jask looked back across to the quadrant, scanned his pack until his eyes fell to where Dione sat by the small bundle that lay at her feet. Her eyes were glazed as she rocked. He fought back the escalating fury that burned his throat.

He had to keep it together.

He fought to keep it together.

'No one's got an army like that in Blackthorn,' Jask hissed. His attention snapped back to Corbin. 'Did they give any indic–'

But catching the scent in the breeze, Jask's attention snapped to the whispers of smoke in the distance. Smoke coming from the outbuildings beyond the arch.

Heart pounding, he marched across the quadrant towards it, not even registering if Corbin or Phia were following.

He picked up pace through the arch, took an abrupt left through the gate.

And froze.

What was left of the greenhouse was a burnt shell. The herbs and the plants – their lifeline – were nothing but ash.

He snatched his gaze back to Corbin as he drew level.

'We did what we could but it was futile.' A new pain flashed in Corbin's eyes. 'Jask, they took some of our young.'

Jask couldn't move. Everything around him blurred into some unreal distance.

'They didn't say where. They didn't say why,' Corbin added. He looked to the dense sky, closed his eyes to compose himself, and took a steadying breath before looking back at Jask. But his attempt to contain his tears didn't work.

Jask hadn't seen Corbin cry since the night they lost Ellen. Pain seared through him, his own tears scorching the back of his eyes.

'Tuly was amongst them,' Corbin finally declared. 'They took my baby girl. The bastards took my baby girl, Jask. And there was *fuck* all I could do about it.'

Jask stepped forward to grip Corbin's neck, before pulling him against him, holding him tight, the only comfort, reassurance he could offer him.

He looked across at Phia, tears equally filling her distressed eyes as she stood motionless watching them. He reached for her, wiped a tear from her cheek.

'Jask…' Corbin began. But he couldn't finish.

Jask pulled back enough to look at him – had sensed it in his tone. He'd heard that tone once before, and it tore through him now as it did then. His heart rate slowed to a painful thud. 'Rone?'

The look of confirmation in Corbin's eyes may as well have gutted him.

Jask's gripped his best friend's arm. 'Where is he?'

'He wouldn't back down, Jask,' Corbin explained.

'*Where?*' Jask demanded.

'I'm sorry.'

Jask shoved his way through both Corbin and Phia, all but falling through the gate as he scanned the courtyard.

He didn't need an answer once he was out there. Three of his pack emerged from the holding block. And when Samson's gaze met his, he knew.

Jask didn't feel the ground beneath his feet as he burst inside. The holding room was empty. He skimmed the steps, staring into each of empty rooms to his left as he did so.

But he could smell the blood. He could sense the pain. As Sera exited the third room with a bloodied bowl in her hands, as her eyes met his, he took the last few steps.

Solstice was stood beside the stone table, gazing down at the figure laid out on it, her hand gently sweeping Rone's curls back from his forehead.

Jask braced his arms on the doorway, unable to bring himself to step across the threshold as he stared down at the bloodied, beaten body of his son.

His eyes snatched to Solstice's, her tearful blue eyes gazing back at him.

Then he heard his son take a breath. A laboured breath, but a breath all the same.

His heart leapt and he lunged forward.

But Solstice was between them before he could get there, her hand on his chest. 'He held on for you,' she said softly. She eased onto tiptoe to whisper in his ear. 'There's nothing we can do. Not with the herbs gone. There's ten out there now trying every witch in Blackthorn. We could only hope you'd get back in time. He doesn't know,' she added. 'He doesn't know it's all gone.'

Jask was by his side in seconds, one trembling hand clutching the stone table, his other on Rone's chest just so he could be sure the movement hadn't been an apparition.

Rone opened his eyes – eyes that were sunken in his swollen face. He was barely recognisable. His breathing was shallow and, from the tension, the pain was too intense for anything more than that.

He stared down not only at his son's beaten body, but his *tortured* body.

Fury burned deep, but not as deep as the guilt.

Rone held up his hand a little and Jask instantly grasped it.

'I'm sorry,' Rone said, even the small movement making the splits in his lips bleed. He gasped for air, at least one lung evidently punctured. 'I let you down again.'

Jask shook his head, but waited patiently as Rone gained enough breaths to talk again.

'I tried to be you,' Rone said. 'To save them. But I couldn't.'

Jask could barely swallow against his constricted throat.

'He tried to get the young down here and tuck them away in the recesses in the containment rooms,' Solstice said. 'But they caught up with us. He tried to protect Tuly. He tried to protect me. Your son is a hero, Jask.'

He looked across at Solstice and Corbin in the doorway, Solstice's arms wrapped around herself, the distress clear in her eyes.

She'd been Rone's mother in Ellen's absence. She'd been the parent Jask had failed to be. Now she rested her head back against the doorframe, selflessly there again to be his comfort despite her own child having been snatched away.

Jask attempted to swallow, but there was nothing fluid in his throat. He looked back down at his son, gently cupped his face. 'You did exactly what I would have,' he said. 'You put yourself at risk to save your pack – I couldn't ask for more bravery.'

Rone caught his breath again. 'I know you wish I'd died that day. That Ellen had lived. That maybe my brother… was more than I could have been.'

Jask's tears dropped onto his son's arm.

'I wish I could have been more,' Rone added, looking at him with eyes that were the image of his mother's.

'You never needed to be more,' Jask said, reaching to hold his son's face. '*I* needed to be. You didn't fail. You've never failed.' He pulled one of the packets out of his pocket and held it up for Rone to see. 'We got it, son,' he said. 'Thanks to you we got the turmeric we needed. You *did* save us.'

Rone tried to smile, but it only made him wince.

'You…' Rone gasped for air. 'Get our young back,' he said, clearly using the last of his strength to grip his father's hand – a hand that was icy cold now. 'No one–' He gasped for air again. 'Fucks with… our pack… right?'

Jask nodded. 'No one.'

Rone tried to smile again. He didn't quite make it.

His hand fell lax.

His chest stopped moving.

Jask's throat scorched. He couldn't breathe. The image of his son blurred behind the water filling in his eyes.

Water he was drowning in.

He fell to his knees. Every defence mechanism told him it wasn't real, that it hadn't happened.

The yell that escaped was disturbing even to him, almost as if it was coming from someone else. A gut-wrenching yell that came from somewhere deep and feral and visceral inside. Something that screamed for blood.

Something that screamed for vengeance.

❊ ❊ ❊

Sophia flinched and recoiled from the doorway.

She'd only seen glimpses of what was going on – both Corbin and Solstice blocking the way. But she'd strained enough to hear everything.

And the war cry that echoed from within the chamber stabbed her like a blunt blade direct into the heart.

She slammed her hands to her mouth and backed against the wall.

It had been enough seeing the aftermath out on the lawn, to see the desecration of their crops, to hear they had taken the young – taken Tuly. But knowing now what she knew about the relationship between father and son, her own war cry resounded from within – a silent cry of fury like she'd never felt.

And as Jask's emotional agony, pain and grief ricocheted around the chamber, she could think of nothing but getting to him. Of holding him. Of doing whatever was possible to give him any fraction of comfort that she could.

She pushed herself from the wall, almost stumbling into Corbin as she tried to squeeze through the gap between him and Solstice. But Corbin was having none of it.

He braced his arm across the doorway as an impenetrable barrier. 'No, you don't.'

She took a step back, her hands clenched. 'I need to see him.'

'No,' Corbin said. 'You need to leave him be.'

Despite knowing it was futile, she stepped forward again, ready to shove Corbin aside if she had to. But Corbin's hands locked on her upper arms as he pressed her back against the wall, Solstice promptly quietly closing the door to shield Jask inside.

Corbin's eyes weren't lycan eyes laced with the familiarity she had come to know and trust with Jask – his was the warning glare of a stranger. A stranger who was barely holding it together in his own anger and grief. 'He needs time alone.'

'I want to see him.'

'It's not about what *you* want. He's not safe right now.'

'He won't hurt me.'

'Don't,' he said, his tone laced with impatience, his eyes narrowed. 'Don't talk like you know him. You know *nothing* about him.'

'I know what Rone meant to him.'

His eyes flashed but then he frowned again. 'Then you'll also know what Tuly means to me. So you'll know that right now is *not* the time to be arguing with me. No one goes in there.'

The resentment that emanated from him so profusely forced her to be silent for a moment. Just long enough for Solstice to step over and place a hand tenderly on her partner's arm.

'Let her go, Corbin. We've had enough conflict for one night.'

Corbin stared Sophia down for a second longer before he turned away. He stepped back over to the door, leaning against the architrave, clearly listening to whatever was going on inside.

The bangs and thuds, the splintering of wood within, made her flinch again.

'Get some fresh air,' Solstice said to Sophia, everything about her surprisingly composed despite the lingering distress in her own eyes. 'Jask will find you when he's ready.'

An act of kindness or just one of civility on Solstice's part, it still made Sophia's chest clench. 'I'm scared for him.'

'Jask is strong,' Solstice said. 'We need to give him time to remember that.'

Sophia pressed her lips together. She glanced back at Corbin. She was an outsider – that's what she had to remember. She wasn't part of the pack – not like Jask had said, not like she'd started to feel herself to be.

They resented her. Hated her even. She'd taken Jask away from them when they'd needed him most. She'd led him on her quest and he'd subsequently abandoned his pack to fend for themselves.

Solstice hadn't said it. Corbin hadn't said it. But she'd seen it in their eyes. Their little girl had been taken because of her. Lycans had died that night because of her. Jask's world had fallen apart because of *her.*

'I'll get her back,' Sophia said. 'I'll help. We'll get them all back – Tuly, the others–'

Corbin spun towards her with a speed that made her recoil.

'This is not some fantasy adventure, you *stupid*, naïve little girl!' he snapped. 'This is real. This is Blackthorn. People die. People out there *have* died. Good people. Don't you dare fucking stand there like you can even begin to know what you're talking about!'

He marched back over to the door, no doubt the only thing he could do to restrain himself.

How did she even think she was going to try to console a lycan? A lycan who had had his compound invaded, his son murdered, because of her.

She *was* stupid. She *was* naïve. Corbin was right.

Sophia backed away before turning towards the steps. She had to do something. Do something to make it better.

'Wait!' Solstice called out.

She turned back around.

Solstice caught hold of Corbin's arm as he stared bewildered down at her. 'Let her have five minutes with him,' she said.

'He doesn't–' Corbin began, but Solstice only squeezed tighter.

'Let *him* decide,' Solstice said. 'Maybe she's exactly what he needs.' She opened the door and indicated for Sophia to enter.

Heart racing, Sophia slipped between them and into the room.

Only then, seeing Rone fully, the caskets destroyed, Jask's coat torn to shreds, the bags of turmeric thrown at the walls, did she understand the full extent of Jask's agonising cry.

Now he sat silently on the floor, his back against the stone table, knees bunched against his chest, his head wrapped in his arms that rested upon them.

She couldn't think what else to do.

She lowered to her knees, reached out and laid her hand on his arm.

He'd know it was her – not just by her touch but by her scent. He could swat her away if he wanted to, as she no doubt deserved, but it wouldn't stop her trying.

She prised his arm away from his knees, squeezed between them.

His response had been instant. But instead of shoving her away, he pulled her tight to his chest.

She wrapped her arms around him, looped her legs over his thigh, as he buried his head in her neck.

Laying her head against his chest, she could hear ragged breaths echoing from deep within, the slow, rhythmic beat of his lycan heart. A heart she now knew had been torn apart for a second time. She pressed her palm over the top of it. If she could have stitched it back together, she would have. But she knew this wound needed to be raw and open. He needed to bleed for a while. And she wasn't going to leave him until that bleeding stopped.

She couldn't think of anything else to say because there was only one thing – one thing that burned inside her. Words that she uttered without restraint. 'I love you too,' she whispered.

And Jask's hold tightened.

Chapter Thirty-Six

Jask hadn't wanted to let Phia go. Just for that short time he'd held her, he'd lost himself. Lost himself in the comfort of her touch, in the words she'd uttered so softly, so honestly. Words he'd needed to hear like never before.

Words that had given him strength.

And strong is what he needed to be, now more than ever. He'd crumbled last time he'd felt that much pain, that much grief.

But not this time.

This time he wasn't coiling in on himself, losing himself to the darkness of his own self-pity and anger. He would grieve and he would mourn when he was done, and not before.

And instead of lashing out at whoever got in his way like last time, *this* time only those who were responsible would pay. Because they *would* pay. And wallowing in his anguish would not make that happen.

The pack needed him now more than ever. He was their leader and he would pull himself together. This was about strategy, about moving forward quickly.

And this time he had more than them as reason enough to pull through – now he had Phia.

He gently eased her away from him. 'I'm all right,' he said, seeing the concern in her eyes. He pushed back her hair and gently cupped her face. 'Are you?'

'I'm sorry.'

He frowned. 'For what?'

'Taking you from your pack.'

'I took *myself* from my pack, Sophie, because I had no choice. But I'm back now.'

He looked out of the doorway to where Corbin, having been pacing, came to a standstill.

His friend took his cue to enter.

Phia equally took her cue to take her seat to the left of Jask, as Corbin assumed his to the right.

Jask rested his head back against the stone and looked back at the wall ahead, avoiding the pain in his friend's eyes – anything that would further intensify his own.

'Who the *fuck* would do this? And why?' Corbin asked. 'What have they got to gain by destroying our lifeline like that, unless they want to destroy us?'

'You know as well as I do that this stinks of the authorities. I don't know whether the TSCD are directly involved or just turning a blind eye, but they *are* involved somehow.'

'Do you think it *is* revenge? For going up against them?'

'If it is, they're looking for an all-out implosion.'

'Do you think that's what they want? Finally turn us into the monsters they need –have the perfect excuse to slaughter us all?'

'I haven't ruled it out.'

'Tuly is out there somewhere with no meds,' Corbin reminded him. 'In a matter of days, every bone in her little body will break. Every tendon and muscle will be stretched to excruciating lengths. She will become an animal not knowing what to think and what to feel or how to control all the primal urges surging through her. We *have* to stop this.'

'And we will,' Jask said, meeting and holding his friend's gaze.

Jask pulled himself to his feet, ran his hands back through his hair and clutched his skull, his back to them as he stared at the wall.

Though how the hell he was going to go up against an invisible army and protect his pack at the same time, especially when contained within the walls of Blackthorn and Lowtown, he had no idea.

He needed to think.

'Go to Caleb,' Corbin said. 'Tell him that The Alliance were paid by someone to kill him and Jake. Get him on side. If anyone can infiltrate this district and find out what's going on, it's him. If anyone will go up against the authorities besides Kane, it's Caleb. He's the only vampire around here besides Kane who's fucked-up enough to do it.'

'I'm not going to Caleb.'

Even if he could, he wouldn't. He wasn't turning to any vampire for help.

'Then go to Kane. Tell him what's happened. This is an invasion of *his* territory too. He could be one hell of a powerful ally again.'

'And look what happened last time I made a deal with him. He let me down once; I won't be giving him that opportunity again. He could even be the reason *why* we're suffering this retaliation,' Jask said, turning to face them. 'And if he is, he–'

Jask had sensed it, but left it too late, the alien scent now corroborated by movement in the corner of his eye.

Daniel stood in the doorway, the gun poised directly at Jask's head.

He'd let his guard down. He'd fatally let his guard down.

But a second later, another figure stepped in behind the assailant, Daniel's gun-holding arm wrenched to the side as he took a shot. The figure looped his arm around Daniel's throat in a choke-hold, squeezing until every one of Daniel's limb tensed.

'I don't think so,' Kane whispered in his ear.

Chapter Thirty-Seven

Kane Malloy remained at the threshold, less than ten feet away and, from the expression in his eyes, Sophia knew it had taken him less than a second to sense what she was.

From the slight, brief tilt of his head it looked as though it took him another second longer to believe it.

Sophia's skin prickled as the master vampire's narrowed gaze remained locked on hers whilst she stumbled to her feet. In that moment she could see exactly, *exactly* why he had the impact he did on so many. Kane was powerful enough in reputation, but in the flesh, locked in eye contact with him, he was mesmerising.

This was why, in all the research she had conducted into serryns, the witches would take on any vampire without hesitation – except for Caleb Dehain it seemed, and master vampires. Masters were reserved for the most powerful serryns – the most experienced, the most intrepid, the most lethal. And, stood there, frozen to the spot as she stared back at him, she realised how much she lacked in all three.

And knowing the same, Jask yanked her behind him, creating a barrier between her and Kane.

Corbin, soon on his feet despite the pain, was immediately by his friend's side.

And she could do nothing but stand motionless amidst the pending bloodbath.

'As if the night wasn't complicated enough already,' Kane remarked, his gaze switching back to Jask.

'What the fuck are you doing here, Kane?' Jask asked.

'A simple thank you would suffice,' he said, slamming Daniel's wrist against the architrave, forcing him to drop the gun – amidst Daniel's pained gasp – to the floor.

Kane kicked it into the centre of the room, metal skidding across stone, before throwing Daniel to the floor between them.

Daniel instantly drew his wrist to his chest, confirmation it was either broken or badly sprained, before glowering up at the lycans in front of him.

Glowering at them with the cold glare of the assassin he was.

She'd forgotten he was there. But amidst the chaos, Daniel had clearly made the most of the moment – awaited Jask's return and took the opportunity.

It was only what she would have done less than three days before.

And she would have lost Jask to him, of that she had no doubt, if Kane hadn't intervened. Corbin would have instantly killed Daniel as a result – not even a gun-toting assassin being quick enough to take out two lycans in such close proximity. But Daniel wouldn't have cared about the risk. He would have given it his best shot and died in the process if he had to.

It was what The Alliance was all about. What they *had* been about. What *she* had been about.

As Kane stepped into the room, a lycan came hurtling in behind him – a lycan Sophia recognised as Phelan.

Despite his startled wariness at Kane's presence, his attention was soon on Daniel, then Jask.

'He got out of the room,' Phelan said, indicating towards Daniel. 'He must have taken Connor unaware. He shoved a knife in his back, rendered him paralysed before slitting his throat. I just found him. Saw he'd taken his gun.'

Jask tucked Sophia behind Corbin before taking the few steps towards Daniel. Before she'd had time to protest, he kicked him with a force that made Sophia flinch, knocking Daniel out cold against the stone floor.

Jask raised his boot, his intention clear, to crush Daniel's skull beneath it.

But Sophia couldn't let him do it.

'Jask!' she called out, breaking the silence.

As she captured Jask's attention, only then did she take a breath. 'We might need him,' was all she could think to say.

Jask hesitated. The fury and pain in his eyes told her he wavered. But he lowered his foot and took a step back.

Kane raised his eyebrows a fraction. '*We*?' he echoed. 'Seemingly even more complicated than I thought.'

'*What* are you doing here?' Jask asked, his voice dangerously low.

'We need to talk.' Kane glanced at Sophia, down at Daniel, before looking back at Jask. 'And it looks to me like the agenda is growing.'

There was another moment of silence.

'Take Dan outside,' Jask instructed Phelan. 'Make sure he's secure. The same goes for the compound. I want all the exits marked from now on.' She knew from the look in Kane's eyes that Jask had returned his attention to him. 'We can't just have anyone wandering in here.'

Kane folded his arms, before tonguing his incisor behind the shield of his closed mouth.

Phelan nodded. 'Onto it.' He hoisted Daniel from the floor, flung him over his shoulder with ease before disappearing back outside.

'Dan, huh? So you know him then?' Kane remarked.

'Two weeks, Kane – two weeks you've fucking disappeared for,' Jask said, taking a step towards him. 'You *and* Parish. And now you come back demanding my attention? Well, you'd better be here with news that she's dead – that you finished the job.'

Kane didn't even flinch, his eyes calmly attentive. 'Like I said, we need to talk.'

'I'll take that as a no. Well, take a good look around, Kane. Do I look like I have time to talk right now? Do you think the fact I gave evidence against the TSCD has nothing to do with this?' he demanded, his pointed finger thrust back towards Rone. 'Evidence I had no choice but to give because *you* pulled out of our deal.'

'I didn't pull out of anything.'

'Xavier Carter was going to die – that's what you said. The soul ripper was going to tear his soul out before you turned on Caitlin Parish. That was the deal. They were *mine* to avenge as much as yours, but I trusted you when you said you had a more effective way. Instead, you turned soft, bedding the girl you were supposed to make suffer so that *they* suffered. *Instead*, you did nothing but ensure they're all safely locked behind bars. I kept to *my* side of the deal, Kane. I could have let you go on the rampage that night you found Arana. I could have let the TSCD win. I could have let you give them the massacre they wanted, but I did what was best for my pack, for you, for this district. And *you* broke that deal. Which meant I stood in that stand, gave evidence to the very system I loathe, to support those members of my pack who were wronged. All because it was the only thing I could do under the circumstances *your* actions had created. So please excuse the lack of red carpet here today.'

'She already knows all of this, I take it?' Kane said, indicating back at Sophia.

'You need to leave,' Jask declared, folding his arms. 'Like you said, this night doesn't need to get any more complicated.'

'Come on, Jask – you know me better than this. You must have known in your gut that this isn't over.'

'Then why? Tell me what changed.'

'Carter was working with the Higher Order.'

'The TSCD and Higher Order are right up each other's arses. What's new?'

'They were leaking information to him.'

'What kind of information?'

'The kind of information that meant I needed to keep Carter alive a little longer.'

'And Parish? Why's she alive?'

'Because I want her to be.'

Jask exhaled tersely. 'Get the fuck off my territory, Kane,' he said, daring to turn his back on him. 'I have a pack to worry about.'

'And I'm being liberal here on account of that. The attack on your compound was a targeted operation, Jask,' Kane declared.

'No shit,' Jask remarked flippantly, stepping back over beside Sophia and Corbin.

'I know who's responsible.'

Jask's scowl deepened as he turned around to face the vampire again.

Kane's gaze was steady, sullen, unflinching. 'So, do you want to talk about this civilly? Or shall I walk away and leave you to work this out for yourself? Only with what I know, I'd *strongly* advise the former.'

Chapter Thirty-Eight

Entering the holding room, Jask and Corbin took their seats at the heads of the table, Kane taking his to Jask's left.

Jask guided Phia to sit adjacent to him on the opposite side of the table to Kane. That way, if Kane went for her, he'd have the table to contend with first, let alone two lycans, before he even got that far.

But everything about the way Kane leaned back in his chair, one bent arm resting loosely on the broad back, his legs casually parted, told him this was not a time for a face-off. Not yet.

And for once, despite the deadly look in Kane's eyes as he meticulously assessed Phia, she'd thankfully opted for the sensible choice of silence.

But he couldn't be sure how long it would last – not just because Phia was Phia, but because he'd seen twice now the effect the proximity of vampires had on her. *She* knew playing ball was the best option, but whether the serryn in her agreed was a whole other matter. And more the reason why Jask needed to conclude this as quickly as he could.

'So this is an interesting, if not very unexpected, scenario,' Kane said. 'Where did you find her, Jask?'

'I stumbled on her by accident.'

'By accident?'

'That's right.'

'Where?'

'I'm going along with this for now, Kane – that doesn't mean I'm fucking accountable to you.'

Kane's jaw tensed, he lifted his eyebrows a fraction before he leaned forward on the table, turned his head to look him in the eyes – a move that made even Jask's stomach churn. 'You've got a serryn in your compound. You'd better fucking believe I want answers.'

Jask wasn't stupid enough to push him, but his days of compromise were over. He just had to hope that somehow there was a way forward, or blood was going to spill before dawn ignited. And if it was Kane's, they'd not only have an invisible army closing in, but a hundred times as many vampires that dominated the district.

Still, there was no way anyone, not even Kane Malloy, was taking Sophia from him.

'*My* compound,' Jask reminded him. '*My* territory. *My* business. She has nothing to do with you or anyone else.'

'No? When they find out you've got her, she soon will have.'

The tepid light from the window caught Kane's face, igniting his navy eyes. It had not been a day unlike that when Jask had first tracked him down and told him what the lycans had confessed to. He'd resented going to Kane, with every iota of his being, but he'd known it had been the only way to save lives – many lives, not least those of his pack.

This was another of those days.

Jask's skin prickled. 'What's that supposed to mean?'

'What's she doing here, Jask? And who was the assassin she protected?'

'You first.'

Kane held his gaze to the point Jask half expected him to lunge across the table, pin him to the floor and demand the answers he wanted.

But he didn't. Instead, Kane folded his arms and leaned back in his chair. 'Sirius Throme.'

It was two simple words. One simple name. But it said more than either of them needed to share explanation on.

It was Jask's turn to lean onto the table, his fists clenched as he locked gazes with Kane. 'You're telling me the Global Council did this to my pack?'

'We've got a problem, Jask. A huge fucking problem.'

'This is because of the court case, isn't it? This is their punishment. For stopping their evoked massacre in Blackthorn – *this* is their punishment.'

'Fuckers!' Corbin hissed, standing abruptly, kicking his chair halfway across the room.

Phia jumped.

Jask had already sensed it coming.

Kane didn't even flinch.

'It's not punishment – it's the start of a war,' Kane declared. 'And you're their example of what's to come, Jask. According to Sirius, an easily justifiable example considering you're the reason they never got their hands on me in the first place.'

His heart skipped a beat. They were the words he had always dreaded. That every resident in Blackthorn dreaded. It was a day they had all known would come. 'They're closing in on us?'

Kane nodded.

'Why now?'

'Because they're ready for me.'

Jask stared at him, then fell back into his chair with a curt exhale. He shook his head before glaring back at Kane. 'So this *is* all about you? This *is* down to you?'

'That's what they want everyone to believe.'

'Well that's how it fucking sounds to me.'

'This war was happening one way or another. What happened here today is just the start. Next will come the call for me. If they get what they want, if they get me to surrender, they have the perfect reason to destroy the place. If others surrender me, the same still applies. Or they'll come in and destroy Blackthorn until they find me.'

'They'll start a global uprising. They can't do that.'

'If there's an uprising, they'll destroy sister districts too. This is going to be zero tolerance, Jask – and Sirius is holding the reins.'

'Why does he want you?'

'The same reason the Higher Order want me – they want what I know. In the case of the Higher Order, it's how to make the healing permanent so they don't lose their purpose. Sirius, however, is one step ahead it seems. He wants to build an infallible Global Council. He wants soul transference. And I'm the missing link.'

'Soul transference? Like what you did with Caitlin?'

'Only on a much bigger scale,' Kane added. 'And now he's calling the shots to get it. At least he thinks he is. It depends what we do from here.'

'Hold on a second,' Jask said. 'There is no *we*.'

Kane frowned. 'Did you not hear what I said? There is no get-out clause here, Jask. They're not just coming for me; they're coming for us all and they want this district to implode in the process. Everyone within these walls is expendable, whatever the outcome. They get what they want, and there is no more Blackthorn, no more Lowtown, no more third species. This is what these walls are all about – containing us for this very event. One way or another, whether justifying it through this or the rising of the chosen one, they were never giving us a way out.'

'Burning down our greenhouse,' Jask said. 'They *want* us to morph, don't they? That's how they're going to justify coming in here if you don't play ball.'

'The same as I'm guessing they've hidden your young here in Blackthorn, waiting for you to rip the place apart trying to find them. They're toying with you. They're toying with us all.'

'Do you know where they put them?' Corbin asked, stepping back towards the table from his position by the window.

'No,' Kane said, glancing at him. He looked back at Jask. 'But we'll find them.'

'I keep telling you, there is no *we*,' Jask reminded him. 'We'll find them our way. We don't need you, Kane.'

'Jask, there is only one way this is going to work. We either pull together or they win. We made a pact, remember, should this day ever come.'

A pact that said the third species would never turn on each other. A pact that Jask had agonised over since the trial, since Kane's betrayal. And no more so than since Phia had landed in his lap – a potential of vengeance once he'd done what he needed to.

Until he'd fallen for her.

'As if I'd ever trust you again,' Jask said.

'You need to,' Kane said. 'With what the Higher Order, more specifically Feinith, let slip to Carter – our beloved ex-head of the TSCD.' Kane glanced at Phia then back at Jask. 'The truth about the vampire prophecies.'

Phia frowned. 'Why did you look at me when you said that?'

His navy eyes narrowed slightly as he looked back at her. 'Why do you think?'

Phia scowled back, staring Kane down despite the intensity of his mutual glare. 'I wouldn't be asking if I knew.'

Kane frowned. 'Keep a rein on that temper, serryn.'

She exhaled tersely. 'You don't tell me what to do.'

Jask knew that look in her eyes only too well. It was one of the triggers – conflict. The second her blood started pumping and the adrenaline started to flow, once she started to relax into her own sense of power, the serryn would begin to out.

As she stared the master vampire down, there was something else he noticed – her pupils were constricting, not dilating, despite the circumstances.

And, more to the point, Kane had noticed too.

Jask knew that look in the vampire's eyes, that expression. The same expression that brought a casual, relaxed smile before he thrust his fist up under someone's ribcage and tore out their throat.

Jask reached out and grasped Phia's wrist, a reminder that he was there because, for that moment, she seemed to be losing sight of everything but Kane. 'What does any of this have to do with Phia, Kane?'

'Why don't you tell him?' Kane said, his glare still troublingly locked on Phia.

'I would if I knew but I don't.'

'Like fuck you don't,' Kane hissed.

But Jask knew confusion and shock when he saw it in her eyes. And he believed it.

'Whatever you think she knows, she doesn't,' Jask said. 'She's been a serryn less than two days. I found her the same night the line jumped to her.'

Kane's attention snapped back to Jask. 'Jumped?'

'From her sister,' Jask added. 'I found her in the ruins of an old building over on the east side.'

He raised his eyebrows slightly. 'My territory?'

'I needed her, Kane. This isn't the only trouble my pack is in. The latest remedy didn't work. You know as well as I do that the blue moon is pending. I needed turmeric. Using Phia was the only way I could get it.'

'And did you get it?'

He nodded. 'Not that it makes any difference now. Not now they've ruined the rest of the supplies. We'll never get what we need in time. Now tell me what any of this has to do with her?'

'And the assassin?'

'Kane…' Jask warned.

'Tell me how you let an assassin through here, what he has to do with her,' he said, cocking his head towards Phia, 'and I'll tell you what you need to know.'

'I was part of The Alliance,' Phia cut in. 'The same as Dan out there. We were killing off key players in the third-species underworld. Until we got ambushed. We're all that's left.'

'I was using him for leverage,' Jask explained. 'Until things went wrong.'

'Just tell me why you looked at me when you mentioned the prophecies,' Phia demanded.

Kane waited a few seconds, to the point Jask was sure Phia was going to explode, but then he spoke. 'The chosen one, a Higher Order vampire, remains as such until the transformation is complete.

For the transformation to be complete, they need to drink a serryn to death. They take her to the Brink, steal her soul and return the Tryan. And the prophecies begin.'

Jask snapped his attention to Phia, but her silence, let alone the look in her eyes, told him the shock was even greater to her. 'You didn't know this?'

Phia shook her head, her eyes wide. 'No,' she said, staring back at Kane.

'And as she's already here,' Kane continued. 'It seems we've now got double the problem to deal with. The serryn emerges within days of the chosen one being selected. Both were destined to appear here in Blackthorn.'

Jask frowned. 'The prophecies have started?'

'Seems that way.'

'Is this why you chose Blackthorn?' Jask asked. 'Is this why you're here?'

Kane's silence said it all.

'But you said it's a problem. Why would that be a problem to you?' Jask's heart pounded, an uncomfortable darkness leaking into the room. 'This chosen one – tell me it's not you.'

Kane exhaled tersely. 'Oh, it's most definitely not me.'

'Then do you know who?'

'I wish I did. Let me be more specific – I'm here to make sure the prophecies never happen.'

The room closed in, darkness masking the edges. Everything within him went numb. Nothing would have prepared him for the gut-wrenching sickness that curdled the pit of his stomach, the very pit of his being. 'Why?'

'This isn't going to be a peaceful political move, Jask. Not like the rumour the Higher Order have spread for their own ends. It was never going to be that way. We're talking about a full-blown uprising. We're talking about an apocalypse.' He glanced back at Sophia. 'And your new girlfriend is the key to it happening.'

Chapter Thirty-Nine

Kane clearly wanted to kill her.

Not only did she have Caleb Dehain on her back but Kane Malloy now too. And Jask was the only one standing between them.

Jask who, because of her, was now caught in the middle.

Exhaustion, anxiety, stress – she didn't know which one was winning out, but the room became hazy. Sophia shoved back her chair, needing to get out of there. 'I need air,' she said, turning towards the door.

She stumbled outside of the room, pushed open the main door and gasped in the courtyard air before falling back against the wall, sliding down against it before clutching her lowered head in her hands.

This was what Leila had been talking about. This had to be what Leila meant when she said it was complicated. There was nothing Leila didn't know about prophecies. And for some reason she'd warned her to stay away from Caleb. She'd warned her of the implications should he find her.

Caleb had to know – somehow he had to know about the role of the serryn in the prophecies.

But he'd let Leila go. He'd *let* her go.

It didn't make any sense.

She knew his footsteps, and she knew the touch that caressed her forearm.

'Hey,' Jask said.

She eventually looked up at him. 'Do you think he's telling the truth? About everything?'

'Kane's many things, Sophia – but he's not a liar.'

'Not just one war, but *two*? Jask…'

'I know,' he said, lacing his fingers in hers, gripping her hand. 'Fucked if we do, fucked if we don't.'

'How does he know so much?'

'It's the way it's always been with the masters – in-built as much as read.'

'But the stuff he was talking about – the Global Council, the soul transferring… Jask, what's going on?'

'I'm going to find out.'

'He wants me dead, doesn't he? One less problem.'

'He needs me, Sophie. We need each other. And having seen the way I feel about you, he's not going to do anything to jeopardise that for now.'

'It sounded to me like he's talking about pulling an army together, about not waiting for them to strike first. Jask, you know the implications of this.' All she could hear was her own pulse in her ears, her surroundings shrinking and expanding as her curt breaths starved her brain of oxygen. 'This is it, isn't it? This is all over. One way or another, this is going to happen.'

He tightened his fingers within hers. 'Where's that warrior, huh?' he asked, with a faint smile. 'Where's that assassin spirit?'

'It's not quite as easy when you care.'

He cupped her face, the surprise clear in those beautiful azure eyes. 'No,' he said. 'But it's what makes you fight harder. And we *are* going to fight this.'

She squeezed his hand back, lowered her voice. 'How do you know you can trust him? I heard what you said about what happened with the TSCD. If he did you over, then…'

'I need to hear him out.'

And she needed to finish hearing Leila out. Before she said anything more, before she did anything, she needed the rest of the story from her sister.

She looked past Jask's shoulder, only then seeing Daniel strapped to the railings across the courtyard.

He was conscious. More than that, he was looking right at them.

Jask followed her gaze.

'There's someone I need to hear out, too,' she said.

Jask helped her up. 'You sure you want to do that?'

'I want to kick his arse for what he tried to do to you, Jask, but I think that would make me something of a hypocrite, don't you?'

As she gently eased her arm away, he let her.

Daniel watched her the whole time she approached, his head resting back against the railings.

She looked back across her shoulder a few moments later to see Corbin had replaced Jask in the doorway – clearly Jask not wanting to leave her unguarded.

'Very cosy,' Daniel remarked, as soon as she was in earshot. 'And there was me coming to rescue you.'

'Which was just as much about killing Jask, right?'

'He *was* our next job, Phia.'

Her stomach flipped. She glanced anxiously over her shoulder at Corbin, hoping she was out of earshot. She lowered to her haunches. Lowered her voice to a whisper. 'The Alliance were going after Jask next?'

'What, you didn't work that out? Abby had put me in charge of it. The operation was starting after we lay low for a couple of days. Until everything kicked off.'

'And you just had to see it through.'

'Some of us don't go soft over pretty blue eyes, Phia.'

'I saved your life in there. Those pretty blue eyes were ready to smash your skull in for what you did to Connor.'

'Connor? Who the fuck is Connor? First-name terms now is it, Phia?'

'That's the difference, Dan – I've learned they have names.'

'Oh, how poetic,' he said with a sneer.

'The Alliance is finished, Dan, so what cause are you fighting now?'

'The right one. The one you *were* a part of. Just tell me you're playing him. Tell me I didn't see what I just saw then.'

'I joined The Alliance for one reason – to make a change, to break the web of corruption in this district.'

He exhaled tersely. 'And the rest,' he snapped. 'You were as much on a tirade of vengeance as the rest of us. We've all lost someone to this fucked-up system, Phia. This was as much about *you* as the corruption, so don't play the martyr.'

'You don't become a martyr until you're dead, Dan. And I've got a lot I want to do before then.'

'With him? With one of those third species *responsible* for the corruption.'

'It's not like that. There's more going on. Much more. This isn't about them and us anymore – humans and third species. This is about right and wrong.'

'And how do you know the difference? What makes you so arrogant as to *believe* you know the difference?'

'I know Jask. And I know this pack. And I know we were wrong about them. And that means I know we've been wrong about a lot of things. That's not arrogance – that's about open eyes.'

'So you're teaming up with one of them? Teaming up with one of the third-species leaders. One of the very leaders who tore our Alliance apart in the first place? Maybe we should have left Jarin in charge of us – he clearly does a better job at assassinating his own than we do.'

Her stomach flipped. 'What did you say?'

His eyes widened, then he glowered down at the floor.

She tilted her head to the side to try and recapture his attention, her knuckles cold against the hard floor. 'Who the fuck is Jarin, Dan? Is he the one who paid us to go after the Dehains?'

He met her gaze again. 'I never said that.'

'You don't have to. You said "his own" – he's a vampire? Why are you protecting him?'

'I'm not.'

'Then what the hell do you call this?' she demanded in a curt whisper. 'You've known all along, haven't you? You lied to me.'

'It would make no difference even if I did tell you. He's untouchable, Phia.'

'You let me head out on a rampage, Dan. Why not stop me?'

'I tried. And then I was going to tell you after you'd called your sisters. But we got ambushed.'

'You had plenty of time after that. When Jask and Corbin were in the kitchen – you could have said–'

'Because I didn't know you wouldn't tell him: Jask. Like I said before, I saw the way you were looking at each other. And I know how you go off on one. How you splutter things out when you're angry. If you told Jask and Jask told Caleb, then Caleb would go for Jarin and Jarin would know it was us who had disclosed the very truth he's killing us to cover up. Taking on the third species undercover is one thing; having the Higher Order baying for your blood is another.'

She stared at him. 'Jarin is a *Higher Order* vampire? That's why you're scared.'

'I'm fucking petrified.'

'But why did he go after Caleb? Why are the Higher Order turning on their own?'

'I don't know. Abby let it slip to me in her panic the night after you disappeared, when it all started. For fuck's sake, Phia, just untie me, will you?'

She glanced back across at Corbin in the distance.

'Phia!' Dan said more curtly.

She snapped her attention back to him, back to his wide blue eyes.

'They're going to kill me if you don't let me go,' he said.

'Jask won't do that.'

Daniel exhaled tersely. 'I tried to kill him.'

'I'll talk to him.'

'Are you going to talk to Kane, too? For fuck's sake, Phia,' he snapped, his wrists straining against the leather bindings. 'I was there for you. You got into The Alliance because of *me*. I gave you purpose and I gave you means. And I've saved your life more than once. I've known you almost a year. You've known him less than two days.'

And in two days her world was turning upside down in ways she couldn't ever have imagined.

Because if the Higher Order were involved and they worked out, just as she had, that only a serryn could have saved Jake, then, if what Kane had just told her was right, they too could already have worked out the key to the prophecies was in their midst.

And if they questioned Caleb, they could find out about Leila.

She could barely breathe, barely think.

She turned on her heels and ran.

Chapter Forty

'I don't need to explain what you're in the middle of here, do I, Jask?' Kane said, as Jask re-entered the room. 'I need to take her off your hands.'

Jask resumed his seat, but this time directly opposite Kane. 'She stays with me. You owe me this much. And if you want my co-operation, you owe me it even more.'

'You know that if it was anyone else, I wouldn't be giving them the option.'

'But you know she's safer here with me than anyone else.'

'And are you willing to keep her contained, whatever it takes? Because if either Sirius or the Higher Order find out you have her, what they did here tonight is nothing more than the pre-warm-up.'

Jask looked across at Corbin. 'She's heading across the courtyard. Will you watch her for me?'

Corbin nodded, taking his leave, closing the door behind him.

'You have to get your pack to safety, Jask. Or they will use them against you. Take my offer.'

'I look after my own. And you don't touch her, do you understand me?'

'Don't worry,' Kane said. 'She's too useful for that. The same as I have no more intention of disclosing her than you do.'

'What game are you playing?' Jask asked, frowning.

'I'm not,' Kane said. 'I'm long past playing anything.'

'You said you want to stop the prophecies. That means you're going up against your own.'

'I'm trying to save my own. There's a difference.'

'And is that why Caitlin Parish is still alive? Is she somehow useful in all this too?'

Kane sent him a hint of a smile. He lowered his gaze, licked his incisor before looking back at Jask.

'It's true, isn't it?' Jask said. 'You *have* gone soft on her.'

'Let's not ruin my reputation now, Jask. And I won't ruin yours. Because from the way you were looking at that serryn, it seems we're both making moves above and beyond what's required.'

Touché, Jask thought, but he didn't quite trust Kane enough to confirm it, despite the shared moment of understanding. Kane was still a law unto himself. Always had been. And there was still enough potential for this to be all about Kane's survival instincts for him not to maintain his wariness.

'So can I count you as being on side?' Kane asked.

'I'll think about it – if you can eradicate another problem first.'

'Which is?'

'Caleb Dehain.'

Kane frowned. 'I've not heard of Caleb having a problem with your pack.'

'He will have – if he finds out I've got the serryn he's looking for.'

He hadn't seen that troubled look in Kane's eyes for a long time. It did nothing to abate his own.

Kane leaned forward to rest his forearms on the table. 'He knows about her? How?'

'Jake's accident – where he drank that girl to death – was down to Phia. He and Caleb were targeted by The Alliance. Only Caleb found out. And now he's after her. Only he knows she's a serryn too.'

'You know this for sure?'

'Phia's sister told her. The sister the serryn line jumped from. She was the one who saved Jake Dehain. Caleb had her. He knows she lost it and now he's after Phia, the next in line.'

Kane's frown deepened. He turned his head to the side slightly as if finding it difficult to process what Jask was saying. 'You're telling me a serryn saved Jake Dehain?'

'Seems that way. I'm guessing that's why Caleb let her go.'

Kane's eyes widened. 'He what? She's still *alive*?'

But before Jask had time to answer, the door flew open, a breathless Phia bursting inside. She slammed her hands down on the table, glaring Kane direct in the eyes.

'Why do the Higher Order want Caleb Dehain dead?' she demanded.

Jask stood and immediately forged a barrier between them, despite Kane's previous assurance that he wouldn't touch her. Arm across her waist, he eased her back from the table, keeping her back, sending a warning glance to Corbin who was now rejoining them in the room.

'Dan just told me who hired us,' Phia declared. 'The same one responsible for torturing and murdering my entire squad. So why are the Higher Order going after their own? Why did they hire us?'

Kane didn't flinch, despite Jask detecting the storm building behind his eyes. 'Do you have a name for this Higher Order vampire?'

'Jarin. Mean anything to you?'

'I know *of* him,' Kane said. 'I hear Caleb's been embroiled with his betrothed, Feinith, for decades. Only Jarin's never been one to confront Caleb in the flesh. Trying to kill him let alone his brother, and failing? Yes, he's going to want to cover his tracks. No one fucks with Caleb and gets away with it – not even the Higher Order.'

'But if Feinith is embroiled with Xavier Carter and the TSCD like you said she is, does that mean Caleb is too?' Jask asked. 'Will he know about the serryn role in the prophecies?'

'Only Higher Order vampires are supposed to know. But it seems secrets have been leaking out all over the place.'

'What if the Higher Order discover Sirius's plans?' Phia asked. 'Surely it'll be more important than ever that they find me? I'll be their best weapon. Maybe their only weapon.'

'She's right,' Jask said to Kane. 'We need to talk to Caleb and find out his role in this. Something tells me we're about to be hit from all angles.'

'He was next on my list.'

'Do you think you can get him on side? Call him off Phia?'

'If not, avoiding that implosion might not be as straightforward as I first hoped.'

'You can handle Caleb, though, right?' Phia asked. 'Only he's got my little sister.'

'Jask tells me he let your other one go – the serryn. Do you know why?'

'No. She said it was complicated. That she'd explain when she came back.'

'Came back? From where?'

'Home. Summerton.'

'He let her escape to Summerton?'

She nodded.

Kane exchanged glances with Jask.

'What?' she said. 'Why are you looking at each other like that?'

Jask knew why. Something he had not yet dared utter to Phia, having not wanted to burst her bubble, on seeing her relief back in the alley that her sisters were alive. He knew as well as Kane did that Caleb was guaranteed to have an ulterior motive – something that was becoming ever more probable with the latest revelations.

Kane shoved back his chair and stood. 'Your big sister should be dead, darling – especially as he already knows he's got a backup in you. If he let her go, there's something in it for him. Something big enough to warrant it. He's got more to gain somehow. He's not done with her yet.'

Sophia tensed in Jask's arms, her lips parted in horror.

'I'll call you tomorrow night,' Kane said, turning his attention back to Jask. 'If you want your pack somewhere safe in the meantime, there are plenty of places on the east side I can sort.'

'If you're going to see Caleb, I'm coming with you,' Jask said.

'And give him proof you have Phia? No way,' Kane said. 'This is one for me to handle alone. But I *will* find out what's going on. You just watch her,' he said, indicating towards Phia. 'And keep her out of sight. She might not just be the Higher Order's best weapon – she might be ours too.'

'You get Caleb off her back and come back here and tell me what's going on, and then, and only then, will we have a deal,' Jask declared.

Kane flashed a fleeting smile. 'You're going to make me work for this, aren't you?'

'We have a lot of ground to make up.'

'And we will,' he said, crossing the room.

But he stopped at the door and turned to face Jask again.

'I'm sorry about Rone,' he said, his navy eyes laced with sincerity – another moment of complete understanding, and revealing the side of Kane that few ever saw. The side of Kane that Jask had trusted all those years before. 'Join me and we'll bring the fuckers down, Jask. All of them. For good this time.'

And with that, Kane disappeared through the doorway, out into the subtle glow of dawn light.

Chapter Forty-One

Sophia leaned against the tree trunk, not far from the poolroom, as she watched Jask mingling with his pack.

The atmosphere was dense enough to wade through, but the lycans were active again. Graves were being dug, the lycans monitoring the peripheries had a look of grit determination in their stance, others were carrying various tools through to the exit.

Jask wasn't just keeping them focused and distracted; he was making preparations. He wasn't going down without a fight – that much was obvious. But first he was going to lay those of his pack he had lost to rest and, at the same time, make sure the rest were protected any way they could be.

As he strolled back across the quadrant to join her, she stood up straight, ready to greet him. The breeze in his fair hair, the late morning sun backlighting him, his azure eyes fixed on her, she couldn't look anywhere but at him. Couldn't look anywhere but into the eyes that had first scrutinised her in the ruins back at a time that now felt like months ago.

She thought how easily Daniel could have killed him. How she could have lost him just a few hours before. Three days ago she'd have killed him without hesitation. Now she couldn't imagine life without him.

'We don't have long, do we?' she said, as he drew level. 'Before you all change.'

'Six days. Five days until we'll need to be contained.'

'Six days to change the world. No pressure then.'

He shrugged. 'No pressure at all.' But the faint smile on his lips didn't manage to make it to his eyes. 'We'll do whatever we can to keep your sisters alive. And once we know exactly what's going on, we'll decide what to do about it.'

'But Caleb Dehain versus Kane Malloy is something we need as much as a full-scale war.'

'Which is in both of their interests to avoid. And they know it.'

'I don't trust him, Jask. I don't trust either of them.'

'I trust Sirius Throme, the Higher Order and the TSCD even less. And one way or another, they're coming whether we like it or not.'

She glanced back over his shoulder at his pack, preparing to say goodbye to their loved ones. 'Well, I don't know about you,' she said. 'But I'm up for a hell of a fight if they think we're going to make this easy for them.'

This time he did smile. 'Warrior spirit's back, eh, Phia?'

'Which they'll see for themselves soon enough.' She looked back at him. 'No one hurts the people I care about, Jask. *No one*. Been there, lived through that, and I'm not going back there. Like you said, I'm part of this pack now. We'll find your young. And I'll make sure, whatever it takes, that I'll get our pack the supplies it needs to make sure none of you have to morph. What's the point of having a serryn on your arm if you can't pull a few strings?'

He caught hold of her hip and pulled her closer, taking hold of her hand in the other. The minute her skin touched his, he interlaced their fingers. He gently cupped her neck with the other hand, sliding his thumb across her jawline. 'You coming into my life was the best thing that could have happened to me, Sophie.'

'Because I'm going to make sure they regret fucking with the wrong serryn?'

He managed another smile, and this one caught her deep in the ribs.

'Because you've reminded me of who I am,' he said. 'And why the fight is worth it.'

She smiled back, despite anxiety still lurking in the pit of her stomach. 'They really don't know what they're taking on, do they?'

He lifted the hand he'd been holding, tightened his fingers in hers as he held it up near their shoulders, moving in as close as he could get.

'Are you okay with this?' she asked, indicating over his shoulder towards his pack. 'Being with me so openly. I'd understand if–'

He caught her lips with his, his hand slipping around the back of her neck, kissing her deeply, stopping her breathing for those few seconds.

She snatched back a breath as soon as there was a gap of air between them again.

'The pack know you tried to save them,' he said. 'I made sure they did. They believe me that things are far from over. An angry pack is one thing. A pack with hope in their veins is a force to be reckoned with. And I'm going to keep that hope alive. Above all else, I'm *proud* to be with you.'

'So you should be,' she said. 'And don't you forget it.'

He smiled again. 'I'm sure you'll keep reminding me.'

'And how does Corbin feel about us?'

'He's wary of you, but he trusts my judgement. Always has done.' He led her towards the tunnel. 'He just needs a bit more time with you.'

'And what do you need?'

'Time to think. Once we start this, there'll be no going back.'

'But would you want to go back?' she asked. 'Do you want things to stay like this?'

'No. This has been a long time coming.'

'Win or die trying.'

He looked across at her. 'Now, that *is* warrior talk.'

'I meant what I said, Jask,' she said, coming to a standstill. 'When I was holding you down at the stone table. I wasn't just saying it.'

'I know. Just tell me you believed me when *I* said it. Because we're going to have to trust each other, Sophie, if we stand any chance of pulling through this.'

'I do trust you.'

'Tell me you believed me.'

'I don't think you could have said it if you didn't. I don't think those words have fallen from your lips often enough.'

'They haven't.'

'Well,' she said with a small shrug, as she looked down. 'Once more won't hurt.' She glanced back up at him.

He cupped her neck again, gazed deep into her eyes to the point she could see nothing but him. 'I love you, Sophie. More than I thought I was capable of.'

She traced her fingers over the leather straps at his neck. 'And I love you too. So go and do what you have to do. I'm right here with you.'

His gaze lingered for a few moments longer. She knew he was putting it off. She could feel it in the way he reluctantly pulled away.

She wanted to go down there with him, but knew Jask wanted to face it alone. Needed to face it alone.

She wrapped her arms around herself against the chill, as the only thing she could do to comfort herself.

When he re-emerged minutes later, his shrouded dead son in his arms, Sophia almost choked on her tears.

But Jask was controlled. Jask kept his head up. Kept focused.

She followed him back through the tunnel to join the rest of his pack, to where the others they had lost were being lowered into their graves.

She kept back at first as Rone was laid on the fabric, Jask, Corbin, Samson and Phelan each taking a strap at one of the four corners.

Once he was in the ground, Jask shovelled the earth back in, before taking a step back, his head lowered.

Words were said for them all. Words she couldn't hear from her distance.

But when Jask looked across his shoulder at her, held out his hand for her to take, it took her no hesitation to join him.

She noticed his necklace had gone, the one with the pendant. As she glanced down at the mound of earth, she had no doubt who now wore it.

Jask looked across at Corbin on the other side of the grave, his second in command clutching Solstice's hand as tightly as Jask clutched Phia's.

'They started this,' Jask said, his voice terrifying calm. 'And we're going to finish it.'

'Too fucking right,' Corbin said.

'The district, the system they created, will break them,' Sophie declared.

Corbin looked across at her, before returning his attention to Jask. 'Now I see what you mean.'

'Oh, believe me,' Jask said, capturing Phia's gaze. 'You haven't seen the half of it.' He looked back at his friend – his second in command. 'Neither have they,' he declared as he squeezed Sophia's hand. 'But before we're done, they most *definitely* will.'

Epilogue

The engine stopped rumbling. She could hear the opening of doors.

The only thing that stopped Tuly rolling around in the small coffin-like box as it was slid over metal was being strapped to all four of the sides of the rough-sawn wood. Her breathing was equally restricted by the tape across her mouth.

She felt herself being lifted, accompanied by a male grunt. The motion made her feel sick, the sedative only just starting to wear off.

The movement and pace told her she was being carried by one set of footsteps, distinct in the silence.

But then there was another approaching in the distance.

'In here,' another male voice said.

She heard the unbolting and unlocking of a door.

A few moments later her container was dropped onto a surface, her whole body jolting with the sharpness of the drop.

'How many?' the male voice asked.

'Nine in total,' the other answered.

'How long for?'

'As long as it takes. Couple of days. Maybe three. Then they're all yours. Might be worth keeping some of them alive for the whole five. I heard the entertainment is impressive when they start to change – especially the young ones. You could sell tickets. Especially if you lock them in together. You could have your own makeshift dog fight. Or should I say puppy fight.'

The other male laughed. Deep. Unsettling. Cruel. But it was fleeting. 'Just make sure Throme comes good. I want what he promised or I'll be letting things slip to their owners, you hear me?'

'All the alcohol, cigarettes and food that you want. And, of course, every penny you make on the pups is yours. He deems that payment enough.'

'And it will be,' the male voice said. 'As long as I don't get those fucking lycans sniffing around here.' There was a momentary pause. 'Let's take a look then.'

Latches were lifted on all four sides of the box.

A bright light suddenly made the insides of Tuly's container glow. She didn't want to squint – she wanted to see who was out there. But she had no choice as the lid was lifted off, the white overhead bulb blinding her.

A male hand, warm, clammy, grabbed her jaw as his other ripped the tape off her mouth. He squeezed her jaw open, pushed up her lip to examine her canines, before letting go just as sharply.

'Bring the rest in,' the male voice who'd removed the tape said. 'Put them down in the basement. We've got a cage all ready.'

The other male's footsteps disappeared into the distance.

'Hey, little sweet thing,' her captor said.

Now he was nothing more than a dark outline, his features still indistinguishable. But he wasn't a vampire, she knew that much. There was something familiar about his smell. Something... human.

And then she saw them – on the inside of his arm as it rested on the edge of her container. A sequence of tattooed numbers.

She blinked against the light, now masked as he leaned over her.

She stared up into his cold grey eyes.

'You ever been to The Circus?' he asked. And he smiled. A smile like she had never seen before. A smile that turned her insides cold. 'We're going to have *so* much fun.'

LETTER FROM LINDSAY

I really hope you enjoyed Jask and Phia's story and their revelations about the world of Blackthorn. Please feel free to get in touch and let me know if you did – I love contact from readers.

If you did enjoy *Blood Torn*, I'd also be grateful if you'd consider writing a review on Amazon. It's a great way to encourage new readers to try this series.

If you'd like to be one of the first to hear about my latest books, you can sign up for e-mail updates at:

www.lindsayjpryor.com/lindsay-j-pryor-e-mail-sign-up

And if you're intrigued to know more, please visit my website for all the inside information on Blackthorn so far – no spoilers, of course!

As for what comes next for Blackthorn… you have one final couple to meet before the impact of these relationships unfolds. You can get a sneak preview on the next few pages, with the first chapter of *Blood Deep*. Welcome to The Circus!

Lindsay
www.lindsayjpryor.com

BLOOD DEEP

Chapter One

Eden stood alone in the darkness, habitually flipping the mint in his mouth over and over again with the perfected rhythm of his tongue. The night air was fresh against his face, the breeze slightly stronger from his viewing point on the flat roof of the derelict shop.

The van in the alley thirty foot below was still being unloaded. Whatever the crates contained wasn't heavy, not from the ease with which the lone guy lifted each onto his shoulder in turn. He followed the same pattern every time – lift the crate, carry it inside, be gone for three to four minutes, then unload the next.

When he disappeared inside for the eighth time, Eden scanned the roofs of the row upon row of terraced houses. The graffiti-emblazoned buildings, sat amidst their maze of back alleys, were once an inhabitable residential area of what was classed as a city decades before.

Now, aside from the district's hub where the third species hung out, this was the second most lethal place to be in Blackthorn. This was The Circus: home to the convicts abandoned by the penitentiary of Lowtown across the border, and forced to reside within the confines of the third-species-dominated core of the locale.

Returning after disposing of the ninth crate, the guy slammed the van door shut and reversed back into the side alley from where he'd come. The same alley where he'd passed Eden – his van lights off, opting for the tight squeeze as opposed to the main road only a few feet away. It had evoked Eden's curiosity enough to take the external fire escape steps up onto the flat roof – an advantageous viewpoint of the buildings he'd been heading for anyway.

He flipped his mint over in his mouth again as he watched the van back up to leave, when the figure to his left caught his attention.

'You spying?' the petite blonde asked, remaining a sensible twenty feet away. Her hands were tucked in the pockets of the black cropped leather jacket that hung half off one skinny shoulder. Right hip cocked slightly higher than the left, her thin, parted legs ended in biker boots to complete the defensive stance.

'You know this place?' he asked.

'You agency?'

He slid his open-cuffed jacket sleeve up to expose his inner arm, the numbers tattooed there – numbers that indicated the penitentiary he had come from as well as the categories and frequency of the crimes he had committed.

She folded her arms as she walked towards him to take a closer look, her vest top low enough to reveal the lace cups of her well-padded bra.

Her eyes – hollow, sad eyes, barely visible through her shaggy bob – were indicative of the system she was no doubt locked in. And those blue eyes flared as she examined the condemnatory array of numbers that stretched higher than his restrictive sleeve would allow her to see.

Blowing back her fringe, she raised her eyebrows, her subsequent half smile as blatant as the length of her tight skirt. 'That's a *lot* of bad behaviour.' She tilted her head to the side slightly. 'And yet you look so sweet.'

'Where does that door go?' he asked, cocking his head to where the crates had been taken.

She stepped alongside him and glanced down at the alley. She shrugged her small shoulders. 'There are doorways all over this place since they knocked all the houses through – some blocked up, new ones put in both inside and out. I've been here three years,' she added, 'and I don't know half of this maze.'

Three years. At least sixteen years his junior, she couldn't have been a day over twenty.

She took a packet of cigarettes out of her top pocket and offered him one.

Eden refused.

'You know how hard it is to get your hands on these around here?' she asked.

'I don't smoke.'

'I suggest you take it up.' She placed one between her badly painted lips, her skinny fingers trembling in the cold – fingers worthy of piano playing, tipped in chipped baby-pink polish that conflicted with the tough biker look. She sniffed and wrapped an arm around herself, dropped her cigarette-holding hand loosely to her side to flick off some ash. 'Saying that, some reckon they fill these with all sorts of shit before shipping them in – that they'll kill us off that way if not with the booze and food they supply.'

He'd heard the conspiracy theories a hundred times before and they didn't get any more interesting with a change of teller. 'Do you know what was in the crates?'

She shrugged again and blew out a curt stream of smoke that promptly dissipated in the cold night air. 'You're new here, right?' She raked him swiftly again. 'Only I'd remember you.'

'New as of a few hours ago.'

'They just dump you off on this side of the border? Shit, isn't it? No money. No provisions. No directions.' She took another swift inhale before exhaling just as brusquely. 'Do you know what percentage of cons dropped off here make it to the second night?'

'Do you?'

She shrugged again. 'Nah. Still, it's better than the penitentiary. At least you get to do what you want around here.'

'You're a con?'

She slid her jacket sleeve up her arm with her cigarette-holding hand to give him a quick flash of her own numbers.

He knew exactly what they meant. 'Murder?'

She shrugged again. 'Stopped him cheating.'

He didn't know whether he was saddened more by the indifference in her tone, or the lack of expression on her heavily made-up face.

'You don't get sent here just for murder,' he said.

'I killed one of the penitentiary guards who reminded me of him.' Her jacket sleeve dropped into place again as she wrapped her arm back around her waist.

He didn't doubt it was more than bravado. The capability consumed her morally apathetic eyes. He knew the type only too well. Had handled enough.

'I don't remind you of him too, do I?'

She smiled, revealing surprisingly good teeth. 'Good looking *and* a sense of humour. Nah, you're all right.' She stepped up to the edge to look down at the alley before turning to face him. 'Building up the courage to go in, huh? You'll be all right – unless you're planning to make your mark and get beaten to a pulp for it. My advice: keep your head down. And don't flash those numbers too much. Some might see it as competition.' She lifted the cigarette back to her lips and exhaled as she assessed him from head to foot again. 'Messing up that handsome face, let alone that body, would be a crime in itself.' Her gaze lingered before she sauntered back over. 'I've got a room in there. You can bed down with me until you get yourself straight.'

'And where *does* someone get themselves straight around here?'

'This patch is Pummel's. If you've got something to offer, he might give you a room. If not, you can try one of the abandoned buildings, but security ain't good. Any further afield and you're going to find yourself with vamps as neighbours or a rogue lycan or whatever other third species crawls the back alleys of this district.'

Anywhere beyond the thin margin of the south that didn't belong to anyone other than the squatting cons.

'Pummel?' he asked, despite already knowing he was in the right place.

'That's what he's known as around here. For good reason.'

'He sounds like a charmer.'

She smiled again, but this time it didn't reach her eyes. 'So you want that room?'

'With my history?'

She exhaled a steady stream of smoke as she sidled closer. 'This place gets lonely. Besides, whatever those numbers say about you, I'm a good judge of character. Hang around long enough and you get to know types around here.'

Clearly not that good a judge.

'As much as I appreciate the offer, you don't want to be bedding down with me.'

She smiled as she closed in, her overpowering perfume surrounding her like an aura. 'Why? You got some kind of fucked-up kink or something? Only I'm open-minded.' She looked back down at his arm before looking him in the eyes again, lingering with a confidence only experience brought. 'Just how far up do those numbers go anyway?'

Eyes that, despite their confidence, looked on edge, almost impatient.

He glanced over at the fire escape and back at her. As he'd guessed, her impatience escalated.

'Or we can stay up here,' she said, discarding her cigarette before running her hand down his arm, guiding him to face her, his back to the fire escape, as she pressed her lips together. 'That's quite a body under that jacket. I bet you know how to take care of yourself. And me.'

It was subtle. And she was good. But not good enough for it to do anything but confirm he'd been right to sense the signs of an ambush.

'And taking care of me is the only thing I'm interested in right now,' he said, removing her bony hand from his arm, a hand he could so easily crush for what he suspected, before backing away.

'At least let me show you around,' she called out louder than she needed to, catching up with him as he crossed to the steps. 'Hey! Wait! You'll want to know where you're going in there.'

'I'll take my chances,' he replied, descending.

She clunked down the fire escape behind him. 'What's the problem? You not into women or something? Or am I not good enough for you?'

'Don't take it personally.'

'In case you haven't noticed,' she said, grabbing his shoulder. 'I'm offering it to you on a plate here.'

'And lucky for you, I don't have an appetite tonight,' he said, shrugging her off.

At least he'd got to the bottom of the steps before they appeared.

There were two of them at first. Then another two appeared from behind them.

He glanced back over his shoulder at the blonde who remained four steps up, her arms now tightly folded, her eyebrows raised smugly to perfectly complement her smirk.

'You're done, Mya,' one of the males said.

'No way,' she insisted. 'Not when I did all the work again. I want to watch this time.'

Eden glanced back over his shoulder at her again, the thought of putting her over his knee and giving her a damn hard spanking, and not for his personal pleasure, reeling through him. 'Sugary little thing, aren't you?'

'Fuck you,' she sneered.

'Oh, darling, you wish,' he said, turning his attention back to the four squaring up ready to attack.

If there was one thing he abhorred it was pack hunting. If he was going to be taken on, he could at least grant some respect to an opponent willing to take him on alone. But these reeked of cowardice, a guarantee to send his adrenaline pumping.

Only two types fought in packs in Blackthorn – cons and lycans. And there was nothing lycan about these. Lycans didn't hesitate, and they sure didn't use honey traps to do their dirty work.

In fact, there was nothing third species about them at all. These were humans – his own kind – convicts that clearly didn't intend to ask questions or need a reason for their intentions. This was about entertainment. He could see by the look in their eyes that they wanted to hurt him, and he'd been in that situation *far* too many times before.

He crunched the thin remainder of his mint as strategy instantly kicked in. The two guys on the periphery were the weakest link. They'd be easy enough if they fought fair.

But Eden first turned his attention to respond to the one who had spoken – clearly the leader. He dominated his five-foot-ten adversary by at least three inches, unlike the other three who were clearly the muscle of his little gang.

'Any of you Pummel?' Eden asked, already knowing that the answer was no. But it wouldn't hurt to play innocent.

The leader's thin lips broadened into a chilling smile. 'You ain't going to get that far, pretty one.'

Eden had the feeling the con believed it. He frowned for effect. 'Is that some kind of come on? Only I'm not into possessive types.'

The leader didn't laugh. Neither did the others. The leader's slitty eyes narrowed – eyes that emanated sadism. 'What the fuck did you say?'

'Hey, I'm not questioning your taste,' Eden said. He glanced at the other three guys. 'Unless I'm the anomaly and *they're* your usual choice.'

It took a moment for his insult to sink in.

When it did, just as he'd suspected, they didn't come at him in an orderly queue.

With a single nod of the leader's head – a nod that indicated he intended to sate his minions' taste for blood first – the three attacked.

Eden didn't take his eyes off his first target. One clean and powerful sideways kick to the windpipe and number one was down long enough for him to turn his attention on the second. A swift, solid, precise fist to the attacker's groin and number two was on his knees, curled over with pain.

The third took his opportunity and punched Eden clean in the jaw – but only enough to throw him off balance rather than take him down.

Eden ploughed into him before the attacker's fist had a chance to make second contact. He rammed his attacker against the wall only for him to shove back with equal retaliation, slamming Eden backwards onto the metal fire escape steps.

Mya squealed in disturbing delight, almost skipping as she slipped past them to avoid the onslaught whilst number three, pinning Eden to the steps with his weight advantage, applied two sharp blows to Eden's side and another to his jaw.

Eden spat out blood into his attacker's face, surprised, from the force and angle of number three's blow, that a tooth hadn't exited with it.

The blood shower only incited more vicious pounding, the leader also closing in ready to pounce.

Eden gritted his teeth, lifted his knee and kicked him clean off. Using the steps as leverage, he got back onto his feet.

But so did the other two he had taken down in round one.

Eden wiped his bloodied mouth with the back of his hand, spitting out more blood as he rethought his strategy.

Clearly they didn't take the hint. Clearly they intended to kill him. And he never took to that kindly.

This time, a second blow to number one's windpipe was intentionally fatal. A swivel kick to number two knocked him clean against the protruding rusted pole jutting out from the wall.

Their comrade's impaling only slowed number three and the leader for a couple of seconds before they bared their teeth and closed in on him again.

Eden shook the tension from his shoulders, rolled his head left and right, nimbled up, ignoring his waning energy before taking a defensive stance.

Unfairly fresh to the fight, the leader eventually took advantage. Several poundings later, he'd weakened Eden enough for number three to get a grip on him. Wrenching Eden's arms back, number three exposed Eden's torso for the leader to make several more dangerously impactful blows.

Eden knew he had no choice but to sag, the move allowing him to regain a few inches between him and his captor, the latter loosening his grip just a fraction as he'd hoped.

Not wasting any time, Eden used the leader as a walk-up, kicking him hard in the jaw and simultaneously slamming him against the brick wall in the process. He concluded the manoeuvre by pivoting over the one who held him and taking him to ground with the force, his opponent's head cracking on the floor beneath him as he used him to soften his own fall.

Stumbling back to his feet, Eden spat out another mouthful of blood as he looked across at the leader now also upright again, his slitty eyes filled with rage.

This time Eden was out of patience. A full-on fight in under three hours was not what he had planned for. And he most certainly hadn't accounted for dying. This time the leader was going down.

But another con emerged from around the corner. One who clearly wasn't expecting to walk in on the floorshow but, from the way he smirked as he discarded his cigarette, was all for interaction.

The newbie and the leader fought together and they fought dirty, Eden taking several more blows for the many more he defended. He struck them both hard enough to draw blood several times, but not enough to floor either of them for long.

His body ached, his eyes blurred as he took a smack to the nose. But as the newbie wrapped his arm around his neck, jammed his other arm behind his back, Eden hadn't expected the leader to play *that* dirty.

He rammed the blade into Eden's side. And twisted.

'Fucking do it again,' the one holding Eden hissed.

Eden felt the blade leaving his numbing body, before the leader rammed it in again.

When he felt it withdrawn once more, Eden knew the next one was going to be fatal.

He took a steady inhale to build up the last of his strength, ready to shove back against his captor with all his force.

A split second later, the leader's head was twisted sharply to the side, his limp body slumping to the floor. He heard further crack of bones from the newbie, his hold loosening.

Eden fell to his knees on the floor. He clutched his side as he squinted up through blurry, bloodied eyes, barely able to make anything out but a girl stood above him – a tall and shapely female with dark, waist-length ringlets.

That distinctive feature along with the fact that, whoever she was, she clearly wasn't human, told him he might have found what he'd come for.

If he lived long enough to see it through.

Printed in Great Britain
by Amazon